The Rose Bowl

THE ROSE BOWL

Judy Gardiner

C

CENTURY

LONDON SYDNEY AUCKLAND JOHANNESBURG

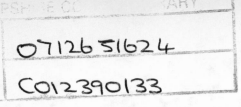

Copyright © Judy Gardiner 1993

All rights reserved

The right of Judy Gardiner to be identified as the author of this work has been
asserted by her in accordance with the Copyright, Designs and Patents Act 1988.

First published in Great Britain in 1993 by
Random House Limited
20 Vauxhall Bridge Road, London, SW1V 2SA

Random Century South Africa (Pty) Ltd
PO Box 337, Bergvlei 2012, South Africa

Random Century Australia Pty Ltd
20 Alfred Street, Milsons Point, Sydney, NSW 2061
Australia

Random Century New Zealand Ltd
18 Poland Road, Glenfield, Auckland,
New Zealand

A CIP Catalogue Record for this book is available from the British Library

Typeset by Deltatype Ltd, Ellesmere Port
Printed in Great Britain by
Mackays of Chatham plc. Chatham, Kent

For Bunny, who loves roses

You see, sweet maid, we marry
A gentler scion to the wildest stock,
And make conceive a bark of baser kind
By bud of nobler race.

The Winter's Tale

In the warmth of a June afternoon the old man and the young woman stood looking at one another. Slowly he held out his hand.

'How do you do,' she said, taking it. 'I'm Nanda O'Flynn.'

His hand was very large, almost shovel-size, the skin of it hard and dry. They continued to stare at one another, then the old man said, 'Yes, I imagined you must be.'

He turned without further comment and led the way along a path bordered by shrub roses in full bloom. The young woman paused to examine one, then followed after him. The old man must have been very tall in his youth; he was still tall now, although age had given him an angularity and had bowed his shoulders a little. He continued to walk ahead of her and she carefully noted the long legs, narrow old man haunches and thin, blue-veined arms. He was wearing a pair of heavy cotton trousers, leather sandals and a bright blue open-necked shirt with the sleeves rolled up, and the effect was one of immaculacy casually assumed.

'Nice roses,' she murmured politely.

'I'm supposed to be famous for them,' he said.

She wondered with a slight feeling of depression if he was going to be difficult. Certainly that was not his reputation; everyone in the office who had spoken of him had said what a dear old chap he was. Easy, helpful, courteous, and so on. Ah well, he couldn't be worse than her previous assignment. Mary Dalrymple the Aldeburgh novelist who was tiddly before midday and legless after it, and who was incapable of disentangling honest fact from her ghastly fiction. Once during the interview she had hurled a pair of shoes at the representative from the *Ipswich Bystander*; not just one shoe, but a pair, Nanda O'Flynn recalled with a slight renewal of resentment. No, he couldn't be worse than Mary Dalrymple.

They turned a corner. The house came into view, and it was impossible to judge its age, size or style for the almost impenetrable covering of roses. They swarmed up every wall, the

1

more daring of them scaling the roof and reaching long leafy arms towards the chimney stack, and their clusters of blooms reminded the young woman of laughing mischievous faces. She had seen children with faces like that: beautiful and unblemished, their perfection lit by the innocent fun of pulling the cat's tail.

The path took a left-hand turn and the house and its roses became partially obscured by the dark green of cypress. The old man halted and turned to face her, and she became freshly conscious of his scrutiny. His eyes were wonderfully bright for his age and she felt his unhurried gaze encompassing her smoothly cropped hair, vee-necked T-shirt and faded, well-laundered jeans.

'I thought we could sit in the arbour,' he said finally. 'Free from interruption.'

She acquiesced, and he then appeared to notice the briefcase she was carrying. 'Please, allow me,' he said, taking it from her. He had a polite and rather pedantic way of speaking, and her sensitive ears caught the hint of Suffolk singsong in his voice. The *old* Suffolk, that her father had learned to imitate in his youth.

She saw the arbour on the far side of a stretch of lawn bordered by more rose beds, and the scent from them came towards her on the ghost of a breeze. They walked side by side without speaking; there were daisies on the lawn shining white as peppermints, and high in an ash tree a blackbird gave an introductory trill before settling down to a spell of serious singing.

The arbour had been constructed from rough baulks of timber, most of them invisible beneath further torrents of roses. Pink, white, lemon and scarlet, they tangled into each other and wreathed rapaciously in a joyous excess of well-being. Motionless, the young woman stood staring at them, their leaves patterning her face.

'Do please sit down,' the old man said, and pulled out one of the four basket chairs that stood round the old round iron table. She did so, and he carefully placed the briefcase down by her feet before seating himself opposite. They looked at one another, smiling rather warily, then her gaze transferred to the glass bowl standing in the centre of the table. It contained six roses, all of a different colour and all of them semi-open, and whereas the climbers, ramblers and tall shrubs that surrounded them delighted with their cascading exuberance and their weight of numbers, the

2

six specimens on the table were six examples of total perfection. They seemed to Nanda O'Flynn to be regarding the world with patrician serenity; we are we, and that is the end of the matter.

'You know, I'm not really keen on all this,' the old man said abruptly. He indicated the tape recorder she had extracted from the briefcase and placed on the table, together with a notebook and pencil. 'It's very kind and flattering, of course, but at eighty-five I'm too old to be interesting.'

'Even after what's just happened?' She looked at him ironically. 'It must have been the thrill of a lifetime – ' She broke off, as if his name was somehow difficult to pronounce.

'So what do you want to know?' He folded his big hands patiently.

'I think I said when I phoned that we wanted to do a feature article on your most famous roses – someone happened to notice that they were all named after women.' There was courtesy in her tone, but not quite enough to cover the impression of slight disdain.

The old man sat considering her; the neat workmanlike clothes and the nice young face – intelligent and proudly unadorned by make-up – and the capable hands with their short-clipped nails. Everything about her breathed intelligence and a rather prickly self-sufficiency.

'Are you what they call a *Guardian* woman?' he asked mildly.

'I read the *Guardian*, but I work for the *Ipswich Bystander*,' she said sternly, then added, 'Right. Shall we get on with these women of yours?'

'They're all there,' he indicated the glass bowl. 'Those two won the Royal National Rose Society's Gold Medal, the white one was awarded the Clay Challenge Vase and the one facing you was lucky enough to get the President's International Trophy.'

She flicked her eyebrows by way of comment, fiddled briefly with the tape recorder, then said, 'Yes, great. But now can we get down to the human interest?'

'The human interest,' the old man repeated. He sat back and closed his eyes. 'My God, you don't expect me to strip my soul bare, do you?'

'Not to me,' Nanda O'Flynn said with a businesslike smile. 'Just to our readers.'

3

1913

He was small for his age and his anxious face was half-concealed beneath a baggy tweed cap. The cap was new and so were his boots, which were authentic working boots with iron-studded soles and long laces which tied at the back of the ankle. The trousers and jacket had belonged to his elder brother Grigg before being handed down to Willie, who was next in line. Grigg was now married and gone to Australia and Willie had had very little wear out of them, having died of diphtheria when he was fifteen. Now, they constituted young Thaddeus's first working clothes. The trouser legs were still too long and upon Ma's instructions he had tucked them into the tops of his new boots. His shirt was his own, and the red spotted handkerchief had been given to him by his Grandma. 'It belonged to your Grandad,' she said. 'He bought it for the ole Queen's Jubilee and never wore it but the once.'

The handkerchief, tied in a double knot beneath his chin and still smelling faintly of naphtha balls, imparted an air of false jollity to its wearer as he tried to match his father's obdurate bowed-shoulder march along the wide empty track that led to the Home Farm. His father had worked as horseman at the Home Farm for almost forty years, each summer seaming his face a little deeper, each winter knifing his limbs a little more cruelly with rheumatism. But that was the way of it, God having ordained that almost every man and woman living in the small village of Marling and its hamlet should work up at the Big House in some capacity or other.

Only Miss Ball and the village postmistress and the vicar's family remained independent, although Brigadier Sir Wilton Fitzhardy's influence (if not his benevolence) extended to their territory as well. He chose the hymns and read the lesson in church, chided the postmistress for allowing dogs in the shop, and as school governor descended twice yearly upon the village school kept by Miss Ball in order to hear the nervous chanting of tables and the Catechism. Thaddeus had only once drawn a personal

4

comment from Sir Wilton, and that had been withering in ‹
extreme: 'Ten years old, you say? Not much to show for it.' It had
made Thaddeus the butt of many jokes and jibes, the least
offensive being the suggestion that he should try putting horse
muck in his boots, and the thought that he, like all the other village
boys, was destined eventually to become an employee of Sir
Wilton was less happy than it was inevitable.

'Step out, young Thaddy,' his father said on that first September
morning. 'Garden work's a sight easier than farm work, and Nable
Sims ain't a bad little ole boy only for Gawd's sake don't call him
Nable call him Mr Sims, and touch your cap like I told you.'

Thaddeus said that he would, then in order to prolong the
comfort of conversation, added, 'You never said why he's called
Nable.'

'Ah now, that'd be telling,' his father kicked at a loose flint lying
in his path. 'Something to do with his wedding night, they say.
Doubtless you'll hear one day.'

There were lots of jokes about mating in its various forms; cows
and bulls, mares and stallions. Thaddeus had heard a great many
of them whispered and sniggered over behind the row of earth
lavatories in the school yard, yet the older generation (his parents
included) always preferred to think of the young as pure and
unsullied. No one was supposed to know the reason for the
creakings and pantings coming from their parents' bed, often in
the same room, although they were conversant enough with the
inevitable outcome. The midwife arriving on her tall bicycle and
Dad going off to the Carpenter's Arms until it was all over. Then a
new brother or sister, red-faced and squalling in a square of
blanket, and Mum looking tired and dank-haired telling the eldest
girl to make a cup of tea for nurse and ask her if she'd like a bit of
ginger cake.

Most of the cottages in Marling and Marling Hamlet belonged
to the Big House; they had small drowsy-eyed windows set
beneath untidy thatches, flowers in the front garden, hens and
vegetables in the back and a wooden privy set in the shelter of the
hedge. Artists from London sometimes came down to paint them
for this was famed Constable country, but they only painted the
more agreeable aspects: the roses, not the rats; children with red
cheeks rather than rickets.

5

But there was beauty enough for those with the time and the right sort of eye to see. Great flaring sunsets bathing the fields and woods in Old Testament red, the slow flight of a heron across the harvest moon, the placid progress of the river on its way to the sea at Harwich.

'September's a tidy ole month to start work,' Thaddeus's father observed as they passed the newly stubbled fields upon which Sir Wilton's pheasants and partridges were feeding. 'Not much growth going on now – break you in nice and easy.'

Thaddeus nodded in silence. He was keen to become a gardener, and only the thought of Sir Wilton and Mr Sims made him moisten his lips apprehensively.

His father walked with him past the newly filled stackyards and through the iron gate that led to the glasshouses and potting sheds. 'Got your dinner safe, have you? And a bitta something for bait-time?'

'Yes, Dad.' He indicated the small canvas haversack.

'Right, then. So do you be a good lad and mind what you're told and I'll meet you here knocking-off time.'

'Yes, Dad.' He stood for a moment watching his father stump away towards the stables then turned and walked into the yard, his new boots ringing bravely on the cobbles.

He counted ten of them there. All bigger, all older – fathers and uncles of boys he had known at school. Fenny Brewer was nearest his age; a large-boned youth with rubbery features who was an unofficial cousin of the Noggin children according to rumours of a moonlit encounter between a Brewer and a Noggin some seventeen years ago. He greeted Thaddeus with a brief nod, then the men straightened themselves and those smoking pipes knocked them out as Mr Sims appeared.

In keeping with the rank of head gardener, Mr Sims wore breeches and stockings instead of trousers secured below the knee with straps. He also wore a black jacket, from the neck of which glistened a round white celluloid collar and a narrow black tie. His small neat cap was placed upon his head with great exactitude and his eyes were the colour of Suffolk flint.

He saw Thaddeus immediately. 'You the new lad?'

Thaddeus acknowledged that he was.

'And what use you reckon you'll be to us, then?'

6

Taking this as a reference to his size Thaddeus shuffled nervously and said he didn't know but he'd try. Then added that he wanted to learn to be a gardener.

'Ho, yes?' Mr Sims's tone softened. 'Like gardens, do you, lad?'

Thaddeus said that he did, and Mr Sims asked what in particular he liked about them.

'Well . . . reckon I like all the flowers and that,' Thaddeus said, then remembered to add 'Sir'.

'So we'll start you off with some nice flowers then,' Mr Sims smiled kindly. 'We'll put you to work picking some nice dahlias and chrysanths to take home to your Mum, shall we?'

With a fatherly hand on the back of Thaddeus's neck he moved with him towards one of the large greenhouses. They went inside, where shafts of early morning sunshine were splintered and diffused by a forest of richly carved leaves. Gazing upwards, Thaddeus saw the swelling bunches of blue-black grapes hanging motionless, a million globules of glowing, glistening fruit, the richness of whose taste he had heard, but never sampled. It was stiflingly warm in there.

'*Boodaful*, aren't they?' Mr Sims said softly. 'And they're all for the Big House. Every one of 'em. And if one single bunch goes missing, Sir Wilton'll know. Ho yes, he'll know all right.' Mr Sims bent down and peered beneath the peak of Thaddeus's cap. 'Sir Wilton knows everything, just like God does. Because Sir Wilton *is* God, in these parts. And he'll know if a bunch goes missing. He'll know if one single little grape goes, and what's more, he'll know who took it. Which means that any young shaver as tries it on get's turned off with a beating, see? A terrible beating as draws blood. Ho yes, it draws blood all right.'

He fell silent, while continuing to stare deep into Thaddeus's eyes. And Thaddeus, transfixed, stared back while visions of young shavers beaten to the consistency of raspberry jam filled his mind.

Then Mr Sims stood erect and cleared his throat, and his tone became as brisk and flinty as his eyes. 'In the meantime, we've got a touch of mildew threatening. Only a touch, mind you, but mildew destroys grapes faster than you can say Muscat of Alexandria, which is what these here are, so we're going to take precautions before it gets a hold, see? And we're going to do it by

7

painting all the hot pipes you see in here with equal parts lime and sulphur. And when I say *we* – I mean *you*.'

He led Thaddeus outside again, and one of the men took him into a shed and showed him how to prepare the quicklime and sulphur, then provided him with a brush and told him to look lively. Steam rose in the bucket as he carried it back to the grapehouse, squatted down and began very carefully to paint the two thick iron pipes that ran one above the other round the walls.

A short while later the rising fumes began to make his eyes water. He wiped them on his cuff and continued. A few minutes more and he began coughing. Balancing the brush across the top of the bucket he went over to the door and opened it. An outraged face looked in, roared something about making a draught on the grapes and shut it again.

Thaddeus persevered with narrowed eyes through which the tears continued to squeeze. He tried to paint faster, dabbling the witch's brew on the pipes, between the pipes and some of it on the floor. By the time he was halfway round it hurt to breathe. His chest felt raw and constricted and the heat given off by the pipes was overpowering.

It was bait-time when he stumbled out of the grapehouse with empty bucket and splattered clothes. Mr Sims was nowhere to be seen, and the other men who were sitting in a row with their backs against a wall eyed him with amused sympathy. One of them offered him a swig from his bottle of cold tea but the strong liquid made fresh tears rush to his swollen eyes.

'They do say first day's the wust,' someone observed laconically.

'Reckon you done the wrong thing when you said as you liked flowers,' added an elderly man in a black slouch hat. 'Now then, if you'da said you liked painting pipes with lime and sulphur he'da most likely put you to a nice bitta hoeing.'

'Awkward ole bugger,' someone else murmured. 'But he don't mean no real harm.'

It proved to be a long, long day, and when it was finally ended Thaddeus plodded off home. Except for his father, the family was already seated round the kitchen supper table and his mother gave a loud squawk when she saw him.

'Gawd alive, boy, pray look at your face, do! You bin stung by a hornet?' She grabbed him, hauling him this way and that as she examined him more closely, then began to pull off his outer clothes. 'You stink worse than a privy in a heatwave!'

Drawing water from the big iron kettle on the range she told him to wash, then snatched up his discarded garments and hurried away with them. Wearily he did as he was told, and one by one his siblings lost interest in the scene and returned to spooning up potato and onion soup. The smell of it made Thaddeus feel hungry for the first time that day.

But his supper was further delayed. Reappearing from the garden with a large handful of fresh herbs Mrs Noggin set about making a poultice for his eyes, and he accepted with resignation the soggy splodge of boiled greenery slapped over them in a bit of torn-off sheet.

Half an hour later it was removed and he sat down to eat; he had taken no more than two spoonfuls when the backdoor latch clicked and his father came in.

'Where were you, then?' Ignoring the others, his eyes went straight to Thaddeus. 'I told you to meet me knocking-off time, didn't I?'

Having been on the verge of describing the rigours of his first working day, Thaddeus looked mutinous. 'Reckon I was too tired.'

'Too tired?' His father flung down the old canvas satchel in which he always transported his day's ration of food. 'So you never give a thought to me wondering where you'd got to? I went all round looking for you.'

'Sorry.'

His father grunted, sat down and removed his heavy boots. Then he looked at Thaddeus again and his expression changed. 'Give you a hard day, did they?'

'A bit.' The boy lowered his head, suddenly on the verge of tears. The tiredness in him felt like a deadly illness and it still hurt to swallow.

'Tell us, Thaddy boy.'

The rest of the family fell silent. All eyes turned on him again and he had to wait for a moment or two to ensure that his voice would be steady. 'First I done all the pipes in the grapehouse with lime and sulphur, then I swept out all the sheds and barns and the

9

apple stores ready for the picking, and then after dinner I cleaned out two big manure tanks and then started them up again.' His voice strengthened and grew in confidence as he met the eyes of his family. He was glad that his father was there. It wouldn't have felt the same without him.

'They got the tanks set in the ground about six foot deep and I had to climb down into 'em and git all the sludge and stuff out and when they was all nice and clean I had to fill 'em up with buckets of water from the back pond and then git the manure. To make a good tank of manure it's got to be one part well-rotted muck and two parts water and I'm to stir it up every day 'til it's ready for using.'

His father nodded over his raised soup spoon. 'One part muck to two parts water sounds about right.'

'Cow and bullock,' Thaddeus said. 'But not chicken.'

'No, chicken'd be too strong,' agreed his mother, cutting more chunks of bread.

'Is pig all right?' asked Eric, the youngest Noggin child.

'Little ole boy Levett's got a heapa pig looks like *black tabacca* . . .'

'No wonder he grows marrers two foot long . . .'

The conversation turned to other matters, but when they rose from the table Thaddeus's father put his hand on his shoulder in what amounted to a rough caress. 'Reckon on going back tomorrow, do you?'

'Might as well.'

'Good ole boy.' And the words were a blessing on his new status as working man.

There were six members of the Noggin family, not counting Willie who had died of the diphtheria and Grigg who was in Australia, and they were packed into the four-roomed cottage like starlings in a drainpipe.

Both Joe and his wife Beatty came from Suffolk, and while he was tall, lumbering and slow-speaking, with a ragged yellow-grey moustache and faraway blue eyes, she was small and thin, with a bright beady glance and darting whisking movements like a jenny wren. She spoke sharply and briefly, and managed the family's affairs with obsessive stringency coupled with furious energy, and

10

without joining in any local activities always knew what was going on within a five-mile radius of Marling Hamlet. Although slow to praise or condemn, she was always among the first to recognise any situation that might possibly be turned to advantage.

If anyone died, Ma Noggin would invariably be first on hand with an offer to tidy up the deceased's home and purchase for a copper or two any small article that happened to take her fancy. Bedding or oddments of china perhaps, or winter boots or Sunday suits if the dear departed had been a man. She had purchased the Widow Bean's six bantams for fourpence ha'penny apiece before their owner was cold in her bed, and on the morning of the funeral their voices rose with one accord and each laid a little brown egg. She made physic and liniment from roots and berries, brewed nettle beer and dandelion wine and could snare a rabbit or knock off a pheasant as well as any man.

With Grigg and Willie gone, Thaddeus was now the eldest child. Next to him came Marjorie, and then Dora, both still in pinafores and pigtails and scorning boys as clumsy and uncouth. Marjorie wanted to be a lady's maid when she left school, while Dora, not yet emerged from the mists of make-believe, wanted to be Florence Nightingale. ('Don't be so daft, how can you be somebody who's already *been*?')

They bickered and made up; told tales and exploded into giggles at private jokes, and unless they were feuding went everywhere hand in hand.

Eric, at five, had just embarked upon the phase of life that would henceforth be dominated by Miss Ball at the village school. Like Thaddeus, he had been equipped with a new pair of boots, but was less pleased with his coat, which was an old one of Marjorie's with the sleeves turned up. He trudged the half-mile to and fro twice daily in company with his sisters and when his legs grew tired they would sometimes give him a bandy-chair. Otherwise he had to toil along as best he could, and learn not to grizzle same as everyone else.

The village of Marling lay cradled in the valley of the river Stour, its close-cuddling cottages dominated by two large and august buildings. One was the church, a soaring tribute to the glory of God built by fourteenth-century wool merchants and the other was Marling Place, familiarly known as the Big House,

11

which had been built by a hero of the Napoleonic Wars in tribute to himself. Three generations of Fitzhardys had now been born to preside over Corinthian columns and rolling parkland, and if the church spire seemed to be raising an admonishing finger, the windows of the Big House that overlooked the valley appeared to be holding the village in a long stare of cold dislike.

Viewed from where the Noggins lived at Marling Hamlet, the house itself was obscured by a belt of woodland but its presence was still felt. As a large and powerful machine devours fuel, so Marling Place devoured local people and spat their cold cinders into the row of almshouses adorned with the Fitzhardy coat of arms. It was one of the facts of life and, like the weather, accepted as such.

It was a long, lingering autumn that year, the trees slowly catching fire in a glory of red and gold while the hedges blazed with berries and bubbled with old man's beard. Ploughing was well advanced, rooks and seagulls feeding in the wake of men like Joe Noggin, second horseman, who plodded tirelessly behind his team of Suffolks. The clink of harness and the quiet swish of the ploughshares cutting and turning the heavy soil were the only sounds; there was no birdsong, and only the occasional rasp of a pheasant relieved the monotony.

Under the flint eye of Mr Sims young Thaddeus was serving his initiation with a series of either disagreeable or boring jobs. He undertook each one with inbred stoicism, and with the shortening of the days and the coming of the first frosts he was allotted a twig broom and ordered to join the army of leaf sweepers. The system of hierachy reigned supreme in the Fitzhardy world, the older men entrusted with sweeping the flower gardens surrounding the house while the youths and one or two simpletons were ordered to clear the drives and carriageways.

Assigned to several acres of parkland planted with oak and beech, Thaddeus swept carefully and methodically, a small lonely figure in big boots and baggy cap. Mr Sims had ordained that some leaves were to be burnt and rendered into potash while others, oak and beech among them, were to be carefully heaped ready for collection and stacking for compost.

His seventh heap was half completed when he became aware of the quick drumming of hooves and the sound of voices. A man and a woman were riding towards him and Thaddeus felt a stab of alarm at the thought of finally coming face to face with his employer. Head lowered, he went on sweeping with great diligence until a voice cried 'Hey – *you!*'

It was a young voice, crisply self-assured, and belonged not to Sir Wilton but to his only son George, whom Thaddeus had never encountered either. He stood to attention, holding his broom with one hand as the two riders halted in front of them.

The young man stared down at him from his elevated perch, then told him sharply to doff his cap in her ladyship's presence. Fumbling hastily, Thaddeus did so, and the woman riding side-saddle on the big bay mare leaned forward to pat its neck.

'What's your name?' Sir Wilton's son demanded, flicking his riding crop against his polished boot.

'Thaddeus Noggin, Sir.'

'Not very big, are you?'

'I believe we have several Noggins,' her ladyship said. 'The name is quite familiar.' As she was wearing a bowler hat and a tight-fitting veil it was difficult to decipher her expression, but she seemed less peremptory than her son.

'My Dad's second horseman on the Home Farm,' Thaddeus was anxious to be polite, 'and my Auntie Bessie was scullery maid afore she married my Uncle Percy, and then my Uncle Harry started off as gamekeeper until he hurt his leg . . .' Something warned him not to continue. His voice died.

'We didn't ask you for a family history,' the young man said coldly, 'and the sooner you learn to speak when you're spoken to, the better.'

Spurring his horse he moved away. His mother remained for a second longer, contemplating Thaddeus from her Olympian heights. 'You really are very small,' she said, and he imagined that he saw the suspicion of a smile behind the veil before she too departed.

Still standing to attention, cap in one hand and broom in the other, Thaddeus stared after them as the horses quickened their pace to a canter. Hazy sunshine lit the two upright, slim-shouldered figures and caught the whirl of scattering leaves as they rode through each of the six completed heaps. He heard the sound of jolly laughter.

For some reason he made no mention of the encounter when he reached home that evening, but during the succeeding weeks his thoughts constantly returned to it. There was no sense of grievance or resentment, merely a wonderment at having seen, at such close quarters, two almost mythical creatures. It was as if Father Christmas or the Phoenix had suddenly confronted him, and he pondered their magnificent apartness to the lonely swish of his broom.

Flowers. Hundreds of them. All cut to the same length, all perfect, and all massed in careful bunches that seemed, on that sunless November day, to encompass a marvellous light of their own. The colour and scent, and above all the uniformity of their flawlessness amazed him. He stood motionless as the gardener carried the wicker baskets out of the glasshouse and dumped them down beside him.

'Gittaway loading then, afore the petals start dropping.'

One by one Thaddeus lifted them and placed them carefully on to the clean sacking that lined the barrow.

'What's these called, Mr Taplin?' He touched a fluffy yellow ball that left a fragrant powdering of pollen on his finger.

'That's mimosa. And all them's carnations and picotees. That there variety's the *Princess of Wales* with the red edge to her and that there one's the *Baroness Burdett-Coutts*. Reckon they're all right, eh?'

Thaddeus nodded, without taking his eyes from them. 'Are they all called after women, Mr Taplow?'

'Ladies,' corrected Mr Taplin. He straightened up, and regarded the boy with a tolerant smile. 'No, not by a long way. Your *Scarlet Bizarres* – them three lots there – are *Admiral Curzon*, *Robert Houlgrave* and *Robert Lord*. Then in what we call your *Scarlet Flakes* there's *Henry Cannell*, *John Ball* and *Matador*. That's your *Matador* there, look.'

He looked, and the brilliance of its colour astonished him afresh.

'Takes a whole day to arrange them up at the House, and I hear they look a rare sight all set up with great ole garlands of smilax and ferns and stuff. Never less than forty sit down to supper on her ladyship's birthday.'

14

Mr Taplin dusted his hands together then went back into the glasshouse. He returned a moment later carrying the final basket and set it down in the remaining space in the barrow.

'Them's never roses!'

'They're not red hot pokers, son.'

There must have been fifty of them. And although the carnations and picotees had exquisite form and colour, they seemed to Thaddeus to stare past him with haughty Fitzhardy unconcern whereas the roses looked straight up at him. They were all the same colour, a soft silver pink, and the high-rolled petals were just beginning to relax a little in readiness for full opening.

'That's *La France*,' Mr Taplin said. 'The most beautiful rose in the world, and what they call an HT.'

'What's HT mean, Mr Taplin?'

'Gawd knows, boy. I only looks arter'em.'

Upon Mr Taplin's instructions he wheeled the barrow along the cinder paths that led to the servants' quarters. He had never been so close to the Big House before, and its majesty was awesome. It made an insect of him.

He knocked on the closed door painted dark green. A maid in blue and white stripes and with her sleeves rolled up told him to go to the garden entrance, then slammed the door. He trundled on, and the carnations and picotees stared over his head. The next door remained tightly closed even after three bouts of knocking. Apprehensively he continued round an embrasure in the wall and to his relief came to a kind of stone tunnel, the door to which was propped wide open. He heard the sound of women's voices, and after a moment or two someone saw him. She came hurrying towards him, an elderly personage wearing a voluminous dark dress and a small white lace cap.

'You'd better bring them in – not in the barrow, you fool! – bring the baskets in . . . careful now . . .'

A bunch of keys clinked at her waist as she hurried ahead of him, and from small chill rooms on either side of the tunnel he caught the confused sounds of activity. The splash of water, the clatter of iron utensils, the sound of voices. The atmosphere of bustling crisis infected him and he began to walk faster, the basketful of *Baroness Coutts* nodding swiftly.

'In here.' The elderly personage indicated another open door,

15

and his scattered wits gathered themselves sufficiently to tell him that she must be Mrs Repton the housekeeper, a character almost as remote and splendid as Sir Wilton himself. 'Set them down there.'

The cold stone room was empty except for shelves and a large brownstone sink flanked by slate draining-boards. A single brass tap shone in the gloom.

He unloaded all the baskets one at a time, and the last one contained the specimens of *La France*. Lingering in the cold damp, not wanting to leave them, he still couldn't believe that they were roses. The old familiar rambler that clung to the thatched roof at home every year bore sprays of small bunchy roses, each flower a haphazard jumble of pink petals surrounding a white centre. Like country girls in clean pinafores they were pretty enough in their way, and even as a very small child he had always enjoyed seeing a jugful of them standing on the kitchen table – but these had a cool sweet beauty that impressed without intimidating. Very gently he touched one, then recoiled violently as a voice bawled at him from the doorway.

'Caught you, haven't I? Thinking you'd pinch one, weren't you?' Mr Sims strode forward and gave him a sharp blow on the ear.

'I wasn't – ' Thaddeus concentrated on retaining his balance.

'Ho yes, you were! Don't tell lies because liars always get found out, don't they?'

Accustomed by now to Mr Sims's habit of addressing his inferiors in a series of questions that were not designed to be answered, Thaddeus gazed down at his boots.

'Any more of it and you'll be turned off. And where d'you reckon you'll go if you're turned off – hey?'

With a final withering glance Mr Sims turned on his heel and strode out. After a discreet pause Thaddeus followed, comforting himself with the promise that one of these days he was going to have a whole great bush of *La France* all to himself in his own garden.

Although the staff at the Big House took no part in her ladyship's birthday celebrations (apart from having threepence per head clipped off the current week's wages for a voluntary birthday present), it was difficult to remain unaffected by the atmosphere of expectancy and the glimpses of steadily mounting grandeur. Housemaids scurried with brooms and feather dusters, cook and her assistants sweated and steamed over the two great iron ranges, and Mr Willis the butler retired to his pantry with a purloined bottle of Old Tawny.

The same atmosphere of nervous excitement spread to the outdoor workers. Despite the lateness of the season the lawns were rolled and the gravel drives carefully raked into half-moon patterns, and young Thaddeus, chilblains tingling, tried to imagine the climax to all this furious preparation. Fenny Brewer's auntie, who was a parlourmaid, said that her ladyship always wore white at her birthday ball: white lace that set off her lovely dark hair and her emeralds. She had beautiful shoulders and narrow little feet and her waist was no more than two hands' span even though she had a son of twenty.

'I'm going to be like her when I'm grown,' Thaddeus's sister Marjorie confided, and the family turned on her in good-natured derision.

'What – *you*, gal? You got feet like two bricks and a nose like a parsnip. You got ginger hair and enough freckles to please a courting frog and you got no fancy ways of talking . . .'

They took her to pieces, comparing each component part of her with either some vegetable or some small and unlovely non-human species, yet the analysis was not intended to wound. The merriment was tribal; each guffaw reaffirmed her closeness to them even as it dismissed any fancy ideas about stepping over the social boundary and marrying up with young Mr George. Us is us and them's them.

As zero hour approached, carriages were dispatched to the railway station at Bures St Mary to collect the house guests, then the string orchestra arrived by charabanc from Colchester and was given tea and meat-paste sandwiches in the housekeeper's room. Darkness fell, and the carefully raked drives became clogged with a variety of local conveyances ranging from Commander Plympton's de Dion Bouton to the curate of All Saint's bicycle parked discreetly behind a clump of laurel. Crystal chandeliers obligingly illuminated the sumptuous scene for the group of villagers, mostly young girls, who had crept through the cold starlight and concealed themselves among the shrubs; one of them, Hannah Smart, claimed to have witnessed every detail of both supper and ball, but when Thaddeus asked her whereabouts the pink roses had been, she shrugged and said, 'Stuck in with all the other flowers, I reckon.' She had always been daft at school.

For although like everyone else Thaddeus had found himself imaginatively involved in her ladyship's birthday celebrations, for him it was the roses that took precedence. To him they were far more than a mere part of the decorations, they were elegant guests in their own right. A week later he plucked up courage to ask Mr Sims if he could work in the rose hothouse, but Mr Sims said no.

As a country child, Thaddeus was automatically familiar with the killing of animals: a hen's neck wrung in preparation for the pot, a snared rabbit banged on the head, a brown trout poached from the Stour and gasping on the bank. Unwanted kittens were drowned, and the old dog Castor shot when his legs refused to hold him up any longer. It was all done methodically and without fuss, but that first winter up at the Big House made him aware of another reason for killing.

He still remembered clinging to Ma's skirts outside the cottage gate as the hunt went past, splendid, in red, black and white. He remembered the atmosphere of bravery and gallantry, the reek of excited horseflesh as the heavy-legged hunters trotted past, each bearing a member of the gentry who acknowledged the bared heads and respectful cheers with an Olympian raising of the hand. He remembered the splodge-footed hounds with their noses to the ground, and it was all a moment of brief beauty before they turned off the road and began to canter across the open country, the horn tootling and the hounds baying into the distance. The world seemed a grey place after they had passed, and only Ma Noggin had the common sense to shovel up the horse-droppings in a bucket, knowing that muck from thoroughbreds was twice as rich as that from the average ole nag.

But now, officially categorised as a working man, it was time for Thaddeus to become more closely acquainted with the various pursuits organised to keep winter tedium at bay. He saw her ladyship perched light as a butterfly on a great chestnut gelding as the hunt met for a stirrup cup outside the Big House; he watched the impatient wheelings and stampings of horseflesh ready for action and he listened to the braying jollity of the immaculately breeched and top-hatted Sir Wilton, who was Master.

Shortly after, he was briefly instructed in the duties of beater, and ordered to present himself at the annual pheasant shoot. He was keen, but his keenness dwindled as the day wore on and the remaining birds were driven again and again towards the guns, and the wearied dogs brought back yet more limp bunches of feathers. There were far, far more of them than any one family could hope to eat and the carnage began to depress him. He noticed for the first time how many of the ladies wore birds' plumage in their hats.

But it was different again on the day that Fenny Brewer, unofficial cousin, sidled up to him in the yard and asked Thaddeus if he would like to come to a bit of good cheer over at Blankwall Farm that evening. Conscious of the raw empty cold of endless January Thaddeus accepted, but for some reason he was unable to explain told no one at home of the invitation. He merely polished his boots, slicked down his hair with Vaseline and said that he would be back later.

'Thaddy's going courting,' tittered his sister Marjorie.

'He'd have a job to find a girl who couldn't pick him up with one hand,' observed Dora, who was darning stockings with her head bent close to the oil lamp.

'Reckon he'll make twopenn'orth of straw outta most lads afore he's done,' their father said, 'so hush your clackbox, gal.'

Blankwall Farm lay back off the road, and was a rundown, poor-looking place with tiles off the roof and weatherboard barns in need of repair. Thaddeus had never been there before, but remembered having heard tales that the farmer was a drinker and his wife funny in the head.

A bitter wind soughed through spindly trees as he approached, but the moon gave enough light to see the shadowy figures of fellow guests moving towards a small brick-built barn. There was something strangely clandestine in the atmosphere that made his heart quicken its beat and he hoped that the forthcoming entertainment wouldn't be something embarrassing to do with women. Edging his way half-taught and totally inexperienced through the emotional minefield of adolescence, it was impossible to imagine with any clarity the kind of thing he dreaded.

19

But inside the barn he felt reassured. Golden light from hurricane lamps showed Fenny and some three or four dozen others sitting round in a circle on thick shuffs of straw. Fenny waved, and several others acknowledged him with a friendly nod of the head before he found himself taking a seat next to one of the other gardeners from the Big House: the man called Neddy who had offered him the swig of tea on his first morning at work.

'Seems no time since you was a sprog of a boy,' he said kindly. 'And now, here you are.'

Thaddeus agreed, and again wondered uneasily if the forthcoming events were to involve women in some way.

Clay pipes were lit and bottles of beer placed handy, and Thaddeus gazed firmly at the roughly swept circle of brick floor in front of him. The place smelt of potatoes, sweat and black shag tobacco. Then the hum of conversation died as two men came in, each leading a dog. Both animals were muzzled, and the silence was broken by a burst of cheers.

'Good ole Towser! Git arter him!'

'Givvim what for, Sultan – goo on in there, boy!'

The two dog owners conferred for a moment, then shook hands. And then bent to remove the dogs' muzzles.

'Towser's Tom Laker's dog,' whispered Neddy. 'That's the white one, half bulldog. The other's got mastiff blood in it and never bin beat so far.'

The atmosphere became tense as the two dogs stood a little apart, as if sizing one another up. Slowly they moved closer, touching noses, their ears pricked. The brindled animal called Sultan attempted to sniff his opponent's anus and was warned off by a low growl. They stood face to face again, heads lowered and the fur slowly rising along their spines. Thaddeus watched, absorbed.

Towser opened the proceedings. As the low thunder of his growl continued his lips curled back to expose glistening teeth, the canines ready to strike. Sultan drew back a little, both dogs snarling now, then they flew together with a thud, yelping as each sought to seize hold of the other. Their jaws interlocked, then with an effort Towser broke free, shaking his head. Shouts of encouragement broke out and Thaddeus saw Sultan's owner standing with arms folded, lips compressed. He saw Fenny take a quick swig of beer.

The two dogs circled then sprang again, and the blood flowed from a bite on Towser's neck. The scent of it seemed to inflame both dogs to madness. In the pride and splendour of their savagery they bore no relation to the average family mongrel lounging idly in the village street and Thaddeus heard the sharp intake of his companion's breath as the dogs, tails curled between their legs, skirmished and struggled in a mutual grip. Sultan broke free, and in the light from the hurricanes his eyes shone as red as the blood splashing about them. The audience watched in silence, beer bottles clenched tight in ham fists.

'Sultan'll win,' rasped the man on the other side of Thaddeus. 'He's never bin beat.'

But Towser, insensible to everything except raging hatred, plunged again and again at his adversary. There were cheers from the spectators as he ripped off part of Sultan's right ear. It flicked to and fro between their desperate feet like something alive in its own right.

Suddenly Neddy stood up and began to hurry away. Instinctively Thaddeus followed, stumbling over legs and bottles and shuffs of straw. Men cursed him without removing their eyes from the scene.

'Reckon I can't face all of it,' Neddy said apologetically. He leaned against the wall and moonlight glistened on his sweating forehead.

'I'm not too keen neither.' Thaddeus strove to sound offhand.

'Rare good sport, though.'

'Reckon it's that, all right.'

They fell silent, feeling the cleansing chill of the wind and listening to the bloodlust roars coming from inside the old barn. Thaddeus sensed an affinity with Neddy, although he was older, and he remembered again the swig of tea on his first morning up at the Big House.

'Go back in, shall we?'

'Don't mind.'

But neither had any intention of moving. Flinching, Thaddeus heard the shouts rising to a hoarse crescendo, and then fall silent. It was possible to catch the faraway cry of an owl. They went on standing there in the shifting flickering moonlight, then the doors opened, letting out the golden bobbles of light from the hurricane lamps.

21

Towser's owner headed the solemn procession, carrying the dog with all the portentous dignity of a priest carrying a holy relic. He gazed down at it proudly, reverently, and Thaddeus saw the glistening mess where its lower jaw had been torn away. Its white coat was barely visible beneath the blood, but from the juddering spasms of its ribcage it was still alive.

They crowded round it, awed and full of praise, then it was the victor's turn. Tightly leashed, he stumbled at his owner's heels with blood from the torn-off ear now matting his eyes. There were wounds in his throat and a deep tear on his shoulder. He looked dazed and exhausted, and refused the titbits of raw meat proffered by his admirers, who seemed in no hurry to disperse. There was still beer to drink and details of the fight to discuss and no one noticed the departure of Thaddeus and Neddy. They walked in silence, and parted without saying goodnight.

Joe Noggin had two loves in his life. One was his family and the other was horses. All his forebears had been connected with them in some way or another – as carters, stablemen, grooms or blacksmiths, but the majority had worked with them on farms, like Joe.

And they all began as young lads, and worked to an unrelenting schedule until they were eventually upgraded to horseman's mate and then finally to horseman, or baiter, with sole responsibility for a pair of Suffolk Punches. These great animals, weighing in excess of a ton, had a sweet amiability and a capacity for work that was characteristic of their breed; one of Joe's earliest memories was being held up to the stable door to see a newborn foal tottering bravely in the shadow of its dam.

He left school when he was eleven, and was fortunate to be put to work with Arthur Beal when he was second baiter up at the Big House farm. He learned to accept the long hours and disciplined routine involved in good horse management as a young colt learns to accept the bridle and bit, and Arthur taught him with the same kindliness with which he handled his pair of Suffolks. He learned the art of grooming and feeding – a stone of mixed oats and beans as the daily basic, and a pinch of dried tansy for bringing up the bloom on the coat – and he sat on a three-legged stool polishing harnesses and buffing up brasses with housewifely pride. But most

22

of all he learned the art of communication through tone of voice and touch of hand which could lead to that strange and precious empathy between man and beast.

He was learning to guide a plough when Arthur was upgraded to head baiter, and to celebrate the event young Joe smoked his first black shag roll-up. It made him feel very ill, and Arthur prepared an emetic with the same scrupulous concern with which he would prepare a bottle of horse physic.

To be made head baiter on a large Suffolk farm could almost be compared to being given command of a regiment. The position carried great formal dignity, and at no time was this more apparent than at turn-out in the morning, and then the return to stables when the day's work had been completed. True to his title, the head baiter's team always led the procession, coats gleaming, brasses clinking and twinkling, and Arthur's appearance was equally spruce. Velvet-fronted waistcoat, brightly patterned neckerchief, and over his cord breeches a pair of knee buskins for added warmth. His heavy boots were polished daily and his clay tobacco pipe was stuck jauntily in the band of his billycock hat. There was an indefinable air of swagger among the horsemen on a farm which set them apart from the ordinary labourers, and when young Joe became elevated to first baiter's mate, his new twill shirt crackled like a bonfire when he moved. He was determined to succeed Arthur when the time came.

Yet increasingly he loved the horses for themselves, and the year he married Beatty at the age of twenty-three he was put in charge of his own team: a pair of chestnut geldings with a white blaze on their foreheads and their names were Boxer and Bowler. Despite the attractions of the nuptial bed he was up every morning at four and on his way to the stable to prepare the first feed of the day.

And they would be waiting for him, large eyes glowing in the sombre light, velvet noses lifting and wrinkling with pleasure. He loved the warm pungent smell of them, the rough shoving caress of their great heads, and was sensitive to their personal idiosyncracies; Bowler preferred not to pass a certain red may tree when it was in flower and Boxer was unnerved by the smell of pigs. Joe knew all these things and many more, some by careful observation and some by intuition, for horses were in his blood. Particularly the Suffolks.

It was a hard blow to his pride when Arthur Beal finally retired, and was replaced by a young horseman brought in from over Pebmarsh way. True enough, he knew his work and was conscientious in all matters, but he had usurped the role that belonged by traditional right to Joe Noggin. Joe, now the father of six, was still second baiter, and still stood aside in the twice-daily procession to and from the fields while the young chap from Pebmarsh led the way.

With Grigg married and gone to foreign parts, with Willie dead and buried and Thaddy preferring to be a gardner, it seemed to Joe as if the age-old Noggin involvement with horses might be coming to an end. Hopefully he watched little Eric for signs of wanting to follow in his father's footsteps in the ploughed furrow, but Eric was a tucked-away, fanciful child who played imaginary games about being a fisherman, although he had never seen the sea except in a picture book.

So Joe continued to bide his time, and was civil to the young chap who had come over from Pebmarsh to fill the place that was rightly his own. March came in, roaring across the fields and driving the soil ready for the horseman to start drilling the oats and barley. The sowing of cattle beet and mangels came after, and when the winds had turned from the east it was time to harrow the winter wheat.

The soft blue air was full of birdsong, full of the sense of eager young growth, and Joe, marching at a steady two miles an hour behind Boxer and Bowler, saw all the evidence of a fine harvest to come that year. He had no means of knowing that some eight and a half million young lives were also due to be harvested.

In the meanwhile with the season of field sports blood-letting at an end, foxes, badgers, hares and game birds were allowed to go about the process of procreation in peace, and down on the Stour young otters played unhindered, diving and surfacing in a cloud of silver bubbles.

And with disconcerting suddenness, young Thaddeus began to grow. With bony wrists shooting from the cuffs of his jacket he seemed to grow almost hourly, and as the distance between head and feet increased with such rapidity he found it difficult not to bump into things. He seemed to trip over other people as

24

frequently as they tripped over him: 'Gather y'self together boy –
do!' the family would cry, but the more he strove to marshal his
limbs into some kind of compact order the more they appeared to
sprawl and gangle of their own accord. He crashed his head on
every doorway in the cottage, whirled things off the table with his
elbows, and even in bed there was no respite, for his feet stuck out
at the bottom and flickered pale defiance at him.

The change in his voice was equally spectacular. Helplessly he
would hear himself plummet from boy soprano to seasoned
baritone all in the space of one sentence and his sister's giggles did
little to soothe his embarrassment.

No one else of his age seemed to be suffering as he was, and
when in a fit of mutinous despair he said as much to his mother she
replied that it was his own fault for starting so late. Then she
reached up to pat his shoulder: 'Don't you take on, boy. Ash buds
stay black 'til April but they last longer than most the others do.'

So he tried to ignore the physical embarrassments and to
suppress the fluctuating moods, for in the meanwhile there were
the gardens up at the Big House.

He was now allowed to hoe some of the less conspicuous
herbaceous borders, but not to set out the new summer bedding
plants. He was instructed in the art of unobtrusive staking and
tying, and he trundled the two-wheeled galvanised tank full of
manure-water to wherever it was required. He weeded paths on
hands and knees, and was finally entrusted with the task of dead-
heading the early pansies so they would bloom again in August.
He was slowly becoming familiar with plant life in the same way
that his father, years ago, had become familiar with Suffolk
Punches, but so far he had not been allowed to work in the rose
garden. This was the exclusive territory of Mr Sims and two of his
most favoured gardeners, and Thaddeus, caught peering
enviously through an archway in the yew hedge, was ordered to go
and thin onions in the kitchen garden if he had nothing better to do
with his time. He went, his mind still dazzled by the scent and sight
of a thousand roseheads basking in the sun.

And in the benign warmth of that first glorious summer, the
family at the Big House became visible as they strolled on the
terraces, wandered through the shrubberies, sauntered by the
lake. Large hats and lacy parasols bloomed like great white

25

peonies and the gentlemen's straw boaters glistened a deferential accompaniment. Thaddeus grew accustomed to the click of croquet mallets, the lazy plash of oars and the murmur of gentry voices as they gathered for afternoon tea beneath the cedar of Lebanon. The family entertained a great many house guests, but among all the softly draped, willow-waisted women who lingered and leisured through the gardens there was no one as beautiful as Lady Isobel.

There was no one like her at all, and peering guiltily through barricades of clematis and honeysuckle Thaddeus marvelled at the poise of her head, and the graceful fall of her skirts that ended in a trickle of lace at her heels. She seemed to move over the smooth sunlit lawns like something effortlessly in tune with nature itself, and he could only compare it to the easy flow of the Stour on its way to the sea.

He saw her strolling with her son George, smilingly, with her arm linked through his. He heard the jolly boom of Sir Wilton's voice as he called to the two gambolling brown Airedales that lived as part of the family, and he wondered what it would be like to be a rich young man with a mother like Lady Isobel. Sometimes at night he wondered what it would be like to be her husband, like Sir Wilton, then hurriedly turned his thoughts away.

Mid-afternoon torpor had fallen over the gardens on the day that Thaddeus, in cap and shirt-sleeves, was making his way back to the potting sheds. There was no one about as he passed the high yew hedges that enclosed the rose garden. Dreamy silence filled the world, and on impulse he stole cautiously through the nearest archway. The roses, plump with well-being, crowded the big rich beds between the narrow gravel paths and their mingled scents intoxicated him. Dazed, he turned his head this way and that, catching traces of nutmeg and lemon spiking the sweetness of peaches and honey, then, awkward with his new height, bent to sniff the opening heart of a salmon-pink hybrid tea; as he did so, a large white rose from the next bush released a slow flood of petals at his feet with what seemed like a tired sigh. There was something in the gesture that made him think of a beautiful woman letting her skirts fall about her, and when he heard a soft footfall and looked up to see Lady Isobel slowly approaching, he blushed scarlet.

It was too late to retreat. Snatching off his cap he stood in the required attitude – head bent, eyes lowered.

26

Lady Isobel paused, then gave a slight inclination of the head. 'Good-afternoon.'

In an agony of shyness and guilt, Thaddeus mumbled good-afternoon in return, then gathered himself for flight.

'Do you like roses?' The clearness and the amused ease in her voice seemed to him extraordinary.

He raised his eyes, and the gentle folds of her white gown were dazzling in the sunlight. They reminded him of his feeling at the fall of the white rose petals, and his blush deepened. She smiled at him and he saw the gleam of her eyes beneath the shade of her large-brimmed hat.

'Yes – thank you, My Lady.' He swallowed convulsively.

'I dare say you help to grow them, do you?' She seemed interested, and in no hurry to move away.

'No – well, I just help to prepare the muck, like . . .' Instantly mortified by his mention of the word muck in her ladyship's presence Thaddeus dropped his cap and stood staring at it blindly.

Lady Isobel's laughter was like the musical trill of a bird. 'In that case we must see that you reap some of the benefits.' She came a little closer. 'Does your mother like roses? I take it that you have a mother?' She seemed to find him increasingly amusing.

'Yes . . . she likes them fine . . .'

'Then you must take her some,' Lady Isobel said lightly. 'Here –' she detached a small pair of gold scissors from the wide blue belt that encircled her waist. Drowningly he recalled Fenny Brewer's auntie saying that her waist was only two hands' span. He remained motionless, fresh waves of confusion mounting.

'Go along. Do as I say. Cut some.'

He took the scissors, small and ornate and still warm from her person. His fingers were so big that he could only insert the tips of them through the holes. He stood looking at her helplessly. 'Which ones must I. . . ?'

'Whichever ones you think she would like. Take some of those –' she waved towards a bed filled with butter-yellow blooms. Thaddeus bent to snip one, and it lay warm and quiescent on his hand like something that was living and breathing.

Lady Isobel came closer, and the scent she was wearing mingled with that of the roses. Her eyes still gleamed, and the brim of her hat made a pattern on her shoulders.

'You must cut more. One is no use. Take her some of the pink ones, and what about those over there . . . and there . . . look, there are hundreds of those red ones just beginning to open.'

The moment during which they had stood facing one another in the sun-drenched garden had seemed to have no feeling of time, but now a strange and mutual sense of urgency appeared to seize them both.

'Go along!' she said sharply, with a sudden little movement of her head, 'cut them, cut them. Do as I say.'

He obeyed, crouching untidily over the exquisite blooms as the little gold scissors poised on the ends of his fingers severed the warm juicy stems and the roses fell like silken prey into his grasp.

She was still urging him on when there were too many to hold, and he had to lay them in a reverent pile on the edge of the path. Stricken by their loveliness, he fancied that they were panting out their lives like the shot birds of last winter, and when he glanced up and saw the suffused face of Mr Sims confronting him through the archway his heart jumped with fear. From the corner of his eye he saw Mr Sims taking in the terrible scene – he appeared to be counting every rose with a perceptible nod of the head, then abruptly he was gone. Lady Isobel seemed not to have noticed him.

'That's a wicked great heap,' Thaddeus said desperately. 'I daresn't cut n'more.'

'Are you quite sure?' She stood looking at him with kindly curiosity.

He nodded, incapable of further speech, and began to gather the pile of roses lying by the path. One of the thorns gashed his finger. Lady Isobel noticed, and asked if it hurt. Wiping away the blood, Thaddeus nodded.

'Beautiful things invariably cause us pain,' she said, a little sadly. 'Now, take them home to your mother, rose boy, and should anyone question you, you may refer them to me.'

He thanked her and stumbled away. Bowed beneath a tumult of feeling he forgot to pick up his cap.

His mother greeted the armful of roses with cries of astonishment. 'Thaddy – you *never* – !'

'No, of course I never!' Indignation drove his voice to a high squeak.

'You don't mean *Nable* givvem to you?'

'Yes,' he said recklessly. 'He was sort of showing me how to prune them, like.'

He was in love with Lady Isobel. And the power of it seemed to spring partly from the sheer impossibility of his loving her. There were no hot dreams of seduction – he shrank even from the thought of touching her – but she was now with him day and night like a serene and lovely ghost. Her phantom presence enriched him, and opened his eyes to the casual beauty that lay all around him. Even chipped cups standing in odd saucers took on a pleasing aspect in her secret presence. His world seemed to expand, to blossom with a thousand innocent delights because of her.

And the roses filled the cottage with their fragrance, and filled each poky, low-ceilinged room with a radiance that matched his new inner life. A brown earthenware jug containing six of the white blooms he had cut under Lady Isobel's supervision stood on the washstand of the bedroom he shared with young Eric, and as he watched them glimmering in the grey summer darkness they seemed more and more to encapsulate the elusive enchantment of Lady Isobel herself. He mourned the slow falling of each petal like a little death, and ignored family hints that he must be in ole Nable's good books, and might soon be elevated from gardener's boy to under-gardener up at the Big House.

But while Mr Sims for some reason refrained from mentioning the appalling scene he had witnessed in the rose garden, he gave no hint of forthcoming promotion either, and Thaddeus continued with the humble labouring tasks allotted to him. He made a point of staying as far as possible from the rose garden, but feasted his eyes on the lovely vision of Lady Isobel whenever she was in the vicinity. It was not easy to do so because of the cardinal rule that gardeners must contrive to work while remaining unseen by their betters.

The sight of a shabby, perspiring man mulching the marguerites or staking the delphiniums was considered unappealing and therefore best left to the imagination, but it was still possible with a little ingenuity to loiter for a moment or two behind an extravagantly flowering shrub and see her mingling with guests on the croquet lawn, to watch her slow graceful movements as she approached the ball then lightly tapped it through the hoop. There

29

was a wonderful airiness about her whole demeanour that enchanted and enslaved him during the course of that long hot summer, and during his romantic idealisation of her she became increasingly associated with the remote beauty of the rose *La France* from the hothouse, and with the glistening chalices of the high summer blooms that had graced his bedroom for a few precious days. Roses and Lady Isobel were now synonymous in his mind.

It was mid-July when the idea came that he might possibly grow some roses of his own. The idea filled him with a stealthy excitement, and when during one bait-time he was able to snick a dead rosehead between thumb and forefinger and transfer it to his pocket he felt that he had made a good beginning.

He took it home, and after tea prepared a small pot of loam and secreted it up in the bedroom. Eric was playing in the road outside as Thaddeus sank down on to the side of his bed with the dead flower in his hand. Very carefully he pulled it apart, noting the different components with care; little black whisker-things and a small green container like a round box. He shook it next to his ear, hoping to hear the rattle of seeds, then very gently pulled it apart. The seeds – if they were seeds – were disappointingly small, pale and sticky-damp, but he scooped them out very carefully and covered them with a layer of damp loam in the pot. Knowing that seeds develop best in the dark, he hid the pot under his bed. Under the impression that he was trying his hand at growing mushrooms his mother chucked them away and told him to wait until September when they'd be thick as daisies all over Pedlar's meadow. He refrained from confessing the truth.

He tried again later, and this time secreted them in a seedbox beneath the staging in one of the hothouses. A small green shoot appeared which he watered with care, but on the day the world found itself plunged into the first global war, he discovered that it was only a weed.

It seemed at first as if nothing could break the spell of that slow, languorous summer.

Harvest was the next event in the country calendar, but when Sir Wilton summoned his entire staff to the entrance to the stableyard and repeated in a barked staccato the injunction that

England expected every man to do his duty, a quiver of excitement ran through them. They remembered the old childhood tales of valiant knights going forth to fight, and several employees, including the gardener called Neddy, bravely volunteered to join the colours without even the ability to locate Kaiser Bill's Germany on the map. Sir Wilton awarded them half a sovereign each, which he took from a leather purse.

Abruptly they became heroes, those clumsy, sun-scorched and self-conscious young men, and tentative romances blossomed at speed as the day for departure came closer. Mothers wept proudly and the young volunteers read the glimmer of envy in their fathers' eyes. A silver band saw them off at Sudbury railway station and Ma Noggin grasped Thaddeus by the elbow and said 'Pray oh pray it'll be over afore you have to go.' Patriotic sentimentality had little place in her life.

Young George, the son of the Big House, was one of the first to offer his services; he allowed himself to be seen in officer's tunic and sharply cut breeches and brandishing an even more lordly demeanour before departing for the unknown shore they called Flanders. He looked very handsome and heroic as he strolled through Marling and its hamlet, and Thaddeus's sister Marjorie suffered a sharp attack of fantasy passion which she confided to her elder brother while they were picking blackberries one Sunday afternoon. He sympathised, without disclosing any hint of his own longings.

It was a splendid harvest that year, the golden fields yielding a richness of dry ripe grain, and Joe Noggin, walking to and fro from the stackyard at the head of his team, wondered what German farmers were like. Much the same as Suffolk ones, he imagined, plus a kind of sly wickedness. Every now and then he eyed the young chap from over Pebmarsh way who had taken the place of Arthur Beal as head horseman, and wondered whether he too was going to volunteer, and if he did so, who would take his place. Disappointment still ached behind the magnanimity.

They had cut and carted the seed clover and pulled the cattle beet when the news came about Tom Lake's son being killed while on active service. The telegram was passed from hand to hand round the village, and the Lake family's loss was their own. Mrs Lake borrowed a black coat from her sister when the vicar's wife

31

invited her to tea and her motherly pride only melted into sobs when she passed the family grave in the churchyard and realised that her boy would not be laid to rest in it. He would be all on his own in some place she couldn't pronounce the name of.

As tales of atrocities in Belgium found their way through the placid Suffolk countryside, the mood of rather larky enthusiasm hardened to a patriotic hatred. Spurred on by ladies knitting socks and rolling bandages, the young men queued at the recruiting offices, each imbued with the determination to give ole Kaiser Bill what-for, and two housemaids from up at the Big House cast aside their caps and aprons and went off to Colchester to work in munitions. They didn't qualify for half a sovereign as Sir Wilton considered that their duty was to Keep the Home Fires Burning: his own in particular.

Even by 1915 the workforce on the land was becoming noticeably depleted. Those who remained were exhorted to put their backs into it for the sake of King and Country, and Thaddeus was returning to the potting sheds one afternoon when he saw a group of men standing close together by the yard gate. As he approached they moved aside, and he recognised his friend Neddy wearing a bright blue suit. Hunched on a pair of crutches, his empty left trouser leg had been folded and pinned neatly above the knee. He looked strange and embarrassed, and laughed with uncharacteristic heartiness at the brave jokes, struggling so hard to hide his old workmates' awkward sympathy.

'Not too proud to know me, are you, Thaddy?' His eyes held a yearning, almost animal appeal which reminded Thaddeus uncomfortably of the dog-fight at Blankwall Farm which squeamishness had forced them both to leave before the conclusion. Swallowing hard, Thaddeus said that of course he wasn't too proud, and gave an inconclusive dab at Neddy's arm.

'So what's all this then, Neddy?'

'Some blooming ole Jerry took it offa me at Wipers. Reckoned he'd keep it for a spare.'

They all laughed loudly, Thaddeus included, because they sensed that laughter and not sympathy was what Neddy was silently begging them for. He had never played the clown in the old days but now had evidently decided that it was henceforth to be his chosen role: the funny man hopping about on two sticks. All he had to look forward to now was the indulgent applause normally bestowed upon a third-rate circus performer. He had decided – and they accepted his decision in the absence of a better one.

Thaddeus went home in thoughtful mood, and expressed no comment when it became known that Sir Wilton had recommended Neddy to a home for mutilated ex-servicemen somewhere up on the coast near Southwold, where he would be taught genteel new skills like embroidery and building models of the Houses of Parliament out of spent matches far away from everyone he knew. He hoped that Neddy wouldn't go, but he did. Characteristically, Sir Wilton continued to sweep away whatever major or minor decision a subordinate might make.

Neuve Chapelle, Festubert, Loos, Gallipoli . . . each name took its place in the roll of battles being fought Over There, and the vicar procured a large map of the Franco-Belgian border and pinned it up in the porch of All Saints' for the benefit of his parishioners. Conscription was introduced, and farmworkers (but not gardeners) were exempted; to volunteer was for them a matter of conscience only.

Working alongside the other gardeners Thaddeus heard the younger men making up their minds, and heard their decisions for going discussed with their elders at bait-time. Patriotism, although still strong, now appeared to be slightly in the minority compared to other more homely reasons: Jeff Waskett had fallen out with his girl, Harry Cousins wanted to see a bit of the world before he settled down, and Fenny Brewer, who owed seven-and-six to Amos White, thought that Sir Wilton's half-sovereign would come in handy.

So they went off in their Sunday clothes and with a flower in their buttonholes, joking and guffawing just a shade uneasily as they waited for the train, and Thaddeus, left behind, was finally allowed to hoe and dead-head in the rose garden.

He worked under the flint eye of Mr Sims, who maintained a tight-lipped silence apart from curt instructions about cutting to the nearest outside bud-point and using the hoe on a shallow slant in order not to disturb surface roots. Yet despite close supervision he managed to secrete more spent blooms with their promise for the future into stealthily prepared pots of loam hidden under hothouse staging. To grow a perfect rose like *La France*, or the white rose who had so seductively dropped her petals on that stolen afternoon, became the summit of his life's ambition. The war was raging somewhere out there beyond the Stour valley, but the fixed purpose which held him and supported him through adolescence was his determination to watch a rose come into being; to struggle upwards from the soil, a solitary green shoot almost comic in its vulnerability, stretch upwards and branch outwards and form rosebuds that would open their faces to the sun. And it would be his rose. A work that he had helped to fashion through care and skill, and it would have nothing to do with hatred and killing and dying silly proud deaths. He became known among the men who remained up at the Big House as a funny shy sort of lad with no real harm to him.

The autumn of 1916 came in dank and grey. Rain fell and westerly winds swept the gardens, tearing across the abandoned croquet lawn while the lake ruffled its face in alarm. The fires of geraniums and dahlias were doused and the last roseheads hung sodden and sullen with discomfort. Mildew attacked, and one afternoon when the clouds parted to disclose a watery gleam of hope, Fenny Brewer, clad in the now familiar suit of hospital blue, came tapping his way into the yard on a white stick, his milk-coloured eyes upturned and with a silver plate in his head.

He was particularly proud of the silver plate, and pointed to its exact location as if they were unable to see for themselves the patch of skull where the hair would never grow again, and the way his features had become eerily displaced; those on the right side a bit higher than those on the left.

'Gotta ding on the head,' he told them with the same beseeching laugh that Neddy had offered. 'Come to three days arter, and didn't know nuthun 'til they told me I'd copped a Blighty one.'

They laughed with him, admiring the squinting white eyes and grotesquely rearranged features, and Thaddeus brooded upon what seemed like a wayward human preference for pain and disfigurement. The torn and screaming fox that had given a good run for its money had a toast drunk to it; he remembered the admiration bestowed upon the dog Towser when its lower jaw was ripped away, and now men like Neddy and Fenny and all the others coming back from Over There distorted and unsightly but

34

obviously brave, qualifying in their turn as objects of awed veneration.

Then on the 2nd of November the telegram arrived to announce that young George Fitzhardy had lain down his life for his country.

Time stopped, frozen in its tracks. No one could believe it, because despite the march of progress there was still a natural order to dictate who should qualify for suffering and who should remain exempt; Fitzhardys, like all gentry, were taken as belonging to the latter category.

Dead. Killed outright on something called the Somme. Aghast, they watched the dark blue holland blinds close down over each Big House window, and Mr Sims was ordered to stop the hands of the stable clock. Grief's heavy silence fell everywhere, and Thaddeus took his place in the queue waiting silently to receive one of the black armbands ordered from the haberdasher in Sudbury. Weeping housemaids wore black streamers round their mob caps, and Lady Isobel's forthcoming birthday celebrations were cancelled, together with all sporting events planned for the coming winter. The vixen ran free on the hillside and game birds strolled unhindered in the lanes, but Sir Wilton and Lady Isobel were invisible, broken, it was whispered, by the weight of their grief.

'Stuffed up in the dark in that gret ole place can't be doing them n'good,' observed Ma Noggin.

'Won't be doing poor Georgie much good, neither,' added Dora, with a sly glance at her weeping sister.

Like everyone else, the Noggin family was bowed beneath the momentous shock, then like everyone else, began to come back to life with the news that the body was to be brought home and given a full-scale military funeral. The local shop ran out of black dolly dye-bags and word went round that the Suffragan Bishop would be coming to take the service. In the meanwhile the gloomy work of autumn proceeded in a more sporadic fashion than usual.

Thaddeus had left the task of lifting and storing dahlia tubers in order to slip into the hothouse to check the pot of tiny rose seedlings hidden there, when a soft footfall made him turn sharply.

Hatless, and wearing a long black coat with a shawl collar, Lady Isobel was walking smoothly and blindly as a sleepwalker.

Immobilised with shock, he stood watching as she wandered through a tracery of ferns and creepers, up one tessellated path and down another. Her face was bloodless, and his sense of shock changed to a profound unease when he saw her lips moving as if she were talking to herself.

His first instinct was to hide, to close his eyes and his mind against anything about her that was unseemly and therefore hurtful to him, but he remained incapable of movement. She turned towards the final path, where he was standing, and when he saw the tears on her cheeks he instinctively stepped out in front of her and said, 'Please, don't take on.'

She looked at him vaguely, as if she were no longer part of the world, then he saw recognition stir in her wet brown eyes, and her tears increased. She stood with her head bent, abandoned to sorrow like a child.

Setting down the pot of seedlings he timidly took her hand and led her unresisting to a seat. They sat down, and her helpless weeping distressed him so much that, unaware of what he was doing, he put his arms round her and drew her close to him.

Submissively she leaned her head against his shoulder and he sensed her abandonment to a grief that gave her neither rest nor hope of deliverance. It was like a separate entity, that grief of hers; a monster of pain that obliterated the old familiar world of beauty, leisure and security. Without either of them being aware, it also obliterated the old established order, and as he held her with inexperienced young arms he was conscious not of her identity but only of her suffering.

Her weeping grew wilder as broken words and phrases tumbled out. 'My ch-child and he was all I ha-had . . . they took hi-him from m-m-me and they took – they took away his l-l-life . . . so full of ha-ha-happiness and promise and it was all for nu-nu-nothing . . .' It went on and on, disjointed and repetitive, and he held her tenderly, lovingly, with no sense of propriety to wither his urge to comfort her.

She stopped trying to talk, and when at last she raised her head he took his handkerchief from his pocket and gently wiped away her tears. Wincing, he saw that he had left a little smear of soil on her cheek; she appeared not to notice when instinctively he moistened his finger and wiped it away. The world outside was cold with autumn, cold with death, but among the tropical garlands in the hothouse bloomed a strange little hybrid relationship, a mere flower of an hour, that was able to comfort and console.

The storm of weeping came to an end and Lady Isobel pushed his arms away and stood up. Thaddeus also rose to his feet, and with the abrupt return to normality, automatically assumed the correct posture of straight back, lowered head, and gaze directed at the toes of his workboots. Already the sense of reality had drained from the last few minutes, leaving him confused and appalled.

'What is in the pot you were holding?'

His heart sank at the tone of her voice. 'Rose seedlings, my lady.'

'Did Mr Sims order you to grow them?'

'No, my lady.'

He loomed over her, gangling and ungainly as he waited for the words of dismissal: they would be cruel and bitter because in her own eyes she had made a fool of herself. Then, to his stupefaction, she threw her arms around him and held him to her with a wild and desperate strength. For the first time he became distractedly aware of the scent of her skin, the warmth of her body. It overwhelmed him, and he wondered if he was going to faint.

'But they shan't have *you!*' she was crying against his shoulder. 'They have taken my son but they shan't take you! I shall forbid it – I can, you know – my husband is a JP and he also has influence with the War Office – he has met Douglas Haig several times . . . I *refuse* to allow any more young men – the flowers of our country – to be maimed and killed – it's a madness – a madness!'

'All killing's a madness,' he said. 'Wanting to kill is wicked and anyhow, it don't do n'good . . .'

Her sense of distracted horror communicated itself to him in a kaleidoscope of brutal imagery – the dog-fight, the stricken game birds plummeting from the sky, the hateful, pleading expressions on maimed human faces – he realised instantly that nothing would induce him to be part of the war. That there was no sense of valour in him, no willingness to be humiliated by pain and ugliness for the sake of empty words like heroism and self-sacrifice. The feeling had been there all along, but suddenly it had been made tangible, something that could be put into words and spoken aloud.

'They shall not have you! – they have taken away so many others, including my son, and I *refuse* to allow them – '

'It just don't seem to do n'good, all this killing – '

'People should concentrate on creating, not destroying!' she raged against his shoulder. She was trembling, and he had to put his arms round her to hold her still. Their voices rose, colliding among the listening plants.

'What they done to poor ole Neddy had no sense to it at all. His leg's off just above the knee and he'll be hopping round on a coupla sticks for the rest of his life – can't hardly work at a decent job like that, can you?'

'My son had everything ahead of him, like so many other young men. He would have taken over the estate – '

'Then what about ole Fenny? Poor ole Fenny, they really done for him, didn't they? Blind as a mole now and a face on him nobody likes to look at n'more than once – '

'But they shan't take *you*!' Lady Isobel released her grasp of him, and his own arms fell away from her as she stepped back to look at him. Her dark eyes blazed in her beautiful ravaged face and despite the chaos of his own feelings he sensed that she was close to madness. 'You shall stay here in the garden, growing roses! Do you hear me, now? They have taken millions of other women's sons and fed them into their war machine but I refuse to let them have you. You are not going to the war – I personally will see to it that you do not . . . No more, no more . . . and if anyone questions my word, you may refer them to me!'

The sense of decisive authority in that frail-seeming body moved him almost unbearably, and he stood motionless as she suddenly turned on her heel and walked rapidly away. The doors of the hothouse crashed behind her, shivering the giant leaves of a Dicksonia tree-fern.

And although the strange and desperate contact between them had carried no hint of carnality, his love for her manifested itself for the first time that night, and he woke from sleep with wet loins and a triumphantly pounding heart.

He loved her, and his love would last unchanging through the multitude of years that now lay ahead because he was not going to the war. She had said so, which meant that she must love him, just a very little, in return.

They were up at five on the day of the funeral.

Long before it was light the horsemen had been at work in the stables, and Joe Noggin, second baiter, had added a helping of ground red carrots to his team's first feed of the day. Cold rain beat on the stable roofs but Joe worked in shirt-sleeves, grooming his two Suffolks with long rhythmical strokes of the brush then bringing up the final bloom with a bit of rag moistened with paraffin. Their hooves had been polished and their manes and tails bound with black and purple braid.

They sensed that something was up. They stamped restlessly, throwing up their great heads and snorting while Joe took his own bait nearby: a bit of cold mutton pie smeared over with pickle and washed down with a bottle of tea. Munching with a slow and dogged persistence he sat thinking of what lay ahead, and wishing that it was over. Making a public show of your boy's death wasn't right somehow, even if he was a Fitzhardy. Any case, it wouldn't bring him back.

The stable door opened and the head baiter, the young chap from over Pebmarsh way, came in with two long black feathery things.

'Plumes,' he said, handing them to Joe. 'They want them fixing on the bridles, upright between the ears.'

Joe received them in silence. The young chap lingered for a moment, then rubbed his hands in attempted cheerfulness. 'Reckon they could've picked a better day for it.'

'It's gunna be a wet ole day in more ways than one,' Joe said heavily.

Down in the village and its nearby hamlet, preparations were well under way. Martha Green and her daughter Mabel had swept the church and polished the brasses, and when the doctor's wife bustled in with the floral decorations and dropped arum lily petals on the altar steps Martha had disposed of them wearing an expression of resolute control. Then the verger had come in and fussed about draping the Fitzhardy pew with laurel and ivy, during the course of which a lot more mess was made. It was dankly cold in the church and their breath lay on the air like wreathing ghosts.

As the morning wore on towards eleven, villagers arrayed themselves in their carefully assembled mourning; Marjorie Noggin looked unexpectedly pretty in her late grandmother's black two-piece and her sister Dora wept mutinous tears at being ordered to wear Aunt Cissie's big black coat which came down to her ankles and smelt of mice. Young Eric accepted his allocation of black tie, black cap and black woollen stockings with equanimity, being at the age when clothing had little meaning beyond the requirements of warmth and comfort, but he admired his mother's hat artfully fashioned from a black velvet cushion cover that had once belonged to the doctor's wife.

They surveyed one another anxiously and a little doubtfully when the transformation was complete, then drew down the blinds and went out to take their place in the road where all the other blinds were drawn and the thatched roofs dark with rain. The church bell was already tolling as neighbours nodded and smiled, then, remembering the occasion, readjusted their features and gazed stoically at their feet.

They heard the sound of the regimental band before the cortège came into sight, winding its way along the narrow twisting road from Bures St Mary's railway station. It sounded hoarse and sonorous, and so unlike the cheerful voice of Sudbury's silver band that whatever small amount of gossiping and fidgeting was taking place, ceased abruptly.

The khaki-clad figures slow-marched past the school that bore sodden black ribbons on its closed gates, past the general shop and the alleyway that led to the allotments. Raindrops fell from the peaks of their caps and slid down the polished surfaces of trombone, trumpet and tuba, and young Marjorie searched the passing faces of poor Mr George's battalion for signs of grief. She felt her own tears pricking, and groped in the pocket of her grandmother's two-piece for a handkerchief.

The coffin, draped with the Union Jack and covered with flowers, was resting on a large flat-sided cart from the Home Farm. The wheels glistened with a fresh coat of black paint while the floor of it had been covered by a pall of purple and black, and it was drawn by four Suffolk Punches. With carefully observed protocol, the head baiter's team was in the lead, and he marched at their head with rigid spine and a set expression. Joe Noggin was directly behind with Boxer and Bowler, the rain drumming on his new black cap, and there was such poignancy in the scene that handkerchiefs fluttered freely.

40

The motors came next: a fleet of black Daimlers with pearl-grey blinds closely drawn and wide black ribbons stretching the length of the bonnet. One or two of the older women lining the street dropped an involuntary curtsy as the first one passed: the one that would contain Sir Wilton and Lady Isobel, poor souls.

Thaddeus had been placed in the estate workers' guard of honour that lined the way between the main gates of the Big House and the family's private entrance to the churchyard. The vicar was waiting with the visiting bishop beneath a large black umbrella; he looked pinched with cold, and kept worrying at his nose with a conspicuously white handkerchief while the bishop, unctuous in purple, gazed blandly ahead.

The sound of Chopin's Funeral March, heavy with doom, came gradually nearer and Thaddeus automatically straightened his shoulders, conscious that everyone else was doing the same thing. He watched the soldiers pass, and his heart quickened at the sight of his father walking protectively close to his team. The black plumes on their heads had been thinned by the rain but their effect was still curiously intimidating; they had turned two gentle old friends of his childhood into creatures with a hint of prehistoric menace.

He watched the coffin go past and noted the heaped wet flowers that covered it, but his thoughts were centred on the first black limousine crawling in its wake. She would be in there, steeling herself to play a major part in the solemn ritual of burying the body of her son; she, who couldn't stand the thought of wars and killing any more than he could. Clenching his fists he tried to send her courage and love, but averted his eyes as the fleet of Daimlers passed.

Wiping the rain from his eyes he felt as if the day would never end, as if the dull thudding of the church bell would hammer itself into his brain for ever more.

The service was over. The orotund tones of the Suffragan Bishop had condemned the enemy and lauded the young man who had so willingly laid down his life for all that we hold dear, and the congregation had tried hard not to stare at the Fitzhardy family in their mournful dark-leaved family pew.

Many people cried unashamedly during the singing of 'Abide

with Me', and Thaddeus, standing at the back of the church among the other gardeners, shuddered at Mr Sims's loud braying of the terrible words 'Hold Thou Thy cross before my closing eyes . . .' Every death in the world since its creation seemed to be encompassed in that rectangular box, flag-draped and heaped with living flowers; every death from the past and every death still to come, because the war wasn't over yet. Perhaps it would never be over; perhaps the killing would go on and on until there were no more men left to fight, no more guns, no more bullets . . .

But at least he wouldn't be going. He wouldn't be conscripted. She had told him so, hugging him close to her as if to keep him with her by force.

The rain had ceased during the service and a brief glistening of silvery light lit a path through the churchyard. Estate workers had carried the coffin into the church, but now four soldiers from young George's regiment shouldered it and slow-marched with creaking boots and bare heads towards the Fitzhardy family tomb while the organist played some quietly searing music and the bishop led the way intoning 'I am the resurrection and the life . . .'

He saw her then for the first time, standing tall and black-clad, her face no more than a pale gleam behind the heavy veiling that flowed from her feathered hat. Her arm was held by Sir Wilton, who was splendidly accoutred in a scarlet and navy-blue uniform. The silver light died and the rain began falling again; falling gently and sadly upon the hastily reopened umbrellas. Wrenching his gaze from Lady Isobel, Thaddeus looked round at the dank yew trees and at the gravestones padded with lichen. Raindrops were coursing down the cheeks of a stone angel nearby, and he saw that Neddy and poor ole Fenny Brewer were standing in what was obviously a place of honour reserved for disabled ex-servicemen. There were a dozen or so, some he knew and some he didn't, all of them very neat and respectful looking except for Fenny, whose white upturned eyes roamed in their sockets as if seeking a way of escape.

The bishop ceased praying, and as the coffin was interred a bugler began to sound the Last Post. The sense of desolation in the notes was so acute that Miss Ball the schoolmistress broke down utterly and had to be led away.

At last it was over. All over. The bishop stood with bowed head as if acknowledging inaudible applause, then walked briskly away with the vicar at his heels like a faithful dog. Unable to bear any more, Thaddeus broke away from the crowd and walked distractedly across the churchyard, away from the main path that led to the lych-gate. The wet grass squeaked beneath his boots as he tried to banish the vision of black umbrellas grouped like hungry birds of prey and the whole unctuous panoply and emotional torture of a military funeral; tried to soothe himself with the knowledge that he would never play a part in that world.

He walked to the end of the churchyard then turned and followed the ancient brick wall that enclosed it. With lowered head and hands clasped behind his back he arrived at the small wicket gate that led to the grounds of the Big House. He found himself face to face with Lady Isobel and Sir Wilton: they were alone, as if they too had urgent need for escape.

Hastily snatching off his cap Thaddeus stood aside, then made a grab at the gate and held it open for them. They passed through in silence, then Sir Wilton suddenly paused and looked back at him.

'You,' he said, looking him up and down. 'Do you work here?'

'Yes, Sir. Sir Wilton.'

'Don't recognise your face. What's your name?'

'Noggin, Sir Wilton.'

Sir Wilton continued to scrutinise him, and Thaddeus felt himself caught in the choleric blue stare like a stoat in a gin-trap. It was the first time he had ever been in the presence of his employer, and his senses, already overwrought, swam in fresh confusion. The moments passed, and trying to ignore the motionless figure of Lady Isobel standing at her husband's side, Thaddeus blurted that he was very sorry about the young master.

Instead of placating, the words appeared to precipitate an avalanche of violent emotion in the older man. His face reddened, his body stiffened, and Thaddeus noticed with a fresh stab of apprehension that he was wearing a sword.

'*Sorry.* You're sorry, you say. May I express my humble gratification upon the expression of your kind sentiments. Really most kind of you. And now perhaps you will be good enough to tell me what course of action you intend to take to avenge your young master's sacrifice?'

Thaddeus opened his mouth and then closed it again as the relentless bombardment continued.

43

'Well? Unable to answer? Struck dumb, are you?' He came a step nearer, impelling Lady Isobel to move with him. 'Then I will tell you what to do. You will take the only course possible – you will go out there and personally avenge him. You will go out there and slaughter twenty – forty – *sixty* Huns in his memory. This is your personal duty. My son made the supreme sacrifice of laying down his life for England, for his parents, for his home, for all that he held dear. And that included not only his love of the great and the glorious and the good, but also the humbler things. The peasant at his door. The unskilled labourer, the ignorant yeoman, the unschooled rustic. In other words, *you*, Sir.'

Obscurely aware that this was a man brought near to madness by grief, Thaddeus let the words pour over him. White-faced, he glanced at Lady Isobel during the course of her husband's tirade but she remained motionless and unprotesting, her face hidden by the black veiling like the moon behind a cloud. He glanced at her again, and then again, until it slowly dawned upon him that the scene in the hothouse might never have taken place.

'How old are you? I asked how old you are – why don't you answer?'

Dragging his wits together, Thaddeus mumbled that he was just turned seventeen.

'Eighteen, I hear you say? Excellent. Here is your half-sovereign, and I shall not expect to see you again until you have done your humble best to wipe the Hun from the face of the earth.'

Sir Wilton turned on his heel and stamped away, leaving Lady Isobel to move in his wake like a sad and graceful ghost. Clutching the half-sovereign, Thaddeus stood motionless; watching, and desperately hoping. But she didn't look back.

Ploughing had been completed two weeks before Christmas and the horses were resting. Soon the men would be threshing the first of the seed-barley, and during the preceding lull Joe Noggin asked permission to take a couple of hours off.

'Nothing wrong, is there, Joe?' The young chap from over Pebmarsh way looked at him concernedly. His second-baiter had never asked for time off before.

'Nothing as can be helped,' Joe said shortly. In the privacy of the stable he combed his thinning hair, buttoned his shirt collar

44

and put on his jacket. He walked out of the yard, and the obdurate set of his shoulders discouraged further questioning.

There had been a frost overnight but now the air had softened and the glistening soil lay upturned, waiting for spring. His boots scrunched on the narrow winding road that led to Bures and he wished he had given them a bit of a shine-up before leaving. Halfway there, he paused to consult his old turnip watch, then gave a satisfied nod; twenty-five minutes would do nicely, and give a couple of spare.

He marched through the village and over the bridge that straddled the Stour, but when he reached the railway station the family was already there, standing huddled defensively up on the draughty platform.

'Reckoned you wasn't coming,' Ma said laconically.

Joe made no reply because at that moment he only had eyes for the tall, ill co-ordinated figure that stood in their midst. He seemed to tower above them, yet the gawky vulnerability of him made his father wince.

Wearing the ginger-coloured tweed coat that his Ma had salvaged from Gawd knew where and the baggy black cap that he had had new for the funeral, Thaddeus was nursing his small wickerwork suitcase between feet which even to Joe's uncritical eye looked extraordinarily large. Proper fighting men he had always visualised as muscular and neatly compact, but Thaddy would only need to stick his head above the trench once to get it blown off. Brushing his tearful daughters aside, Joe went up to him and determinedly shook his hand.

'Gunna be off, then? Train due any time now, I reckon.' With the other hand he took out the turnip watch again and studied it fixedly.

It had shocked him when Thaddy had said without preamble that he had taken Sir Wilton's half-sovereign. Shocked him, because Thaddy had always been a peace-loving boy and because money never seemed to mean much to him. But now here he was, looking as if a north wind would blow him over, and with a strange new look in his eye like a horse being faced with a dose of physic. Sometimes Joe had the feeling that the older he grew the less he understood.

They continued to stand on the cold platform, the two girls now

45

trying to chivvy young Thaddy, and Thaddy responding with broad, brave smiles while his Ma tweaked restlessly at the folds in his coat and reminded him that she had packed a tater pie in with his clean clothes. Eric was there too, smiling dutifully when required but otherwise watching the men at work in the signal box. Godlike they were, moving slow and indistinct behind their glass window in readiness for the approaching train.

They heard it coming, the laboured shuffling of it coming down from Ipswich, and as Thaddeus picked up his suitcase Eric danced a brief little jig of delight before remembering that this was a serious occasion. Thaddy was going off, most likely to get killed in the war.

The train stopped, covering them all in steam for an instant. Thaddeus climbed aboard, struggled for a moment to let down the window and then stood there smiling down on them. They smiled back at him, for there was nothing left for them to do but smile and offer the last-minute platitude.

'Come back safe – '

'Don't do anything I wouldn't do – '

'If you can't be good, remember the date – ' Inappropriate advice, but as he didn't know what it meant it didn't matter.

Carriage doors banged, the guard's whistle blew, and a fresh burst of steam sent young Thaddeus on his way. They left the platform in silence, and with no more than a muttered word or two Joe went back to the farm to give his team their evening bait.

The young chap from Pebmarsh came into the stable, and Joe noticed for the first time that he had silver horseshoe buttons on his weskit. Being first horseman had made him a bit of a dandy.

'Everything all right now?'

'Reckon so.'

'Joe,' the first horseman said, leaning back against the door. 'Joe. All this time and I still can't git over that ole funeral. I git off to sleep then sure enough it all comes back to me. All them people in black and all so sorrowful, Joe, and that little old boy blowing the bugle like that, well, it went straight through me. It was a real terrible day that, Joe.'

'Reckon you're right.' Joe bent to inspect the inside of Boxer's left foreleg while the horse munched in unison with Bowler.

'Some things you can git over and some you can't. I mean, up 'til now this was just a place of work to me. I got on with what I was set to do, and I reckoned that them up there did the same. They had their place, us here had ours, and that was the end of it. But it's not like that, Joe. The funeral made me see that.'

Joe made a wordless sound and replaced Boxer's leg on the ground; the horse stamped it gently, as if to get rid of the human touch.

'We're all in it, Joe. Not just us, but them as well. And now when you think there's no son to take over here, well, I reckon it's . . .' he shook his head, 'well, I reckon it's just plain wicked.'

'That's so.' The older man straightened up and stared across at him. He hadn't bothered to light the lamp and the stable was almost in darkness. 'So what you gunna do about it?'

'I already done it, Joe. I bin into Sudbury and enlisted.'

'You're exempt,' Joe said heavily. 'You're a landworker.'

'I know I am!' There was torment in the young chap's voice. 'But we gotta keep on, hain't we? We gotta keep *on* – '

'Oh yes. We gotta keep on.'

'And I mean, Joe, I can't just stay on here nice and safe now, can I? I mean, not after that funeral.'

Joe stared at him through the thickening shadows and made no comment.

'Not as if I've got a wife and kids, Joe. There's only me to think of except for me Auntie Florrie and I hain't set eyes on her for a bull's moon.'

Go on then, Joe's face said. Go on and join all the others. All that swarm of bees, all that senseless streama frogs crossing the road from one pond to the other; go on then, do what all the others is doing, including my son. Go out and git yourself killed along with all the rest on 'em . . .

'I've told them up at the Big House,' his companion was saying. 'I went up and said my piece just afore you got back, and what's more – ' he paused for a moment, then added gently, 'what's more I told'em you was due to be made head baiter. You should'ave bin head baiter over me when I first come here, I told them that and they agreed I was right. They said I was right, Joe – and the job's yours now.'

'I don't want it!' Joe roared suddenly, fists bunched and face dark with rage. 'I don't want your job nor nobody's leavings! I seen my boy off this afternoon and now you're going! Soon there won't be nobody left 'cept me and a handfulla broken ole creatures crawling about on sticks – I'm not stepping inter dead men's shoes not for nobody I'm not!'

'I'm not dead yet, Joe,' the young chap attempted a rueful smile. 'I hain't even gorn.'

'No matter,' Joe growled. 'I don't want the job. It's too late now and I'll stay how I am.'

Seizing his jacket from its nail he shoved past the young chap from over Pebmarsh way and marched, a broken man, back to the home that no longer contained his favourite child.

1921

'What I really had in mind was a gardener-handyman cum general factotum,' confessed the Reverend Bonamy Fiske, rector of Shilling Tye. 'Unfortunately one can no longer afford to employ a separate expert to deal with each domestic subject in which one is a self-confessed ignoramus – the war has changed a great many things, some of them no doubt for the better . . . Can you oil locks, stoke boilers and unfreeze pipes in addition to hoeing and mowing and clipping the hedges?'

Standing tall and straight in the vicar's ramshackle study Thaddeus said that he could; and (seeing that employment was difficult to obtain) that he would be pleased to lend a hand wherever it might be needed.

'Stout fellow!' cried the vicar. 'Fifteen shillings a week and midday meal provided. Mrs Palfrey my housekeeper is an excellent plain cook . . . other than her, I am reduced to one parlourmaid.'

Making a polite sound indicative of sympathy, Thaddeus ventured to ask when it would be convenient for him to start.

'Tomorrow morning at nine,' the Reverend Fiske said promptly. 'I see that I've arranged to take Communion at eight but I don't suppose many will turn up – ' reaching across the littered desk he seized the younger man's hand and shook it warmly. 'How *nice* of you to join us, Noggin.'

Nice of you to join us. The words echoed in Thaddeus's mind as he cycled back to Marling Hamlet. They hadn't said that to him the day he started work up at the Big House as a nipper. They hadn't said it to him when he joined the 3rd East Anglian Regiment either, and gone over to France with the rest of them. But all that was over now, all the killing and the casual hardship, and he had come back unscathed among the stream of wearily triumphant men looking for the old life they had left behind. Only the lucky ones found it. The rest of them, after the first hectic rejoicings, were left to blunder along as best they might in a country sickened and impoverished by the longest, most fiercely concentrated war in history. The abrupt transfer from trench to civvy street sometimes proved less than idyllic, the change from hero to figure in a dole queue something of a mockery.

Thaddeus had been more fortunate than many, although changes had taken place at home during his absence. Marjorie had been courting with poor old Fenny Brewer's brother until he went into the navy, after which she had swiftly changed tactics and married a maltster's son from Sudbury. She was quite well-off now, and sometimes drove over in a pony and trap with the remains of a fancy pudding or half a Victoria sponge, which Ma, tight-lipped, fed to the hens as soon as her back was turned. She had had her hair cut off and wore flesh-coloured stockings with fancywork up the sides.

Dora was working as a draper's assistant at a funny old shop in Stoke Abbey, two miles downriver from Marling. She seemed content with her lot, although the pay wasn't much and dusty bales of cotton rep and calico made her wheeze. Eric had left school and apprenticed himself to a boatbuilder near Manningtree, but the old hand-carved chair that stood at the head of the kitchen table was empty now. From about the time of Thaddeus's departure Joe Noggin had seemed to decline.

'He dwindled,' Ma said. 'Couldn't seem to do nothing. Wouldn't eat no more'n a hen's noseful because of pains here and pains there, but the doctor reckoned there wasn't much wrong. Givvim some pink stuff in a bottle – it lays there on the shelf still – but your Dad reckoned he'd be best off in bed and that's where he went and that's where he stayed until he was too weak to move a finger. We thought as they might give you leave for the funeral – Elsie Pain wore big pearl earrings and when I said they're a bit loud for a funeral, aren't they, she said Oh *no*, pearls are for tears, Mrs Noggin dear . . .'

'I didn't know,' Thaddeus said. 'We didn't get to hear much news at Passchendaele.'

The death of his father affected him deeply, and filled him with a profound regret that he had never talked to him more, never really got to know him as a friend. There had been an instinct for friendship between the two of them, he now recognised, that should have been explored and encouraged with words; but words had not come easily to either of them, so perhaps the instinct, the silent understanding, had been sufficient in itself. He hoped so, because now it was too late.

So he settled back to life in the family cottage with Dora and his mother, determined from the very first that he would not go back to the Big House to work. If the fragile, boyish love for Lady Isobel had been crushed by the brutality of war, so had the timid deference expected of him. The old world had crumbled within the space of four years, and although no one was sure what might come in its place, there was an unspoken feeling that people like the Fitzhardys were, in a curious way, doomed to extinction before long.

And although he had kept out of the war, Nable Sims had evidently become part of the new order because he hailed Thaddeus in the pub one evening, bought him half of bitter and told him a couple of jokes at which Thaddeus laughed with genuine pleasure although he had heard them both before. He also knew now that Nable stood for Not Able, apparently in reference to his wedding night.

He also discovered that work was scarce. After the agricultural boom of the war years, farms were already showing the first signs of neglect and no one in the Stour valley could work out why it was cheaper to import wheat than to grow it. Gardeners were even less in demand than ploughmen, and Thaddeus resigned himself to a stint of odd-jobbing round the villages until he saw the rector of Shilling Tye's advertisement in the local paper.

So he began work on the 6th of April, and discovered that the Reverend Fiske was an ardent rose-grower.

'*Neu desint epulis rosæ* . . . the dear old Romans were absolutely potty about roses,' he told Thaddeus as they walked through the garden, 'and furthermore, according to Athenæus Cleopatra had her floor covered one and a half feet deep in them, as you probably know.'

Thaddeus didn't know, and made a mental note to ask the Reverend Fiske who Cleopatra was, when he got to know him better.

'No one to beat the ancients, Noggin. They are the fount from whence our wisdom flows.'

'Reckon that's right.'

Although very large, the Vicarage garden had none of the meticulous regimentation so assiduously practised up at the Big House. Tulips and narcissi ascended from clouds of wild violets and forget-me-nots and the budding arms of roses flung themselves about unchecked. Fat primroses starred the lawns, and when a cock blackbird flew down at their feet the vicar crumbled a bit of bread from his pocket and dropped it before him. 'His wife must already be sitting,' he observed as the bird flew off with loaded beak.

The waving branch of a pillar rose hooked itself into Thaddeus's sleeve and Reverend Fiske watched with approval as he carefully released it.

'That is *Belle Lyonnaise*, a daughter of *Gloire de Dijon*. Not quite as beautiful as her Mama, but a rose of distinction nonetheless.'

Thaddeus admitted rather gruffly that he was interested in roses and would like to try his hand at propagating them one day, and his new employer gave a sudden merry little skip and said, 'In which case, my dear Noggin, we will settle down to a life of propagating together!'

It all seemed too good to be true, but it took Thaddeus only a short while to discover that the Reverend Bonamy Fiske was indeed a man of natural charm and unclouded temperament. With a halo of fluffy white hair, pink cheeks and bright eyes, he was the product of a classical education, unmarried, and apparently untroubled by lack of a close relationship to lean upon. The incumbent of Shilling Tye for more than thirty years, he seemed to skim through the days blithe as a bird, and in the evenings he played patience and sometimes amused himself by composing Greek iambics, cuddled into a knitted shawl of his own creation if the Vicarage draughts were proving extreme.

They were returning to the house by the back way on that first morning when Thaddeus saw the girl pegging sheets on the washing line. Her back was towards him, but he became aware of the curve from hips to upstretched arms, and of the loosely tied blonde curls escaping from beneath her maid's cap.

'Polly,' explained the Reverend Fiske. 'Parlourmaid-in-chief and second-in-command to the redoubtable Mrs Palfrey.'

The girl turned round, removed the clothes-peg gripped

between her teeth and smiled. 'Morning, Mr Fiske. Sun's lovely, isn't it?'

'A benediction upon us all,' Mr Fiske agreed, then added, 'Now you must come here and meet Mr Thaddeus Noggin, who is our new gardener-handyman.'

The girl did so, putting out a pink young hand that seemed still moist from the washtub. A little clumsily Thaddeus shook it. 'How-do, Miss?'

'I do well enough,' she said demurely. 'And I'd do even better if someone'd see to that ole mangle – the top roller keeps on a-slipping.'

'I'm perfectly certain that repairing a mangle will be child's play to Noggin,' the vicar said, beaming. Then putting his hand on Thaddeus's arm, he propelled him towards the kitchen door. 'Now you must come and meet Mrs Palfrey, my *éminence grise* and the secret power behind the incumbency.'

The middle-aged woman making an apple tart was large, white and dimpled like a loaf of bread risen ready for the oven. She smiled and nodded to Thaddeus. There was a slow calm about her that was totally unlike the air of nervous hysteria he remembered from up at the Big House. Once again it all seemed to be too good to be true.

Swiftly he settled into a working routine devised largely on his own, for the Reverend Fiske showed little inclination to issue commands or to criticise tasks that had been accomplished. The training that he had received under the watchful eye of Mr Sims was proving of inestimable benefit, and the touch of sun-warmed soil on his fingers came like a blessing after the bloodshed of Flanders.

He was patiently disentangling the eager new growth of a clematis growing against the dining-room wall when young Polly came up to him with a brown paper package in her hand.

She gave it to Thaddeus with a demure grin. 'Mrs Palfrey says please will you take these down to the blacksmith for the usual?'

'What's the usual?' He turned to face her. Her butter-yellow curls were bunched under her cap and he noticed the faint dusting of freckles on her nose. It was a small nose, soft and pliable looking as a child's.

'None of your business.'

'Do you know what it is?' He wanted to keep her talking for a little while longer.

''Course I do.' She was finding it hard not to laugh.

'So why not tell me?'

'Because it's something private between women.'

'The blacksmith's no woman, I don't reckon.'

Polly began to giggle, controlled herself with an effort, then burst into a peal of laughter. Her cheeks turned pink.

'Is he?' Thaddeus persisted, grinning back at her.

'I can't say, I'm sure.'

'So what's it all about?'

'Ask no questions and you'll get told no lies.' With a little twitch of her shoulder she turned on her heel and flounced away. He stood watching her go, smiling appreciatively. Beneath the white bow of her apron she had a little round bum that swung from side to side as she walked.

The brown paper parcel was long and thin and light in weight, and when he had finished dealing with the clematis Thaddeus cycled down through the village to the blacksmith's forge. Together with the nonconformist chapel which stood opposite, it was the last building before the woods and fields took over; Shilling Tye was closer to the Stour than Marling.

The blacksmith had just finished reshoeing the milkman's horse and was pausing to roll a cigarette. He was a large, heavy-bellied man with a low jutting forehead that sheltered small, hot brown eyes. Three other, younger, men were lounging nearby and they turned a slow bovine gaze upon Thaddeus as he entered.

He laid the brown paper package on the anvil in front of the blacksmith, who stared down at it with his hands on his hips.

'What's this, then?'

'From Mrs Palfrey, up at the Vicarage. She wants the usual.'

'Up at the Vicarage, hey? You the new chap, then?' The blacksmith stared hard at Thaddeus, then slowly unwrapped the parcel with huge fingers. Half a dozen bent and buckled strips of metal about the length of a footrule were disclosed. One of the onlookers snuffled with suppressed mirth and moved away.

'Know what these are, do you?' The blacksmith subjected Thaddeus to another hot brown scrutiny before moving away to thrust a hammer into the glowing heart of his fire.

'No,' replied Thaddeus. 'She didn't say.' The memory of Polly's dimpling grin returned. 'So what are they, then?'

Without replying, the blacksmith wiped his hands over his leather apron, waiting for the hammer to reheat. When it had done so he seized the first strip of metal in a pair of tongs and began to beat it flat.

'Busks,' he roared above the clanging. 'Busks outta the ole gal's corsets.'

Thaddeus joined in the laughter.

'Reckons on having 'em straightened out three times a year. Powerful-figured woman, ole Ma Palfrey.'

'Like working up there, do you?' One of the blacksmith's companions turned a considering eye upon Thaddeus. Thaddeus said that he liked it fine.

'Rare little ole boy, the vicar,' observed one of the others. 'Goes round his garden talking to roses.'

'Reckon he's queer in the head, talking to things as can't answer.'

'But there ain't n'harm in him, Will,' said one of the others above the clangour. 'That little ole boy's done a right lot for this parish – and he don't never preach at you, neither.'

'Oh no,' Will agreed. 'He don't never preach.'

They fell silent, under the spell of the great iron hammer smashing down rhythmical blows upon Mrs Palfrey's busks. When they were finished the blacksmith gathered them together and replaced them in the brown paper.

'Right you are,' he handed them to Thaddeus. 'Reckon they'll keep her upright a bit longer.'

'How much?' Thaddeus put his hand in his pocket but the blacksmith brushed him aside.

'Don't fret about that, mate. She's got an account with me.'

The laughter was more friendly now, the eyes less suspicious, but as Thaddeus reached the doorway one of them said casually, 'Reckon you must know young Polly Monday.'

'Only by sight. Just seen her flitting to and fro, like.'

'Flitting to and fro,' repeated the man who had not spoken so far. He had ginger hair and gooseberry green eyes. 'Reckon that's about it.'

A small and ruminative silence fell, which Thaddeus finally

55

broke by wishing them all good-day and departing with Mrs Palfrey's corset busks tucked under his arm. He thought about Polly all the way home.

'*Deforméd, unfinished, sent before my time into this breathing world, scarce half made up* . . .' murmured the Reverend Fiske, holding a large and luscious caterpillar between finger and thumb. Gently he placed it in a small tin box.

Spring was deepening into summer and the rosebuds were fattening. Once again it looked as if *Roseraie de l'Haÿ* would be showing colour before her near neighbour *Louise Odier*, and each year the vicar enjoyed the fancied spirit of competition between his darlings. He lingered in the sunlight, his old panama hat tilted over his nose, and when a tall shadow fell across the grass nearby he looked up and said 'Ah, Noggin . . .' in a satisfied tone.

'Been looking over the sweetbriers,' Thaddeus said. 'Reckon they could take a bit more surface-dressing. Those ole poplar trees take all the benefit – I wonder we don't root 'em out this autumn.'

'God gave us trees as well as roses,' the vicar said, a shade reproachfully. 'And the poplars shelter us from the north-east wind.'

'Yes, God gave us that an' all, didn't He? Begging your pardon, Vicar.'

His employer straightened up and pushed his panama back from his eyes. He stood contemplating the young man in front of him. Now aged twenty-two, Thaddeus carried his height with casual ease. His shoulders had broadened, his limbs had lost their painful gangling quality, and all the old shadows of childish apprehension had disappeared, leaving smiling blue eyes in a tanned country face.

'Are you happy working here, Noggin?'

'Yes, Vicar. Very happy.' Thaddeus's smile broadened.

'And have you succeeded in putting the war behind you?'

'Pretty fair. Don't get the dreams I used to when I first come back.'

'The world has learned its lesson. Protracted violence gets us nowhere, and the wise man returns home to cultivate his garden. Are you familiar with Voltaire, Noggin?'

'No, Vicar. Can't say I am.'

'Then I must lend you my copy and you can read it in the evenings.'

'Thank you, Vicar. Much obliged.'

'Noggin,' said the vicar, depositing another smaller caterpillar in the tin box. 'What are you smiling at?'

'Nothing special, Vicar. Nothing special at all.'

Thaddeus returned to the sweetbrier hedge and hoed gently round the base before applying the mulch of compost. There was plenty to smile about, for young Polly had agreed to go for a walk with him that evening.

'Reckon Thaddy's courting,' Ma Noggin said to her daughter as they sat over the supper table. The evening was warm, and through the open kitchen door came the high repetitive song of a thrush. A striped cat lay curled in slumber on the old chair that had once been Joe's.

'Is he?' Dora appeared uninterested.

'Third time he's bin out this week.'

'Who is she, then?'

'Don't rightly know, but I reckon it's a gal from over Shilling way.'

'Shouldn't have thought there's many to choose from,' Dora said.

'No call to sound sniffy.' Briskly Ma clapped the lid over the cheese dish, then poured herself another cup of strong tea. 'Anyway, it's high time you was doing a bit of courting on your own account, else you'll end up an ole maid.'

'Could be worse ways to be.'

'Suit yourself.' Her mother sipped, elbows on the table and holding the cup with both hands.

Dora studied her without appearing to do so, and wished she would refrain from wearing her hat in the house. Particularly at the table. Although Marjorie had persuaded her to have her long hair cut off, Ma had never been noted for the luxuriance of her tresses, and what had once been a small screwed-up knob of lacklustre brown was now a thin and rather greasy bob protruding an inch or two beneath the dusty old beret she had taken to wearing from the time she got up until the time she went to bed. Her features had sharpened even more with the years, and two

57

little yellowish channels led from either nostril because of taking Dr Gentry's Remedial Snuff.

'I will suit myself, so there,' Dora said, suddenly irritated beyond endurance. She left her place at the table and marched out of the door.

'And shut the hens up while you're about it,' Ma called, 'else the old fox'll be doing a bit of courting an' all.'

Dora loathed hens, and Ma knew it. Pouring a third cup of tea, her thoughts turned to Thaddeus. And to the idea of him courting.

Well – natural enough at his age, and he was nice-looking enough for any girl. Tall and straight and strong like his father had been before work bent his back and bowed his shoulders. She had always loved him in the same rough and monosyllabic way she loved all her children, but the sudden thought that he might be planning to leave home chilled her. Pushing away the new and guilty realisation that he was her favourite child, she went out to see if Dora had shut the hens up properly.

The stretch of meadowland that lay between Shilling Tye and the Stour was dotted by giant willows and great mounds of blackberry, and intersected by a belt of ancient woodland that ran from the road down to the bank of the river. The whole area had a casual, comatose appearance, probably because there was no Big House to keep a watchful eye on it.

On that first evening Thaddeus and Polly Monday strolled decorously along the footpath that skirted the far side of the wood, and talked about the weather. She was wearing a blue cotton skirt with a crocheted blouse and her straw hat had a pink ribbon round it. When they had exhausted the weather he complimented her upon it. She told him that it had been given to her by Mrs Palfrey, then added the additional information that Mrs Palfrey had also made her blouse. They agreed that Mrs Palfrey was a rare ole gal, and when Thaddeus had gallantly helped her over a stile they said that the vicar was a rare ole boy and all.

Conversation languished. Tall grasses brushed against their hands like silk, and the constraint might have lasted for ever if Polly hadn't suddenly limped to a halt with a stone in her shoe. She clutched at Thaddeus's arm with one hand while she tried to remove her shoe with the other.

'Here, let me do it.' He led her, hopping on one foot, to the hedgebank and made her sit down. It was a shabby little shoe that he removed, with a scuffed toe and worn-down heel, and he carefully ignored the piece of cardboard that covered the hole in the bottom of it. He shook it, then ran his fingers down the inside to make sure that the stone had been dislodged.

'Didn't hear that come out.'

'Oh, I did,' she said. 'That went in the cow parsley.'

He took her bare foot in his hand and it barely covered the palm. She had plump little toes and tender pink toenails that seemed to Thaddeus as if they were smiling. Regretfully he slid the foot back into its shoe, fastened it and then helped her up. 'That better?'

'Yes,' she said. 'Reckon that's fine now.'

The physical contact had banished the sense of diffidence. He called her Polly and she called him Thaddeus, and when he helped her back over the stile there seemed no good reason to let go of her hand afterwards. He saw her back to the Vicarage, then collected his bicycle from the old stableyard and rode home in a glow of delight.

They went walking again on the following evening and on the one after that, and when Thaddeus ventured to ask where her home was she said she reckoned it was the Vicarage.

'I mean your real home.'

'Haven't got one.' She turned to face him, the evening sunlight touching her with pink and gold. 'They found me outside the police station when I was a few days old. I was lying in a fish box and there wasn't anything to say who I was or anything. So they took me to the orphanage and called me Polly after Matron's dog because it had just died and she wanted to keep its memory bright, and they said me surname might as well be Monday because that was the day they found me on.'

There was no self-pity in her voice, and no sense of tragedy, but the stark facts touched Thaddeus deeply.

'I dare say I'm a bastard,' she said.

'If you are, you're not the only one.'

'Reckon there's a lot of it about.' She looked him squarely in the face, and he saw the dimples in her cheeks begin to deepen and her blue eyes kindle with laughter. 'If you don't want to know me any more I'll understand.'

59

He kissed her then, for the first time. It misfired. Instead of the gravely courteous symbol of acceptance it was a hasty and inconclusive dab that landed somewhere close to her ear and knocked her straw hat crooked. He withdrew, red-faced with embarrassment.

'Shall we try again?' she asked, and the sight of her standing there small and unwanted by the world, with her face upturned and her eyes closed as she waited, swept away the last of his caution. He put both arms round her and the sweet softness of her drove him mad with joy. He lifted her off her feet and swung her round, crushing her to him. Her hat fell off and she tightened her arms round his neck as if she would never let him go.

They kissed, drinking deeply of one another, and she seemed to dwindle and dissolve in his embrace. When at last they released one another it was with the realisation that the world had become transformed.

He held her by the shoulders, away from him, and stared into her eyes. 'Will you walk out with me, Polly?'

'Yes, Thaddeus.' Her eyes were blue as cornflowers, and although her hair was golden her eyelashes were tipped with sable brown. *Variegated*, Thaddeus thought. 'Walk steady, I mean.'

'I thought we already were,' she said simply.

They told no one immediately, preferring to revel in the intimate delight of secrecy. If Polly had cause to address Thaddeus within earshot of the Reverend Fiske or Mrs Palfrey she would call him Mr Noggin, and only the play of dimples in her cheeks would hint at the true state of things. And Thaddeus played the role of taciturn gardener-handyman as he hoed and mowed and cut down the rich swathes of cow parsley with a scythe.

'If he *is* going out courting every night it'd do him no harm to tell us,' Dora complained.

'He'll tell us when he's good and ready.' Her mother chucked a dead rabbit down on the table. Its body was still limp, and Dora recoiled.

'One of these days you'll be had up for poaching, Ma.'

'You like rabbit pie, don't you?'

'Not all that fussy,' Dora replied, and removed herself from the vicinity.

*

'Roses may be propagated in three ways,' the Reverend Fiske said
to Thaddeus. 'By cuttings, by budding, or by the natural way
wherein pollen is transferred from the stamens to the stigmas.
Once upon the stigmas, each pollen grain puts out a threadlike
tube which grows down the style – here, d'you see, Noggin? – until
it reaches the ovum, where in due course, safe as a babe within the
womb, it will develop into a seed.'

'Yes, Vicar.' Thaddeus peered closely into the heart of the
Madame Isaac Pereire held out to him.

'Oh, what a *gorgeous* dame she is!' cried the Reverend Fiske,
abruptly overcome. 'Wife of a Parisian banker, and so graciously
willing to share her innermost secrets with a young acolyte! *O,
token flower that tells, what words can never speak so well . . .*'

Having become a little more proficient at extracting nuggets of
knowledge from thickets of romantic poetry and classical allusion,
Thaddeus was now learning a good deal about rose management.
Under the joyless, fear-ridden tutelege of Mr Sims up at the Big
House he had learned the rudiments of good garden management
and these would never desert him, but now he was plunged into a
new world packed with knowledge and experience and un-
ashamed delight that was helping to drive out the horrors he had
experienced in France.

The Reverend's roses, lightly pruned and liberally fed ('I find a
little night soil very beneficial, Noggin'), were left to grow largely
as they pleased. As the summer progressed they flung limbs of
ever greater abundance over hedges and shrubs, and swarmed up
trees from which their flushed and lovely faces smiled down upon
lesser mortals. Old wrought-iron arches reeled beneath their
weight and a rose-drenched arbour set beside the neglected tennis
lawn collapsed with a tired sigh. The scent of them – honey and
almond, tea and lemon and nutmeg – blended deliciously and lay
over the garden on still summer evenings like a laudation. And as
the summer progressed the Reverend Fiske carefully supervised
Thaddeus's first attempts at budding: making the T-cut in the bark
of the rose stock and then carefully inserting the shield-shaped
fragment containing the bud of the chosen species, and then
binding the two together with a strip of moistened raffia.

He made a mess of the first four, but the fifth met with his
employer's approval. 'Well done, Noggin!' he cried, then abruptly

clapped his hand to his mouth. 'Oh, my giddy aunt, what's the time? I think I'm supposed to be taking Evensong – '

And then in the evenings, when work was finished, there was young Polly. Young, adorable Polly who made his heart contract whenever he first caught sight of her waiting at the entrance to the footpath that followed the edge of the wood. She was generally wearing the same skirt and blouse, but somehow she always managed to introduce some subtle little difference to her appearance: a wild flower carefully threaded through the crochetwork of her blouse, or a bit of bright ribbon tied round her waist. Sometimes she bunched her butter-yellow curls up on top of her head in the old-fashioned way and he would wince at the sweet, tender curve of her neck; other times she would let the curls spread loose over her shoulders, which made her look like a demure little girl, and he would remember about her being found in a fish box and brought up in an orphanage and swear to himself that he would make up to her for all the deprivation she had suffered. He was planning to propose to her as soon as he had saved enough money to set them up in a cottage of their own.

And Polly would sparkle and giggle and blush when she first saw him sauntering down the footpath with his hair brushed neat, his clean shirt with the sleeves carefully rolled above the elbow and a juicy stem of grass between his teeth.

'Evening, Thaddy.'

'Evening, Polly.'

'All right?'

'Reckon so. You all right?'

'Yes, I'm all right, Thaddy . . .'

They would kiss formally, solemnly, as if renewing a sacred contract, then wander off hand in hand, forever conscious of their physical closeness as they made carefully trite conversation.

'Ole cock was a-crowing afore dawn this morning. That means rain.'

'Could do with a drop or two.'

'And Mrs Palfrey's sister's in bed with her veins.'

'Nasty ole things, veins.'

'I took her a bunch of pinks out the garden. Vicar said I might.'

'That was nice. Rare good smell, the ole clove pinks . . .'

Then silence. A bank of pink and green cloud shielding the

setting sun. A lone heron flying back to the river, neck stretched and legs trailing. And Thaddeus loosening his hand from Polly's and sliding it round her waist; the beauty of the evening world was inseparable from the beauty of their feelings for one another.

But solemnity never lasted for long with Polly. Suddenly she would break from his loving hold, tap him lightly on the shoulder and cry '*Tig!*' before running from him like a hare. He would pursue her, big feet thundering while she sped light as dandelion seed across the meadows, in and out of the trees and round the great hummocks of blackberry. Childhood would come back to them: the delirious enchantment of hide-and-seek and catch-me-if-you-can, and their breathless giggles would startle the partridges nested in the long grass and they would take off with an abrupt whirring of wings . . .

But longer legs and superior strength would win the game and she would collapse against him with her ear pressed to his drumming heart and he would hold her fiercely, almost cruelly, with all the strength of loving and the desire to possess.

It happened on the night she tripped over a tree root and fell headlong. They had been staying out later and later, and now it was almost dark. In a panic he rushed up to the small, prone figure lying face down beneath the willow and fell on his knees. Fearfully his hands passed down her shoulders to her hips.

'You all right?'

'Think so.'

She turned herself over while his hands hovered uselessly, then with a cry she flung herself into his arms. He held her protectively, her yellow curls beneath his chin and the sweet country scent of her closer than it had ever been.

'I love you, Thaddy,' she was crying against the buttons of his shirt, 'Oh Thaddy dear, I do love you so much . . .'

So he found himself having to soothe someone he adored from the pain of loving him too much; the idea was too momentous for him to grasp. He held her in his arms and rocked her like a baby, and her distress at being in love with him was so terrible that he felt his own tears gathering.

He kissed her again and again; when she lay back on the warm earth beneath the willow her arms tightened round him and he seemed barely conscious of what was happening. Of what he was doing.

When it was finished he laid his aching, spent body beside hers and groaned 'Polly, oh Polly, I didn't mean to . . .'

She lay stroking his hair and gazing up into the darkling willow leaves. 'It was bound to happen sooner or later.'

'You're not angry?' He raised his head, staring at her intently because of all the tales he had ever heard about women being sacrificed to men's lust. He hated himself.

'Reckon I could put up with worse,' she said, then gathered him to her and they lay warm and unmoving until they heard the church clock chiming midnight across the fields.

They made love every night after that; sometimes hastily, and on fire with the urgent need for immediate gratification, other times with a sweet and unhurried rhythm in which there was time to murmur endearments and even talk about the future.

He asked her to marry him, and she accepted. He told her that he had an eye on a cottage set by itself up by Glover's Spinney which he reckoned he could get for six bob a week.

'Six bob's a lot, Thaddy.'

'Not if we're both working. Not if you keep on for a bit too, and my ole Ma'll help out with this and that. There's a nice little table been stood out in the shed for three years or more . . .'

'I'd like to have a cuckoo clock,' she said dreamily. 'I've always fancied having one of them.'

'Might get one for a wedding present . . .' Words fading to kisses. An owl calling far away.

'Come to think of it, we haven't got much in the way of friends, have we?'

'Come to think of it, no, we haven't.' He positioned himself between her parted legs and heard her give a sigh of pleasure.

Later, when it was over and they had rolled apart, she pulled up her knickers and said, 'I'd like to have Hoppity May for me bridesmaid. Talking about friends, she's the only one I've got.'

'Why's she called Hoppity May?' He regarded her fondly.

'Her name's May, and that's how she walks because she's got one leg a bit longer than the other. She was one of the big girls at school when I was little, and she was the only one not to look down on us that came from the orphanage. She helped me learn the alphabet and taught me how to tie me hair in a bow at the back.'

'She sounds all right.'

64

'So can I, Thaddy?'

'Can you what, my little dearie?'

'Have her for me bridesmaid?'

'Her and Mary Pickford for bridesmaids and I'll have the Prince of Wales for me best man . . .'

Dreams. Dreams that touched reality with no more insistence than the occasional brushing of a moth's wing.

Dora took down the heavy bale of brown casement cloth and unwound a turn or two with a soft thump. She stood back from the counter and said, 'This comes a bit dearer at one and eleven three-farthings.'

The customer drew in her lips, then took the edge of the material between her fingers. 'Don't reckon I can run to that, gal.'

'Good quality,' Dora said tonelessly, then turned back to the shelf. 'Don't know if you care for green?'

'Green?' The customer removed her fingers from the previous material and used them to pinch the end of her nose. Her eyes reflected the torment of indecision. 'What does this come out at?'

'This one's only one and three. Quite a nice colour.' Dora displayed it, pushing the other bales further down the counter.

'How much did you say the first one was again?'

'One and six-three. Quite a popular one, really.'

'But this one's only elevenpence, didn't you say?' The customer rummaged among the billowing samples. She fingered it again.

'Eleven-three,' Dora corrected. 'Not good quality like the others and it won't wash well . . . depends what you want to pay.' If there was a hint of acerbity in her voice, her customer chose to ignore it.

'I'll have three yards of the green. No I won't – I'll have the one and eleven.'

'One and eleven-three,' Dora corrected. She reached for the appropriate bale while her customer stood silently wrestling with her conscience. Dora was aware of the twitching fingers, batting eyelids and worriedly computing lips, but remained indifferent because she had seen it all before: the quiet anguish of housewives trying to make one shilling do the work of two because the country was in a bad state after the war. Sometimes you'd think the other side had won, not us.

65

Having paid for her purchase, one coin at a time from an old concertina purse, the customer departed while Dora began to rewind the rejected materials back on the bales.

'Everything all right, Miss Noggin?' Mr Bunting, the proprietor, came round the back of the counter. 'Here, let me help.' One by one he lifted the bales back on to the shelves.

'Thank you, Mr Bunting.' Dora's cheeks flushed a delicate pink, and she tried to breathe without wheezing.

'Is your throat troubling you again?' Mr Bunting was too much of a gentleman to say *chest*, for which Dora was nervously grateful.

Her employer was in his fifties; a pale man with handsome, rather saturnine features beneath a stiffly greased quiff of hair. He wore a black suit with old-fashioned high lapels and a wide celluloid collar against which nestled an impeccably folded cravat, for the newer, more relaxed fashions for gentlemen had barely penetrated the small towns and villages of East Anglia. If they had, it was doubtful whether Mr Bunting would have taken advantage of them, for not only was he the proprietor of Bunting's Drapery Emporium, he was also a long-standing communicant of the Ezekiel Chapel in Sudbury.

'No, it's better today, thank you,' Dora said, then dusting off the counter with her sleeve added, 'How's Mrs Bunting getting on?'

'She's coming along quite well, thank you Miss Noggin. Rather a restless night but much improved after a nice bowl of bread and milk.'

Mr Bunting spoke bravely, gallantly, and Dora's young heart contracted with renewed love and pity. In her early days as apprentice shop assistant she had been nervous of him in the same automatic way that she had been nervous of the vicar, the doctor and Miss Ball the schoolmistress. He was Authority: one more remote and godlike personage who held the power to destroy with a word or glance. But Mr Bunting had made no attempt to destroy. He had treated her with extreme politeness, always asking instead of ordering, and on the day she made her first unaided sale (six pearl buttons and a yard of knicker elastic) he had congratulated her and left it to the other assistant to explain that knicker elastic was known in polite circles as ladies' elastic.

Miss Pugh was old and short-sighted, and when she retired Mr Bunting made no attempt to replace her, for trade had been dwindling even before Bowers Bros had started the weekly motorbus service into Sudbury every market day.

Now Miss Noggin, aged seventeen, was the sole assistant in the Drapery Emporium that sold not only material by the yard but also men's calico workshirts, ladies' nightgowns and long woollen combinations for either sex. It stocked babies' layettes next to the knitting wools and the haberdashery counter, and in the long pauses between customers Miss Noggin refolded and retidied, dusted the counters, swept the lino-covered floor and sometimes ran errands for pills and potions for poor Mrs Bunting.

Naturally, Mr Bunting had never explained what was wrong with her; in fact, Dora had never even set eyes on her, the only sign of her existence being an occasional heavy thump on the bedroom floor above and the fortnightly visit from the doctor who would come down through the stair door into the shop, shaking his head and murmuring, 'About the same, Mr Bunting, but at least no worse.'

It was all very sad, and mystery added a touch of romantic fantasy to the situation. Dora pictured a willowy, ghostlike woman with tumbling Pre-Raphaelite hair stretching out a wan hand to poor Mr Bunting on his knees at her bedside with his face buried in the folds of her nightgown (feather stitched and lace trimmed at four and eleven-three). It was only the thought of marital devotion that prevented Dora from abandoning herself hook, line and sinker to a passionate love of Mr Bunting. Or, more accurately, it prevented all hope that one day a widowed Mr Bunting might love her on a reciprocal basis. Faithfulness was the keynote of romantic love, and such is the cussedness of the human heart that Dora would have stopped loving him if he had stopped loving his wife.

But the subject of love occupied her thoughts endlessly, and on Wednesday afternoons when the Emporium was closed she would cycle to Sudbury library to exchange last week's Ethel M. Dell for a Ruby M. Ayres.

The love life of her brother Thaddeus suffered a severe blow on the evening when Polly flung herself into his arms and sobbed that she was in the family way.

67

It was impossible to feel surprise after the summer evenings they had spent together, the nearest approach to contraception being the age-old belief that this will never happen to us, but now he felt a chill of dismay that instantly communicated itself to Polly.

'You don't really want to marry me, do you?' She looked up at him tear-streaked.

'I do, I do. Of course I do.' He drew her close again, and patted her back while he tried distractedly to refashion the lovely lazy plans they had made. Of course they would marry; he loved her, and wanted above all things to be married to her, but . . . 'When?'

She tightened her arms round his neck and her hot tears dampened the front of his shirt.

'I reckon it must have been at the beginning. I never felt nothing particular – never once bin sick, I mean – but I know that's what it is, Thaddy . . . I can feel that moving about in there!' Her sobs intensified.

'How d'you know it's not wind?'

'Never had the wind in all me life – '

'There's a first time for everything,' Thaddeus said with diminishing hope, and flinched when she suddenly released her clinging arms and punched him on the jaw.

'You don't care, Thaddeus Noggin! You're same as all the rest – just have your bit of fun in the hay and when it comes time to reckon the score you pretend it never happened! Nothing to do with you! It's always the poor girl's fault – reckon that's what happened to my Mum – it's the girl's the one who's got to carry the blame and all the shame while the chap gets off scot-free and goes romping off with someone else.'

She turned from him and ran. The strap from one of her shoes broke and after floundering on for a few steps she angrily kicked it off, leaving him to stare after her in dismay.

She was panting heavily by the time he caught her. Gently he took her by both arms and made her sit down. He wiped her eyes, smoothed back her hair, kissed her and then proffered the discarded shoe.

'Now, givvus your foot.'

'It's no use,' she said dully. 'It's old and busted, same as me.'

He smiled, tried not to, then roared with laughter. 'Oh my word, you poor ole dearie!'

'You can laugh, it's all right for you . . .' But her anger was fading. 'You're not the one who's having it, are you?'

'Our baby,' he said, putting his arm round her shoulders and hugging her close. 'It's ours. Yours and mine. And we're getting married on the first day we can get it fixed. I love you, sweet Polly, and everything'll be all right.'

'I love you too, Thaddy.' Her blue eyes were honest and trusting as a child's. 'And I'm sorry I got in a state just now.'

'I'd have bin the same if it'd bin me.'

'I felt I'd let you down, Thaddy. It was my fault . . .'

'Of course it wasn't your fault – takes two to do what we've bin doing . . .'

They walked back to the Vicarage in the glow of a new, wordless tenderness. After a sleepless night Thaddeus went back to work early, fidgeted ineffectually in the kitchen garden for an hour, then squared his shoulders and marched through the back entrance of the Vicarage and knocked on the Reverend Fiske's study door.

He was at his desk, pince-nez crookedly astride his nose.

'Ah, Noggin. Is all well?'

'Yessir.' Thaddeus had removed his cap, and stood massaging it in both hands. 'Well, there is one thing, Sir. I'd like to ask permission to marry Polly.'

'Marry Polly?' The vicar looked surprised. 'But my dear fellow, you are perfectly free to marry whomsoever you choose.'

'Yes, but . . .' Thaddeus floundered, then recovered. 'I mean, I'd – we'd like to git on with it as soon as we can . . . the arrangements, that is.'

'Aha! You mean that you're asking if I will perform the ceremony? Certainly I will, my dear Noggin – only too delighted!' The Reverend Fiske passed his hands through the litter of papers on his desk and unearthed his diary. 'Now, let's see. We're nicely placed between Whitsun and St Swithun – I always hold St Swithun in particular esteem Noggin, for mid-July is when our darling roses are in most need of rain in order to refresh their labours . . . St Mary Magdalene – St James – St Anne – the Horticultural Show on the 28th – the choirboys' outing . . . so now we come to August . . .' The vicar fluttered his diary leaves. 'August which gives us Lammas . . . Transfiguration . . . and so

69

on to the beheading of St John the Baptist – *awful* shame that, Noggin – then the harvest in full swing . . . how about September?'

'I reckon that – I was wondering if we could make it a bit sooner, please, Vicar.' The peak of Thaddeus's cap creaked between his anguished hands. 'I mean, well . . . time's getting on . . .'

The vicar stopped fluttering the pages of his diary. He looked sharply at Thaddeus. 'How soon?'

'As soon as possible, please, Vicar.'

'Am I to understand that we are contemplating what they call a shotgun wedding, Noggin?'

Thaddeus nodded, his face crimson.

'In that case,' the vicar said, 'how about next Saturday?'

Hastily Thaddeus agreed, thanked him and stumbled from the room. He was halfway down the passage when the vicar called him back. He went, with dragging steps and bowed head.

'And when I have tied the knot, Noggin, where do you propose to live?'

'Hadn't rightly thought, Vicar. With my Ma, most likely.'

For the first time during the interview the vicar showed signs of irritation. Banging his chubby fist down on the desk he said, 'You can't. I won't allow it. A new marriage is a tender young plant that needs nurturing in a place of its own. It needs peace and privacy, and space in which to grow. You cannot take Polly to live with your mother, Noggin, however admirable a woman she may be.'

Thaddeus said nothing. He had nothing to offer. A bee buzzed in through the open window, hovered and then departed.

'There is the old coachman's cottage,' the Reverend Fiske remarked finally. Removing his pince-nez he twiddled them between his fingers. 'It hasn't been lived in of course since poor old Hobart died and the pony was sold . . . a bit cobwebby by now I dare say, but *omnia vincit amor* as Virgil said, and with a bit of a clean-down and a bowl of roses in the window it should prove adequate for the time being.'

'Thank you, Vicar. Thank you very much,' Thaddeus mumbled. Gratitude beaded his forehead with sweat. He swallowed hard.

'I believe we may also have a few articles of furniture stored up in the attics,' continued his employer. 'We must make a reconnaissance with your future wife. And Noggin – ' he replaced the

70

pincenez on his nose and gazed sternly through them at Thaddeus – 'take my advice and be guided by her when it comes to choosing any article of a domestic nature. Although I may be said to lack practical experience of the marital state – I have never actually been married, Noggin – I have been an active participant at more weddings than I care to remember, and I have seen more than one knot which I have tied firmly and decisively come irretrievably undone over a matter of what one might term household goods. Homes and their contents are of paramount importance to women, Noggin, and this is a fact which you must forever bear in mind. The fringing on a bedspread, the pattern on a teapot, can cause untold anguish to a nesting woman. The exact placing of a chair can prove a matter of far greater importance to her than the Treaty of Versailles, if you follow me, Noggin, and the man who wishes to preserve and enrich his marriage is the one who will understand this fact and pay due attention to it.'

'Yes, Vicar. Reckon so.' Thaddeus wiped his cap across his forehead.

The bee, or perhaps it was another one, zoomed back through the window and began to examine the welter of papers littering the Reverend Fiske's desk. It settled upon an invitation to the Mother's Union jumble sale.

'And that which cannot be found in the attic,' continued the vicar, eyeing it, 'will doubtless be run to earth at some worthy charitable affair or other. We are all here to help, Noggin, in any way we can, and I confess that my heart warms at the prospect – ' he turned beaming eyes upon his gardener – 'of uniting two young people who already mean a great deal to me, and whose future I will watch over with a father's loving care.'

'Yes . . . well. Thank you again, Vicar.'

'So I will keep you no longer.' The Reverend Fiske reached for his diary and proceeded to make a note of the wedding date. 'It is now up to you to ascertain the reactions of your betrothed to the arrangements I have tentatively suggested.'

There should have been words to express his thanks, his boundless gratitude and sudden effervescing joy. He couldn't summon them, didn't even know them, but when the Reverend Fiske stood up and offered his hand Thaddeus seized it and all but crushed it to boneless pulp.

71

The news was out within hours, and that evening Thaddeus took Polly home to meet his mother, mounted side-saddle on his bicycle while he pushed her all the way to Marling Hamlet. She was wearing her best blouse and skirt and a large home-knitted cardigan lent by Mrs Palfrey to disguise the tell-tale swelling of pregnancy.

'I'm scared, Thaddy,' she said. 'Always bin scared of people's mothers.'

'No call to be scared of mine,' he comforted, and suppressed the thought of the wringing of necks, the drowning of kittens. 'She wouldn't hurt a fly.'

Ma was in the front garden, ostensibly pulling up a root of groundsel, when they arrived. Wiping her hands on her skirt she came forward as Thaddeus helped Polly to alight.

'Well,' she said, 'you're a comely young mawther an' no mistake. No wonder Thaddy's going on like a man tranced.' Then she smiled and seized Polly's quiescent hand in wiry brown fingers. 'Come on in, gal, the neighbours is staring fit to bust.'

Confusedly aware of cottagers standing in small, carefully negligent groups by their garden hedges, Polly hugged Mrs Palfrey's cardigan close to her and followed her prospective mother-in-law round to the back door.

The kitchen was tidy; fresh-baked bread stood resting on the old marble slab, a jam jar full of aquilegia stood on the white cotton tablecloth and the canary was trilling the last song of the day in its cage. To Thaddeus's relief there was no sign of blood, guts, fur or feathers.

With lingering hands he helped Polly to the old hand-carved chair that had been his father's – his half-finished bottle of pink medicine still stood on the shelf above – and when he stood back he saw that her face was illuminated by a shy and rosy pleasure he had never seen before.

'Oh Thaddy,' she whispered, 'you never let on you had such a lovely home.'

The way she lingered over the word *home* brought back to him the vicar's words of advice: *Homes are of paramount importance to women*, he had said, and the renewed picture of sharing four walls and a roof with sweet Polly filled him with an almost tearful sense of joy.

72

Ma came back to the table with three tumblers and a large stone bottle. She removed the bung and said, 'Elderflower. Five year old.'

Discreetly holding hands, they watched her pour the clear pale liquid. Five years old. 1916. Verdun. The Somme. The year young Fitzhardy got killed and the year Thaddeus confusedly accepted Sir Wilton's half-sovereign ticket to hell. . . He brushed the memories aside, raised his glass and said, 'Ah well, all the best to one and all.'

'All the best,' agreed Ma, and seizing a handful of his hair gave it a sudden hearty tug. Then she reached across to Polly and touched her cheek. 'So when's it due?'

There was a moment's discomfort; the canary stopped singing and bent to fiddle with its toenails, then Polly relaxed the protective folds of Mrs Palfrey's cardigan and said, 'It's still quite a long way off yet.' Her voice trembled, as if she were on the verge of apologising. Then, 'How did you know?'

'Reckon it's one of the reasons for getting married,' Ma said drily. 'We noticed young Thaddy was courting hard – clean shirt every night, shaving after tea, rosebud in his buttonhole and smiling like a gret ole fool – '

The back door opened and Dora came in. She looked pale and tired, and she stiffened slightly when she saw Polly.

'This is my sister,' Thaddeus began awkwardly, and motioned with his hand, 'and this is – is my intended.'

'Pleasedtermeetcher,' Polly said politely, and half rose from her chair.

'Good-evening,' Dora responded with something of her formal haberdasher's assistant's manner. Then seeing the three glasses on the table, added, 'congrats and all that.'

'Your tea's in the meat-safe,' Ma said. 'Lettuce and tomato and a nice bitta pie. Have a droppa wine, will you, gal?'

Dora began to shake her head, but Thaddeus had already reached for another glass. It was a smaller one, because they only had three glasses the same. 'No harm in drinking our health.'

'I'm teetotal,' Dora said to no one in particular, and dumped her fresh library books on the table.

'Same as Mr Bunting, eh? He's on the water wagon too, so I've heard.'

'Mr Bunting signed the pledge,' Dora said, pink-faced. 'He's an elder at the Ezekiel Chapel and they don't hold with drink. Same as me,' she added defiantly.

But mother and son appeared to ignore her words, and while she pretended not to watch, Polly saw Dora take a small pale sip before saying, 'I don't feel like pie and lettuce.'

'Bread and cheese, then. Or a tinna sardines.'

'I'll have something later.'

'Suit yourself.'

Conversation was brusque; words were not wasted, but the sense of a close-knit family was very strong. As if through the pores of her skin Thaddeus's fiancée sensed all that she had missed in the orphanage. So she sipped her glass of flower-fragrant wine and assented gladly when Mrs Noggin invited her to see the hens and the ole pig a-lazing in her sty. They passed the row of tins painted bright red to keep the birds off the blackcurrants and Polly admired everything earnestly and sincerely. Only occasionally would a strange little flicker of dubiety flicker across her features. Then they went back indoors and ate fresh crusty bread with Cheddar cheese and spring onions and tomatoes washed down with a large pot of tea. Dora, who was eating a ladylike boiled egg, gave Polly a smile from which the primness was receding and asked if she liked reading books. And Polly smiled back a little uncertainly, and with memories of following beneath each line with her forefinger said yes she did, quite. She envied the smooth plaits coiled in earphones on either side of Dora's head.

Thaddeus wheeled her slowly home to the Vicarage with his white shirt-sleeves glimmering in the dusk and a warm reedy smell rising up from the Stour. Although the whole world was theirs now, and they were accepted as potential man and wife, they seemed already to have moved beyond the wild and wicked desire to make love; to strip off their clothes, run naked and then plunge into one another's eager panting flesh. Maturity had suddenly dropped a cloak over their first youth as they made their way soberly and responsibly to the gate where Polly slid from the bicycle saddle and they kissed briefly and fondly before parting.

They might have been married for ten years, and their love was deeper than ever.

*

74

Their new home stood in the Vicarage stableyard, which was swept and tidy but otherwise deserted; the old, high-wheeled gig still stood in the open cartshed and the two loose-boxes still bore the names of the last two occupants, Blossom and Hugo. Not a wisp of straw remained, but sometimes a little ghost of horse scent would catch the nostrils of the sensitive passer-by.

The cottage was attached to the stable on one side and to the high wall of the yard on the other. To indicate its status as human dwelling, it had pretty borders of knapped flint round the windows and door.

There were two rooms, one up and one down, plus an outshut kitchen at the back, and upon opening the door they found the place strewn with a miscellany of dust-laden junk. With little crows of amused surprise the Reverend Fiske unlocked ancient trunks, rifled the contents of wooden boxes and flipped through a pile of yellow newspapers. There was a sofa with three legs, a collapsed iron bedstead ('Poor old Hobart's, I don't doubt') and a couple of china washbasins and ewers, cracked and chipped.

'They all must go!' the vicar cried with a wave of his hand. 'They are all old sad and broken things that have no part in a new life – '

So they all went, carried off on a trotter's cart from Bures St Mary, and the happy demon of creation overcame the new occupants; they swept and scrubbed and Thaddeus distempered the walls a nice pale yellow while Polly sat on the floor sewing brass curtain rings on half-price chintz remnants from Bunting's Emporium, courtesy of Dora.

Appropriate furniture was found in the Vicarage attics, as the Reverend had promised. A beautiful double bed with fruitwood inlay and a billowing feather mattress. A kitchen table and two chairs, an oil stove for cooking on and a couple of large wooden cupboards. Mrs Palfrey donated two rag rugs made by her married sister in Bury St Edmunds and a nice coloured print of *Sunset Over the Marshes*, while Ma Noggin provided saucepans and blankets and a pair of calico sheets. Thaddeus's sister, Marjorie, gave them a full tea service made of bone china. As the word got round, small wedding gifts arrived from old friends whom Thaddeus thought he had left behind: a whistling kettle from ole Neddy who had lost his leg in the war, and a woven dressing-table mat from poor Fenny Brewer, who had made it himself at the St Dunstan's place where

75

he was now. The mistakes in the pattern made Thaddeus's eyes fill with stupid tears, but then he was acting stupid most of the time these days; singing and laughing like a clown and loving Polly and the idea of the baby and them all being together in the coachman's cottage.

For Polly herself, those few brief days before the wedding passed in a dreamlike state. To begin with she had tried hard to make herself believe in the truth of the situation, but as time went on reality became more and more obscured as it appeared that more and more people loved her. Really loved her. She couldn't understand it, couldn't believe it. Up until now there had been no reason why she ever should: no family, no friends except one, and only a pretty, blundering child's instinct to guide her towards longed-for relationships.

But now there was not only Thaddy holding her gentle as a bit of cotton wool and stroking her hair back with his lips, there was Mrs Palfrey on her knees with a mouthful of pins while she hastily fashioned a white wedding dress from a taffeta petticoat and a pair of Nottingham lace curtains. And Mrs Noggin, who looked thin and hard as a nail, saying, 'Now then gal, reckon you better call me Ma same as the others', and giving her a smile that showed her little yellow ferret teeth which matched the yellow stains of snuff. All sorts of people loved her now, and shadows from the past seemed to be melting in the warmth they offered.

At the heart of it, as if he were leading some kind of merry dance, was the Reverend Fiske. In battered panama and trembling pince-nez he hurried over with an armful of books which included a current copy of *Whitaker's Almanac*, *Green's Short History of the English People* and Popple's beautifully illustrated *British Flora and Fauna*.

'If the baby's a girl shall we call her Flora?' Polly asked Thaddeus.

'If you like. But I don't reckon too much on Fauna if it's a boy.'

The vicar also gave them a silver salver inscribed with the name of a forebear in memory of Trafalgar, and on the evening when the decorating was all but complete he arrived with a glass bowl brimming with roses. Polly threw her arms round his neck and kissed his cheek as if he had been her father and not her employer and spiritual mentor. He held her carefully and inexpertly; when

76

she drew away from him she looked at him with loving child's eyes and said, 'You're so good and kind – why didn't you ever get married, Sir?'

'I think it must be because no one asked me,' he replied.

Thaddeus was nailing lino on the kitchen floor on the evening Polly came in with a young woman he had never met before. She was not very tall, neither was she particularly well dressed, but his attention was immediately caught by the homely face smiling at him from beneath an old-fashioned straw hat. He rose to his feet, wiping his hands on the backsides of his trousers.

'This is Hoppity May Farrinder,' Polly said. 'I told you, didn't I, that she's going to be my other bridesmaid.'

They said how-do-you-do rather gravely, then Hoppity May looked round the almost completed home and exclaimed, 'Oh, haven't you made it pretty! It matches you exactly, Polly dear!'

They showed her round, pleased as two children, and she clasped her hands, her face shining warm with delight under her straw hat. She mounted the wooden stairs one at a time, but with a rapidity that told of long being accustomed to her physical impairment. When she had seen everything they boiled Neddy's whistling kettle on the oil stove and made a pot of tea.

'May comes from Tarrent's Row,' Polly said, 'and we met at Sunday School.'

'It was my job to try to teach the scriptures,' May said. 'Some pupils were more receptive than others.'

'What was Polly?' Thaddeus rumpled her hair.

'I thought she was one of the good ones until I found her drawing pictures of fashionable ladies in the back of her bible.'

'They weren't ladies, May, they were angels.'

'Without any wings?'

'You didn't give me time to draw them.'

May shook her head in mock sorrow, then reached up and removed her hat. Seen without it, she had fine dark hair coiled in a loose knot at the back of her head, and smiling dark eyes set in the shelter of a slightly blobby nose. It was an ordinary face, notable mainly for its open, pleasantly receptive expression. Sipping his tea, Thaddeus slid a glance towards Polly, who was sitting so close to him, and marvelled again at the matter-of-fact quality of her springtime beauty. He hoped the baby wouldn't do anything to spoil it.

77

They talked of this and that, easy as three old friends. When they turned to the subject of the wedding May asked if her pink flowered frock would be all right with a nice sash instead of the belt to make it look a bit special. She could also wear the little seed-pearl necklace her mother had left her.

Polly asked Thaddeus if he knew what Dora, the other bridesmaid, was going to wear. He confessed that he didn't, any more than Polly, as Dora (never noted for cosy affability) had remained polite but noncommittal on the subject. Polly, still nervously in awe of her, had not liked to ask.

'Never mind, you'll be a rare sight for sore eyes,' Thaddeus said, then added a after a moment's consideration, 'all of you will, I mean.'

'I haven't been a bridesmaid since I was a little girl,' Hoppity May said, 'so I'm looking forward to it very much.'

She spoke more ladylike than Polly; a bit like Dora had picked up at Bunting's but more natural-sounding. He looked at her with renewed interest, but could only recall Polly telling him that her friend's parents had died when she was small and that she had been brought up by an aunt somewhere near Long Melford. He knew Tarrent's Row, a terrace of cobblestone cottages with big windows – weavers' cottages they had been originally – standing down by the old ford. He thought he might have seen her once or twice before, but there was only really her limp to set her aside from other girls. Anyhow, Tarrent's Row was normally out of his way.

May left soon after, hopping precariously on to an old high bicycle, and they waved her out of the stableyard before closing up the cottage for the night.

It was some minutes before Thaddeus realised that Polly seemed different. As if the light had gone out of her. She stood by the window with her head bent, idly touching the petals of the Reverend Fiske's roses, and didn't answer when he spoke.

He went over to her. 'I just said, only two more nights then we don't have to lock up and go separate.'

'Oh.'

'Looking forward to it, are you?' He put his arms round her, and was disconcerted when she remained stiff and unyielding. 'What's up?'

'Nothing.'

He could see only the top of her head, the white parting winding a careless path through the exuberance of yellow curls. 'Come on, little gal, what's up?'

He tried to raise her chin in his fingers but she jerked her head away. 'I don't want to marry you, Thaddy. I thought I did, but I don't.'

He let his hand fall, and stood blinking helplessly. 'You're kidding. Go on, you're kidding.'

She shook her head, moving away from him and leaving him to stare blindly at the bowl of roses.

'Why don't you? What's different? For God's sake, Polly – '

'I've just changed my mind, that's all.' She attempted a dry little laugh. 'They say it's a woman's right, don't they?'

'But *why*? Why've you changed so sudden? You were talking about the wedding and everything bright as a bird only a while back, and now you say you don't . . .' he shook his head dazedly.

'I just don't, that's all.' Her voice was sulky; the voice of someone else.

'Do you mean you don't love me any more?'

She remained silent, her back turned.

'Is that what you really mean – what you're really trying to tell me? You've just gone off me all of a sudden?' His voice was rough with shock.

'Yes – no . . . don't ask me.'

'But I've a right to know, for Chrissake!' Then his voice softened. 'Is it the baby, Polly? Making you feel all in a bother-like? That's what it is, isn't it?' He moved towards her, and at the same moment she turned and flung herself against him. In a state of confused relief he heard her weeping.

'Poor little gal – Oh, my poor sweet Polly . . . bin working too hard and all the excitement and flutter and then the baby coming . . .'

He let her go on crying because he knew it would ease her; would wash away all the tiredness and over-excitement that had been accumulating during the past week. He was unprepared when she pushed herself away from him and said in a choked voice, 'I'm sorry, I can't marry you because I love you too much and because I'm not sure the baby's yours.'

79

He let her go. He stood staring at nothing with his arms by his sides while he tried to absorb what she had just said. She wasn't sure the baby was his.

'Who was it, then?' He spoke with difficulty.

'I don't want to say.'

'You've got to.' He clenched his fists, a little pulse beating in his cheek. He didn't want to touch her any more.

'Sam Potter,' she said finally, and hid her face. Her tears had stopped now, but there was a terrible forlornness about her bent head and the droop of her shoulders.

'Sam Potter?' He looked at her blankly, then closed his eyes. 'Oh, Chrissakes not *him* . . .'

If she attempted a reply he failed to hear. His attention was centred wholly upon the image that filled his mind. The blacksmith. The big beer-swilling belly, hairs on his arms thick as spiders' legs and a brutal forehead overhanging small mean eyes. All that, and old enough to be her father. 'Not him, Polly. Don't tell me . . . not him.'

'What difference does it make?' she asked tonelessly. 'I bin unfaithful to you. At least, I was before . . .'

'Before we met?' A gleam of hope, perhaps.

'Before I began to love you, I mean.'

He shook his head in fresh confusion, unable to work out if that made it better or worse.

'I'm sorry Thaddy.' She turned to face him, looking so small and piteous that his confusion turned to rage. He couldn't stand the thought of her looking like a little beaten animal. And he still couldn't bring himself to touch her.

'I'll go now.' Her voice was barely audible.

'Where?'

She shrugged. 'I'll find somewhere.'

'What about Saturday?'

'Saturday?'

'Saturday was the day we were getting married.' The bitterness in his voice made her catch her breath. As soon as she looked at him her eyes filled with fresh tears. 'I'm sorry, Thaddy.'

'Sorry? I reckon you should be. After all we done to this place and everybody looking forward to . . . I mean, what are we going to say to 'em? The wedding's off because the baby you're

80

expecting mightn't be the bridegroom's? Right ole fool I'll look, won't I? . . . But Sam Potter – ' he banged his fist against his forehead, 'Christ, every time I think of him I want to sick up – him of all people, the great hairy old bastard – '

'You've never known what it's like to want somebody to care for you so bad you'll settle for anyone. Wanting to belong some- where.' The tears were trickling down her cheeks although her voice was quite steady. 'I used to ask God for somebody to say they loved me. Just to let me hear the words and know they were being said to *me*, and nobody else. I've tried hard to be like Hoppity May who's happy on her own, but I can't. I just can't. Being brought up in an orphanage with nobody of your own is like not living in the real world. You're just looking at it through the window.'

'Did he say he loved you?'

Her face showed signs of crumpling and she tried to hold it taut with her hands. 'No. He didn't say anything much.'

'Just got on with the job, eh?'

She nodded, almost imperceptibly, and the anger slowly drained out of him. The room they had prepared with such pride was dissolving in the summer dusk, its contents receding like their own future. The cuckoo clock he had bought for her was ticking away the last wooden minutes and soon they would be stranded in the dark. And for them, there would be no tomorrow.

He opened his arms and she crept into them.

The day began like liquid gold spilling out of a pink and blue casket. Pearly mist rose up from the river and melted in the strengthening sun. Larks sang, and so did Mrs Palfrey *sotto voce* as she arranged a jug of roses and lilies at the side of the altar steps. Roses for love, lilies for purity. Well . . .

She had boiled a ham and arranged a big bowl of salad for the wedding breakfast. The cake, hastily baked and the icing barely hard, stood on the Vicarage sideboard ready for the ceremonial cutting. It was a shame the way everything had to be so hurried but there you are, that's how life goes and she wasn't the first, poor little dear. But with the gathers carefully arranged in the front of her Nottingham lace it shouldn't be all that noticeable.

She hurried back to the Vicarage through the garden, where the scent of awakening flowers made her pause for a moment. Delphiniums raised their calm spirals and the roses – Oh, the ole vicar and his blessed roses – turned smiling faces from among the froth of aquilegias and pink and white campion. Campion was a weed, but the vicar would never have it pulled out. Not him. Campion's a flower of God same as all the others, Mrs Palfrey, he would say.

Of course flowers were people to him, she mused on her way back to the kitchen. Before now she had caught him bending over a border of white pinks and saying 'Good-*morning* my dear Mrs Sinkins! I trust you spent a restful night?' Nearly every garden in Shilling Tye had a root or two of cottage pinks, but none of them smelt anything like so lovely as the Reverend's Mrs Sinkins.

Over at the Noggins' cottage at Marling Hamlet, Dora was up in the small airless bedroom she shared with her mother, unrolling her hair from rag curlers. She didn't like her hair in curls but felt in an obscure way that she owed it to Thaddeus. She wasn't sure about her frock, either. More and more local girls were going in for the new short straight styles just as they were having their hair bobbed, shingled or bingled, but Dora was unwilling to join the merry band. So the frock was the one she had bought for the charabanc trip to Lowestoft two years ago – navy blue with little white flowers, long sleeves and a mid-length skirt.

Her future sister-in-law still had long hair and wore long skirts but then Polly wasn't exactly an arbiter of fashion. Polly, Dora had swiftly discovered, was less endowed with worldly goods than even the poorest cottager, and depended on casual cast-offs and clumsy make-do's with which to clothe herself. Presumably it was God's way of adjusting the balance to give her a pretty face and tumbling fair curls that looked right on her.

Curls didn't look right on Dora, and she surveyed herself in the small dim mirror with misgiving. In place of the usual neatly plaited earphones, large snail-like portions of hair had risen palpitating from her scalp. She was unsure how to deal with them. Tentatively she began to comb them and they rose in a dense and concerted forest above her forehead like the soaring wig of Marie Antoinette.

She seized the hairbrush, and the forest repaid her rapid strokes by separating into a frenzy of finely articulated fuzz. She brushed harder, bending double and furiously sweeping her hair from the back of her scalp and over her small hot face. Teased and tormented from its usual docility, tufts of it remained defiantly perpendicular while other portions grouped themselves defensively together and stuck out sideways like the arms of a many-faceted windmill.

With a little sob Dora tipped more water into the china washbasin and plunged her head into it. With relief she saw the dreadful foreignness of frizzy hair returning to the familiar little fronds of unobtrusiveness with which she felt at ease. Cool water swished against her temples, soothing away all vexation, and Ma's voice from the open doorway might have been coming from a shell pressed against her ear: 'Gawd alive gal – don't tell me you caught nits?'

Amara sapere vix deo conceditur, thought the Reverend Bonamy Fiske, scraping a razor across his pink cheeks. To be in love and to be wise is scarce granted even to a god.

I hope Noggin will be wise. That he will remain simple and sensitive, for only true simpletons are ever sensitive, and that the love he bears this girl will not degenerate into brutish lust inflamed by Adnam's ale and raucous jokes in the Fox and Garter. I hope that their child, the flower of their love, will esteem them in its youth and cherish them in their dotage.

The bell-ringers were calling the first hesitant notes before swinging into the customary wedding carillon. The Reverend Fiske sloshed water over his face before drying it. It was going to be a hot day and he hoped that Mrs Palfrey had remembered to cool the fruit cup down in the cellar until after the service.

Struggling into a clean shirt and snapping his clerical collar in place the vicar mentally checked through the coming ceremony: organist ready in his loft, Mr Lacey the churchwarden supervising the choirboys, bible in place on the lectern – a small simple wedding, with pitifully few in the congregation on the bride's side, he feared. Which was why he had insisted upon there being music –a Bach toccata to open with ('And don't forget to give it *socks*, Miss Evans!'), then the lovely anthem 'Cleave unto Joy and Depart not Away' which the boys had learned to sing very nicely . . . He paused abruptly, hairbrush suspended in mid-air. Oh my

83

giddy aunt, who is supposed to be giving the bride away? In stockinged feet he sped down to the kitchen to find Mrs Palfrey in order to confer.

Ma Noggin, dressed in the gabardine costume that had belonged to Fanny Upton before she passed away, saw Thaddeus standing alone in the back garden among the raspberries and blackcurrants. There was a curious stillness about him, head bent, hands in the pocket of his new suit as if he were listening intently for something. Trying perhaps to catch a hint of the future that was due to start at midday prompt.

He made no sign of awareness until she was almost level with him, then looked up in surprise.

'Not feeling frit, are you, boy?'

'No. I was thinking about Dad.'

'He'd have liked her fine. Always had an eye for a pretty young mawther.'

Something in her tone caught at his mood. His eyes softened in a smile. 'Bet you were a little queen when he married you.'

'Reckon at best I'd pass in a crowd.'

'Git*on* . . .' He slipped his arm round her shoulder, a thing he had never done before. Her bones had the sharp fragility of a bird's.

'Save your glozing for the bride,' she said, and patted his hand before moving away. 'Reckon I'd best go and put me hat on. Eric'll be here any minute.'

Eric had learned to drive a car since being apprenticed over at Manningtree, and in the capacity of best man had hired a Dodge of ancient vintage and uncertain temper. He drove up in a cloud of dust, and while the machine stood panting and throbbing outside the Noggin's gate, helped his mother up on to the back seat and indicated that the bridegroom should perch beside him.

They set off for Shilling Tye in a series of convulsions with half the dogs of Marling Hamlet galloping joyously behind. People waved as they passed and Ma clung on to her hat with both hands.

'Ole boy's having the bells rung for you!' she exclaimed as the car's roar died. 'Just hark to 'em, Thaddy.'

The lych-gate was open, and after helping his mother to alight Thaddeus straightened his tie and smoothed his hair. The sun was hot on his shoulders.

'Doing all right?' Eric enquired.

'Sweating like a horse.'

The three of them proceeded rather cautiously towards the porch. As they entered they could hear beneath the clashing of bells the sound of Miss Evans warming up the organ in a series of long, droning chords that made the soles of their feet tingle.

'That's a nice tune,' Ma said admiringly, and scurried hastily into the nearest pew. Although God-fearing in their way, the Noggins were not regular communicants, and the dozen or so already forming the congregation stared at her. I feel like a trapped weasel, she thought, and then a voice hissed sharply in her ear, 'You're on the wrong *side*, Mother! You're supposed to be in the front pew over there, with *us*!'

Her elder daughter Marjorie loomed over her in a pink cloche hat and a powerful waft of Evening in Paris. With a cluck of irritation Ma followed her. They settled themselves alongside Ken, Marjorie's husband, and their two little boys who were wearing grey flannel suits and oiled-down hair. Marjorie turned her attention to her mother's appearance.

'What on earth's that thing on your head?'

'Me hat.'

'Wherever did you dig it up from?'

'I didn't. I made it meself.'

'Looks like a buncha weeds on a gatepost.' Although she had worked assiduously at her diction since marrying Ken, true Suffolk was still apt to intrude.

'Well, yours ain't no more'n a po downturned on a muck heap – '

'*Mothah!*' Marjorie regained her improved cadences. They both shut up after that, and Ma concentrated on the figures of her two sons standing close together by the altar steps. Thaddy in particular was a fine boy; very tall, very straight, and with the same gentle ways as his Dad . . . Her thoughts wandered, then jerked back to the present as the organ left its vague wanderings and began to play a proper tune while the Reverend Fiske, a rosy apple nestled in a crisp white surplice, led his village choirboys up the centre aisle. She saw Thaddy look round, and she caught Eric's cheerful, surreptitious wink. Yes, Eric had grown into a nice boy too.

85

A few more had joined the congregation, but the pews on the bride's side remained starkly empty except for the imposing figure of Mrs Palfrey sitting defiantly in the middle.

'Rather awkward isn't it, her having no family,' breathed Marjorie, releasing another blast of scent.

'She'll have one afore the morning's done,' said Ma, and watched as the choirboys settled themselves in their stalls and the Reverend Fiske positioned himself at the top of the altar steps with his small hands folded.

Funny ole bugger, thought Ma, and the Reverend Fiske thought I do wish we could have found someone a little less macabre to give the poor child away to, but this is what happens when one does things in a hurry. *O maxima mea culpa* . . .

It seemed an eternity before Miss Evans snapped off the tune she had been playing and began a new one. With a little rustle of expectation the congregation rose to its feet as Polly Monday in her lace curtain wedding dress entered upon the arm of Reuben Ashpole, a bouquet of the Reverend's roses resting lightly upon her pregnancy.

The two bridesmaids followed close behind, and Dora, embarrassed, tried to accommodate her pace to the little dipping, bobbing movement of Hoppity May. Everything about Thaddy's wedding was embarrassing her: the bride was pregnant and had no family or friends except the Reverend's cook-housekeeper and a girl with a funny limp, and surely they could have found someone better than a gravedigger to give her away. Although the old man had spruced himself up and put a flower in his buttonhole you could sow potatoes down his fingernails.

It was a long, slow walk to the altar steps, and to soothe her discomfort Dora tried to imagine what it would be like if she were the bride and Mr Bunting the man waiting to claim her hand. It would be a jolly sight different to this; she, Dora, would be wearing white, but with proper entitlement to it. She would be a virgin going unsullied to her bridegroom. And Mr Bunting in a tailcoat would be standing gravely to receive her; gravely, yes – but with a pounding of his heart and a tightening of his throat . . . Dora began to blush uncontrollably and hastily switched her mind to other things.

Standing close beside his brother, Thaddeus had never felt so lonely in all his life; lonely, and filled with the nervous desire to bolt like any animal in unfamiliar surroundings. Never before had he been so conscious of his hands, heavy and red as two bricks. He folded them in front of his crotch; unfolded them and began to shove them into his pockets, but it didn't feel polite in church. So they hung down at his sides once more, two great ole hams slung on a couple of meat hooks.

Then everything changed. He sensed her arrival at his side. Glancing under his lashes he saw the white lace and one little pink hand half buried in a great mass of roses. Fleetingly, drowningly, he recognised *Fantàin Latour* and *Celeste* and the incomparable scent of *Louise Odier* . . . and he knew that Polly and roses would be forever inseparable in his mind.

The service proceeded, and with her there it was all quite easy. The Reverend spoke the words in the same sort of ordinary way he spoke when they were going round the garden, and Thaddeus repeated the promises after him without stumbling. Polly did the same. Her little voice was all but inaudible, but the Reverend's grasp was surprisingly strong and very reassuring as it joined their two hands together. After Eric had fished the ring out of his pocket and it had lain for a spell on the Reverend's open book, Thaddeus pushed it firmly down over Polly's finger, which was as pink and trembling as the roses she held.

They knelt, ostensibly to pray, but the bridegroom's thoughts whirled in a dazed kaleidoscope and only regathered themselves when the words *Those whom God hath joined together let no man put asunder* rang round the church and fled away up into the hammerbeam roof. After that there was a psalm, and when the Reverend called upon God to assist with His blessing of these two persons that they might be fruitful in procreation Thaddeus dared to slide his hand into the bouquet of roses and squeeze the fingers of his wife. They squeezed back.

Then it was over. The final formalities were accomplished, Miss Evans let fly with a bursting fanfare and the bells seemed to tumble over each other as the Thaddeus Noggins moved ceremoniously down the aisle.

Deeply relieved, the bridegroom flashed his mother a quick grin, then glancing across to the opposite pews saw that Mrs Palfrey was no longer the sole occupant. His grin faltered when he recognised the lowering forehead and small glittering eyes of Blacksmith Potter: he was standing to attention with his hymn-book held in both massive paws, his bull neck tightly constricted by a mercilessly starched Sunday collar. And his expression was that of a bereft child fighting back its tears.

Confused and incredulous, Thaddeus grasped his wife more tightly as he recognised the others – Billy Dewey, Bertie Fox, and the chap who came round selling paraffin once a fortnight. There were two he didn't know the names of, but he knew Percy Cattermole from the baker's and Dennis Wiston who was supposed to be walking out with Amy Hume. They were all there; all scrubbed and shaved and dressed in Sunday serge and they were all paying homage, all speaking a sad and loving farewell with their eyes. The eyes of men yearning after a treasure, after the sweet unattainable. He saw them, each one of them as he passed, moist-lipped and dreaming the sweet dreams of youth that would never fade, never die, so long as this darling child of nature with the irrepressible gold curls and tip-tilted features fashioned in the soft pink and white of classic shrub roses should walk the winding lanes of Suffolk.

Yes. But even so . . . Suspicion sharpened: had she in fact always been the sweet unattainable? He knew about Potter, but what about the others? Not Billy Dewey, of all people. Not Percy Cattermole, for Chrissake. And what about all the others? All the others standing there with the Reverend's prayerbooks clutched tight in their meaty, sweaty hands while they watched her go by. How much did they know of her? How much had they. . . ? How many. . . ?

His hand tightened round her fingers, bruising the rose petals in which they were buried. He sensed her wince, and they were near the end of the long ceremonial march when she glanced up at him and he saw that her brimming eyes were luminescent with a love that was as unmistakable as it was heart-rending.

Bracing his shoulders Thaddeus marched her out to the porch, a dog with a prize bone, and the bells greeted them in a tumbling tumult of joy.

They had ham and salad and freshly baked rolls and there were bottles of beer as well as the fruit cup when they all sat down at a long trestle table under the trees in the Vicarage garden. Although there seemed to be no clear demarcation line between guests and gatecrashers there was plenty for all, including jelly and custard for the choirboys.

There were no speeches, but when the cake was cut everyone raised a cheer. As the day dwindled Dennis Wiston produced his old concertina, and the older ones, brushing the last of the crumbs away, were the most eager to form up for the Black Nag and Betty-Trip-Lightly. The young held back, vaguely discomforted by the knowledge that old country dances had given way to Ragtime and the Charleston, but the lilt of the music overcame their scruples and everyone joined in, choirboys buzzing like mosquitoes in and out of the ever-changing pattern. Thaddeus saw Sam Potter spit on his hands and rub them together before making a grab at Mrs Palfrey.

The ground shook as they thundered past, monumental as a couple of traction engines, and the darkness of suspicion and jealousy was blown away on a gust of laughter. His mother and the Reverend danced past gay as bouncing robins, and he saw Marjorie partnered by her husband Ken and poor ole Dora smiling fixedly as she tripped past with Eric. Dora was a nice gal in her way, but she could do more with herself. Curl her hair up, or something . . .

Polly danced too, but refused to let go of her bouquet. She clung to it as if it were some kind of lucky charm, and when Mrs Palfrey advised her in an undertone that she didn't really show all that much Polly turned pink and said that it wasn't that – the roses had all bin chose by Thaddy because they were his favourites and she wasn't going to let go of them, not ever.

The only one who didn't dance was Hoppity May. She remained at the trestle table among the picturesque ruins of the feast with her head nodding and her foot tapping in time to the music. She had taken off her hat and her dark hair had loosened at the nape of her neck.

'Hullo, May.' Percy Cattermole slumped down beside her, laboured breath whistling through tobacco-stained fangs. 'All right, gal?'

'Yes. Wonderful.'

'Make a good couple, don't they?' His eyes were fixed on the bride.

89

'I love them,' she said, and the simplicity of her words embarrassed him. Suffolk people didn't talk about love, even when they were making it. He got up and wandered away.

Eventually the dancing declined, and Dennis Wiston changed from country jigs to the slower, sadder tunes that survived from the war no matter how hard some people tried to drown them out with Yankee stuff. The sweet melancholy of 'Long Long Trail' and 'Keep the Home Fires Burning,' so grievously evocative for some, so meaningless for the young ones, blossomed and faded into the twilight of the old garden where the roses glimmered and the owls called.

No one appeared to notice when Thaddeus took his wife's hand and led her away. Not towards the coachman's cottage ready and waiting in the stableyard but out through the gate, down the lane and along the narrow track past the woods. They walked slowly and without speaking, Polly's white lace dress gleaming ghostlike in the lingering dusk.

'Tired?' he asked eventually.

'I could go on all night.'

He held the gate open that led down to the water meadows and they could sense the presence of the river; its rich moist smell, the faint mist rising through the spires of butomus and typha.

'Got a surprise.' His voice was casual.

'Oh? What?' Without replying he moved slowly with her through the soft damp grass until they came to the bank of the Stour. 'Look, the Reverend's given us a loan of it.'

She peered down without letting go of his arm, without letting go of her bouquet. 'Oh, Thaddy – can we go in it?'

The simple, urgent longings of childhood returned: to eat cake with icing on it, to ride on a donkey, to own a doll that said *Mama*, to go in a boat.

'Can we really go in it *now*? I've never bin in a boat yet – '

She hung on his arm, tugging it imploringly. And if she was the artless and ingenuous child he was the wise and beneficent adult touched by her innocence. 'Reckon that's what that's there for.'

He opened his arms with the idea of helping her down into it, but instead he crushed her close to him and a flutter of petals fell from the rose caught between them. Then he picked her up and gently placed her on the small seat in the stern. It rocked deliciously beneath his weight as he took the other seat, and she watched him untie the painter then push away from the bank with one of the oars.

'Didn't know you was a rowing man, Thaddy.'

'Only know enought to get by. Eric's the one for boats, not me.'

Eric. Who was now her brother-in-law. Not as tall as Thaddy and more gingery in colour, but very nice. He had smiled at her and said how glad he was to meet her, then wished her all the best for the future.

She lay back with her legs stretched out and her elbows on the gunwales while she considered the family she had acquired through marrying Thaddeus: a mother, two sisters and a brother. Well, sort of. Not quite the same as your own, perhaps, but she was hardly in a position to compare. Mrs Noggin had told her to call her Ma same as the others, but so far she had been unable to. It didn't feel right. But most likely it would come in time.

She liked Mrs Noggin, sensing beneath the sharpness a magnanimity, a kind of laconic affection that might one day grow into real love, but she was still uncertain of her two sisters-in-law. Dora was nice to her, but a bit distant. But then Dora had a good job in a draper's and earned fifteen shillings a week, so it was rumoured, and shop assistants were superior to maids of all work, even when they worked in vicarages. She didn't know of any of the girls from the orphanage who had gone to work in shops; for them it was domestic service or the workhouse. But she felt sure that Dora would be her friend in time; perhaps on her half-day she would come over to tea and in the winter they would sit close to the fire and play with the baby . . . And one day Dora would get married and then their babies would be cousins.

The baby had got two cousins already, of course. The two little boys who belonged to the other sister, Marjorie. And if Dora tended to be distant, Marjorie had a bright smile which she bestowed upon the world in general and no one in particular. She was very good-looking, with blue eyes same as Thaddy's and her hair was shingled at the back and clung to her cheeks in two kiss curls. She had worn a lovely frock at the wedding with a fringe round the hem and Polly remembered with admiration the heavy gold bracelet worn round her upper arm with a lace handkerchief tucked inside it. Very smart and very rich, but apart from saying

'Hullo dear – congrats and all that' she hadn't taken much notice of Polly. Her husband had been nice and friendly though, kissing her hand and asking which rosebush Thaddeus had found her under, and the two little boys had joined in the dancing with her although for some reason they wouldn't mix with the choirboys.

But it had been a wonderful wedding, something she had never dreamed of, and if one or two people had turned up a bit unexpected, well, there hadn't been any awkwardness, and after all wedding days were meant to be happy for everyone.

It was a warm night. Thaddeus was allowing the little boat to drift along by the bank where the Stour was crinkling black and grey beneath the overhanging trees. The only sound was a faint plash as an occasional pike or gudgeon rose.

'I'll never get over this. Never,' Polly murmured. The dying remains of her bouquet rose and fell slowly as she breathed. 'And you don't reckon it mattered, me having ole Reuben give me away? Him being a gravedigger, I mean.'

'Never been one for superstition, meself,' Thaddeus gave a gentle pull on the oars, 'and there's no harm in gravedigging, is there? It's a good honest job, same as mine.'

A little night wind stirred the reeds, riffling through them like a sigh.

'One of these days I'm going to be me own boss,' Thaddeus continued. 'I like the Reverend fine – if you've got to have a boss you couldn't have a better – but one day we're going to set up on our own and I'm going to grow roses. Nothing but roses. They're what I understand most, and what I know I'll do best.'

'And then when he's left school you can teach the baby how to grow them too, can't you?' She closed her eyes to trap the new dreams. 'He could be your partner . . . Thaddeus Noggin and Son.'

'How d'you know it's a he?'

'I just know.'

The wind increased, rustling and fumbling along the banks like a predator; the dark face of the river was no longer friendly. Abruptly Thaddeus leaned forward. The intensity of his stare, sensed rather than seen, made her sit upright.

'You'll never let me down will you?' Apart from the outline of his head she could only see the whites of his eyes in the darkness.

His voice had an eerie sound against the wind. 'Promise you'll never let me down, Polly.'

She shivered, then reached forward to link her arms around his neck. 'I'll never let you down, Thaddy dear.'

'And you'll never go away?'

The madness of the idea startled her. 'Whatever would make me do that?'

'But you promise me you won't?'

'I promise you, Thaddy. I promise.'

She released her arms and they sat peering at one another with painful intensity, striving to pierce the shadows. It struck her that the promise she had just made out here in the darkness in the little boat was more solemnly binding than the vows she had repeated in church. Everyone said the other ones; the words must be so worn thin with use by now that it would be like binding people together with a bit of old frayed rope. This was different: this was their own private vow made out here on the river with no one else to hear.

'I promise I'll never leave you, Thaddy,' she repeated. 'Now you say the same.'

'I'll never leave you, sweet Polly. That I do promise.'

The moment was so strange and serious that she gave an unvoluntary giggle, then the moon sailed free of cloud and transformed the darkling river into a network of shining silver. There had never been anything so beautiful.

Slowly Thaddeus took up the oars again and said, 'Time we went home. We're getting near the first ole lock before Nayland.'

They reached the stableyard as the church clock was striking – Thaddeus reckoned it must be half-past eleven – and they stood together at the open door, listening to the silence resettling over the garden and the sleeping black hulk of the Vicarage.

'Rare ole wedding, that,' Thaddeus said meditatively. 'Don't reckon royalty could've had a better send-off.'

'But I should have helped with the clearing up, shouldn't I? I shouldn't have gone off like I did.'

'Nobody clears up on their wedding day,' he said, then led her inside and firmly closed the door behind them.

'Not bad, Noggin! Not bad at all,' said the Reverend Fiske, squinting through his pince-nez at the small white rose topping the four-inch-high plant. 'Now my boy, have you thought about budding from it? If you have, take my advice and cross it with a hexaploid – it has forty-two chromosomes, as I think I explained – and it will give fertile offspring in plenty if your seedling is diploid, which I rather believe it to be . . .'

Thaddeus listened intently as he watched the little potted plant slowly rotating in the vicar's fingers. Last autumn he had taken the seeds from an old cottage rose in the garden at home and straight away planted them in compost. A week after he started work at the Vicarage – the 12th of April, to be exact – the seedlings had appeared. Seven nondescript little shoots with oval first-leaves which he carefully potted on and transferred to the Vicarage greenhouse, and now, only eleven weeks later, they were examining the first hesitant bloom. A bare inch in diameter, it had a shy, uncertain look as if doubtful of its reception.

'Eighteen petals,' said the Reverend, counting. 'Between sixteen and twenty is what we are looking for, and I dare say the colour will vary a little with successive flowerings until she settles down. But as charming a firstborn as one could wish – speaking of which,' he handed the pot back, 'how is Polly?'

'Doing nicely, thank you Vicar. And if – well, just supposing I got a new rose offa this – one nobody's ever seen before, I mean – I'd like to call it by her name.'

'A splendid idea!' The Reverend removed his pince-nez and beamed at him, 'although I fear the results will not be in time for the accouchement. We can hurry the process by budding during the first year, although we will need a steady hand and eye to deal with such a tiny creature, and even if all goes well we must not expect any blooms before next July.'

'No, Vicar. But it still makes me want to have a go at it.'

'Then fire away, Noggin!' cried his employer. '*Tempus* is forever fugiting faster than we give it credit for . . .'

Thaddeus agreed, and they parted. The idea of creating a brand new rose and naming it after his wife kept him company for the rest of the day.

Hoppity May was at the cottage when he returned from work. She quite often called round in the afternoons, and the two girls would sit outside in the old stableyard sewing and gossiping and drinking tea from the big brown teapot that had been a wedding present.

94

'Look, Thaddy – May's taught me feather-stitching!'

He went over to his wife and admired the bit of flannelette sheeting she was brandishing like a flag. 'Much too good to use,' he said. 'Reckon we oughta frame it.'

Polly crowed with laughter, then explained as if to a lovable half-wit. 'No dear, this is a draw-sheet. Nice and warm for the baby to lie on because he's going to be born in the winter, isn't he? And babies have got to be kept warm, no matter what. So we've got four draw-sheets, and look – May's done that one with little lazy-daisies in the corner, but his top sheets are going to be proper hem-stitching. May's showing me how. And your Ma's given us a bag of real duck down for his little pillow to rest his head on . . . isn't it *lovely*, Thaddy?'

He agreed yes, it was lovely all right, and across Polly's bent head caught a merry wink from her friend Hoppity May. *She's just a child*, the wink said, *and we're sharing in her triumph and her joy, aren't we?*

Yes, the gravity of his smile replied, *she is a child who has been denied all but the barest necessities of life.*

Then Polly chucked her sewing aside and ran to make his supper. Two fresh boiled eggs, tomatoes warm from the sun and bread carefully cut and liberally spread with fresh butter from the farm.

But her running was no longer that of the young girl Polly he had chased laughing across the meadows in the joy of early summer; now the increasing bulk of the baby encumbered her, and the movement was more that of a waddle. Turning suddenly she caught his expression, and her smile faltered into uncertainty. He saw how it happened and he understood, and sent his love and tenderness flowing across to her before seating himself at the table. She stood behind him as he ate, with her hands on his shoulders and trying not to run her lips across the hair curling close to the nape of his neck while Hoppity May sat peacefully sewing.

Summer was fading, slipping away like sand through the fingers, and when Thaddeus had finished eating May folded up her sewing, removed her thimble and said that it was time she went home. The evenings were drawing in. Yet they lingered, content in each other's company, and when Polly suggested that they sit outside again for a bit, Thaddeus fetched the other kitchen chair they had recently acquired.

The air was warm and very still, and they sat listening to the commotion of blackbirds preparing to roost.

'Why do they always call pink-pink-pink?' Polly asked.

'Well now, it's like this,' Thaddeus said slowly. 'Way back in the Garden of Eden, ole Adam got all the living creatures together and told'em it'd be a good idea if they was all to choose a different colour to act as a sign of danger to their particular species, being that some things are dangerous to some kinds of creatures and others not. Us humans'll have red for danger he said, grabbing the best colour quick because – well, he was a human, wasn't he? Then all the others chose – horses have yellow, cows have blue, but only after a bit of argy-bargy with some of the bulls because they wanted red same as humans – but what they didn't realise was that all the blackbirds were out foraging and hadn't heard about the meeting. So when they got back and they found there was no colours left, they were in a fair ole sweat. Then ole Adam come up and says, Well now, I enjoy hearing you a-whistling up in the trees come springtime, so I'll tell you what I'll do; I'll slosh a bitta water in a bucketfulla my red and you can have pink. Which is what he did, being a man of his word, and the one time-a day when blackbirds get nervous is when it's getting dark and they're afeared of being trandled and stuck in the pot by some ole human who don't appreciate them the way that Adam did.'

'A lovely story,' May said. 'And I believe every word.'

The twilight deepened and still they remained. From the corner of his eye Thaddeus saw a small agile figure slip through the gateway and come across to them on noiseless plimsolled feet. It was Ma.

'Gor dear, what bring you over at this time?'

'Had to tell you soon as I heard else I'll never sleep.' In the lavender dusk her eyes shone bright with enjoyment. 'So brace up for a shock.'

'Go on, then?'

'The Big House is up for sale. Pore ole Fitzhardys have gorn bust!'

It was like the end of the world to anyone who had come from Marling or Marling Hamlet. Although the family's power had waned considerably since the end of the war they had always been there, and presumably always would be, even though young

96

George the son and heir had copped it on the Somme. Somehow it had been assumed that there would always be Fitzhardys; cousins or nephews would be produced like thoroughbred rabbits out of hats in place of the Old Man when he went, but their reign would last for ever. They were immutable as time itself.

But now they were gone. Broke, like so many others after the war, and the Big House with all its pomp and circumstance was up for sale. Thaddeus had never set eyes on Lady Isobel since the day of the funeral. Had only carried a picture of her in his mind during the blood and mud of Flanders until the picture had faded like a Victorian daguerrotype in harsh light.

'You and your Dad used to work up there, didn't you, Thaddy?' Polly's voice broke the silence.

'Yes,' he replied tersely, then rose to his feet. 'Cuppa tea or glassa nettle beer, Ma?'

But already she was preparing for departure, as if delivery of the stupendous news had proved sufficient in itself. May rose to accompany her.

'So where's Her Ladyship going, then?' Thaddeus spoke gruffly. 'Foreign parts, or somewhere?'

'Most likely London, they reckon. But nobody knows the truth on it yet.'

His mother waited while May collected her bicycle from where it leaned against the wall and they walked out of the yard together.

'A few years ago there'da bin real hardship in the village if they'd gorn. Most everybody worked up there, but things is different now. There's day work in Sudbury and parts, where you can call your soul your own, and there's no more going on about . . . well – '

'Loyalty?' suggested May. The light from her cycle lamp wavered dimly between them.

'Aye, that's it. Although in the ole days we was happy enough with what we'd got. We just made do.' Her feet pattered silently and energetically along the glimmering lane. Then she peered narrowly at May: 'Your Pa was to do with learnin' or suthun', weren't he?'

'He taught history at a boys' school in Halstead. He and Mother passed away within a year of one another.'

Giving a brief cluck of condolence, Ma came to a halt. 'Reckon

I'll leave you here, gal, and go the quick way – ' As May paused, Ma dropped to the ground and burrowed like a small nocturnal animal through a hole in the hedge and vanished from sight.

Giving a series of little hops, May mounted her bicycle and rode off towards home in Tarrent's Row.

During the weeks following the wedding Polly had been like a child with a wonderful toy; a little girl given a doll's house.

Tirelessly she had arranged and then rearranged the furniture in the cottage, always pausing in whatever she was doing to listen to the clock strike and to watch with clasped hands as the little wooden cuckoo flew out of its door. She swept and dusted and cleaned the windows; she washed and ironed and tried her hand at making cakes and puddings. Some were successful, but Thaddy was always very kind about the failures, too.

'Nothing wrong but what a bit of practice won't put right,' he would tell her while chumping determinedly on sunken sponge or rock-hard pastry.

Blissfully ignorant of convention she often wore her wedding dress because it was far too beautiful to put away, and also because it was yet another powerful symbol of happiness. So she greeted Thaddeus on summer evenings after work, waiting for him in the sunset glow of the old stableyard with her curls bunched up in a ribbon and the long white dress shimmering against the grey of the coachman's cottage.

And Thaddeus, because of Suffolk taciturnity and new husbandly dignity, would acknowledge the picture with no more than a brief nod before asking what they'd got for tea. Yet half an hour spent in the magic of the cottage – clean towel laid ready for his ablutions at the brownstone sink, his healthy face emerging brick red and shining – was enough to break down the masculine sense of constriction, and after the meal, *Your Ma brought us them lovely duck eggs, Thaddy*, the old habits of courtship would return. After washing the dishes they would wander back down the meadows and the old footpaths ringing with evening birdsong.

They would talk with their arms round one another, close as if they were one indissoluble person, and the kisses they exchanged became as tremulous and sweetly uncertain as the early ones. But they no longer played tig, or any of the other childish games of pursuit that had seemed so natural in those days; partly because of the baby, but also because of the deepening seriousness of their relationship. Now, they were a married couple with their baby to consider. As the evenings began to draw in Thaddeus would bring roses home and explain to her about them.

'This one's what they call a Bourbon. She come out in 1843 and she's called *Souvenir de la Malmaison*, and that one there's a Damask. Very old the Damasks are, and the Reverend reckons they come down from the *Rosa gallica* . . .' Polly would listen and try hard to remember, sitting close to him and smiling at the tenderness in his big work-thickened fingers.

As autumn crept away and winter took its place she would light the fire early and lie back in the chair watching the flames flicker and dance and a sense of peaceful lethargy would envelop her. She became conscious of her body almost as a separate entity, with the baby that was now so close to the world stretching her skin drum-tight with the power of its growth. In this new half-comotose state the past became blurred in dreams of the future; she had never seen the future so clearly before – had never really bothered to think about it – but now it was extending in front of her like an enticing pathway and she had only to follow it hand in hand with Thaddy and their son. The possibility that the baby might not be her husband's had long since faded from her mind, together with memories of the orphanage and being Polly Monday. She seemed drugged with tranquillity during those short and firelit days.

For the first time she began to wonder about her mother and father; who they were, and what they looked like. She wondered whether it had grieved her mother to leave her outside the police station in a fish box. They reckoned at the orphanage she had been about three or four days old, but if they had any other information about her they had not thought fit to disclose it. It wasn't supposed to be good for orphans to know too much about themselves.

Since being old enough to understand what it meant, she had taken it for granted that she was illegitimate; most of the other inmates of the orphanage were, but Matron had taken the view that although being born out of wedlock was a sin and a social disgrace there was no use crying over spilt milk, and the only thing to do was try to make the best of a bad job.

She hoped now that her parents, whoever they were, might have been as happy as she and Thaddy, if only for a little while.

She was never lonely during those waiting months because Hoppity May continued to call quite frequently, and several times Mrs Palfrey came across the courtyard with a freshly baked loaf or a little bit of something she had knitted for the baby. They would make a pot of tea and sit with it close to the fire while Mrs Palfrey told Polly about the new maid: 'She frames about well enough, but we don't have half the laughs we used to in the ole days.'

The Reverend himself also appeared, knocking deferentially on the door as if the cottage was really hers and Thaddy's and not part of his Vicarage. He too stayed for cups of tea, and when Christmas came she went with Thaddeus to the carol service and lingered dreamy-eyed by the crib that had been set up by the font.

The first snow came late that year, and on the afternoon Thaddeus arrived home with a last handful of brave little rosebuds, the labour pains had begun.

He took her by the arm, almost rough with the sense of urgency. 'You'd best go to bed . . . it's best to be lying down . . .'

She shook him off, and continued to walk up and down the room, holding the rosebuds close against her face although they had no scent.

'You all right? Be all right, will you, while I go for the nurse?'

She nodded, and smiled at him. Alarmed and deeply loving he put his arms around her and kissed her hair, then hurried out to his bicycle.

The snow was blowing in his eyes as he bent low over the handlebars, shoving at the pedals with his heavy work boots, and his alarm became tinged with excitement at the thought of the baby. Any doubt concerning its paternity had faded from his mind too.

The nurse was at home. She gave her cat some milk and banked up the fire with slack before gathering up her midwife's bag. Putting on her hat and coat she asked whether Thaddeus had timed the pains. He confessed that he hadn't.

'Her first, isn't it?'

'Yes,' he said humbly.

'You'll learn.' She turned the lamp down low.

She offered him a lift in her Morris two-seater but he had to refuse because of his bicycle. So he set off ahead of her, then turned back at the sound of the car's gasping cries of resistance to the cold wet snow.

'Here –' He had never tried to turn a starting handle before, and this one knew it. With the white flakes slamming against his back he bent over it, trying to persuade, to induce, and finally to bully. Bullying won. The Morris coughed and shuddered into life, and stood pulsating in the lane while the nurse climbed regally aboard, bag in hand.

She overtook him after the first hundred yards, splashing him with churned brown snow. By the time he reached the coachman's cottage she was already installed and in charge, apron-clad and with sleeves rolled up.

'There's nothing you can do,' she said to Thaddeus. 'Might as well go down the pub.'

'In this weather?' He tried to sound jocular.

'That's what all the other fathers would do.'

'I'm not the same as all the other fathers.'

'I started to make you a nice tea, Thaddy –' Polly began, and was immediately shushed by the nurse.

'No call to worry about hubby's tea now, dear – you've got other things to think about. I'm sure he can get his own just this once,' and she turned upon Thaddeus an eye like a metal button.

He wasn't hungry. So he washed his hands and face at the sink with the nurse clucking and fidgeting behind him, then went back to the living-room and drew the curtains against the hurling snow. Polly was walking from chair to chair with the roses held against her nose as if they contained anaesthetic.

'All right, are you?' he asked in a low voice so that the interloper wouldn't hear.

'Yes, I'm fine,' she whispered back, her smile colliding with a grimace of pain.

'They say that if men bore the child there'd never be a second,' the nurse said. 'I hope you've got clean sheets on the bed, have you?'

Polly nodded, and the nurse placed a muscular arm around her and led her upstairs. Left alone, Thaddeus listened to the footsteps overhead and the closing of the door, before sinking into the chair by the fire where a big pan of water was simmering, put there by the nurse.

She hates men, he thought despondently. Reckons it's all our fault, all this. Staring into the heart of the flames he tried to hate

101

her back, but the hatred wouldn't come. Instead, he felt guilty, ugly and gross – precisely the way she wanted him to feel.

Warm for the first time that day, he fell into a doze while listening for any meaningful sounds coming from above – then jerked confusedly awake when a high, rough-edged squealing bit into his eardrums. He leaped for the stairs, ready to murder the nurse for hurting his wife, but stopped abruptly outside the closed door.

'It's manners to wait 'til you're invited,' the nurse said, opening it, 'but since you're here you'd better come in.'

The room was warm from the paraffin heater. Polly was lying back on the bed still glistening with sweat, and on the chair close by was a tin bowl containing something that looked red and murdered. He rushed towards her, then the nurse stepped in his way and offered him a small object wrapped in a bit of blanket. Its eyes were little squinting slits and it was damp and still streaked with blood, but the nurse's face was aglow; transformed like everything else in the room at that moment.

'Your son,' she said. 'A lovely healthy boy and the dead spit of you, Mr Noggin dear.'

She sent him downstairs to make a nice pot of tea while she concluded her duties. Both Polly and the baby were washed and gowned and the placenta had been wrapped up in newspaper ready to be burnt by the time he returned.

Sitting on the foot of the bed he looked at Polly while he drank his tea and tried to fix a permanent image of her in his mind. Some rose varieties had that same delicate bloom that seemed to come from within the petal's composition like a thin coating of light. The *Portland Rose* had it, so had the *Queen of Denmark* and particularly *Madame Pierre Oger* . . . Polly's light glowed in her eyes and suffused her skin and he wanted to touch her but daren't in case he obscured it with his clumsiness. In case the petals should fall in a spent shower.

'Are you pleased with him, Thaddy?' Her voice broke into his thoughts and he watched her lay her cup and saucer aside and bend over the crib standing at her bedside.

'Rare pleased with both of you.' He wanted to add the word *darling*, but couldn't, especially in front of the nurse.

'One of the quickest confinements I've known, especially for a first.' Sipping her tea with her sleeves rolled down, the nurse seemed to have assumed a different persona; homely and comfortable, like a familiar pair of shoes. She didn't seem to despise Thaddeus any more.

'What are you going to call him?'

The parents exchanged a loving glance. 'Joseph Bonamy,' they said in unison.

'Joseph after Thaddy's father and Bonamy after the Reverend,' added Polly.

'That's nice,' said the nurse in the same way that she said it to everyone.

A lot of boys were being christened Brian and Derek and Leonard these days, so it made a nice change. But she wasn't too sure about Bonamy; all right for a clergyman but a bit outlandish for an ordinary working-class chap. She hoped he wouldn't get teased at school.

I'm an auntie three times now, Dora thought, tidying the button drawer in Mr Bunting's Emporium. I wonder if I'll ever be a mother?

If it depended upon the object of her adoration, the answer seemed more and more like no. Apart from the unalterable fact that he was married to Mrs Bunting, her employer now seemed to maintain an even greater distance between them. Once upon a time he had sometimes smiled at her and made homely little remarks about the weather, but now he spoke only if it were strictly necessary, and even then he refrained from looking at her.

Naturally she had no desire to act fast, or to lead him on in the way some girls would, but it was very hard when the gentleman you silently loved and honoured regarded you as no more than a black-clad shadow meekly selling ladies' elastic to impoverished farm labourers' wives.

He didn't even seem to like her enquiring after Mrs Bunting any more. In answer to her admittedly dutiful request for news he would merely say that Mrs Bunting was progressing favourably and leave Dora to speculate about the increased visits from the doctor. During the week that followed Thaddeus's wedding she had felt unsettled and dissatisfied almost to the point of giving in her notice, but one sidelong glance at Mr Bunting's pale and noble features beneath the impeccable quiff was sufficient to melt her insides with love and she would resolve to bob her hair and wear stockings with fancy patterns up the sides and try to behave more like other girls. The sort of girls who knew what they wanted and saw no point in noble self-sacrifice.

But she didn't. Couldn't. She just wasn't the type to play fast and loose with married men so she continued as before, silently efficient and seeking to content herself with whatever meagre crumbs might come her way. And now she was an auntie to Thaddeus's and Polly's baby, conceived out of wedlock and welcomed with a wicked pagan joy she found difficult to share no matter how hard she tried.

When she called at the coachman's cottage with six rust-coloured chrysanthemums Polly was sitting up in bed, pink in the face with pleasure and excitement. She held out her arms to Dora as if she were one of the people she loved most in the world. Dora returned her embrace awkwardly, conscious of the warm animal smell coming from her, then smiled dutifully in the direction of the crib and said what a dear little baby Joseph was.

'And that all went off wonnerful easy,' said Ma, who was sitting by the washstand with her old beret on. 'Coupla yelps and that sprung out like a jack rabbit.'

'I'm very healthy, that's why,' Polly said, bunching her curls up on top of her head. 'And we're going to have lots more, aren't we, Thaddy?'

'Reckon you're the boss,' he said, and Dora had to look away from the expression of adoration in his eyes.

Hoppity May called too, bringing a little angora matinée jacket she had knitted; watching her bob swiftly across the room Dora thought, that makes two of us. Her and me, both set to be old maids.

The room was very warm in spite of the iron cold outside and Ma was the first to notice that the rose pink of Polly's cheeks was turning to a darker shade.

'Get too flushed up with excitement and you'll curdle the milk,' she warned, and punching the pillows into shape she made the girl lie down. They tiptoed out, Thaddeus last. Polly watched him turn down the lamp, then closed her eyes.

She still seemed tired the next day. 'What they call reaction,' the nurse explained when she called in. 'Common enough with a first baby.'

She should have been feeling better by the third day, but a new sense of lassitude seemed to be smothering the old eagerness and sense of joy. She lay passive and becalmed, and when they gave her the baby she held it dutifully rather than lovingly. The rush of milk dwindled and the baby sucked at its fists and bawled. Concerned, the nurse asked the doctor to call. He appeared on the following day, clumping up the narrow stairs and shaking the room with his presence.

He took Polly's temperature, left a prescription for some physic and advised that the baby should be fed on diluted cow's milk. 'We call it reaction,' he said. 'Common enough after a first delivery.'

She seemed better on the sixth day, and murmured that it was high time she set herself to rights. Propped up on the pillows she tried to tidy her hair, tried to drag the comb through the sticky blonde curls that tickled and tormented her face and neck. Before she had finished she slipped sideways and seemed unable to right herself unaided.

'Having a baby makes you real fagged out,' she murmured apologetically and asked the nurse for another drink of water.

'No more water, dear,' the nurse said. 'There's no goodness in it. I'm bringing you some nice hot bread-and-milk in a minute.'

It came in a pudding basin and lay untouched on the bedside locker, the bread slowly swelling and disintegrating until it sank beneath a skin of heavily sweetened milk.

She kept asking for a cold wet rag to hold on her forehead but they said it would give her a chill. She must keep warm, they said, you don't realise that it's fair perishing outside, but the heavy fumes from the paraffin stove finally made her vomit. She began to feel frightened and curiously alone in spite of the loving concern with which she was surrounded, and wept bitterly when the nurse said it would be better if her baby slept in the room downstairs. He would be with her hubby, who was going to be fine sleeping on two chairs just for a night or two.

'Everybody's leaving me . . .' Distraught, she clung to Thaddeus and her tears seemed to scald his hands when he tried with clumsy tenderness to lay her back on the pillows. But when bedtime came he spread the downstairs heathrug at the foot of the bed and composed himself for sleep covered by a couple of old overcoats.

Next morning she seemed better, but during the evening her temperature rose sharply and she confused her mother-in-law with the Matron of the orphanage. Downstairs in the untidied, undusted living-room Hoppity May assumed charge of the baby's bottle-feeding. It fed slowly and thoughtfully, staring up at her with dark blue eyes that occasionally squinnied with wind, and she stared back at it, smiling a little at the unfolding features of a second Thaddeus.

Next day it was officially admitted that Polly had a touch of fever, the doctor rigorously quelling any undue signs of alarm in her family.

'A common enough occurrence,' he said, glancing round the small, hot room, 'but all will be well in a day or so.' Then he caught sight of Dora, who was sitting by the bedroom window, sewing.

'I've seen you before, have I not?'

'Yes, Doctor. I work at Mr Bunting's Emporium.' She began to blush uncontrollably at the mention of his name.

'Ah yes – poor woman, poor woman,' the doctor shook his head. 'And such a devoted couple . . .' For a moment it seemed as if he might brush aside medical etiquette and say something about the nature of Mrs Bunting's malady, but instead he wrote out a fresh prescription, signed it with a flourish and ordered it to be made up at the chemist's first thing in the morning. 'It will reduce the fever and flush out the poisons.'

Poisons? They looked at one another after his departure, uneasy now, and unsure of themselves in the presence of this new and sinister word. The church bells rang for Evensong.

The nurse came in later, a thing she never did normally on a Sunday evening, and sweeping them all out of the kitchen began to make hot clay poultices, wrapping the baked yellow splodge in strips of white cloth and hurrying upstairs with them. She asked Ma to make a cup of Benger's Food for Polly, who refused it, querulously pushing the cup aside and turning her head away. She was breathing fast and her eyes were closed.

'This is the crisis,' the nurse said, taking her pulse. 'Tomorrow morning she'll be over the worst.'

And she seemed correct in her assumption. Drawing back the

106

curtains, Thaddeus saw early sunlight dancing over patches of blue-white snow and a stray beam of it penetrated the hot little bedroom and drove a golden pathway across the bed.

'Summer's come,' Polly said, and smiled tiredly.

She was tired as if she had walked for miles and spent nights without sleep. She no longer tossed and turned but lay motionless, watching through half-closed eyes the way the sunbeam quivered on the coverlet, and when Thaddeus put his arm round her to help her to sit up he was startled by the thinness of her shoulder bones.

He saw then that her eyes were different, too. Large, very large and faraway, yet at the same time they appeared to be staring at him with a strange and speculative expression, as if she were trying to understand something. But the fever appeared to have passed; her hands and face seemed damply cool and her breathing was slower. He hurried downstairs to make her a cup of tea.

In the living-room the baby woke up and began to howl, rubbing its little fists against the sides of its head. He picked it up and began inexpertly to rock it to and fro and its head banged against his cheek as if it were only lightly attached to the stalk of its neck.

Ma arrived, slinging her bicycle against the wall outside and puffing white feathers of breath in the cold still air.

'How's the gal doin'?'

'Better,' he said. 'Seems a good bit better.' Then he glanced down at her feet. 'And you oughter wear proper shoes this time of year. Plimsolls won't keep the cold out.'

'Don't fret about me, givvus the baby afore you drop it – '

She boiled its milk and set the pan on the doorstep to cool, then hastened upstairs to see Polly, who raised her head in greeting while continuing to stare out of the window.

'Doin' a bit better?'

'Doing fine . . .' The words fell flatly, and there was no accompanying smile.

'You'll be all right, gal. The ole nurse says so.'

Polly acknowledged her words with another tired little flick of her hand. There was Suffolk intimacy in the word *gal* which she would have cherished a week ago. Now she was too weary.

'And the doctor reckons you're all right, too. Just want a bit of feeding up.'

Ma scurried busily, emptying the chamber-pot and the washbowl, then added the sad remains of yet more bread-and-milk and cups of rancid tea and gathered up the baby's soiled nappies that had been left by the nurse, whose status forbade her to deal with such things.

'Shall I bring him up to see you?'

'In a little while.'

Polly lay with her eyes closed, wondering vaguely why the baby meant so little to her. Why it seemed so unreal. But they were all becoming unreal, even Thaddy was no more now than a presence looming in a mist . . . Perhaps there was something wrong with her eyes . . . she dozed, and woke in the grip of abdominal pain. She cried out, and clung feverishly to Thaddeus. The nurse hurried across to the Vicarage to telephone for the doctor.

He came during the afternoon and said that the patient had developed an abcess which would have to be lanced. Removing his coat he rolled up his sleeves, and when the operation had been completed the nurse came downstairs carrying red-stained cloths and what looked like a bowl of blood.

Upstairs, the smell of paraffin merged with the cloying stench of ether, and when Polly finally opened her eyes they were blank as stones.

'She's not come round yet,' said the nurse. 'But I don't suppose she'll be long.'

She made it sound as casual and reassuring as if they were waiting for a bus, but when the Reverend called with a bunch of grapes they could only read ill omen in his clerical collar. He asked if he might see Polly but the nurse said no, better not, so he patted Thaddeus on the shoulder and walked mutely away.

They were all there when Polly died. Ma, Dora and Hoppity May sitting motionless in the room downstairs while Thaddeus held her hands pressed between his own and the nurse stood in silence at the foot of the bed. When it was over he laid her hands gently aside and blundered over to the window where a light snow was beginning to fall.

'Why?' he asked quietly. 'Why?'

'Puerperal fever,' the nurse replied, taking him literally. 'Once it sets in there's not much hope.'

'Did you know all along?'

'Yes,' she said gently. 'But in the medical profession you always keep on trying.'

'*Trying* . . .' he repeated. Haggard and unshaven he went downstairs to break the news.

1930

Ma Noggin scrambled out of the ditch with a cock pheasant held by the legs. The body was still warm. Swiftly she plucked out its tail feathers then stowed the bird away in the spacious pocket that lined her old coat. She called to her grandson that they were going home.

He came rustling through the cow parsley, his brown country face brushed with pollen. 'Wish I'd got a gun.'

'Snares are what you want, boy.'

'Reckon a gun'd suit me better.' He rambled along by her side chewing a blade of grass. Although he had the same irrepressible fair curls as his mother, his features were modelled on Noggin lines: straight nose, firm mouth and watchful blue eyes that sometimes took on the faraway Suffolk gaze.

Spring was well advanced and the air was sweet with birdsong, but the fields had been poorly tended since the post-war slump. Most of them lay as rough grassland, and those that were planted were clumped with heavy weed growth: dead nettle, shepherd's purse, coltsfoot and horsetail. Hedges bulged out of control and ditches were choked, while gates and fences, furred with moss, rotted unobtrusively among the brambles. The opportunities for a skilled poacher had never been better, and with a pound of lard now costing fivepence ha'penny Ma was not alone in the view that heaven helped those who helped themselves.

'Arf'noon, Missus.' Turning into the lane that led towards home she came face to face with Rob Turner, who had bought himself a few acres from what had once been the Big House estate. He was a lean, hungry-faced man who used the land to run a few calves among a miscellany of poultry and had built his wooden house with the aid of a Land Resettlement grant. He was said by some to have his eye on Dora Noggin.

Ma returned his greeting with a brief nod, but Bob Turner seemed disposed to linger.

'Weather's warming up.'

She agreed that it was, and stood with her hands folded meekly in front of her coat while young Joseph rambled on ahead.

'Family all right?'

'Doin' pretty fair, thanks.'

'Thaddeus keeping busy?'

'He gets through a tidy bit.'

'And how's Dora?'

'Dora keeps herself to herself. Always has, and I dare say always will.'

Turner digested this curt lack of encouragement in silence for a moment, then said, 'Dunno what's going on but I reckon I lost near a score of duck eggs in the last coupla weeks.'

'Ole fox, most likely.'

'More like a vixen,' Turner said. 'On two legs.'

'Gippos are camped over Wissington way. They'd fancy a few eggs.' Ma prepared to depart.

'And I reckon they're not the only ones,' he called after her.

Joseph had reached home ahead of her, and watched as she carefully unloaded the pheasant. She laid it on the kitchen table, then from the depths of the poacher's pocket drew out four duck's eggs.

A shadow fell across the doorway. 'Beats me how much you can stow away – little ole doddy bit like you.'

Thaddeus removed his cap and his bicycle clips. Now aged thirty-one his good looks had been hardened by life and work. His eyes were watchful, on guard against attack, and the men in Marling Hamlet said that he would be a rare one to pick a fight with.

The weeks immediately following Polly's death had marked them all permanently; not only had they been totally unprepared for the event, the mere idea of someone so loving and so warmly vivacious slipping out of their lives in a cloud of pain had been difficult to accept.

Although death was still a commonplace feature of life – tuberculosis, cancer, diphtheria, septicaemia and food poisoning –it was felt mutely and muddleheadedly that young Polly had been wrongly claimed; that she was the victim of a case of mistaken identity. They wept at the loss, great undisguised country tears mopped on bits of old and unhemmed sheet until Thaddeus

111

roused himself from his stupor and told them all to clear out and take the baby with them.

The nurse drove Ma and Dora back to Marling Hamlet with young Joseph packed in a wicker basket. Snow fell remorselessly as Thaddeus bolted the door of the coachman's cottage and remained inside, impervious to all who came offering comfort.

He remained indoors for four days. Sometimes he would clump upstairs to the room where she had lain and stand smoothing the coverlet with large uncomprehending hands, but mostly he remained crouching over the fire, sometimes letting it die away to ash so that winter crept in under the door and advanced stealthily towards him. He remained dry-eyed and expressionless; he ate nothing, and there were no thoughts in him. Nothing except a great solid coldness, a block of stone pinning him down. He too might have been in the process of dying except that there was no pain, no reluctance to depart.

The cuckoo clock finally roused him. Unwound since before the day she died, it thrust open its wooden door and the bird gave a wheezing death-throes cry that shattered the silence.

Rage tore him from the chair. Seizing the clock in both hands he snatched it from the wall and flung it on the floor. It whirred a feeble protest and his boot smashed down on it, reducing it to matchwood. He smashed it again and again, grinding the splinters beneath his heel then kicking them away. Then he stood motionless, glaring round the room as if seeing it for the first time, and the lust to destroy everything that he had ever loved filled him with sudden murderous joy.

He smashed plates and cups and saucers against the wall; he wrenched down the curtains, tearing them apart in his teeth and his big hands; he kicked over the table and snapping off its legs flung them into the empty fireplace. He rushed upstairs and hauled at the bed, kicking the feet of it and clawing at the covers. Flinging open the small window he tried to push them through it and the rising wind pushed them back at him. He was crying now, great choking gasping sobs while he continued the mad frenzy of destruction, then thundering downstairs again he tore back the bolt on the door and crashed outside.

It was dusk. Pools of melted snow lay in the stableyard ready to freeze with the coming of night. He splashed through them, directionless as a rabid animal. He ran, sobbing and blinded by tears, down the footpath that skirted the wood. The strengthening wind rocked the treetops and he seized the trunk of an ash tree in both hands, wrenching and heaving in a mad effort to haul it from the ground. He put his arms round it and held it close, desperately seeking comfort, then shook it again while he bellowed his pain and grief up at the tossing branches. He woke the birds, and a marauding fox paused to consider him from behind a bank of rusted ferns.

As darkness gathered he revisited all the old places, his legs seeming to carry him of their own volition through the meadows and footpaths that led down to the Stour. The great mounds of blackberry swayed in the wind and the dead grasses gleamed pale and stiff.

He passed the place where they had first made love, crossed the stile that led to the spot where she had a stone in her shoe and passed the bend in the footpath where she had broken the news of her pregnancy.

And he sank down on his haunches with his hands over his face and wondered if he had the strength and resolution to kill himself. Part of him was dead already.

He remained motionless as fresh snow began to fall, the wind driving it against his back and covering his hair. The pain was like a living thing consuming his mind and body, a rat gnawing at living tissue, and he knew that he would never be free of it.

He remained crouched in the same position until cramp shot paralysing barbs through his calf muscles. Straightening up, he turned his face to the wind and found the darkness streaked with driving snow. He stared in dull surprise from beneath clogged eyelashes and saw that there was no place for him here. Summer had gone, and taken her with it.

Slowly he walked back, stumbling through the thickening snow and crying wind. There was a light showing through the fanlight of the Vicarage front door. He knocked, slumped almost unconscious against the side of the porch.

'Sorry to . . .' the rest of the sentence floated away from him.

'Come along in, my boy,' the Reverend said. 'I've been waiting for you.'

*

He attended the funeral, staring grimly ahead and taking no part in it, and the Reverend Fiske conducted the proceedings with merciful simplicity. When it was over and she had been put in the ground by the same old man who had given her away, there was nothing left to do but try to go on living without her.

He couldn't go back to the coachman's cottage. It needed a particular kind of courage that was in short supply with him just then, but one early afternoon he steeled himself to enter it for the last time.

Although an attempt had been made to tidy away the worst of the chaos he was vaguely surprised to see the broken furniture, the absence of china and curtains, and only a crooked nail in the wall where her cuckoo clock had been. He had no more than a confused and dreamlike recollection of his bout of destruction and it held no interest for him.

So he chopped up the broken furniture for firewood and asked the Reverend to stop half a crown out of his wages each week until the damage had been paid for. The torn curtains and bedding he gave to his mother for a jumble sale – 'Don't you try keeping them, now. I swear I'll not set eyes on them ever again' – but Polly's personal effects, including her wedding dress, he carried in a sack down to the water meadows and set fire to them. He stood dry-eyed, watching them burn, as a mild breeze flickered through the blackened fragments and sent them dancing on their way.

After the Fitzhardy demise there had been uneasy speculation concerning the future of all those living in tied cottages until the arrival of solicitors' letters containing permission to purchase them. Fifty pounds was a struggle for all of them, and several families had to pack up and move elsewhere, but with Marjorie rich and a contribution from her other three children, Ma Noggin was one of those just able to make the grade.

It was late February when Thaddeus returned to live with her and Dora. He cycled back to the Vicarage each day and in the evenings he sat in silence by the fire, sometimes reading the local paper but more often staring into the glowing coals, thinking nothing, feeling nothing. If life was a game of Snakes and Ladders he was the player to ascend a couple of modest ladders only to hurtle down the longest snake on the board. A married man with a

114

child, he had been instantly reduced to the lowly status of son who still lives at home.

In the meanwhile Ma was seeing to the baby, seeing to its bottle and its washing and carting it about in a second-hand pram. Once or twice she handed it to him, a warm white-clad bundle that squirmed and made creaking, shuffling sounds, and he would stare into its little blobby unformed face and then silently hand it back.

'Brace up now, Thaddy,' she would say. 'There ain't no amount of grievin' nor sorrowin' that'll bring her back, any more than it did your Dad.'

He knew she was right, but couldn't admit it, and the winter crawled slowly towards the first hint of spring.

In the end it was the roses that saved him. Early red-tinted leaves were beginning to appear on the climbers, ramblers and bushes and it was time to begin the annual task of pruning and feeding.

'More feeding than pruning,' reminded the Reverend, working by his side. 'One can never have too much of a good thing.'

Thaddeus grunted, and continued snipping. A blackbird was pouring out its song from the Vicarage roof.

'Nothing happens to any man that he is not formed by nature to bear.'

'Who said that – God?'

'No, Marcus Aurelius. But speaking of God, it's high time that we thought about christening your son.'

Thaddeus made no comment and they continued to work in silence.

'Just look at the remarkable vigour of that shoot,' the Reverend murmured, displaying it between finger and thumb. 'Unless I'm mistaken, this is going to be a superlative year for all growing things.'

The baby had been about eighteen months old when the doctor came down the stairs at Bunting's Emporium and said to Dora in tones that clanged like a bell, 'Mrs Bunting wishes to speak to you.'

Amazed and flustered, Dora felt her face flood with colour. Further down the counter Mr Bunting, with tape measure hung round his neck, was displaying winceyette sheeting to the woman from the baker's.

115

'Very choice, this line, and only one and three per yard . . .' He made no sign of having heard the doctor's astounding pronouncement.

Mrs Bunting wishes to speak to you. Why? Whatever for? To empty her bedpan? To recite the Nunc Dimittis? In order to question her feelings towards Mr Bunting, Mrs Bunting's lawful wedded husband?

During the whole of her nine years at the Emporium Dora had never met Mrs Bunting and there had never been any suggestion that she should do so. For nine years all she had known of Mrs Bunting was an occasional cough, an odd thump, and the intermittent sigh of bedsprings from the room above the shop. To begin with she had tried to fill the blank with adolescent imaginings of a sadly beautiful Pre-Raphaelite woman stricken with a romantic disease, but as time passed and her love for Mr Bunting grew heavy with longing and gnawed by frustration, Mrs Bunting, the eternally bedridden, had no more meaningful quality than the newel post at the foot of the stairs.

'I see. Thank you,' Dora managed to say, and stood wavering, quavering, as the doctor gave her a dignified nod before departing. And that was also extraordinary, because normally Mr Bunting himself was always on hand to bow the doctor out of the Emporium and to stand hands together in a pose of dignified self-abasement until the doctor had driven away. Today, he went on serving the woman from the baker's as if he had been unaware of his presence. And as if he had never heard the doctor's amazing utterance, which surely he must have done.

Bundling reels of cotton back into their drawer Dora fled to the cupboard-like place of concealment which Mr Bunting had long ago set aside as the Lady Assistant's Rest Room & WC. (The WC was not technically a washdown closet, being a strange design patented but never popular in the early years of the century that let fly with a bucketful of sand when the appropriate handle was pumped up and down.) But it was the place of refuge to which Dora had had frequent recourse in times past, and its dingy interior and smell of Jeyes' Fluid had soothed and comforted many a rush of tears induced by a careless word or thoughtless omission on the part of her employer.

Mrs Bunting wishes to speak to you. The words seemed to

hammer in her brain as she dipped her fingers in the bowl of water on the washstand and wiped them across her forehead. She peered into the clouded mirror on the wall, patting her hair and straightening the collar of her frock. Then she stood motionless, stricken with the certainty that Mrs Bunting, because of her illness, had developed the ability to pry into other people's minds; to forage among their private emotions like some kind of nocturnal animal searching for food.

Mrs Bunting knew that Dora was in love with her husband, had been aware of it all along, and the abrupt summons to her presence had been promoted by the fact that she had at last benefited from a miraculous cure and was preparing to take up her rightful position in the Emporium. And the first thing Mrs Bunting would do would be to sack the lady assistant on the grounds of silent adoration of her husband.

Dora lingered as long as she dared, then left her place of sanctuary and went back into the shop.

Mr Bunting had almost concluded serving the woman from the baker's – her winceyette had been wrapped in brown paper and he was in the act of tying a loop of string for her finger – and Dora cast him a look of desperate appeal for guidance. But he still seemed unaware of her, so with a last drowning vision of his handsome aquiline features and impeccable quiff of hair she slowly ascended the stairs.

She paused on the square of landing, which was heavily timbered like the shop, and didn't know which door to knock on. The old floorboards creaked beneath her feet, then a voice said, 'I'm in here.'

So she tapped politely and went inside and saw for the first time Mr Bunting's wife.

She was in bed, a big high bed that bulged with pillows and fringed covers, and she was wearing one of the Emporium's selection of nightgowns and a thick black hairnet like a spider's web.

'How do you do,' Dora said, choking on the decision of whether to call her Madam or Mrs Bunting or nothing at all.

Mrs Bunting inclined her head; it was a large head with creased and florid features and fluffs of white hair poking through the black confines of the spider's web.

117

'Come and sit down, dear,' she said, 'and let me look at you.'

Dora moved closer; upon receiving a further nod she sank uneasily on to the edge of the bedside chair. Mrs Bunting studied her with a fixed and heavy stare that felt as if it might leave bruises, and Dora studied the wallpaper and thought: This is his wife. This great lump in a hairnet. She smells of wintergreen ointment and witch hazel and he goes to bed with her at night . . . Instinctively her eyes transferred to the place where his pillows would be if they were not helping to prop up his wife, and fresh colour flooded her cheeks when she saw the striped pyjamas folded on the sheet. *His* pyjamas. Three and eleven a pair.

Mrs Bunting continued to study her at leisure, then said, 'Do you like working here?'

'Yes, thank you. I like it very much,' Dora replied, a little more courageously.

'Came here straight from school, didn't you?'

'Yes.'

'And you live over at Marling Hamlet, so I'm told.'

'Yes,' Dora repeated, and tried to smile offhandedly.

'In a tied cottage?'

'Well, it was, but we've bought it.'

'And are you a regular communicant?'

'I don't – I mean – '

'I mean, do you believe in Jesus Christ our Saviour?'

Dora mumbled that she did, and Mrs Bunting nodded slowly. Then she said, 'Pass me that box of pastilles off the washstand, will you dear?'

If being called dear was intended to reassure, it failed. The wolf, Dora reflected fragmentarily, had been very nice to Red Riding Hood before he leaped out of bed and tried to eat her. She found the box of pastilles on the washstand. Mrs Bunting offered her one, poking among them with a swollen red finger.

Dora refused as politely as possible; she watched Mrs Bunting select one and begin to suck it noisily. The idea of her being Mr Bunting's wife was deeply and horribly upsetting. 'I think I'd better be getting back to work now,' she said desperately.

'Not for a minute. There's something I want to ask you.'

Then Mrs Bunting's heavy head fell forward on her chest as if she were deep in thought. Dora waited politely, trying not to fidget, then saw with sickened consternation the half-sucked pastille slip from between her lips and come to rest on her chin. Mrs Bunting breathed with a stertorous sound, suddenly woke up again and said, 'Yes, where was I? What was I saying?' With fat red hands she readjusted the black hairnet.

'You wanted to ask me something,' Dora said.

Mrs Bunting recovered the remains of her pastille with her tongue, then smacked her lips.

'Yes, I wanted to ask you something,' she repeated, and leaning forward, directed her bruising stare at Dora once again. 'Well now, I've heard you're a nice steady sort of girl without any fancy notions, and now I've seen you for myself I feel easy in my mind. I'm going to die very soon, and I want you to promise me that you'll marry Mr Bunting when I'm gone.'

Dora sat rigid, not even blinking. I'm going to faint . . . I'm going to . . . I'm going . . .

The voice came to her as if from under water. 'I've got dropsy very bad and a lot of other things as well, including heart trouble –all my family died of heart trouble – and now I know I'm very soon to meet my Saviour that I adore I want to be sure that someone'll look after Vernon for me. You'll find him kind and considerate and very clean in both his ways and all his thoughts and you must promise me to attend chapel with him every Sunday, morning and evening . . .'

The voice seemed to go on and on, and Dora sat staring at the floor, unable to look at the bloated woman in the bulging bed. 'I don't expect you to say yes or no straight away – after all, it's a big step to take, I know, but I do want to see his future settled before I fly to the arms of my Saviour.'

'Yes. I see. Thank you . . .' With no idea what she was thanking her for, Dora stood up. 'I'd better get back downstairs now . . .'

'There's just one more thing before you go, dear.' Mrs Bunting shifted herself higher on the pillows, groaning with the effort as she did so. 'I hope you're a pure girl, are you?'

With an incoherent little sound, half sob and half gasp, Dora escaped from the room and ran headlong downstairs. It was almost closing time and Mr Bunting was counting the money in the till, a solemn operation in which shillings, sixpences, pennies and halfpennies were stacked in appropriate piles and then stowed carefully away in little drawstring bags.

119

'I'm sorry, I don't feel very well,' she managed to say in a small parched voice. 'If you don't mind I think I'd better go home now.'

'Nothing serious I hope, Miss Noggin?' He looked up at her with concern, but Dora was incapable of further elaboration.

Grabbing her bicycle from the shed at the back she flung herself on to the saddle and pedalled like the wind for home.

She told no one. She was barely capable of thinking about it, let alone discussing it, and because Ma was full of the news that Stan, Ivy's husband from next door, had won ten bob in a sweepstake, no one noticed her silence and lack of appetite. After tea Marjorie and her husband drove over in their new Ford Eight and insisted upon taking Ma out for a short spin. So while Thaddeus was down the garden tying up the tomatoes and watering the late sowing of beans, Dora crept off to bed. But she couldn't sleep. Neither could she think clearly and dispassionately about the astounding interview she had had with Mrs Bunting.

Sudden jagged fragments of it kept cutting into her mind; sudden brilliant visions of the big bedroom with its big bed and big dying woman propped up in it. The smell of wintergreen and witch hazel and then, abruptly, the saintly innocent face of Mr Bunting saying, 'Nothing serious I hope, Miss Noggin?'

She began to weep, hot and soundless beneath the coverlets, but it wasn't until close on next morning that she was able to work out the precise reason for her tears. She was weeping at the death of love, for Mrs Bunting had robbed her of it just as surely as if she had stuck a knife in her heart.

With every instinct imploring her not to go to work next day – to plead illness, stay in bed and feign sleep, even death if necessary, anything to keep the world of Bunting's Emporium at bay – she nevertheless got up at the accustomed hour, sponged her swollen eyes and cycled to work without breakfast. And Mr Bunting, impeccable in celluloid collar and folded cravat, enquired if she was feeling better this morning.

His smile was a torture to her. Perhaps she did still love him after all, or perhaps it was the pain of sudden catastrophic loss. Dusting shelves and rearranging rolls of ribbon she realised that she had lost not only the premier person in her life but also her sense of commitment to the Emporium. Everything had been swept away by the terrible old woman upstairs who proposed handing her husband over to a selected recipient as if he had been a bit of cold meat on a plate, while she herself flew off with Jesus. That in itself would be a sight for sore eyes.

Rage and hate and bitter hurt made her snap at a child sent in by its mother for a card of hooks and eyes, but by closing time she had made up her mind. With her hat pulled down and her coat collar pulled up she walked over to Mr Bunting and said, 'If you don't mind, I'd like to give my notice in.'

He looked surprised, but only mildly so. 'Oh dear, Miss Noggin,' he murmured, 'this is most unexpected. Is there anything the matter?' He continued folding away pairs of men's socks as he spoke.

'I just feel like a change,' Dora said in a stifled voice. 'I'll leave on Saturday, if that's all right.'

He said that it was, although he would be sorry to lose her services. Had she another situation in view? She said Yes, but nothing definite, and they parted without looking at one another.

The week passed with torturing slowness sometimes spiked with apprehension that she might receive a further summons to the bedroom upstairs. Had Mr Bunting told his wife that she was leaving? And if so, would she be so angry that it would hasten her death? On the other hand, might she imagine that she was leaving in order to prepare her trousseau, and because of maidenly embarrassment at the idea of waiting in the wings to claim her secondhand bridegroom? Dora didn't know; anything, she felt, might be construed from such a strange and horrible situation.

She approached the final afternoon with relief mingled with dread. Dread in case she would be coerced into saying goodbye to the dying woman upstairs, and relief that she would be free to forget her stupid love of Mr Bunting. It could never have been real love; more like the sort of thing Marjorie would call a *pash*.

As the hour for departure drew near however, the dreads multiplied like germs in a plague pit. Suppose the doctor called and demanded to know why she had refused to comply with his patient's request? Suppose as she was about to close the shop door behind her for the last time Mrs Bunting crawled downstairs in an effort to stop her? And supposing the final effort killed her and she lay spreadeagled in her spider's-web hairnet among the dusters and huckaback towels? Supposing . . . supposing . . . but when six o'clock finally came, something happened for which she was totally unprepared.

Mr Bunting handed her her final paypacket and burst into tears.

He cried like a child, snuffling incoherently with his hands over his eyes and for a wild moment she was tempted to put her arms round him as she would have done to little Joseph. But behaviour so hideously incompatible with his appearance and his status as employer and proprietor of Bunting's Emporium brought her to her senses. Clutching her pay packet she mumbled that she was sorry and bolted from his presence for ever.

Unknown to her, Mrs Bunting died two weeks later.

That had all happened when she was eighteen. Now she was twenty-four and worked in a sweetshop in Sudbury, which meant cycling to and from the workmen's bus each day, but her employer was a jolly middle-aged woman whose husband worked at the silk weaver's, and this she found adequate compensation for the additional journey.

She still lived at home, as was the usual thing for unmarried girls in those days, and she was shyly, inarticulately pleased that Thaddeus was also seeking refuge there, filling the cottage with his looming height and stirring restlessly at night on the other side of the flimsy partition that had separated brothers and sisters during and after puberty. She would wonder what he was thinking, how much he was grieving. Unknown to him she had also lost a love, and her mind would dwell upon the question of whether it was better to have known fulfilment as he had, or whether she was the luckier, having only known it in her imagination.

Thaddeus thought about her, too; the private and slightly prim sister lying in her small virginal bed with her newly bobbed hair and her vapour lamp for when she had spasms of wheezing. Occasionally a lightness of spirit would come over him and he would tease her, or give her a playful slap, but her reaction was always the same: the instant withdrawal of her smile and a hurt, uncertain look in her eyes that would half amuse and half irritate him. He came to the conclusion that in spite of having been a married man, he understood very little about women. Particularly the sort who never went courting. Women, as all the world knew, were different from men, and at this sexually dormant period in his life he was content to leave it at that. Now it was the subject of

122

rose-growing that occupied his thoughts increasingly, and on the evening Ma came home with the cock pheasant Thaddeus washed his hands and face at the sink and said, 'I've gone and bred a new rose.'

'Reckon that ain't much.'

'Reckon that is. I don't mean I just took a cutting off one and it's rooted, I mean a proper new one. I cross-pollinated it three years back and there's not another one like it in the world. And if I've got a nice bloom ready, I'm putting it in the Flower Show.'

It was a long while since Thaddy had really roused himself up over anything and she was glad, yet the old prevailing streak of hard common sense compelled her to appear unimpressed.

'Do much better to mend the upstairs winda.'

'Not much point, the whole frame's rotten.'

'Can't you make us a noo one, then?' She turned round from the stove, where she was frying bacon and tomatoes for tea.

'I dare say.' He smoothed his hair back with his hands. 'Fact is, I'm thinking of leaving here.'

'Leaving Thaddy?' Instant alarm was hurriedly concealed. 'Whatever you mean by that, then?'

'I'm thinking of setting up somewhere different, that's all.'

'Getting wed? And taking Joseph?'

'Steady on with making plans for me,' he said wearily. 'I only said thinking about it.'

Warned by his expression she said no more, but called Joseph in from the garden. Dora came down from her bedroom and they began to eat in silence.

No one had realised the ordeal it had been for Ma when Thaddeus had left home to marry Polly. Essentially a gregarious and practical woman, her enjoyment of life had been at its peak when the cottage was bursting with family; with Joe in his ole chair with his boots off after a hard day, and the five children – Eric still a baby – filling the place with giggles and squabbles while she cooked, washed and ironed, and sat up late darning and patching and turning sides to middle.

Her quick, rodent-like energy and her opportunism had gloried in the tumult and the problems, and had only received its first check when Willie died. With the others hurriedly evacuated to neighbours' cottages she had nursed him all day and all night, but

123

in the end the diphtheria choked the life out of him and there was nothing for it but to be thankful the others hadn't caught it.

Then Grigg had gone, then poor ole Joe, and after the war so had Marjorie and then Eric, the youngest. And then, finally, Thaddy. Spared by the war, perhaps she had hoped subconsciously that he might also be spared by matrimony, but no. Life had sunk to a low level of tedium during the time she and Dora had been sole occupants of the cottage; Dora was a good little gal, but nobody ever knew what she was thinking after she grew up. She didn't talk much and hardly ever laughed, although she was quite nice with little Joseph, taking him for walks on her afternoon off and sometimes bringing him a few sweets from the shop in Sudbury.

Ma's grief at Polly's death had been genuine, but as she had looked on the bright side after losing Willie, so it had seemed that providence was offering her Thaddy and the baby in compensation. A compensation she had grabbed with both hands.

And now she might be losing them. The prospect filled her with dire gloom until habitual resourcefulness told her to stop mawking and cast about for possible reasons why he should want to forsake a comfortable home. It could only be because of another gal somewhere and she went over likely candidates in her mind.

But there weren't any, unless you counted that rather uppity gal who couldn't walk like other folk. The gal called May who had been poor young Polly's best friend, and she didn't amount to a spoonful of beans.

Thaddeus's plans however, did not include matrimony. They involved the possibility of buying a few acres of land and setting himself up as a rose-grower and hybridiser.

He had become very attached to the Reverend Bonamy Fiske and his ways, and was profoundly grateful for all that he had given him. Kindness, sympathy, amusement, but most of all his rare and intimate knowledge of roses. He had given Thaddeus other things too; things of which he was largely unaware, such as a greater range of the English language to match a wider outlook on life. But now the instinct to move on, to take a new direction, was beginning to tug at him, and when the Reverend took his arm one morning in early June as they walked round the garden and said

124

that the Diocesan Bishop had intimated that it was time for him to retire from the incumbency – it almost seemed as if fate were taking a hand.

So they talked about their plans, two old friends now rather than gardener and employer, and the Reverend said that he had his eye on a nice little house on the way to East Bergholt.

'Reckon you'll miss these.' Thaddeus nodded towards the rose beds billowing with the first excited flush of bloom.

'I shall carry away pictures of them.' The old man tapped his forehead. 'They are all stored away in readiness, but I have no intention of denying myself the pleasure of making another rose garden when I go from here. And you, my dear Noggin, must come and supervise the operation.'

Touched by the Reverend's humility Thaddeus agreed to do so when the time came, which led to the question of Thaddeus's future. He found himself putting into words for the first time the ideas that were now beginning to absorb him.

'I'm not after a big place and I'm not troubled about fancy living, not for a start at any rate, but the soil would have to be right and I wouldn't want a lot of wind raging over it.'

'*To study, culture, and with artful toil, to meliorate and tame the stubborn soil,*' quoted the Reverend. 'So we must both put our backs into our individual plots and make sure that our soils are thoroughly drained, dug and dunged. We must cut our drains with a good straight fall, Noggin, and never less than four feet deep.'

'That's it, Vicar.'

'And manure from the farmyard, both solid and fluid, of horse, cow, pig and poultry. Did I ever tell you, Noggin, how the Romans revered Cloacina, goddess of the sewers?'

'Reckon they knew a thing or two.'

'How right you are, my boy. And now we will go and ask Mrs Palfrey if she will kindly indulge us with a glass of sherry wine in which to celebrate our brave futures . . .'

Still engrossed in future plans, Thaddeus was cycling home on the following day when his eye caught a figure outside one of the Shilling Tye cottages trying to accommodate a large parcel within the confines of a wicker bicycle basket. He recognised her, and instinctively looked the other way. But she had already seen him, and in attempting to wave her hand the parcel overbalanced and

125

fell in the road. She was unable to pick it up without letting go of the bicycle.

He dismounted, and went to her aid.

'Oh Thaddeus, how kind of you!' Her smile was frank and open, and increased his embarrassed discomfort at having avoided her for so long. He had avoided most people after Polly died, and Hoppity May perhaps more assiduously than most. She had been Polly's best friend, and happy times had been spent in her company. She had been bridesmaid at the wedding and god-mother at the christening, the latter inspired by Dora and the Reverend.

Dazed with loss, he had barely spoken to her then, and like an injured man seeking to avoid additional pain, had taken care to avoid her ever since. She had made no attempt to renew the friendship apart from an annual Christmas card addressed to the Noggin family at Marling Hamlet.

'Getting on all right?' He made sure the parcel was firmly lodged in the basket. 'Haven't seen you about much, recently.'

'I've been busy, I suppose,' she said, and it was nice of her to hint at being the one to blame. She indicated the parcel. 'I've promised to reline Minny Thurlow's curtains for her.'

'You do a lot for other people, don't you?'

'Oh, no!' She looked shocked, as if accused of something reprehensible, then laughed at herself and asked how Joseph was getting on.

'A big boy now,' he said. 'Learning his tables and cheeking his Dad.'

'I shouldn't think you'd stand for much of that, Thaddeus.'

'Best come over and see for yourself –' he began to say, and was relieved when she inadvertently interrupted him by asking if he was still keen on roses.

'Very keen. Been doing a bit of hybridising in my spare time.'

'Creating new varieties, you mean?' A bit different from ole Ma's reaction he thought, but she was better educated, which would account for it.

'That's it. And if I've got a bloom ready I might put it in the Flower Show.'

'That would be splendid!' The smile transformed her rather plain face in the way he remembered, and when she held out her hand to him and said, 'Goodness, Thaddeus, it's so nice to see you again after all this time,' he seized it and shook it, infected by her lack of guile. It was stupid to have kept away from an old friend. And a good friend, at that.

'High time we caught up,' he agreed, then added, 'and time you saw something of Joe. Come up for a cup of tea and a bite on Sunday – I went back to live with ole Ma after . . . after . . .'

'Yes, I heard,' she said quietly, and he thought, of course she heard, you great fool. She sends you Christmas cards, doesn't she?

'Tell you what,' he said. 'Instead of coming up to mine, let's go for a picnic. Pack up a bit of tea and stuff and take Joe – he's got a seat on the back of my bike, look.'

She saw it, and nodded. She said that she would like to, provided she had finished Minny's curtains. She had promised them for Sunday morning, before church.

'So what time shall we say?' Suddenly eager, he decided to ignore the question of Minny Thurlow's curtains and concentrate on practicalities. 'I could get Ma to set us up with some sandwiches and a flask of tea, and I daresay she'd make us a bit of scone too –'

'Don't worry about the tea,' she laughed. 'I'll provide that with pleasure.'

He knew that she wanted to come; and knew that they would be pleasantly casual friends again now that time had soothed some of the pain of losing Polly.

He wondered whether he would feel different next morning, a bit of a stupid fool for jumping in like that, but he didn't. On the contrary, that part of his mind that had been asleep for so long now roused itself up and he began planning where they would go for the picnic. Down the river – perhaps as far as Dedham, if May could cycle that far – or maybe find a nice bit of flat meadow where they could have their tea and then perhaps he could teach young Joe a bit of cricket; it occurred to him for the first time that he had never paid much attention to his son, preferring to regard him as a mere adjunct to Ma's domestic responsibilities. A picnic would be a rare treat for him.

Yet Thaddeus remained unsatisfied. The river wouldn't be a real treat because it was already a familiar part of their lives, and there was nothing novel about meadows either, seeing that they lived surrounded by them.

It was late on Thursday night when the great idea came to him and he had to work quickly, but by two o'clock sharp on Sunday afternoon he presented himself at May's cottage in Tarrent's Row with a carefully enigmatic expression and young Joe perched on the back of his bicycle.

'Ready, then?'

'What a lovely day it is!' May was waiting in the open doorway with the assembled picnic. She was wearing a cotton frock with flowers on it, brown lisle stockings and her old-fashioned straw hat secured under the chin by elastic.

'Should do all right.' Thaddeus glanced up at the sky, then touched his cap and helped her to divide the picnic things between them, while young Joe buzzed about between them saying 'Are we going now? Are we going to go now?'

'Just let me lock the door,' May said, smiling at him. 'My word, Joseph, you're growing into such a big boy.'

They set off, loaded string bags dangling from Thaddeus's handlebars and with the contents of May's basket covered over with a white cloth.

'Dad, where are we going? Which way are we going, Dad?' Young Joe drummed impatient fingers on the back of his father's best jacket.

'Home again, if you don't watch out,' Thaddeus replied without turning his head.

It was nearly four miles to Doe's Farm, and they rode into the dusty yard where chickens scratched. A dusty old dog roused itself and came towards them wagging its tail.

Enjoying his companions' doubtful expressions, Thaddeus nodded in the direction of the man who approached and said, 'This is an ole mate of mine, name of Johnny Cousins. Afternoon, Johnny.'

'How-do?'

Johnny Cousins, who had worked up at the Big House with Thaddeus, had been another of the fortunate few to return unmaimed from the war, and had inherited a small farm from his uncle. He had grown cheerful, stout and red-faced during the past twelve years. Politely he wiped his hand on the backside of his trousers before offering it to May.

He led them over to one of the barns and said, 'Well, there she is.'

The car was a 1923 seven horsepower Jowett, hand-painted in yellow and black, which contrasted nicely with the red petrol can strapped on the running board. The hood was folded down and the dicky seat at the rear open in readiness.

'Remember where the gears are, do you? Two for forward and one for back'uds and don't fergit the clutch.' Johnny Cousins demonstrated.

'Are we going in it, Dad? Dad, are we really going in it?'

'Gracious, Thaddeus – imagine you driving a car!'

'Can we get in, Dad? I want to sit in the back – can I, Dad?'

Their reactions were all that he could have desired, and with Johnny Cousins watching critically Thaddeus drove them across the farmyard and down the lane. When he felt capable of driving and talking at the same time he explained that Johnny Cousins was known to lend his uncle's ole flivver out to friends for five bob a day and a packet of fags. 'I got m'self a licence on Friday and yesterday he gave me a couple turns round the lane to get the hang of it. Reckon we'll get there all in one piece.'

'What a surprise.' As she turned to look at him, the brim of May's hat lightly scraped his cheek. 'Where are you taking us to, Thaddeus?'

'That's the second surprise,' he said, and cautiously changed to bottom gear as they approached a gradient. The Suffolk countryside was bathed in after-Sunday-dinner torpor, deep rich meadows shimmering with poplars and willows beneath slow, majestic clouds. Occasionally a horse or a cow would put its head over a gate to stare at them but the villages were deserted.

They spoke little for the first part of the journey, content to sit watching the scenery and the leaves rippling in the hedgerows as they passed; content to go on for ever.

'Where's this, Dad?'

'It says Grundisburgh.'

'Where's that?'

'It's where we are now.'

'Where else are we going?'

'Wait and see.'

Subtly the countryside began to change, becoming flatter and more open beneath a pale enamelled light until Thaddeus indicated a faint bruised line upon the horizon and said, 'There you are. That's where we're going.'

The sea!

The clean tang of it cleansed and intoxicated as the first real sight of it humbled and mystified. It was very calm, a crinkling deep blue touched here and there with pale green and black, and small waves broke on a wide strip of hard and unmarked sand. They stood together on the hummocky dunes that yielded warmly beneath their feet. The breeze stirred the clumps of sedges and rush-leaved fescue and May clasped her hands and said, 'Oh Thaddeus my dear, I haven't seen the sea since I was a child.'

Her words, fluttering back on her lips, appeared to release young Joe from awestruck immobility and he began to run, crashing through the soft sand and rolling down the dunes like some small creature released from captivity. They watched him, smiling, then Thaddeus rubbed his hands together and said 'Now, what about this tea?'

They spread it out on the cloth that May had brought. She had made three kinds of sandwiches, scones, and a date and walnut cake. There was a large flask of tea, and a bottle of ginger pop for young Joe.

They ate slowly and dreamily, with the little boy sitting cross-legged between them, and although the dunes obscured their view of the sea its presence was all pervasive in the salt-crisp air and in the whisper of small waves breaking. It was like being in the proximity of some huge and amiable god. Thaddeus leaned back on his elbows with his legs stretched out and contemplated May with a new and marvellous serenity. They were comfortable old friends linked by a mutual love of Polly, and the memories she stirred in him were no longer painful. He realised how much he liked her and had always felt at ease in her company. In a way, she felt more like a sister than either Marjorie or Dora, and it was pleasant to be friends with a woman who provoked neither desire nor any sense of responsibility.

'Are those roses on your frock?'

'Yes,' she said. 'I wore it specially.'

It struck him as a nice, thoughtful thing to do, and prompted him to tell her more about the proposed rose nursery. 'About three acres to start with, and a good hedge all round and water handy. I reckon to plant a coupla hundred briers first year and bud them the following summer – do you smoke, by the way? Confess I've clean forgotten.' He offered the packet of Woodbines but she shook her head.

'I only tried it once and almost choked to death.'

'Dad, can I have another bitta cake?' Young Joe brushed the crumbs from his mouth.

'I don't know, you'd better ask – ' Thaddeus hesitated between Auntie May and Miss . . . damn, he'd forgotten her surname, too.

'Call me Auntie May, and yes of course you can have another piece of cake.'

The child grabbed it, stuffing joyously.

'Reckon he's got hollow legs,' Thaddeus observed. Woodbine smoke rose in a thin, wavering column above his head.

'He's a healthy growing boy,' May said. Then added quietly, 'I wonder what Polly would think of him now?'

Thaddeus flinched. Then realised that if he and May were to remain friends, Polly's name would have to be mentioned sooner or later. During the first agonised months he had rigorously suppressed all reference to her, silencing even his mother with a look or a curt gesture of the hand, until she had gradually assumed the mystique of a forbidden subject, a taboo to be observed by all. But now it occurred to him for the first time that in his selfishness he had done Polly a grave injustice, almost as if he had condemned her to a second death.

'Reckon she'd think he was all right,' he said, gruffly testing the sound of this first casual reference to her. Then young Joe, tired of sitting still, swallowed the last of his cake and flung himself against his father's back, knocking his cap off and half-choking him with tightly enfolding arms.

Thaddeus retaliated, scrambling to his feet and seizing the boy round the waist. Slinging him over his shoulder he plunged with him across the dunes and ran down to the hard sand. Joe's shouts and struggles increased as they neared the water.

'I'll chuck you in – that's what I'll do, I'll chuck you in!'

'No – *no*, Dad!'

The waves were only inches deep, but for someone who had never seen the sea before, its vastness held an easily aroused terror.

'I'll chuck you in and you'll float all the way to China – '

Shifting the boy from across his shoulder, Thaddeus swung him down into his arms and stood rocking him to and fro as if in readiness.

'One – two – three – ' For one mad moment the compulsion to hurl his son away from him, to cast him into oblivion for killing his mother, and to watch his frantic, tossing form being devoured by the sea, almost overwhelmed him.

He ceased rocking him, and stared down into his face. A little face shadowed with apprehension behind the enjoyable shrieks and struggles. A little face that had his own features and a fleeting glimpse of Polly in its expressions. Thaddeus closed his eyes, held his son close and thought: God forgive me for a wicked bastard.

He set the child on his feet and groped in his jacket pocket. 'Come on, I've brought a tennis ball.'

They played catch, hurling the ball high into the cloudless sky, and the immense emptiness of sea and land filled them both with a kind of drunken energy. They ran and leaped, patterning the pristine sand with their footsteps and shattering the timeless silence with their laughter. Panting, they finally came to a halt, and Joe said, 'Dad – can we paddle? Can we paddle, Dad? Please Dad, can we?'

'Reckon we could.'

They removed their shoes and socks, and Thaddeus was rolling up his trouser-legs when Joe looked up and said, 'Where's Auntie May?' The name came off his tongue as if he had always known her and always called her that.

Then they saw her coming towards them; a lonely little figure in all the vastness hoppiting down on to the flat cool sand. It was not until she drew closer that Thaddeus became aware that she was in her bare feet.

'Can I join you?' It was strange how much younger she looked without her shoes on.

Joe ran up to her and seized her hand, urging her along. Her smooth dark hair had slipped from beneath her straw hat and her arms looked as if they had already caught the sun a little. She was smiling breathlessly and Thaddeus ordered Joe to stop his hustling.

He and May stood looking at one another in silence for a

moment, then holding hands with the little boy between them they walked slowly and gravely into the quietly breathing sea.

'We might be the last people on earth,' murmured May.

'Or the first,' replied Thaddeus.

They walked parallel to the shore, Thaddeus on the outside, and the simple pleasure of walking barefoot in cool water absorbed them utterly. Time had no meaning, and they were scarcely aware of each other's presence in the dreaming blue and gold of that summer afternoon.

The red ball of sun had disappeared, leaving the sky streaked with lemon and plum purple as they drove home. The remains of the picnic had been eaten, and young Joe was curled up in the dicky seat with his head pillowed on his father's jacket, his eyes sealed with sleep and salt air.

Pensively Thaddeus and May watched the warm lanes unfolding in front of them and the moths dancing in the headlights. The first rabbits came out to play and he honked the rubber hooter at them, unwilling to spoil the day with a death. They had reached East Bergholt when May asked him the colour of his new rose, the one he hoped to put in the Flower Show.

'I'm keeping it a secret,' he said.

'What are you going to call it?'

He glanced at the profile half concealed beneath her straw hat and his lips twitched in a smile. 'That's a secret too.'

Young Joe grizzled at being woken up when they left the car at Doe's Farm, and collapsed against his father's back as they cycled the rest of the way. The moon was up, and in place of the sea's tang the familiar reedy smell came drifting towards them from the Stour. They left May at her cottage gate.

'Thank you very much.' Suddenly rather formal, she held out her hand.

With one arm supporting his drowsing son Thaddeus prepared to take it, then changed his mind and touched her cheek with his fingers. It was a nice soft cheek, but nowhere as soft and nice as Polly's had been.

'Thanks for coming,' he said.

The postman always arrived at Marling Hamlet soon after Dora had set off for the Sudbury bus, so she didn't see the letter until Ma retrieved it from a welter of miscellaneous articles on the dresser when she returned at teatime one Tuesday.

'Fancy-lookin' letter for you, gal. That's come from Colchester by all accounts.'

It was a large white envelope containing a large white sheet of crested paper, and attached to it by a paperclip was a smaller sealed envelope with her name written on it. The handwriting made the colour flare in her cheeks.

'Go on – do you read what's in it,' urged Ma, sitting down in readiness.

'Oh, it's nothing special,' Dora said. 'I'll read it later,' and she headed for the stairs.

'Sly little ole thing,' Ma said in a furious undertone. 'She wouldn't give away the time of day, not if she could help it.'

She looked at Thaddeus for sympathy, but he was absorbed in a copy of the Reverend's *Rose Bulletin* from the Royal National Rose Society. He merely grunted.

Up in the seclusion of her room Dora sat down on the bed and opened the smaller envelope first. It was addressed to her in Mr Bunting's handwriting, that elegant, familiar, and once-loved script that had adorned so many bills, receipts and sales tickets in his Emporium.

Dear Miss Noggin, it said, *I take it upon myself to pen these few lines to you personally in order that the official intimation of what I am determined upon will not come as too much of a shock.*

There is no need for me to state what will be much better stated by those specifically qualified to do so, but will content myself by saying that I hope my gesture may to some extent make amends for any hurt or embarrassment you may have suffered during the years in which you assisted me so nobly and selflessly in my place of business. I refer in particular to the unhappy days which preceded, and were the cause of, your departure.

I have always loved you, Miss Noggin, and when it comes time to stand unclothed before my Maker I will confess same to Him and know that in His bounteous wisdom He will understand. Your true friend, Cyril George Bunting.

For a long while she stared out of the window without speaking, without moving. Then very slowly she unfolded the other larger sheet of paper and read its typewritten contents. It was from a firm of solicitors, informing her of the death of their client, Mr C. G. Bunting, and notifying her that she was named as sole beneficiary in his last Will and Testament.

Without change of facial expression she gradually keeled over and lay supine on the bed, staring glassily at the ceiling. There was a long crack in it, meandering as the river Stour, and her eye followed it from end to end. Silently she began to laugh, cramming her fist against her mouth and the brass bed jingled lightly with the vibration; then, when she thought of all the years he had loved her, both before and after his wife died – her tears flowed.

She cried bitterly and soundlessly, then got up and methodically straightened the counterpane before sponging her face at the washstand and combing her hair. She went down to the kitchen as Ma was opening a new jar of pickle to go with the pork pie.

'Nice letter, was it?'

'Oh, nothing important.' Dora seated herself between Thaddeus and young Joe. But she was unable to eat very much.

During the days that followed, the contents of the two letters occupied her thoughts to the exclusion of all else, and it occurred to her that together they constituted a prime example of God and Mammon. At the village school and at Sunday School she had been constantly exhorted to love God; God Himself was supposed to *be* love, and she wondered now whether it included the variety which she and Mr Bunting had felt for one another, or whether it was merely the rather chill ritualism of church worship. Mr Bunting, respected elder of the Ezekiel Chapel, had made it posthumously clear that he regarded both kinds as acceptable. Presumably he had been in love with Mrs Bunting when he first married her, and Dora was unable to decide whether love of God or fear of scandal had prevented him from confessing his feelings for her during and after the time she worked for him. Thou shalt not commit adultery, but it wouldn't have been adultery if she had been his second wife.

Supposing he *had* come to propose to her after Mrs Bunting died – would she have accepted him? She was uncertain, but on the whole thought not. There was something a bit funny about a man who got his wife to do his proposing to her successor, and the memory of him bursting into tears was still very distasteful.

So she was left with Mammon, which was what accepting

135

Bunting's Emporium was all about. The idea frightened her (whatever would people say?), but at the same time she felt a little twitching of excitement. She knew that she was capable of running the business, and the idea of being her own boss was tempting, and yet . . .

She didn't want to go back there, to set foot in the place for the first time after all those years. Although she didn't think she believed in ghosts, it would be very easy to imagine whispering shadows and creaking footsteps. Even more worrying, going back to the old place might make her go back to being in love with Mr Bunting – in this case it would be with his memory – and it might turn her funny in the head. She didn't want that, either.

It was not until the following Sunday morning that she broke the news to her mother and brother. They were both in the back garden repairing the wire netting round the chicken run, and Ma paused to squint at her with one hand shading her eyes.

'I've come to tell you that I've been left Bunting's Emporium over at Stoke Abbey and I've decided to accept it. I know where I can get the keys and I'd be glad if you'd come over with me this afternoon, Thaddeus.'

She turned on her heel and walked back into the cottage before they had time to comment. And before her perilously maintained poise had time to crumble.

They set off by bicycle directly after dinner, Dora staring fixedly ahead and seemingly oblivious to the riot of June wild flowers starring hedges and banks; and equally deaf to the hooting of the cuckoo over in the woods. Stoke Abbey dozed, and lingering aftersmells of Sunday roast hung about open doors and windows. The woman in the cottage next to the Emporium eyed them with dozy curiosity before placing the keys in Dora's outstretched hands.

'Thinkin' of buying the ole place?'

'That's my affair,' Dora said repressively.

She had never been back since the day she left, and she raised her eyes to the frontage with something akin to dread. The three upstairs windows were closely curtained and the dark blue blind obscured most of whatever shop display there might have been. The only thing visible was a line of dead flies littering the floor of the window.

Thaddeus waited in silence while she inserted the key in the door, and after a moment's hesitation stepped inside. It smelt hot and stuffy. Dora stood motionless, staring round at the familiar shelves of calico and casement cloth, lace curtaining, fancy cottons and art silks. Faded newspapers were draped over the modest displays of ladies' wear and baby linen, and she caught her breath convulsively at the sight of Mr Bunting's tape measure hanging on a nail above the till.

Even with Thaddeus there it needed courage to mount the old staircase down which the doctor had come so many times. *'How's Mrs Bunting getting on?' 'She's coming along quite well, thank you Miss Noggin . . .'* The ghostly voices, her own and Mr Bunting's, drifted back to her on the stale air.

'Didn't you know he was dead?' Thaddeus's voice broke into her thoughts and made her jump. 'That must've been in the local papers.'

'I don't read the local papers and I don't listen to gossip.' She sounded snappier than she meant to, but her heart was beating painfully fast as she stood on the square of heavily timbered landing, trying to pluck up courage to open the front bedroom door.

But it wasn't too bad. The big empty bed had been made, the counterpane pulled up over the pillows as if covering the face of the dead. She remembered the wallpaper, and the bedside chair upon which she had sat. Medicine bottles had been cleared from the marble washstand but the smell of wintergreen and witch hazel still haunted the air. For the first time she noticed the big mahogany wardrobe, and hoped fleetingly that it wasn't full of the Buntings' clothes. She would have to pay someone to remove them when she wasn't there.

The other bedroom was a sort of boxroom piled with unused chairs and trunks and old account books. A dressmaker's dummy stood with sad dignity among cardboard boxes half filled with discarded rolls of ribbon, rusted press studs and yellowing gentlemen's celluloid collars of the same impeccable correctitude as those once worn by Mr Bunting himself. She felt the tears rush to her eyes and conquered them with a superhuman effort before returning downstairs.

'Was he courting you?'

137

The rural simplicity of her brother's words almost finished her. 'I don't know what you mean.' Then she sat down on the bottom stair, hugged her knees against her chest and said, 'Well, not until it was too late.'

Without replying he pulled out the little varnished bentwood chair that had always stood by the counter and set it down close to her. Close, but not too close, which was thoughtful.

The atmosphere of the place, the smell of unused drapery and the weight of wasted youthful love brought fresh tears to her eyes, but she blinked them back.

'Yes. I loved him in the same sort of way that you loved . . . well . . .' She was unable to speak Polly's name.

'I know what you mean.' He sat leaning forward, holding his cap between his knees. 'And he'd got a wife?'

'Yes.'

Suddenly it was easy to talk. She wanted to, needed to, and the words poured out. 'I suppose I got what Marjorie would call a pash on him. He was much older than me and the boss and all that, but he was so gentlemanly, so nice-looking and so . . . so correct in everything. And I couldn't help seeing how much he suffered. I know it was awful for her, being an invalid and everything, but he had to run the business – not just serving customers and all that but doing the ordering and all the bills and receipts and everything, and then having to look after *her* as well. Cook meals for them both, see to her medicines and everything else, and when it was time for bed he had to . . . all he had was . . .' The tears, long suppressed, finally overcame her and she sobbed convulsively. 'I mean, some girls have it so simple. Everybody loves them because they're pretty and sweet and they get married to nice young chaps even though they haven't got much to offer and then they . . . they . . .'

'Die for it.' He said the words quietly, swinging his cap between his knees.

'Oh, my God, Thaddy – I didn't mean – ' He had never heard her swear before, and he couldn't remember her using the diminutive of his name since they were children.

'I know you didn't. Any case, I'm pretty well over it now.'

'I don't know that you ever really get over being in love with someone,' she said sadly.

'And you were keen on him too, were you?'

'Yes. For what seemed like years, but his wife put an end to it – Oh, it was awful . . . I felt so ashamed . . .'

Well, I never, Thaddeus thought. Fancy ole Dora getting caught with her knickers down. 'Don't upset yourself, it happens all the time,' he said.

Attempting to comfort her, he was surprised when she suddenly burst into tears and sobbed loudly. 'It wasn't like that – not what you think . . . all men think things like that because it's the way their minds work . . . but it was worse than that! Much, much worse! The doctor called on her one day as usual then came downstairs and told me that she wanted to see me about something, and when I went up and met her for the very first time she as good as told me to marry her husband as soon as she was dead. She even –she even asked me if I was p-*pure*!' Dora wept unrestrainedly. 'I was so shocked and hurt and everything – I mean, it meant that they'd been talking about me – discussing me between the two of them as if I was a roll of calico or a brand of knitting wool – and as if he wasn't capable of making up his own mind about anything . . . and she had this dreadful black hairnet on . . .'

Thaddeus left his chair and sat down beside her. He put his arm round her shoulders and she leaned against him, helpless with weeping.

'It made me hate him. Hate him and despise him. It killed all the things I'd felt, and I felt as if someone had stolen my whole life . . .'

Dear God, her brother thought, we don't know the half of it, do we? Aloud, he said, 'And that was when you gave your notice in?'

'I couldn't stand it there any more. Not after her interviewing me as if I was applying for another job and then knowing that *he* knew all about it but wasn't letting on . . . I bet even the doctor knew and said it'd be a good idea . . .'

He offered her the clean handkerchief he had stuck in his top pocket last evening when he took May to the pictures. Then when she had finished choking and sobbing, wiping and sniffing he released his arm from round her shoulders and said, 'Yes, well. They sound a rum ole pair to me and I reckon you were best out of it. But all that's over now and you've got to think about what lies ahead of you.'

'I don't know what's best to do.' He watched her twisting his handkerchief in her fingers, marvelling silently that this was the chill and self-sufficient Dora speaking.

'I tell you what you're going to do,' he said, staring hard at her. 'You're going to accept this moth-eaten ole place and turn it into something you'll be proud of. I'll give you a hand cleaning it up and shifting all the stuff you don't want – and then while you're busy working here I'll be busy working to build up a nice stock of roses in my own place – didn't tell you, did I, that I've saved up to buy a little bit of land over Maplestead way?'

She regarded him through swollen eyes. 'You don't tell people much do you, Thaddy?'

'Strikes me you don't say too much about yourself, neither.'

They locked the place up and cycled back to Marling Hamlet. Just before they went indoors Thaddeus said, 'When you were a little mite I remember you saying you wanted to be Florence Nightingale.'

She smiled. 'Some hope.'

'Never say things like that.' He seized her arm and held it firmly. 'Just remember you can be whatever you've a mind to. All you've got to do is work at it.'

Ma was depressed. First Thaddy had been going on about leaving, and she knew damn well it was because of a gal somewhere. Otherwise what was to stop him a-growing his ole roses and coming home at night same as he was doing now? No, he was planning on getting wedded again and taking young Joe with him. If not, then why this talk about building a house on the bit of land over Maplestead way?

She still had no clear proof of the gal's identity, and would have been deeply suspicious of her they called Hoppity May if she hadn't had a funny leg. No chap would want a gal bobbing up and down like a cork in a boiling kettle . . .

And now Dora was planning to go, too. She couldn't believe it. Little ole Dora who lived neat as a mouse and never said much, had bin left Bunting's Emporium in a will. She had never met the Buntings and had never been to the Emporium, for Ma's generation contented itself with knowing everything about its immediate neighbourhood and nothing beyond it. If Stoke

Abbey's shops were as rundown as the ones in Marling it couldn't be worth much, but even so it was a shock, and Ma wondered darkly what Dora had been up to with this Mr Bunting. Men didn't generally leave everything they'd got to women who weren't their wives without a rare good reason. At least she hadn't got herself in the family way.

July came in hot that year, with hollyhocks standing sentinel outside cottage doors and apples swelling on the sun-baked trees, and over at Shilling Tye the annual Fête and Flower Show was being set up in the Vicarage meadow.

'Do you come over to it,' Thaddeus urged Ma. 'You haven't been up to much lately, have you?'

She shook her head. 'Reckon I'll not. Ole Shilling Tye's got sad thoughts for me.'

'All the reason why you should end up with happy ones. See my rose I'm showing and say goodbye to the Reverend. Ole boy's leaving at Michaelmas, same as me.'

'I'll see.'

'And I'll give you some money for a new hat,' he coaxed. 'You've had that ole beret stuck on your head summer and winter ever since the General Strike. And Joe can have a bob to go round the sideshows with.'

She remained dubious, but finally came downstairs on the afternoon appointed wearing a green taffeta frock, freshly whitened tennis shoes and a straw hat with a large flat brim.

'Christ, a mushroom on legs,' said Thaddeus, then added, 'You look a rare treat, Ma. And I've brought your bike round and pumped your tyres up fresh.'

They set off, the freshly scrubbed and polished Joe perched behind his father. 'Pity Dora couldn't come as well.'

'Got too far above herself,' Ma said grimly.

They paid threepence each to go in, and there were tents and stalls and swingboats and a shooting range and a fortune-teller from Sudbury. But as in any rural community it was the judging of the flowers, fruit and vegetables that most people had come to see. Bert Adler, retired wheelwright, always collared first prize with his peas, although last year the young chap from Hazel Cottage had run him a close second. Cabbages and cauliflowers lush as bridal bouquets, lusty carrots scrubbed clean as choirboys, and unblemished potatoes arranged on paper doilys . . . the fruit and veg occupied one tent and the flowers (Mixed Bunches, Single Specimens, Pot Flowers) were in another close by.

The blacksmith with slicked-down hair and a clean white cricket shirt was bawling forthcoming attractions through a megaphone as they walked into the field.

'Dear Sam Potter,' said the Reverend, clad in grey alpaca, clerical collar and panama hat, 'what a *formidable* man he is!' He shook hands with Ma, patted young Joe fondly upon the head and then hurried away. The three Noggins strolled round together, then overcome by the lure of the second-hand stall Ma was left behind while young Joe danced with excitement when he saw the rifle range.

'Can I have a go, Dad? Go on, Dad, can I have a go, Dad?'

Thaddeus helped him to steady the rifle and became aware that the boy was tense with eager expectation.

'Don't hold yourself so tight or you'll miss – ' Joe pulled the trigger and the shot went wide of the ping-pong balls dancing on their jets of water.

'Nearly had me ear orf,' complained the man in charge.

'Look, like this.' Thaddeus took the rifle, raised it, squinted and fired. One of the balls faltered, then regained its momentum.

'They go up and down like Auntie May does!' Joe shrieked in ecstasy.

Thaddeus fired twice more, then laid the rifle aside when he was handed a prize of five Woodbines in an open-ended packet. Abruptly Joe's eyes filled with tears. 'I only had one go and you had three – it's not fair. It's not fair – '

Thaddeus paid another twopence and Joe had the next four shots all to himself. He didn't win anything, and to forestall any disappointment Thaddeus jokingly shoved the packet of Woodbines in the boy's shirt pocket, unaware that it was not the prize that mattered, it was the act of shooting a gun.

The Fête was becoming more crowded, and over by the children's races Mrs Palfrey's niece was playing 'The Teddybears' Picnic' on a portable gramophone while bewildered toddlers were being coerced into running towards the line of waiting mothers chirruping encouragement from behind the winning tape.

There wasn't much on the second-hand stall; a few old books, a picture of the Prince of Wales in plus fours, some bits of cracked china and a few old clothes. Ma turned them over with a desultory finger and wandered on. She came to the home-made cake stall, and the gal they called Hoppity May called out, 'Hullo, Mrs Noggin – I say, what a lovely hat you're wearing!'

Ma removed it from her head, studied it thoughtfully for a moment and then replaced it without speaking.

'Would you care to buy a cake, Mrs Noggin?' Wearing an apron over her frock, May indicated her wares. 'Mrs Porter's ginger-bread is nice and Mrs Adler put four eggs in her sponge – '

'More'n I dare do, gal. If I so much as look at a bitta cake I'm sick as a cat.'

'How about a custard tart, then? Or some of Mrs Wilson's scones – '

'I dursn't – honest. I'd be a-writhing all night long.'

Ma prepared to depart, apparently without glancing at the row of confectionery enticingly displayed in front of her. Thick fruit scones, latticed tarts, little iced fancies and close to where she was standing, a rich Dundee cake on a willow-patterned plate.

'Perhaps you'd like to buy something for Thaddeus and Joseph?' May's smile exhibited the gentle persistence of one committed to a good cause. She held a paper bag open in readiness.

'Terrible to say,' said Ma, equally gentle, 'but they neither on'em touch cake unless they want to be up all night.'

'Really. . . ?'

Then another customer appeared and Ma sidled away un-noticed, leaving the willow-patterned plate empty. Depression vanished, and with the old poaching spirit now joyously revived she went off in search of young Joe.

She found him glaring, fists bunched, at a little girl with long ringlets and the lower part of her face buried in a mound of pink candyfloss.

'She shoved me?'

'Well, shove her back!'

He did so, and the little girl staggered, regained her balance and stuck her tongue out at him. Enraged, Joe prepared to take a run at her but Ma seized him by a handful of hair and said, 'She ain't worth it. Reckon you're best off on the swingboats,' and gave him twopence. Evading her grasp, he sped back to the rifle range.

The Baby Show was about to start and the Matron of the Brett Cottage Hospital in company with the Reverend and the Rural Dean, arrived to do the judging. Slowly they passed along the row of young mothers dandling babies on their laps; the Dean was moved to pinch a particularly luscious baby cheek only to snatch his hand back sharply: 'My word, Fiske, it *went* for me!'

'Tamper not with the face of deceit,' murmured the Reverend, smiling genially upon a pair of gurgling twins.

Thaddeus found his mother and son over by the coconut shy, and duly expressed admiration upon hearing that Joe had won a bar of chocolate in the egg-and-spoon race.

'And I bought a rare good cake from that gal whatsername,' said Ma, not to be outdone. She opened her carrier-bag for him to see inside.

'It's not wrapped up,' he commented.

'I told her not to bother. Poor ole gal didn't oughter do all that standing with her a cripple.' Narrowly she watched her son's face for possible reaction, but it gave nothing away. He propelled them towards the tea tent in silence.

Since the day of the picnic he had taken May to the pictures to see a film called *Smilin' Through*, and when Norma Shearer was shot dead at the altar they had both cried, May openly and Thaddeus furtively. He had wanted to take her hand but decided against it. If it had been Polly of course, there would have been no hesitation.

Yet there was something about May that pleased him in a peaceful way. They went for a couple of walks together, but there again, it was nothing like the old days with Polly. Then one afternoon he had taken a basket of strawberries to her cottage in Tarrent's Row. She had insisted that he should share them with her and they had sat in the small neat garden at a little iron table that had belonged to her parents.

Her cottage was very neat and simple inside, and it occurred to him that in essence it was very like May herself: neat and simple – simple that is in her outlook on life and in her dealings with people, although he was also aware of an intelligence most likely superior to his own. Or perhaps she was just better educated.

He liked her, and was also aware that his liking only needed a small shove to precipitate it over the border from liking to loving.

144

They were at ease and comfortable together, a state of affairs seldom achieved until the sex barrier had been surmounted, but so far, all he had done was to touch her hair with a fleeting caress as he passed her chair. He would never forget the way she had caught at his hand, imprisoned it for a moment within his own, and had looked at him with a smile in her dark eyes.

His mind was made up. He wanted to marry her. And because he also wanted this marriage and the whole approach to it to be as unlike the first rapturously rushed one as possible, he refrained from kissing her and instead spent a lot of time trying to devise a novel way of proposing. Various ideas occurred to him, but the right one, when finally it came, was the obvious one.

The bud that he had watched break from the stem had gradually swelled within the protective clasp of its calyx until the five sepals parted and the deep pink of his lovingly hybridised rose pointed an enquiring nose into the world. He watched over it, obsessed by the thought of greenfly, red spider and rose leafhopper. Last year the tortrix moth caterpillar had ruined the Reverend's display of *Rosée du Matin* almost overnight, and experience had taught him that in the nurture of a perfect bloom disaster could strike at any moment.

He had cut the bloom anxiously, and with the Reverend hovering, when it appeared in danger of opening too soon, and they had set it in a jar of water down in the cool dark of the Vicarage cellar. Now, worried that it was not sufficiently unfolded to give a good account of itself, Thaddeus had supervised its positioning in the Flower Show tent upon the trestle table already covered by a white sheet. He had watched as its name was carefully inscribed among those of its fellow competitors on the blackboard and easel standing at the entrance. *My May* it said in the neat script of Miss Owen, the headmistress of Shilling Tye's C. of E. school.

My May. There it was, firmly possessive and deeply resolute, and when Miss Owen had added the meticulous full stop he had said with a face carefully drained of expression, 'Reckon that'll do.'

So he bought his mother a cup of tea and Joe a glass of orangeade, but he couldn't take anything for himself. His throat was constricted with nerves almost as bad as it had been before going over the top at Passchendaele in 1917.

145

'Coming to see the ole rose get judged, then?' he asked offhandedly as she thirstily drained her cup.

'Oh, Thaddy dear! Your noo rose you put in the Flower Show?'

'That's it. Just for a lark, really.'

'And it's going to be judged by all the nobs and them?' He had never seen her look so admiring.

'Well, only the Rural Dean and a gent from the Rose Society who's a friend of the Reverend.'

'Come along, Joseph.' Carefully Joe's grandmother wiped her handkerchief across the boy's orange-stained lips. 'We gotta git a good view of your Dad getting a prize, haven't we?'

If he hadn't been so preoccupied Thaddeus might have suspected deviousness, but outside where the sun was casting its fierce afternoon rays he groaned to think of the heat inside the small Flower Show tent. If every petal hadn't already damn well dropped, then at least the heart of the rose would be showing, and this, the Reverend had said, would certainly lead to disqualification in the big professional shows.

Just outside the tent Ma suddenly raised herself on tiptoe and put her arm round him. The gesture was so unlike her that he wondered whether she was feeling ill. Once inside the tent, however, she seemed to recover, and no one noticed that her other elbow had rubbed fleetingly and with deadly accuracy against Miss Owen's blackboard.

It wasn't all that hot in there after all, but the scent of flowers was almost overwhelming. Roses, sweet peas and lilies were the main contenders in the Single Specimen class and Thaddeus's rose had been numbered 14. It was in perfect condition, its head still slightly raised as if it were listening for something. The petals were a delicate strawberry pink with paler veining, and they were unrolling to disclose a high centre still tightly furled, but already the Damask scent was strongly reminiscent of Bennett's *Lady Fitzwilliam*, a rose which under the Reverend's guidance had played a notable part in its creation.

Standing there alone and unadorned in its narrow glass vase the rose had a simplicity, a purity of being which reduced its grower to a momentary spasm of helpless adoration. For some reason the old days up at the Big House came rushing back to him; days in which cruelty and beauty had played so powerfully upon adolescent feelings.

'Is that it, Thaddy dear?' Ma's voice broke the spell.

'That's it,' he replied tersely.

Young Joe pushed his way in front of them and studied it with close attention. 'It's the same as Mrs Taylor's got next door.'

'No, it's not,' his father snapped. 'This is the only rose of its kind in the world.'

The buzz of conversation around them ceased and the villagers wandering round the exhibits melted respectfully into the background, the three Noggins among them. The Rural Dean and a stout elderly gentleman wearing a monocle were being ushered in by the Reverend, who was holding a sheaf of papers. They stood conferring for a moment, then under the watchful eye of Shilling Tye's amateur gardeners they began slowly to examine the exhibits.

They began with the lilies: the auratums that came striped, speckled or plain – Mrs Wilson's had ten flowers on one stem – and they lingered over the amabiles, martagons and sweet candidums, traditionally the cottagers' lily which is unwilling to flower in grander gardens. They conferred, and the Reverend made notes like an industrious schoolboy before they moved on to the sweet peas.

They stayed for a long while at number 7, which had silver-pink flowers poised like a cloud of butterflies on the stem, and at Mrs Wilson's offering which had petals purple as a dowager's toque. They conferred again, and the atmosphere became increasingly taut because of the work and the planning and the jealous pride that had gone to the making of each specimen. Each one had been brought to birth, nourished and cherished to fruition on window-ledges and in garden corners protected by ingenious arrangements of old corrugated iron and bits of glass. Chicken muck had been saved, laboriously pounded and watered down and then fed to them like Dr Gurton's Elixir Vitae for Infants, and the terror of late May frosts had kept whole families awake and vigilant.

No one spoke. No one batted an eye. Only Mrs Wilson in a halo hat and white ankle socks dared to swat at a fly with her programme. More notes were made, and when the judges moved towards the roses Thaddeus became instinctively aware that the

147

Reverend was striving to ignore the pink rose labelled number 14. They all three looked at it in turn, and to its creator's loving eye it appeared to look straight back at them, then they passed on to the others – hopeful examples of *Dorothy Perkins, Glorie de Dijon, Golden Dawn* and *Etoile d'Hollande*. With agonising slowness they reached the end of the row, and when the gentleman with the monocle walked back to give number 14 a further scrutiny, Thaddeus's nerve almost broke.

'Easy, boy,' whispered Ma, as if speaking to a sweating horse.

At last, after clearings of throats and shufflings of papers, the winners were announced in the three categories of Single Specimen.

'In the Lilium section we have, first prize, Mrs Wilson for her magnificent auratum which is catalogued as number 4. Second prize goes to Mr Digg's trumpet strain – Well done, Mr Digg! – and third prize is awarded to Mr Dolby's dear old lilium candidum – a flower without which our cottage gardens would be sad places indeed . . .'

Number 7 in the Sweet Peas won first prize and Mrs Wilson was heard to give an audible snort at only coming second. Then there was a pause and a little more shuffling of papers before the Reverend announced in a carefully controlled voice: 'Finally, we come to the Rose Section, where we have decided to award first prize to entry number 14, a new hybrid tea rose bred by Mr ah – Thaddeus Noggin . . .'

Without waiting to hear more, and with only a curt, red-faced nod in acknowledgement of the dutiful clapping, Thaddeus strode blindly from the tent and out into the fresh air.

He wanted to find May, but not for a minute or two. First of all he wanted to taste in seclusion the sweetness of victory. His rose had won. It was the best rose in Shilling Tye and most likely the best in all the length of the Stour Valley. And it was the only one of its kind in the world. *Dear May.*

Then rapture was pierced by misgiving. Had the Reverend influenced the other two judges with a secret nudge, a clandestine wink? No – he wouldn't do a thing like that. Where roses were concerned the Reverend was incapable of chicanery, whatever good purpose it might serve.

Thaddeus walked swiftly across the field to where the cricket match was coming to an end. Shadows were lengthening and midges were dancing and mothers with small children were beginning to make for home. He passed two old ladies shaped like tea cosies and their slow Suffolk voices drifted companionably.

'Gonna rain, I reckon. My ole corn's a-jumpin' suthin' crool.'

'Did you see Betty's baby won the competition? Got two teeth, he have . . .'

'Maureen's havin' a noo one in the Noo Year . . .'

Pausing to watch the last of the cricket he heard another voice say, 'Hullo, Thaddeus.' It was Bob Turner, who farmed a few acres of the Big House estate at the back of the Noggins' cottage. 'How's your Ma?'

'Still busy.'

'Reckon she'll always be.' Turner's smile was one of grudging admiration. 'I see her every now and then, but only unofficial like.'

Thaddeus grunted. 'How's things with you, then?'

'Poor. Pretty poor. Not much money about.' His lean body and hungry, wistful eyes endorsed the words.

'Same ole tale everywhere.' Thaddeus wondered whether Bob Turner had heard about the rose, but didn't want to tell him; didn't even want to mention its name – no, specially not its name – until after he had spoken to May.

So they fell silent, watching the cricketers slowly walk from the pitch, the captain of Shilling Tye pulling off his gloves importantly.

'I hear the Vicar's leaving,' Bob said at length.

'He's retiring. I'm the one that's leaving. I'm setting up on my own over Maplestead way.'

'Don't!' Bob said with sudden bitter urgency. 'Whatever you're thinking of going in for, don't. There won't be any money in it and you won't be able to do anything proper because you won't be able to afford labour. I've tried it, and I know. Oh yes, it's a rare good feeling you get telling yourself I'm me own boss. I'm free to work how I like, make all me own decisions an' sod'em all, but everything's agin you. Right from the start everything's agin you. You work all the hours of daylight – all on your own, mind – and when night comes you have to sit over bitsa paper working out the costa this and the costa that and you do nothing but pay out. Everybody's ready to take your money offa you – for seed, for fertiliser, for repairs to your ole bitsa machinery because you can't afford nothing noo, and when you've got what you've grown ready to the market – twelve monthfulla sweat and hard labour – nobody wants it. That's a fact – nobody wants it. There's a glut, they say. We can git it cheaper from abroad. So take it away again mate, and if you've got nothing better to do with it, shove it up your arse.'

'I'm not thinking about farming – ' Thaddeus began, but Bob interrupted him excitedly.

'Listen, I've tried arable – it's good growing land round here. Rich but light, drains well but holds the moisture. But I tell you straight, nobody wanted barley, nobody wanted wheat, nobody wanted beans, nobody wanted clover – I know, 'cos I tried'em all. So I went in for poultry. Then pigs. Then I had a go at market gardening – tomatoes, lettuces, beetroot, soft fruit – all that. Same answer. No, we don't want none of that neither. You can shove that up your arse as well. So now I run a few calves, fatten'em for eight or ten weeks then sell'em again. This lot's all got ringworm but I owe the vet ten quid already – '

Then his excitement died, and he touched Thaddeus apologetically on the elbow. 'Sorry about that, boy. But take my word and stop thinking about going solo. It just don't pay. Nobody wants you no matter what you do.'

'Things could change any time.'

'You don't believe that, no more than I do.' Bob began to move away, then paused. 'By the way, talking about going solo – how's Dora these days? Haven't seen her about.'

'She's living over at Stoke Abbey now.'

'Got her own business, so I hear.'

Thaddeus assented briefly.

'Ah well, so long as it's not farming she'll do all right. Give her my best respects when you see her.' He turned away.

Then he turned back again. 'Don't fancy a quick beer, do you? Beer tent's open at seven.'

'Well, I was just going to meet someone.'

'Ahhh, just a quick one. Be out agin in five minutes.'

Thaddeus hesitated. Bob Turner, thin faced and solitary in his troubles, was gazing at him with all the sad yearning of a lost dog.

'Five minutes, then,' he agreed. 'At least it'll do you more good than staring at a collection of mangy ole calves.'

The stalls were bare now, the takings counted and collected into paper bags. Someone was winding up the white tape used in the children's races and the lady fortune-teller had divested herself of her gypsy costume and wandered outside for a quiet drag. She loved these old local fêtes where everyone knew everyone else, and greatly enjoyed spreading a little harmless mischief between families. *Perhaps I shouldn't say this, dear, but watch your husband. There's a lady – I think she wears a lot of green – who sometimes lends him her* Daily Sketch *at work . . . A tall dark man with heavy eyelids will call on you next Tuesday and try to sell you a vacuum cleaner. Tell him politely that you have no electricity laid on and call for help if he puts his foot in the door . . . Your Auntie Ada – or is it Ida, I can't quite see – will go down with a bad attack of shingles in September . . .* All innocent fun and nothing spiteful.

When her cigarette was finished she ground it under the heel of her silver sandal and strolled over to the nearest tent, pausing to read what was written on the blackboard that stood at the entrance.

Inside, there was a smell of dry trodden grass as she saw that the interior was deserted except for a single dark-haired woman looking at one of the exhibits in silence. The fortune-teller moved towards her and stood by her side. Together they contemplated the single rose bearing the number 14 and a gold card saying FIRST PRIZE. The rose was now fully open, and appeared to be gazing at them wide-eyed.

'Number 14,' the fortune-teller glanced back towards the blackboard and easel. 'Lovely, isn't it?'

'It's the most beautiful rose I've ever seen.'

'And fancy them calling it after their Mum.'

'Yes.'

'*My Ma.* I bet it was some young chap who grew it. Sons are much nicer to their mothers than daughters are. My daughter Pauleen's sixteen and she's a bitch.'

The dark-haired woman made a slight sound of commiseration and moved away with a little bobbing movement. Outside the tent she paused momentarily by the blackboard, but not long enough

151

in the gathering dusk to notice the faint chalk streak where Ma's wicked elbow had hastily erased the letter Y.

Fairy lights were beginning to twinkle and the Fête was assuming an atmosphere that was exciting, mysterious and faintly sinister. In the absence of children, clergy and old folk, young lovers were materialising out of the shadows with their arms entwined. Pretty girls with permanent waves and sticky lipstick, young swains in clean white shirts and new caps, chewing a blade of grass with careful nonchalance. Foxtrots rasped through a Tannoy, and May was preparing to wheel her bicycle towards the exit when Thaddeus's voice made her pause.

'Been looking everywhere for you – couldn't find you, or the other two – ' He sounded aggrieved.

'We've been looking for you as well,' May replied. 'Your mother has taken Joseph home.'

'How could she? One of them'd have to walk, without me.'

'Your mother did. She put Joseph on the saddle and said she'd push him. I wanted to go with her but she wouldn't let me.'

There was no accusation in her voice, none whatsoever, yet it seemed to him to hold a different tone.

'Rotten father, aren't I?' he said, testing her.

'I wouldn't say that.' Her smile looked tired, but maybe it was the shadows. He stood waiting for her to say something more, to say what he had wanted to hear her say since the judging, but she remained silent.

'Well?' He put his hands on his hips. 'What did you think of it?'

'The rose? It's beautiful, Thaddeus,' she said. 'And congratulations on winning first prize.'

'You really liked it?' Impossible now to keep the eagerness out of his voice.

'Yes. I did. And I'm very proud to be your friend.'

'Friend?'

She began pulling on her white cotton gloves, the bicycle resting against her hip. 'Well, yes. I'll aways be that.'

He watched her smooth the gloves over her fingers, and do up the little pearly buttons at the wrist. She did it all very slowly.

'What are you going so early for? I'd planned tonight was going to be special.' Even to his own ears his voice sounded unpleasing, like that of young Joe in a sulk. 'There's going to be dancing, and that.'

She looked at him sadly. 'I can't dance, Thaddy.'

No, of course she couldn't, not with her leg. But he persisted, encouraged by her calling him Thaddy. 'No more can I. I never did get the hang of it but I reckon we could hop round together . . .'

Oh God, that was worse. She knew, and smiled, about being called Hoppity May in the village, but for a potential lover to allude to hopping was shameful. It was all going wrong.

'I'd like to,' she said, 'but I'm a bit tired. It's been rather a long day.'

Helplessly he stood watching as she began to move away, then the pain he felt on her behalf began to harden into an angry self-pity.

'So what about the rose? You haven't said hardly anything about the rose, and what I . . .' He shook his head as if to shuffle the words into a better coherence. 'I worked hard on that, you know.'

She turned back to look at him: a small figure in the gloom holding an old-fashioned bicycle with big wheels and a wicker basket. 'I know you did, Thaddy, and it was the loveliest rose in the world.'

'*Was?* There's going to be plenty more like it, you may depend –' In a sudden fury of frustration he snatched his cap off and flung it on the ground. 'There's going to be hundreds more – all different –and all of 'em better than that one. That was only one of the first – only a poor ole thing . . .' He paused, almost weeping. 'I've got a bitta land, you know. Over Maplestead way. I saved up and bought it and I'm going to build a little house on it and breed roses. Nothing but roses . . .'

She stood motionless, saying nothing. He could no longer distinguish her features. In the distance the Tannoy was blaring a jolly two-step 'I'm Happy when I'm Hiking', and delighted screams rose and fell with the swingboats' momentum.

'So aren't you going to say anything?'

'What do you want me to say?' Her voice sounded small and patient.

He didn't know. At least, not exactly. He rubbed his hand through his hair, then turned away, shrugging his shoulders and leaving his cap where he had thrown it. A few paces further on he halted and turned towards her for the last time. 'So – are you coming? Are you coming – or what?'

As a proposal of marriage it was scarcely in the manner he had intended and he was not surprised at her lack of response. He stared after her, peering through the rich scented darkness at a small, deeper shadow dwindling silently away.

She didn't give a bugger. Picking up his cap he slapped it back on his head and made for the beer tent. He had already had three pints, and three more wouldn't do him any harm.

1940

The Second World War seemed to come at them gradually; a high whirling humming cloud of locusts preparing to alight and devour everything in its path. Already it had devoured the continent, sweeping outwards from Nazi Germany, suffocating with sheer numbers and laying waste with a clash of metallic wings and tirelessly voracious jaws.

They watched for them coming over East Anglia; day and night from church towers and defunct windmills, and Mr Churchill said that we would defend our island whatever the cost might be. We will fight in the fields, he said, and Thaddeus Noggin, now aged forty-one, looked out over the rows of maiden rosebushes visible from his kitchen window and wondered whether this time next week they would be no more than broken twigs beneath roaring tanks and armoured cars.

Contrary to Bob Turner's dire warning all those years ago, his rose business had flourished, not spectacularly perhaps, but with a slow steadiness growing out of the first years of pitilessly hard and monotonous work. And he had done it all by himself, by hand. Had transformed the heavy clumps of coarse meadow grass into a rich and friable soil upturned to sun and rain, and had slept in an old caravan chucked out by Johnny Cousins all the while he was setting up his first stock of roses.

He had already grown a large quantity of *canina* rootstock from seed, and in his first solitary year of budding the sun beat down on his bowed shoulders and the sweat ran into his eyes. He had budded many roses before over at Shilling Tye, but there it had been a comparatively leisurely and enjoyable affair; now he was learning the professional nurseryman's skill with the budding knife – two lightning strokes in the bark of the rootstock, lift with a flick the two flaps of bark and insert the dormant bud of the scion then bind it swiftly and smoothly in place with raffia.

To begin with, he was neither swift nor smooth; still under the Reverend's poetic influence, he was too weighted with wonderment at the power of creation, but that had to go. Creating roses had to become a job like any other, and if he made the cut too deep or inadvertently damaged the tiny shield-shaped bud of the rose he was propagating he would curse because each mistake meant money; meant a threat to the bare subsistence level he had forced himself to accept in those early days.

Sometimes the weather was with him, sometimes not. Wind was the chief enemy, sometimes getting up after dark and roaring towards the small twiggy plants that represented his future as if it were intent upon whipping them out of the ground and hurling them into the next parish. Then there was drought: watching for the clouds massing and waiting for them to drop low and let loose the sweet-scented nourishing rain. Otherwise it was watering by canfuls drawn from the spring that served for his own drinking. In those early days he and the roses lived as one.

Devoid of human companionship yet not lonely; absorbed and intent, he rose at dawn and slept at dusk, collapsing on the caravan's single bunk, often without undressing, and lying up-turned and spreadeagled in dreamless exhaustion. He ate what-ever came to hand, bread and cheese mostly, and his long limbs grew thin and angular, almost back to the way they had been when he first began to grow vigorously at puberty. Only then they had been hesitant, confused and essentially ill co-ordinated in their movements; now they were controlled by experience and the necessity of not wasting an ounce of energy on anything that was inessential.

He washed himself and his clothes in the same bowlful of water and cut his own hair, seizing tufts of it and pruning it back as he would an exceptionally vigorous rambler. The sun burnt his arms and hands and the back of his neck and bleached his hair to a faded straw colour, and as the weather shaped and dominated the land, so it patterned his face and cut pale lines in the taut sun-dyed skin. His eyes, which seemed a sharper blue than before, had neverthe-less acquired the faraway gaze that matches Suffolk taciturnity; with close on five hundred young rose bushes to watch over he had no time to spare for the world outside. The world where Hitler was now German Reich Chancellor.

The only person who persistently pushed her way up the roughly made track to the caravan was his mother, sometimes with a hunk of roast rabbit and an apple pie in an oilcloth bag swinging from her bicycle handlebars. Unless he was at school she was generally accompanied by young Joe, who had now inherited an outgrown bike from one of his well-off cousins. It was a Raleigh with a cheeky rubber hooter, and he spent a lot of time polishing the handlebars and shining up the chromium between the wheel spokes. Joe was growing into a thickset boy with powerful shoulders, and with his father's features softened by his mother's smile.

'What you reckon on doing with that boy, Thaddy?' Ma watched him wandering up and down the rows of young bushes. 'He ain't gunna stay at school all his life.'

'Depends what he wants to do.'

'One of the things he most wants to do is live with his Dad.'

'Yes I know. I'm thinking about it. I'm thinking it's time to start building a house and living a bit better. Then I'll have him, like I said.'

Thaddeus spoke impatiently, and the caravan bounced as he stumped across to light the spirit stove to make a cup of tea. Joe appeared in the doorway; with his hands on the roof he curled his legs up and swung to and fro like a monkey.

'Don't do that, you'll have the damn thing over.'

'Dad's thinking of building his house soon,' Ma said, impassively unwrapping three slices of treacle tart.

'When?' Joe's feet hit the dusty floor with a crash that made his father wince. 'When are you starting, Dad? Can I come and help, and can I come and live with you then, Dad?'

Same kid. Same breathless reiteration of the word Dad; same tumult of eager questions breathlessly repeated. 'Can I? Go on, Dad, can I come and live with you?'

Thaddeus turned round from the stove where the tin kettle was beginning to purr and looked at his son. Really looked at him, perhaps for the first time in two years.

'Yes. You can't stay with your Gran for ever.'

'So can I come and help you build the house? Can I, Dad?'

Smiling in spite of himself, Thaddeus said, 'Depends how strong you are. Can you carry a timber six foot by two? Can you carry a hodful of bricks up a ladder?'

'Yes, Dad! I can pick my best friend up at school and he weighs

157

nine stone because he's fat. He's the fattest boy in our school, Dad! And I can pick ole Gran up under one arm – '

'No call to do that – '

'I'm just telling you I *can* – and I can, can't I, Gran?'

Ma looked at him steadily, thin dry lips pursed, dusty brown beret clamped low down over her head so that only her earlobes were visible. 'Yes,' she said. 'You're a good strong boy.'

They sat out on the caravan steps drinking their tea while Joe talked incessantly through mouthfuls of treacle tart and Thaddeus surveyed the bronzy-green leaves freshly carried by the young rose plants that stretched before them like a ruffled sea. Ma said little, but then she was getting old.

'Reckon we're in for another dry ole summer. Oak come out afore the ash,' she said finally.

'Doesn't always figure.'

'Mostly that does, you may depend.'

'Dad – ' young Joe wiped the crumbs from round his mouth on the back of his hand – 'Dad, can I sleep here tonight?'

'What about school tomorrow?'

'No school tomorrow, Dad, it's Ascension Day.'

'Well, I don't rightly know.' Oddly disturbed by the thought of anyone sharing the caravan, even for a night, Thaddeus turned to his mother. 'Don't suppose he's got the things he needs, has he?'

'Don't reckon he needs much,' Ma said laconically.

Thaddeus was unwilling, his son was jubilantly insistent, but Ma didn't say much, and it was funny that she should be indifferent to the prospect of losing the boy, sooner or later on a permanent basis. After all, she had brought him up from a baby. Still, she was getting on in years and no doubt wanted a bit of peace and quiet to see her out. Thaddeus tried to remember her age, but couldn't.

'All right then,' he said finally. 'If you don't mind dossing on the floor and getting up at six.'

He didn't sleep well, bothered by the knowledge that someone else was within close proximity, and listening to the even breathing rising from the pile of old coats on the floor it occurred to him that he had never been much of a father to young Joe, always preferring to regard him as a stray kid about the place rather than his own son. Ma had done everything for him – women were better with kids than men because it was bred in their nature

158

– but he should by rights have done more for him. Bought him little things, talked to him, taken him about more.

His mind went back to the day when he had borrowed the car from Johnny Cousins and taken him and May on a trip to the sea. He hadn't been to the sea since – hadn't had the time. Joe hadn't been either, to the best of his knowledge. He didn't know about May.

Funny about her. He'd been quite a bit keen on her at one time, and he vaguely remembered being upset over the rose thing until afterwards he learned the truth of it. Someone had rubbed out the letter Y in its name and everyone thought he'd called it after his mother. He now had a couple of dozen of them growing over in the field and they were proving themselves very nicely; free flowering, nice scent and, so far, resistant to black spot and mildew. *My Ma* it was, and that was the name he would market it by when the time came.

Yes. *My Ma*. Nothing wrong with that because she was a good ole gal. As for the other, well yes, she was a nice gal too, and he didn't really know why he hadn't taken the trouble to explain to her what had happened. Afraid of looking a fool, he supposed. Ah well, perhaps it wasn't ever meant to be. He hadn't set eyes on her for a bull's moon . . .

He shifted restlessly, then raised himself slightly and peered over the edge of the bunk. It was dark down there on the floor, but his son's upturned face gleamed like a pale little moon obscured by thin cloud.

What you reckon on doing with that boy? Ma had asked him, a question for which he had been unprepared. And now, his conscience was beginning to nag like a sore tooth. He lay down again, listening to the light wind playing round the caravan and rattling the strip of loose roofing felt with playful fingers.

He was selfish. After Polly went all he had wanted to do was grow roses; to blot out the laughter and the mad-with-love memories behind mountains of them. To drown in hard work, to anaesthetise the pain of loss with the pain of rose thorns puncturing his flesh. When he was a kid he had seen a picture of Jesus wearing a crown of thorns, and in a dim sort of way he had wanted to be like that. To suffer as a way of driving out suffering. And he had never taken much to young Joe because it was Joe that

159

had killed her. Germs had got in and she had gone septic inside, the nurse had explained afterwards, and had been a bit shocked when Thaddeus had asked why the baby couldn't have gone septic and not her.

If anyone had to go like that it would have been much better for it to have been the baby because it was too young to know. Too young to suffer much. He remembered the moment on the picnic when he had swung young Joe to and fro in his arms and said that he would throw him in the sea. He remembered Joe laughing, slightly apprehensive maybe, but happy because he was being played with, and he also remembered the sudden violent compulsion to do as he threatened: to chuck him away because he had no more value than an empty Woodbine packet.

Thank God he'd only felt like that the once, but the memory of it seared him now that the kid was lying trustfully asleep on a bed of old coats.

Leaning over the bunk Thaddeus peered at him again and suddenly remembered the sense of irretrievable loss when he heard that his own father had died. They should have talked more, gone about together more. But they never did, both being afflicted with the habitual reticence of East Anglia. The boy's face was turned away now and all he could see was the silhouette of ruffled hair and a strong young arm upflung on the improvised pillow.

Can I come and live with you, Dad? Please Dad, can I come and live with you, Dad . . . Dad . . .

How the word Dad seemed to rattle out of him, compulsive and convulsive as a hiccough. He never seemed to keep saying Gran like that, and she was the one who'd done everything for him. An ignominious little flame of complacency warmed him, and lying back again he told himself that the kid was all right, and that he must keep on reminding himself that he was after all a bud from Polly grafted on to his own rootstock.

Well, there was nothing reticent about him. He might turn out to be a real winner. In the meantime, they had better make a start on building the house next week.

And over in Stoke Abbey Dora had taken over Bunting's Emporium.

Naturally there had been a certain amount of gossip to begin

160

with, but her decision to ignore it had dealt with it sensibly and painlessly. Thaddeus had helped her in the initial stages as he had promised, but then he had suddenly become immersed in his own affairs over at Maplestead.

Everything connected with rose-growing had to be done at the right time of year, and as a girl reared in a farming community, she accepted it. The day she had cried and told him about loving Mr Bunting had formed a mute but powerful bond between them. Sometimes she sensed that her brother's abrupt departure for the seclusion of Maplestead was based on more than his employer's retirement, but they respected one another's privacy. She would no more have pried into rumours of his courting Polly's friend with the limp than he would have commented on calling at the Emporium one evening and finding her alone with Bob Turner.

Bob had not called as a friend, it goes without saying, but as a prospective temporary employee to take over the jobs that Thaddeus had had to leave unfinished.

She had got rid of the Buntings' furniture and personal effects – giving some to the gypsies and burning the rest in a fiercely vindictive bonfire in the back garden despite her mother's protests.

'God Almighty gal, that's a fur coat you're burnin' there and gimme that gent's black suit outta that other stuff you got!'

They had tussled furiously and rather horribly over Mr Bunting's business suit with the high, old-fashioned lapels, but the roaring spurt of flame kindled by six celluloid collars had reached out to it and Dora had stood panting in triumph while Ma retreated, mopping the heat from her forehead with one of Mrs Bunting's bedsocks.

Then, with the living quarters empty of everything that had once belonged to the Buntings – even mats from under plant pots had had to go – Dora soberly surveyed her new domain. Two bedrooms, one small, one large. A living-room that faced on to a small and crooked back garden now scarred by a large circle of cold ashes, and a dim little kitchen with only a brownstone sink and a brass tap left in it. The food cupboard had gone, so had the deal table and two chairs, the bread bin, the knives and forks and the saucepans – even the string stretched across the front of the paraffin cooking stove where the tea towels had hung had been snatched down and added contemptuously to the bonfire. All she had left were bare floors and walls shadowed by ghosts of Bunting furniture and nail holes where Bunting-embroidered texts had once hung. *Thou God seest me.*

Walking round it, she was amazed to think that she had once regarded their living accommodation as some kind of mysterious and almost celestial region where even mouse-droppings would have a special significance. Love makes fools of us all, she was able to admit that now, and on the afternoon Bob Turner answered her advertisement in the window of Marling Post Office she greeted him with formal politeness. Politeness because his bit of land abutted on to their back garden at home, and formal as an indication that he was not to presume upon neighbourly goodwill.

'I read on your p.c. that you're looking for a hand with some decorating and stuff. Well, I'm at a bit of a loose end just now.' Conscious of Dora's appraising stare, he added, 'What with one thing and another.'

She showed him round while Thaddeus strolled tactfully in the garden, then said that she had other applicants to interview and would let him know. He said that would do fine, any time to suit herself, and marvelled at her acting so hoity-toity.

The other applicants proved disappointing both in quality and quantity: a one-armed man from Wissington, a dried-up septuagenarian who spat on the floor, and a strange youth with staring eyes who had never touched a paintbrush in his life. So she engaged Bob Turner at fifteen shillings a week until the work was completed, and grew accustomed to hearing him whistle and thump about overhead while she made a painstaking inventory of all the goods in the shop and made plans to sell off most of them at half-price.

Now that she had consented to be Mr Bunting's sole beneficiary she wanted passionately to do away with every mortal thing that might remind her of the old days; as the building was being stripped and cleaned and repainted so she wanted to strip and clean out her memory. To take a broom to it, then a bucket and brush to scrub away all traces of the humbly loving, then desperately hurt, and finally the sickened and incoherent girl who had fled from the presence of a fallen idol.

Instead, she parted her hair on the other side, powdered her

162

nose and applied a little lipstick. She bought herself a tailormade costume with new boxy shoulders and shorter skirt, and her sister Marjorie said that she looked like a different person. Deeply gratified, Dora invited her to go to the pictures with her, and Marjorie said OK, but why don't we go to a dance instead?

A dance? Nonplussed, Dora asked if Marjorie's husband Ken would mind being shared between them and Marjorie laughed hard enough to show her dental plate and said, 'My God, we wouldn't take Ken! We'd go on our own and see what we fancied . . .'

Interested, but ultimately repelled by the idea, Dora said she'd think about it. Marjorie stopped laughing and said, 'OK, suit yourself, you S.O.M.'

'What's an S.O.M?'

'Stuffy old maid, amongst other things.'

Any idea of a new phase of sisterly chumminess developing between them died, and they went back to the old tepid relationship of Christmas and birthday cards and the occasional family gathering for Sunday tea. As soon as the new paint was dry in her bedroom Dora had Bob Turner move her bits and pieces over from Marling in the trailer in which he used to take the calves to market, and when asked if he would mind cleaning it out properly first he said no, of course not; he reckoned that went without saying.

Although he was thin he appeared to be very strong, but no man in the world could carry a wardrobe upstairs single-handed. She insisted upon helping, but dropped her end with a thud when she trapped her fingers against the banisters. Manhandling the wardrobe up the last couple of stairs he hastened down again and grabbed at her hand, shaking his head and wincing at the reddening skin and lightly grazed knuckles.

'Cold water. That's the best thing for that – ' He hurried her down to the kitchen and held her hand under the tap. Dora stood mutely watching, as if the hand belonged to somebody else.

She was thirty-seven years old and no man had ever held her hand before.

'Thank you,' she said, withdrawing it. 'I'll be all right now.'

But he recaptured it and dried it on a bit of clean rag that he had in his pocket. 'Funny,' he said, 'what rare little ole hands women

163

have.' It occurred to her that he might never have held a woman's hand before, either.

They finished installing her bedroom furniture in silence, and she stood over by the window watching him re-bolt the bed together. When it was done to his satisfaction he sat on the edge of it and bounced lightly up and down.

'Don't reckon that'll collapse, no matter what you do.'

She smiled without replying, conscious that he had a strange, almost innocent quality that matched her own. He was comfortable to be with, almost as if he wasn't a man. Yet his lean cheeks were shaded with incipient bristle and his bare arms ribbed with muscle. She didn't make the bed until he had gone, and spent the first night in a state of watchfulness in case any last lingering wisp of the Buntings should manifest itself. It didn't; she had banished them once and for all with soap and water and gloss paint where other people might have resorted to bell, book and candle.

Joe had finally gone to live with his father in 1937 when he was fifteen and had left school.

The transition had been gradual, and decidedly cautious on the part of his father. A single day was long enough to begin with – 'Time to go home now, your Gran'll be fretting' – but as the materials for the house were gradually assembled from builders' yards, gravel pits and wood merchants he slowly became aware of pleasure in the boy's company. He still talked incessantly, the words rattling out of him like pellets from a tin can and he still began and ended each sentence with the word *Dad*. He also giggled a lot, and squirmed on the ground in near hysterics when a bag of cement burst open and covered them both in grey powder.

But he was also becoming gratifyingly practical and sensible for his age, appearing to know by instinct how and when to help; he was also keen to learn, and as Thaddeus had never built a house before, the two of them learned together. They dug the footings and laid the foundations in accordance with a book borrowed from the public library, and without worrying too much about plumb lines and spirit levels the walls began to ascend.

Bricklaying was not difficult, merely monotonous, but young Joe seemed happy enough knocking up cement on a wooden board and mounting brick upon brick first in Flemish bond and

164

then in headers and stretchers, which was what the book advised. They bought the window-frames from a cottage that was being demolished, and standing within their house when the walls had risen to an impressive six feet, Thaddeus scratched his head and said, 'Reckon we'd better play safe, boy, and make it a bungalow.'

'Oh come on Dad – we can do better than that!'

'Do you know how to put stairs in?'

'Well, no, but – '

'So we're having a bungalow. Any case, I haven't got time to mess about too long, there's work to do outside.'

Over sausage and mash that evening Joe said, 'Will people want roses when there's a war on?'

'Who says there's going to be a war?'

'The papers do, and so does Gran. She's starting to store up sugar and flour.'

Thaddeus grunted. 'Hitler's a fool, but he wouldn't be such a fool as to march in on us.'

'If he did, I'd join up, Dad.'

'You'd be too young.'

'I am now, but he hasn't come yet, has he?'

'Don't cross your bridges,' Thaddeus said, and reached for the ketchup.

But the conversation came back to him after the boy had gone to bed. Either he or Joe generally bought a newspaper if they went to the village, and that summer knocking-off time usually coincided with listening to the six o'clock news on Thaddeus's old battery set. Nasty things were happening in distant places, like China and Japan being at war and some sort of revolution going on in Spain. Over here a lot of people had got all hot and bothered about the King marrying Mrs Simpson even though he'd left the throne, but Thaddeus couldn't see the sense in it. Leave the poor bugger alone and let him marry who he liked; leave me alone and let me get on with growing roses.

But if by chance there was another war, young Joe was right when he reckoned no one'd want roses any more. Pray to Gawd there won't be one, thought Thaddeus, who wasn't the praying type.

Two months after Joe's sixteenth birthday the Germans entered Austria and Thaddeus sold forty rosebushes to a strange ole gent who said that he was the new owner of the Willows, which he called Zer Veelows. He had arrived from Prague with his family and wanted to replant the garden with roses in the best English style. He was wearing a grey Homburg hat and rimless spectacles on a black ribbon. 'Zer storm iss coming, my friend.' He clapped Thaddeus on the shoulder and his diamond ring flashed.

'It won't come here,' Thaddeus said, striving to sound reassuring. 'And if it does, well, I reckon you'll be all right down your little ole lane.'

Mr Pavlicek said he envied him his certainty, then asked when he would be coming to plant the roses. Thaddeus had to explain that he merely grew them and sold them. Mr Pavlicek gazed at him with his sad outcast's eyes and spread his arms in a helpless gesture. So Thaddeus arranged to have a word with Bob Turner, who might be able to help him out. Like so many other small farmers he was down to subsistence level.

But so far, roses were doing surprisingly well; with the bungalow finished and a handpainted sign at the gateway saying T. NOGGIN ROSE GROWER he was both free and freshly encouraged to set more stock. Wisely he took care to perpetuate the tested favourites such as *Ophelia*, *Albertine*, *Madame Butterfly* and *Penelope*, the old musk rose loved by so many Suffolk cottagers as *Pennyloop*, but he was also trying new varieties – potfuls of young seedlings on the bungalow window-ledges that might one day go towards the making of new and perfect roses, each of them carrying the Noggin pedigree. The failure rate was high and the disappointments multitudinous but it never occurred to him to stop trying. Absorbed in work by day and dog-tired by the evening he was largely oblivious to the world outside, of which his mother was a part.

Ma was now sixty-four; not all that old, but weariness seemed to be gripping her by the throat and draining the life out of her. Alone at the cottage in Marling Hamlet she rose at the accustomed hour of six each morning only to be faced with the dull realisation that there was no longer any reason for doing so.

There was no sense in cooking breakfast for herself; not long ago it had been frying up yesterday's cold spuds with a nice bit of fat bacon and a couple of eggs scrambled into it to see them off warm and comfortable to work or school. But not now. No bait to

166

prepare with its accompanying bottle of cold tea, no planning and conniving to make ten bob do the work of fifteen. Now she had the Old Age Pension and nothing to spend it on except the rates. She didn't fancy eating much; couldn't take more than a hen's noseful, not sitting there all on her own. Dora was gone. Thaddy was gone. And now young Joe was gone too. It was right that he should; a growing boy had no business living with nothing but an ole Gran. He needed men's company and above all he needed his father. Joe was a good boy, and so was Thaddy.

But there was nothing to do. Nothing to see to. So she would pull her old beret further down over her ears and wander on ghostly plimsolled feet round the garden where the beans needed staking and thistles competed with tomatoes, and it all seemed a waste of effort somehow.

People in the other cottages were nice enough, but they were wary of her. 'She'd have the shirt offa your back if you didn't watch her,' the older ones said, and the younger ones, women with a brooda kids to see after, envied her purposeless hours and blissful silence. On bad days they longed to be old same as she was.

She tried to rouse herself. To forget the aches and pains that nagged her by reading the *Daily Mirror* which the woman next door handed over the hedge when the family had finished with it, and the idea of another war coming depressed her even while it filled her with a little trickle of optimism. Perhaps she had better start getting ready. Planning what to do, what to start acquiring and hoarding. Marjorie and Ken were all right, so was Eric who had a partnership in a boatyard now, and she reckoned that Dora was all right too. But you never really knew, not with Dora.

That left Thaddy and Joe. There were times now when she regretted having interfered between him and that gal with the hoppity leg. Anyone else'd have done the same, though; it was natural enough to try and hang on to what you'd got, but Thaddy had gone anyway. To begin with she had made the best of it, and had found comfort in baking pies and cakes and stews he could warm up on the caravan primus, but now . . . the bike ride to Maplestead was getting longer and the little hills steeper, and now they were in the bungalow young Joe was beginning to fancy himself as a bit of a cook.

One Sunday morning she obeyed a sudden impulse and went to

church, smelling of carbolic soap and wearing a bit of fur round her neck that had once belonged to Marjorie's mother-in-law. But a red-faced woman she had never seen before said 'Excuse me, but I always sit there', and gave Ma a shove with her well-upholsterd bum that sent her gliding rapidly to the far end of the polished pew.

The vicar didn't help either. His sermon was taken from Chapter 15 of the Gospel according to St John, *I am the true vine, and my Father is the husbandman*. To begin with Ma listened attentively, her plimsolls resting on the worn blue hassock, but it didn't make a lot of sense, his father cutting off not only branches that didn't bear fruit but those that did, as well. Going on like that he'd have nothing left but the little ole stump.

The vicar leaned heavily on the front of the pulpit and said that it was up to all of us in the name of God to cut off those branches within ourselves that didn't bear fruit – in other words, we must stop being things like vain and greedy and selfish in order that the nice things – here, he looked doubtfully at his congregation as if the possibility of any kind of niceness was distinctly remote – might, with further snipping of the secateurs, eventually bring forth a grape or two.

They stood to sing Psalm 136 *O give thanks unto the Lord for he is good: for his mercy endureth for ever*. Ma left the church unconvinced and uncomforted.

The days shortened. Autumn winds rattled the back door and made the kitchen fire smoke. She let it go out, and sat with an old rug round her shoulders in the hand-carved chair that had belonged to Joe her husband. Sometimes Joe seemed very close; even closer than the woman next door.

She was not consciously unhappy; not really consciously anything, although the pains in her body sometimes made her shift and squirm. She thought about the war that was coming and was dully glad that she had stored a bit of sugar and flour in the cupboard upstairs. She told herself that she ought to walk over to the shop and get a few tins in as well.

She still roused up when the family called round; Thaddy relit the fire for her and got the coal in while young Joe chopped a heapa kindling. Dora brought her two Chilprufe vests from the shop that was now Noggin's Emporium and not Bunting's, and

Marjorie appeared with a large box of chocolates. She was wearing a pillbox hat and an edge-to-edge coat which was plain stupid in November, but Ma couldn't be bothered to tell her so.

The fire went out again, and the woman next door got fed up with the new tactic of poking the *Daily Mirror* under the front door and not getting any thanks. Then one motionless, pale-blue afternoon when the last leaves were down and the bare earth smelt sweet with damp decay Ma went down the garden and out through the gap in the bulging hedge that led to the fields. She thought she might get a rabbit, but couldn't remember for sure if she had set the snares.

The fresh air was doing her good, and she pattered along the hedgerows with something like her old furtive speed until the pain suddenly struck her. She staggered, then held herself motionless, bowed over. The pain eased, then struck again and she couldn't tell which part of her it was aiming at. All of her, even her brain, seemed to be affected by its savage hammer blows.

She slipped on to her knees with her arms folded round her, waiting for the next onslaught. It didn't come, but instinct told her that it was too soon to try standing up again. She remained kneeling, a small bony creature with a face that was suddenly immeasurably old, then very gently she keeled over and lay on her side, curled up like a cat. The relief was enormous, and she lay with her cheek cushioned on a clump of dying plantain. She slept.

Bob Turner found her two days later and burst unannounced into the kitchen of the Maplestead bungalow.

'Cold as cold – there was frost on her coat – and she didn't oughtera gone like that – not all alone like a fox in a ditch . . .'

He cried, haggard with shock, then abruptly pulled himself together and said, 'What about Dora? Somebody's got to tell Dora, haven't they?'

Joe cried too, big bursting, blubbering tears while Thaddeus hurried down to the little police station at Bures and from there to the mortuary at Sudbury to identify the body.

She looked very small and far away when they turned the sheet back an inch or two. Her eyed were closed, her bit of grizzled hair was nicely combed and there was a hint of a smile on her sardonic old lips. They didn't tell him that they had had to break some bones in order to straighten her out from the foetal position in which she had been found.

169

They buried her next to Joe, her husband, and on the other side of her was poor Willie who had died of the diphtheria.

The war came the following year, and young Joe couldn't understand why the army wouldn't take men of seventeen.

'I mean, what's the difference between seventeen and eighteen?'

'Twelve months,' said Thaddeus.

'But I could be training now!'

'Don't reckon it takes much training to stick a bayonet in another man's guts.'

'Trouble with you is you don't give a toss what goes on so long as it doesn't get in the way of your blooming old roses!'

Unlike his father, Joe had a quick temper, which would subside with equal rapidity and leave him smiling ruefully. He continued to work hard, partly because he still retained something of the eager child's love of helping and desire to please, but also because hard work was born in him. The human body, the first practical machine on earth, was designed for a multitude of different tasks and he enjoyed mastering them all in turn. He was sorry when they had finished building the bungalow, and at his own suggestion finished it off with a neat row of palings enclosing a small front garden.

Then as the nursery grew, more barns and sheds had been needed and they built their first greenhouse. When Thaddeus bought another acre of land adjoining the nursery Joe ploughed it with their rattly second-hand tractor, and after it had been planted with specimens of his own breeding Thaddeus took Joe down to the King's Head for a pint of Greene King's best bitter.

'Good health, Dad.'

'And yours, son.'

'Beer's gunna git scarce.' Dolefully the landlord wiped a couple of glasses.

'Reckon he's set on coming, do you?' A very old man left his seat by the fire and peered out of the window as if Hitler might be approaching by bicycle.

Conversation became animated on the subject, and Thaddeus watched with a covert smile as young Joe, beer in hand, listened and nodded and looked judicious like all the rest.

At home, later that evening, he suddenly asked what his mother had been like. 'You never say much about her.'

'Well, you've seen pictures of her.'

Yes, he had, but only one or two small black-and-white snaps taken by his Auntie Marjorie on the wedding day, in which she appeared a tiny, rather doll-like figure dressed in white and clinging to his father's arm.

'Yes, but I mean what was she *like*?'

Thaddeus thought deeply before replying. 'She was the loveliest thing I've ever known, and losing her just about broke me up. Reckon there's no more to say.'

'Wonder if I'll find one like her.'

'Doubt it.'

Sensing that the conversation was now considered closed, Joe said no more, but newly sprung manhood made him wonder whether his father would ever consider marrying again. He was leading a funny ole man's life. His thoughts wandered back to the Auntie May they had seen quite a bit of at one time. He remembered her dark eyes and gentle, amused smile, and her little bobbing walk that had something robin-like about it. He had seen a picture of her in the local paper: *Miss May Farrinder, Area Welfare Officer in charge of arrangements concerning the little evacuees who have been entrusted to us for the duration . . .* She was wearing some kind of uniform, and smiling gravely from the centre of a group of apprehensive-looking children clutching gas masks in cardboard boxes. He told himself that he ought to look her up one day, particularly since she was supposed to be his godmother.

But increasingly the war news occupied his thoughts, and by the summer of 1940 it was impossible for anyone to ignore it.

The collapse of France and the hasty evacuation of the British Expeditionary Force from Dunkirk brought home a sensation of the Germans being almost within shouting distance; certainly the muffled boom of gunfire had been heard from across the Channel, and when the Battle of Britain began on the 10th of July the people of the Stour valley gazed in slow disbelief at the Spitfires and Hurricanes hedge-hopping in furious pursuit of Dorniers and Heinkels. One was brought down at Shilling Tye, and the white-faced young pilot found himself guarded by a ring of pitchforks

171

until the bobby arrived on his bike. He spent the night in the bobby's spare bedroom, and because he looked so young and scared they gave him an egg for his breakfast.

On the day Joe came back from Sudbury with the news that he'd passed A1 for the Suffolk Light Infantry he found his father sitting hunched at the kitchen table staring into space.

'I said I've passed the – '

'I heard you.'

'What's up, Dad?'

'What's up?' Thaddeus stirred himself. 'I tell you what's up. The man's been from the Ministry of Agriculture and said the nursery's got to go.'

'You mean *sell* it?' Joe sat down with a crash.

'No. I mean dig up all the roses and plant bloody cabbages.'

They sat in silence for a moment, Thaddeus staring at his clasped hands, then Joe said, 'You can't. Not after all that work.'

'That's what I tried to point out. Then he took it on himself to point out that the country's at war, which means there's a state of National Emergency – which means that if some sodding Whitehall official tells you to do something and you don't obey, you go to prison.'

Joe sighed deeply, then his face brightened. 'I know what. Pack it all up Dad, and come in the army with me.'

'Once was enough, thanks. Anyway, I'm too old.'

'You're not old, Dad . . .' But there was a certain lack of conviction in his voice which did nothing to dispel his father's gloom.

Old. Well, getting on for forty-three. A rose business just getting nicely established and then some citified bastard in a bowler hat coming down and telling him to plough the whole lot up. Seven hundred bushes or more. Just get rid of them – root them out, burn them and plant bloody cabbages.

Filled with impotent rage Thaddeus banged his heavy fists on the kitchen table, making the salt and pepper leap; he stood up, and tramped from one side of the room to the other, his large working boots clumping heavily on the lino he and Joe had laid so painstakingly. He had been given three weeks in which to complete the task of annihilation, and the savage injustice of the order made his head reel. Any prospect of sleep was out of the question.

Joe commiserated, genuinely concerned on his behalf, but three days after the blow had fallen felt bound to point out the new Ministry of Food's directive about tightening our belts, digging for victory, etc. If we didn't beat Hitler there'd be nobody left to grow roses, anyway. Even more to the point, there'd be nobody left to buy them.

Thaddeus had to agree. There was no arguing with the facts punched home in the new, thinner *Daily Mirror*, or broadcast to the nation in the stately tones of Stuart Hibbard or Alvar Liddell, but equally there was no reason why a man shouldn't rage and weep at a world in which destruction took precedence over creation.

'You're right, Dad,' Joe said, packing a small cardboard suitcase in readiness for departure, 'Can I take your pair of blue socks and leave you my brown'uns? Meant to wash'em but didn't get time . . .'

They said goodbye on Bures railway station where much the same scene had been re-enacted in 1916. Only then it had been November; now it was late July and the roses were in rapturous full bloom.

It was quiet without Joe, and Thaddeus closed his mind against the alacrity with which the boy had gone off to war. Over supper on that first night he tried to recapture his own feelings twenty-four years ago; there had been no jubilation, merely a deep apprehension hopefully camouflaged by the need to appear burningly brave. He had been in a rare ole state over Lady Isobel, he remembered; struggling to change his feelings from love to hate because of her betraying him the way she did.

He washed his supper dishes and put them away, then on the spur of the moment got out his old bicycle and pumped up the tyres. He rode down through Bures again, deserted now in the evening sun, and took the old familiar road that ran parallel with the Stour. There was no sign of aircraft activity and no sound apart from the quiet purring of his tyres. He rode on towards Marling, immersed in thoughts of the past, and when he came to the pompous main entrance to the Big House he dismounted, and began to push his bicycle up the drive.

A deeper silence reigned. Ivy-clad trees stood motionless on either side and slender arms of bramble stretched across the once

173

impeccably swept gravel. He walked on, and the chimneys of the Big House punctured the sky with a pathetic attempt at arrogance.

He stood looking at the scene for the first time since he was a kid of seventeen; dark venetian blinds drawn down like eyes closed in death; the grand portico tilting as one of its pillars crumbled, and cow parsley, thistles and docks clotting what had been smooth lawns round which the carriages and early, elegant motor cars had driven in triumphant arrival.

Propping his cycle against a rotting garden seat he walked round the terrace then struck off through the gardens, and the memories thickened. Mr Sims in breeches and small neat cap; poor ole Fenny Brewer – Fenny was still alive and in his St Dunstan's place, but Neddy who had lost a leg at the second battle of Ypres had died of gangrene some years back. All of them like ghosts now . . .
Yessir, nosir, touch your cap when I speak to you . . .

At first he failed to recognise the entrance to the rose garden. In place of cut yew hedging was a dense and sinister mass of bulging growth, almost black in the evening light. The archway was no more than a slight thinning in the branches. He pushed his way in, his heart thumping with something of the old trepidation.

It was almost impossible to identify the neat paths that had intersected the beds, but some of the roses were still there, struggling for survival against weeds and saplings. Bending to examine one, he saw that it had returned to the brier from which it had originated, and over in the far corner a white rose had managed to raise itself above the confusion like a small imploring hand. He stood motionless, slowly taking in the scene.

Do you like roses? Then you must cut some and take them home to your mother . . .

Her voice seemed to come out of the gathering shadows and he half expected to see the glimmer of her long white dress, the stately charm of her large Edwardian hat.

You must cut more. One is no use. Take her some of the pink ones . . . Do as I say . . .'

The low, well-modulated tones of authority. My lady, who had been the envy of every kitchen maid and the heroine of every stable boy, where she was now? People said that Sir Wilton and Lady Isobel had gone to live in London after they lost their fortune and their only son, and so far as he knew they had never come back to visit the area. And the Big House, after a brief spell as a girls' boarding school, had been left to languish and die like the gardens. All that work, he thought. All that hard work and hard discipline, and what for? What's to see for it now?

A rustling in the undergrowth made him start. A large hare bounded towards him, then paused, half-somersaulted, and leaped away in the opposite direction. He caught a glimpse of its large liquid eyes filled with fear. How many employees' eyes had been filled with the same emotion when the Big House had been at the height of its glory? Dozens, his own included. Doubtless the head cook had only learned how to turn out a perfect galantine after numerous slaps on the ear and bawlings out. Same with Mr Sims: he had acquired his expertise the hard way, and had made sure that the next generation learned their trade in a similar fashion. Perfection based on persecution.

He turned away from the rose garden, but he still couldn't get rid of the memories. Smooth summer lawns and the click of croquet mallets, the gentle plash of oars on the lake – God knows what state the lake was in now – the tinkle of teacups and the tuneful tattle of voices coming from beneath the cedar of Lebanon. All gone. Only ghosts now. And he himself was no more than a kind of ghost stealing through the darkling ruins of the place that had first inspired his love of women and roses.

He rode home through summer darkness pierced by the desultory roamings of a lone searchlight. The place was dead without young Joe. He went to bed without drawing the blackout, and moonlight doused the searchlight and sprinkled a silver pattern on his pillow. He couldn't sleep. Memories of the past and miseries about the future prevented it.

He thought about Joe, probably dossing down in an army tent somewhere, then his thoughts wandered to ole Ma, tough as twine and artful as a fox; a shame about her going on her own like that, yet his own country roots told him that dying in the starched white of a hospital bed would have sent her on her way filled with fear and despair. As it was, he believed that she had known the time was coming and had chosen her own way of acceptance; out across the autumn fields and curled up neat and quiet in the shelter of the hedge same as any other little ole free-running creature.

He missed her. Missed the quick beady glance from beneath the ole brown beret and the rapid patter of her plimsolled feet . . . He had grown up in the shelter of her parsimonious country ways and in the laconic strength of her love. And he had loved her too, although he couldn't recall any occasion upon which he had told her so . . . Thaddeus dozed for a few minutes and when he awoke he was thinking about May. Hadn't really thought about her for years. Funny what happened at the Fête that time, and it made him wonder how it would have been if they had married. He had wanted to marry her then, but perhaps not enough. At least, not enough to find out what had made her change all of a sudden; to go all sad and distant when before she had been so merry in her own gentle way. And then when he had discovered the probable cause – someone accidentally changing the name on the blackboard – why hadn't he gone to her and explained? He didn't know, didn't know.

He turned restlessly, punching his pillow and shutting his eyes to the moonlight that was now streaming across the bed. And the great upsurge of misery that he had so carefully kept at bay almost drowned him in its icy intensity.

In the name of the Ministry of Agriculture you are instructed to plough up your roses and in their place set cabbages and carrots, onions and potatoes. Failure to do so could result in the confiscation of your land under Section God-knows-what of the new Emergency Powers Act. Because of a man called Hitler he was supposed to go out and butcher more than seven hundred young plants, all of them in radiant bloom.

He got out of bed and padded through the bungalow. Joe's bedroom door stood open, the bed glimmering and empty. He decided to make a cup of tea but there was no spring water left in the can. So he lit a cigarette, and then the idea came to him.

It was no ideal solution, but in the circumstances better than nothing. He stubbed out his cigarette. Back in the bedroom he pulled on his working trousers, laced his heavy boots and went out into the moonlight. Hands on hips he stood surveying the scene for a moment, then began systematically to uproot all the white wooden palings that Joe had set a bare twelve feet from the front of the bungalow. There were fifty of them, twenty-five on each side of the front door, and he worked through the night steadily and stealthily, with only owls and foxes for company.

176

By sunrise every paling had been replaced twenty feet in front of its original position and he was left with a rectangular strip of cleanly dug soil. Even under the Emergency Powers Act a man was surely free to maintain a bit of private front garden – freedom was what we were supposed to be fighting for – and if the man chose to cram a hundred of his best and most valuable roses in it, it was surely his affair.

Four days later the operation was concluded. Astonished and resentful, the transplanted roses hung their leaves like worthless green rags, and were only placated by constant cans of water lugged across the meadow from the spring. They were the lucky ones; for their brethren had been ripped up, gathered up and burnt, and only the stray rose petal floating on the wind was left to sing their requiem.

Yet it was OK for some, for on the fifth day Bob Turner sped over on a rattling bicycle with the news that the Min. of Ag. was giving him free seed and a bit of financial help to get the farm back on its feet.

'They want us!' he cried, his hungry face twitching with an almost tearful joy. 'He was a rare little ole boy who called over at mine and laid his bowler hat on the table and told me us farmers are the backbone of Britain. We need you, he said, we need you to feed a nation at war with aggression. Like we need the miners, God bless'em, to keep the home fires burning we need you farmers to fill the larders of Britain so that our chaps can fight their best and our women and children can live healthy on bread and good vegetables until they return victorious!'

'Yes,' said Thaddeus the murderer. 'Nothing like a few Savoy cabbages to put heart into you.'

Enemy bombers on their way to the big cities continued to thicken the air with their droning, yet evacuees from the East End grew increasingly demoralised by the apparent torpor of the country-side. Endless fields intersected here and there by lanes going nowhere, all of it covered by an endless sky uninterrupted by comfortable roofs and smoking chimneys. The kids grizzled for sweets and the women were hungry for love, but with only the occasional skyline glimpse of a man hunched over the wheel of a grey Ferguson tractor while he obediently ploughed for Victory, their hunger remained unsatisfied. Most of them went back home, and Hoppity May closed up her cottage for the duration and transferred to Bethnal Green to help run a mobile canteen amongst the rubble.

Fear and foreboding laced with a certain obdurate defiance was the prevalent mood, and, used as a safety valve, the national fondness for grumbling became elevated to a high art. No beer, no fags, no petrol unless used for work of national importance; can't go here, can't go there; can't do this, can't do that – the military age limit was raised to fifty-one and women's service became compulsory. The war news grew steadily blacker. Singapore fell, so did Tobruk, and while the Germans and the Russians were locked in deadly combat on the Eastern Front Bob Turner went over to Noggin's Emporium and bought two new working shirts and four pairs of socks. As the proprietor was carefully snipping out his clothing coupons he asked her to marry him.

Startled, Dora said no. Then added, 'But thank you all the same.'

'I'm doing all right now. Got twelve pigs and a coupla cows.'

'These socks,' Dora said, folding them, 'are the new Utility range. Look, there's a mark, like two Cs.'

'I'm working all the hours God sends but at least they're paying me. I'm doing all right now, Dora.'

'That's nice. Everything's going to be Utility before long, which means that all goods will be guaranteed to a certain standard and the price will be controlled. The only snag is that the choice of styles and materials will be rather limited.'

'Don't reckon that'll bother me,' Bob said heartily. 'I got the one setta clothes for best and I don't look too hard at what I wear for work.'

'They've also brought Utility in as a way of beating the black market. I think it's wicked of people to try and make a profit out of the war.' Dora folded the socks and placed them on top of the shirts. 'Wrapping paper's a thing of the past, I'm afraid, but I've got a paper bag in the kitchen that hasn't been used – '

'Don't you fret about that, Dora. I got a heap of ole newspaper in the back of me little ole van outside. Seen me little ole van, have you?'

Dora said she hadn't, and deftly rang the money, warm from his trouser pocket, into the till.

'You wouldn't be sorry if you married me, Dora. I mean, I'd give you everything I got, and I'm doing nicely now. Apart from the livestock the Min. of Ag.'s taken over another great chunka land at the back of mine – used to belong to the ole Big House – and they're paying me for working that an' all. I ploughed it and rolled it last week.'

'Yes.'

'You mean, yes you'll marry me?' He tried to grab her hand.

'No.'

'Oh, go *on*, Dora. You won't have to do farmwork nor nothing. Well, maybe you'd like just a few hens – lotsa women seem to take to hens – but you needn't if you didn't want to.' Desperately seeking further inspiration he glanced round the wartime austerity of the Emporium. 'You could even keep this place on. I'd be glad for you to, if that's what you wanted – '

'Yes. I mean, no, thank you very much.'

'You're hard, Dora.'

'No, I'm not.'

'Yes, you are, dear. You're hard.'

'Look, there's your threepence change – '

'You don't mind me calling you dear, do you, Dora?'

'Call me what you like so long as you go. I've got lots of forms to fill in with all this Utility business.'

'I've got lots of forms too, Dora, and I can't understand the half of'em. They're just a loada grunt and I shove'em all behind the clock, truth to tell.'

'You'll get into trouble for that. You could be had up.'

'I know, Dora. But if we could only sit down with our two lots of forms together – '

'No, Bob.'

'Sit down nice and cosy of a winter's night, you and me at the kitchen table messin' about with our forms – Do you drink cocoa, Dora dear? Now are you *sure* you don't mind me calling you dear – '

Somehow she manoeuvred him to the door and thrust his purchases into his arms. She dropped the threepenny bit into his pocket.

'Seen me van, have you? Nice little ole van – got it offa chap in Colchester for fifteen quid – '

She stood in the shop doorway smiling gravely in her neat black skirt and hand-knitted jumper. It seemed like another hour before he stowed himself and his Utility clothing into the interior of the ramshackle vehicle. He lowered the driver's window; it fell the last six inches with a crash.

'I love you, Dora,' but his voice was lost in the sputtering roar of the engine. 'I love you, dear . . .'

She stood watching him go, then went back to the shop. Oh my God, she thought, aren't men *hopeless*. All women want is to be courted nice and *respectfully*.

Anyway, she wasn't sure she wanted to marry, and as blackout time approached she closed the shop, lit the ready-laid fire and sat down to a boiled egg and two slices of toast and margarine. So busy with his practical reasons for marrying her, he might have mentioned the additional advantage of putting their rations together, never mind their forms. Everyone agreed that single rations were very hard to live on – perhaps she and Thaddy and Bob had better combine domestic arrangements for the duration, she thought drily.

But no, she wasn't sure she wanted to marry. Although trade was bad now it would soon pick up again after the war, and anyway, the Emporium was now her world. She was her own boss and she made her own decisions. If ever she thought about the Buntings these days it was with chill indifference laced with a dash of amusement.

The tide of war began to turn in 1943 with the destruction of the German army at Stalingrad, then later with the surrender of Italy.

In rural Britain six million more acres had been added to the twelve million under cultivation before 1939, and Bob Turner, working with the manic glee of an invalid unexpectedly restored to perfect health, applied to the Min. of Ag. for help with the harvest. They sent him some more forms, which he shoved behind the clock from force of habit. Then, reconsidering, he rattled over to Stoke Abbey with them, and Dora helped him to fill them in. They did not sit over a cosy kitchen table, but leaned uncomfortably and far apart over the stretch of counter behind which peacetime knitting wools had been on display.

He posted the forms, and received instructions to await the arrival of Additional Labour (Agricultural) under Section

180

something-or-other of the Emergency Powers Act. In the meanwhile he rose before daylight to feed the stock and milk the two cows and was up on the old Ferguson as the sun's first rays touched the treetops. Dirty stubble covered his cheeks and chin and the dust of harvest covered his hair and clothes. Strained beyond endurance his braces snapped; he chucked them aside and secured his trousers with a length of bailer twine. He took his bait with him on the tractor, swallowing hunks of bread and his bit of agricultural worker's extra cheese as he bounced and jounced to the rhythmical clack-clack of the binder. His Labour (Agricultural) arrived when the harvesting was just about finished, and with the fields stripped to stubble he had time for a quick breather before starting to plough.

The idea came to him when he was sorting through the pile of forms stuffed behind the clock. He stuffed them back again, then got out the pad of lined paper, charged the dip pen from the bottle of Stephen's ink and wrote painstakingly, *Dear Dora, I hope you are well. Myself I am not above middling on account of my bad leg which is why I am writing to ask if you will come over and help me with one or two forms which I must fill up or get prosicuted. I would come over to yours but at this present moment cannot drive. If you thought of coming over on your half closing I would make us some nice tea. Your resperctful friend Bob.*

He drove down to the village to post it, and on returning set to and washed a shirt. While it dried he polished his shoes and got out his best trousers. Still not satisfied, he drove over to Jack Oats, who cut hair in his spare time, and paid fourpence for a short back and sides. Then he bought some fresh bread and made sardine sandwiches of heroic proportions and arranged a selection of clumsy village cakes (unrationed) on a plate that had belonged to his Grandma.

She arrived, as she had said she would, alighting neatly from her bicycle and brushing her gloved fingers together. Remembering to limp he went out to meet her, and tried to look both ill and casually offhand.

'How did you hurt your leg?'

'Tripped over in the stackyard.'

'You weren't looking where you were going.'

'That's a fact. Got something better to do with me eyes these days.'

181

He led her indoors, where the kettle was singing and the tea laid out ready on the table.

'What about these forms?'

'We'd better do'em after. Maisie always likes her tea prompt.'

'Maisie?'

As if on cue, but in reality by mere chance, a girl glad in green breeches and an open-necked shirt came into the kitchen without knocking and said, 'Hey Bob, did you remember to ask about the chicken feed?' Seeing Dora, she stopped abruptly, grinned, and said 'Hi, kid.'

'Good-afternoon.'

'Are you Bob's girlfriend?' Maisie perched her behind on the corner of the table and looked at Dora with friendly interest. She was a well-built girl and all in splendid proportion, with full, firm breasts jutting beneath her shirt and a lot of curly red hair tumbling on to her shoulders.

'No,' said Dora. 'My name is Dora Noggin and I own the Emporium at Stoke Abbey.'

'What's an emporium when it's at home?' Without waiting for a reply Maisie swung her breeches off the table and said, 'Blimey, what a smashing tea! Can we start?'

'If Dora's ready,' Bob said, looking at Maisie.

'I expect you want to wash your hands first, don't you?' enquired Dora, also looking at her.

'Too right!' Maisie agreed heartily, 'nothing pongs worse than chicken muck.'

Sloshing water into the bowl she abluted violently, scattering drops on the floor and emerging from the roller-towel crimson faced. Bob laughed, still looking at her.

'About the forms,' Dora said, accepting a sardine sandwich. 'How many are there? I can only stay for a short while.'

'About six or seven, I reckon. Oh – thanks, gal – ' Maisie was pouring the tea and passing the cups as if she lived there. Which of course she did, presumably.

They ate in silence for a few minutes, then with a visible effort Dora asked Maisie if she came from Suffolk.

'Oh crikey, no, I come from Romford! Used to work in the Income Tax Office and the war gave me the chance to get out. I just couldn't stand being shut in all day.' She took a mouthful of tea, then grinned across at Bob. 'Wouldn't mind settling in the country full time.'

'Have a cake, Dora,' Bob said as he noticed her expression. 'Go on, do you have one of them nice little tarts.'

'I don't think I could manage it,' Dora said. 'I don't normally eat tea.'

'That's what living in an emporium does for you,' commented Maisie, winking at Dora. 'Gimme a load of hens' muck any day!'

Too deeply troubled and affronted to recognise the unblemished geniality and sheer innocent high spirits of Bob's landgirl, Dora asked in a stifled little voice whether she couldn't help her employer with his forms, seeing that she had once worked in an office.

'No damn fear! I said goodbye to form-filling the day I left the Inland Revenue,' Maisie said through a mouthful of wartime currant bun. 'Any case, I expect Bob'd rather you did them than me.' Her smile, playfully sensuous, said *After all, I perform most other services for him*.

'Couldn't do without you, Dora dear,' Bob said soothingly.

'In that case, we'd better get on with them, hadn't we? As I said, I haven't much time to spare.' Dora moved back her chair. 'Perhaps we could do them in the other room – we don't want them smelling of sardines, do we?'

Hastily remembering to limp, Bob took her into the front room and sat in silence while she explained the ramifications, and then filled in some of the more difficult sections in pencil.

'So, it that all?'

'Yes thank you, Dora.'

'There wasn't anything too dreadful, once you put your mind to it.'

'No, Dora. Reckon I'll learn in time.'

They sat looking at one another for a moment and conflicting emotions chased across Dora's face like clouds across a windy sky.

'I must go,' she said finally. 'Say goodbye to – I forget her name.'

'It's Maisie, Dora. Maisie.'

'Maisie, then. And by the way, how's your leg?'

'Still painful. But I'm carrying on the best I can.'

He walked with her, limping, to where her bicycle was propped against the wall. Slowly she pulled on her gloves and stood smoothing the fingers one by one.

'Funny to think you asked me to marry you.'

'What's funny about it?'

'Well . . . things have changed, haven't they?'

'Nothing's changed, Dora. Except – Christ Almighty, I've had me hair cut and polished me boots and cleaned me nails and got a clean shirt on, all because you were a-coming – ' Suddenly exasperated, he turned away. 'What else am I supposed to do, hey? Just you tell me that.'

'You could say you love me,' she mumbled, and scarlet in the face leaped on to her bicycle and pedalled furiously away.

The war had taken another decisive step towards victory when a small army truck drove up to the bungalow at Maplestead. The corporal driver emerged at the same time that Thaddeus appeared round the corner.

'Mr Noggin? Brought you your bod, sir. Mind signing for him?'

Thaddeus looked baffled, then exasperated. 'I said I didn't want anyone. I wrote and said I didn't.'

'Must be a cock-up.' The corporal thumbed through a folder of papers. 'No Sir, it says here Mr Thaddeus Noggin – that is you, isn't it, Sir? – is entitled to one working POW until the end of hostilities and such time as repatriation takes place.'

'I've already made it clear that I don't need anyone.'

'Well, he's a good bloke,' the corporal said. 'Besides which, it's Ministry policy to keep as many of them usefully occupied as we can. Helps pay for their keep, like.'

Thaddeus remained unimpressed.

'Gotta lotta work here, Sir.' The corporal glanced round at the small fields obediently set with potatoes, onions, carrots and cabbages. 'Really do think you could do with some help.' Then he banged his fist on the truck's bonnet and shouted, 'Come on out – let's seeyer!'

The man who emerged was wearing khaki and had coloured diamonds sewn on the sleeves of his battledress. He wasn't a youngster, perhaps as much as thirty-five, and the hollows in his cheeks gave him a melancholy look. He stood silent, as if accustomed to being appraised.

184

'Good worker,' said the corporal, handing Thaddeus a folder of documents, 'and no back answers.'

'Helmut Kubler,' Thaddeus read aloud.

'*Hel-moot*,' corrected the German impassively.

'Get your kit.' The corporal jerked his head at the rear of the truck, then turning to Thaddeus, lowered his voice: 'Won't give you no trouble, mate. Keeps hisself to hisself and this here's his ration book.'

The German dragged a small, travel-worn kitbag from the truck's interior, then stood motionless.

'We'll be keeping an eye on him,' the corporal assured Thaddeus as he signed the receipt, 'but givvus a buzz if he gets funny. Know where we are, don't you?'

Gloomily Thaddeus said that he did; everyone knew that the poor ole Big House had had the worst of its neglect tidied up before being turned into a German POW camp.

The truck roared away, and he was left in sole charge of Helmut Kubler, whom he hadn't asked for and didn't want.

'Come on,' he said with an effort, 'I'll show you where you can sleep.'

'Zleep?'

'Sleep – ' Thaddeus folded his hands and rested his cheek on them.

'Zleep *now*?' The German looked incredulous.

'Do what you bloody well like until eight o'clock tomorrow morning,' Thaddeus said, and led the way to the small outhouse, the first that he and young Joe had attempted to build. It still smelt of apples and there was only an earth floor, but he had placed a row of duckboards between it and the grudgingly improvised bed of chickenwire nailed to four stout wooden posts and covered with an old flock mattress. There were two blankets, a hook behind the door upon which to hang clothes, and, although still hopeful that a POW would not be forced upon him, Thaddeus had arranged a tea chest covered by an old curtain upon which stood a tin bowl, an enamel jug containing water, and a small square of flyblown mirror.

'Best I can do,' Thaddeus said gruffly, and stumped off without bothering to register his guest's reaction.

God knows, this was the last thing he wanted. Accustomed now to living and working on his own, the compulsory infliction of a Jerry POW seemed the final proof that the freedom we were supposed to be fighting for had already vanished beyond recall; been smothered, been certified dead and buried beneath a blizzard of rules and regulations concocted by a lot of bilious half-baked ole London bastards in bowler hats who . . . Rage choked him.

What would young Joe think? Young Joe had survived the evacuation from Greece and had fought at El Alamein; where he was now God only knew, but if he was still alive he wouldn't think too much of some lousy murdering kraut sleeping under blankets that rightly belonged on his bed. What a world.

He finished work early and went back to the bungalow, nervously ill at ease at the thought of the German in the outhouse. What was he doing? Unpacking his kitbag? Lying on the bed smoking? Suppose he set fire to the place . . . suppose he did a bunk? But when Thaddeus returned to the outhouse the German was doing none of these things. He sat sitting on the edge of the bed staring down at his hands, and never in his life had Thaddeus seen a man so hopelessly dejected.

'Eat,' he said loudly. 'Come on, time to eat.'

The German followed him back to the bungalow and his pale eyes seemed to brighten for an instant at the sight of the kitchen. Although it was fairly plain and stark there was a warm glow coming from the stove and on the rag rug in front of it a striped cat lay dozily licking its paw.

'Sit down.' Thaddeus indicated the kitchen chair once used by young Joe, then banged down a couple of knives and forks. Obediently the German seated himself, then said with a terrible effort, 'Zmell goot!'

'Nothing special. Everything's rationed due to the war.' *You do know there's a war on, don't you? And that it was your lot started it . . .*

Resentment flared again, but scrupulously Thaddeus divided the mess of fried-up potato and covered each of the two portions with baked beans. He slapped one of the plates down in front of the German, then cut some thick chunks of bread and passed one on the tip of the knife. *Couple more inches and I'd have this stuck in your gizzard . . .* The German accepted what he had been given with a formal inclination of the head, and began to crumble the bread on the side of his plate. His fingers were thin and surprisingly well kept for those of a soldier and POW. *Never mind, we'll soon change that for you . . .*

They began to eat. The constraint between them was stifling as a blanket: two men on opposing sides of a war sitting on opposite sides of a table, and with no common language to help them define personal reactions. Two men sitting down to supper, one of them the elected conquerer now reduced to the rank of slave-labourer. Staring at their plates they continued to eat; the German surreptitiously impaled the last morsel of bread on his fork and wiped up the final vestiges of food. They both ate an apple, the German peeling and quartering his while Thaddeus took lusty bites and chomped defiantly. The cat got up, stretched, and walked with arched back towards the German's chair. She rubbed against his legs and he caressed her with a lingering hand. 'Poosy. You nice poosy.'

'You know a bit of English, then?'

'Leedle bit English, leedle bit French, leedle bit Italian. Zat iss all.'

'Better'n me, at any rate.' Thaddeus got up to make a cup of tea, and when he turned round from the stove the German was nursing the cat.

'You have cat – at home?'

'Please?'

'Cat. You have. In Germany?'

'Ach, yes. In Germany ve hef many cats.'

At the conclusion of supper Thaddeus offered his companion a cigarette and they disposed of the dirty dishes together, Thaddeus washing and the German drying. It felt ridiculous. When they had finished, Thaddeus pointed to the dial on the kitchen clock and said, 'Six. Six o'clock tomorrow. You get up. We work.'

'Ach, yes,' the German agreed, and departed for the outhouse.

And that was the beginning of a strange relationship. Intimate inasmuch as they worked and ate together, yet miles apart because of the language barrier and because of mutual preference. Then it occurred to Thaddeus that there would have been little point in discussing the war, supposing they had been able to, for their own personal feelings had little part in it anyway; ole Chamberlain hadn't asked Thaddeus Noggin whether or not he was prepared to be at war with Germany and he doubted whether this sad-eyed Jerry had been consulted either. All they could do was to make the best of a bad job.

The German worked conscientiously, although it was obvious that his interest in the cultivation of vegetables was also minimal. His hands blistered, and Thaddeus advised him to rub them with paraffin to toughen the skin. He learned to drive the tractor, to plough and to drill, and the more they became accustomed to one another the less need there seemed for language – hand signs and facial expressions being sufficient for most things.

Sometimes it was like a couple of deaf mutes living together, and occasionally something about their relationship reminded Thaddeus of the strange and fundamental harmony that had existed between his father's two old Suffolks, Boxer and Bowler, up at the Big House farm. He had no particular desire to like the German, but as the months passed there seemed less and less reason to dislike him. Perhaps his attitude was best expressed by the way in which he tended to address him; no longer the impolite and impersonal You, but the half-friendly, half-challenging nationalistic nickname of Fritzy. The German accepted it, and answered to it in the way that a stray dog would accept the name of Fido.

Yet there were times when Thaddeus felt impelled to talk to him. Perhaps after work on a summer evening they would sit outside with a bottle of thin wartime beer and it was natural to speak one's thoughts aloud.

'Roses are my proper trade, but I've had to pack it up for the duration. Nobody wants roses now. These here outside the front are the only ones I managed to save – had to plant 'em much too close, but there was no other way. Most of them took a hold all right, but they're spindly. No proper space to breathe. Still, they'll come in for raising new stock.'

The German would nod, perhaps fulfilled in the same way as Thaddeus.

'I was in the last war, y'know. Maybe I fought against a member of your family. My own boy's in this one. He was mad for me to buy him a gun when he was a kid . . . reckon this lot'll have cured him. Best thing he can do is come in the rose business with me when this lot's over . . .'

He could have asked the German if he had kids too – *How many Kinder, Fritzy?* – but he didn't. Somehow he wasn't sufficiently interested, which was just as well because Fritzy betrayed no apparent urge to confide in him. As a character he appeared polite, hard-working and extremely reticent, and with these three characteristics Thaddeus was well content. His reaction was much the same when in a spell of bitter weather he suggested that Fritzy should sleep in the bungalow and Fritzy politely refused. If he preferred the damp cold and icy draughts of the outhouse, it was his lookout; Thaddeus didn't particularly want him in young Joe's bed anyway.

Yet on the morning he came back from the newsagent's with the daily paper filled with photographs of the Dresden bombing he scanned it quickly and then tore it up. There was no good reason to gloat over mass destruction, and for all he knew Dresden might have been Fritzy's home town.

That was in mid-February, and April was breathing a warm breath over the land when Thaddeus said as casually as possible, 'Looks as if the war'll soon be over now.'

Hoeing between rows of young cabbage plants the German straightened his back with a grimace of pain. 'Zer vor. . . ?'

'Nearly over.'

'Who winning?' There could have been a gleam of humour in his eyes.

'Looks like we are. But I suppose there's still time.'

'Adolf Hitler,' the German said meditatively, 'very bad, very stupid man.'

'You think so?'

'I zink and I know.'

'In that case, I reckon I can tell you. He's just committed suicide. You know . . . killed himself.'

Fritzy received the news in silence. He shrugged, then continued hoeing while Thaddeus trudged back to the bungalow to make a cup of tea.

Eight days later the war was over, and Thaddeus went into the kitchen that evening to hear the six o'clock news. Rather to his surprise the radio was already on, playing some heavy kind of music, and Fritzy was sitting at the kitchen table with his head in his hands.

189

Even out in Flanders Thaddeus was unable to recollect ever having seen a man cry like that. Curse, rage, sweat with pain, but never cry with that terrible silent concentration. He realised then that Fritzy had been trying to make the best of a bad job when he had said that Hitler was a bad and stupid man. Germany had lost the war and he was a German; also, presumably, a patriot.

The music faded, Big Ben struck majestically and the dry tones of the announcer said that it was all over. Thaddeus switched it off, then patted Fritzy awkwardly on the shoulder. 'Don't fret, boy. Reckon you'll be off home soon.' *But what to, Christ only knows . . .*

They had a bottle of beer with their Spam and eggs that night, and it occurred to Thaddeus that technically speaking he and Fritzy were no longer enemies. Perhaps one of the greatest moments in history should have broken the barriers of reticence – almost inadvertently they had now learned to converse in a working idiom of their own devising – but it didn't happen. Not only was Thaddeus reluctant to show triumph in the presence of the loser, he could in all honesty see little reason to rejoice apart from the fact that it would bring young Joe back home. As with the other war, the peace had come too late and the price paid for it had been too high.

They went to bed at the customary hour and the deep silence of rural Suffolk carried no sounds of revelry. Thaddeus lay staring into the darkness while the image of Fritzy's silent weeping burnt into his mind.

He was repatriated the following autumn, and when Thaddeus handed him a five-pound note in addition to his meagre wages he drew back sharply. 'No, I cannot. Iss too much.'

'Go on, take it.' Thaddeus stuck it into the German's work-thickened hand. 'I've quite enjoyed having you here, Fritzy. You've been a good worker and a good mate, but let's get one thing clear: if you and your lot ever try it on again, I'll find you and I'll personally blow your bloody brains out. Understand?'

The German nodded, and began to smile. Amazingly, his smile turned to laughter, the hearty, body-shaking laughter of a man suddenly made free.

'Maybe I come back,' he said, 'but not dressed like zo – ' He grabbed the front of his work-stained battledress and shook it, still laughing.

'OK, come back on a visit, but leave your mates behind – '

'Oh *ja* – I come viz mates but different ones . . .'

They clasped hands, laughing into one another's eyes, and then the army truck arrived. The German clicked his heels and gave a touching, formal little bow to which Thaddeus responded with a salute.

He stood watching the departing truck until it had turned into the lane outside, and an intolerable sense of loneliness enveloped him. Turning away he picked up the walking stick that Fritzy had fashioned from an ash tree branch, and wandered through the small fields where they had worked together in silence for so long. A chill wind licked at him, and he recalled the latest rallying call from the Min. of Ag. *The war may be over but supplies of food are still desperately short. Britain's larder is almost empty. Unless we increase our output it may become necessary to ration bread and potatoes . . .*

No one would think we were the victors. The sense of loneliness became charged with angry frustration, and he swung Fritzy's walking stick at a row of savoys as he passed. It made a pleasing *thwack* as shreds of green leaf flew up. He walked on, swiping to left and right. A rabbit sat up and looked at him in astonishment for a moment before bounding hurriedly away.

At the end of the cabbage field he walked back, gloomily relishing the debris he had caused; the sky was grey, the world was grey, poor ole Fritzy had gone back to God knows what sort of conditions, and over here there was nothing to look forward to except increased austerity and the prospect of growing more bloody vegetables. He was tired, everyone was tired, and apart from the lack of bombs peacetime was proving worse than the war.

Returning to the bungalow he passed through the front garden where the crammed roses were dropping their leaves. Their spindly growth sickened him further. Stooping to pick a couple of late buds he carried them indoors together with Fritzy's walking stick. Later that evening he went down to the King's Head, but the beer was too weak to get drunk on. He returned home as sober as when he set out.

1951

Silver pink flushed with pale gold; very full; well shaped. Fragrant; vigorous upright growth. Dark foliage; young growth bronze red. Known to its breeder as *Rosa X*.

Slowly Thaddeus turned the cut bloom in his fingers, appraising the curl of the outer petals away from the high centre. *Rosa X*. The first peacetime rose he had raised, and who wanted it?

No one, apparently. Although the years of enforced market gardening were over and the nursery had been restored to its rightful occupants, trade was slow. People were too busy watching television and buzzing about in their new Morris Minors to bother about planting roses.

He was now fifty-two. Very tall and spare, with fine lines at the corners of his far-seeing, meditative eyes and a skin dyed by the weather to a tawny gold. Regarded locally as reserved to the point of taciturnity, he would pass the time of day in the village, and in the pub could be impelled to deprecate the rise in the cost of cigarettes, but there it ended. He would cycle back to the bungalow, perhaps prepare a bit of supper then go to bed and sleep the heavy dreamless sleep of one who works out of doors in all weathers.

The roses were all he needed. They were his life, his love, his joy. But nobody needed them.

'You about?' A head appeared round the open door.

'Reckon so.' Thaddeus replaced the rose in its jam jar of water and pushed it away from him. 'Come on in, Bob.'

Bob Turner, now on the plump side, was dressed in a tweed jacket and cord trousers. He was also wearing a collar and tie and his whole presence radiated a modest affluence.

'Bin down to Bures so I thought I'd give you a look.' He seated himself.

'Glad you did. Brought Dora?'

'No, she's busy in Sudbury but she sent you all the best.'

Thaddeus grunted acknowledgement, then got up to make a cup of tea.

Things were going well with Bob and Dora Turner. Married now for almost five years, they were childless but happy together in a rather prosaic and unspectacular way. They enjoyed the same ideal of hard work as a pathway to modest success and both had been seared by life – Dora emotionally and Bob financially. But now they were secure. Agricultural policy was seeing to it that British farming should not be allowed to slip back into the pre-war doldrums, and Dora had bought another shop in Sudbury.

It was another draper's, but run on classier lines than the old Emporium. In Sudbury she sold nylon stockings and long New Look frocks and skirts, but in Stoke Abbey, where change seemed to be regarded with misgiving, she kept to men's working shirts and women's pink calico corsets, but with a nice line in curtaining and knitting wools. She employed a total of five shop assistants and a woman cleaner, and treated them all with kindness sometimes masked a little by shyness. But her business acumen was acute, and only now and then was she suddenly impelled to fling herself into Bob's arms and cling to him as if the strange horrors of the old Buntings could still touch her. 'You *do* love me, don't you. Say you do – go on, *say* it!'

And he would hold her with all his strength, almost crushing the breath out of her because he was concerned and mystified that she should come over all funny in a way that wasn't her at all.

'I love you, Dora dear. Always have and always will, s'welp me if that isn't God's own truth.'

'I love you too!' Then she would free herself and say with a touch of the old primness, 'Sorry about that. Expect I'm just a bit tired, that's all.'

They still lived at Bob's smallholding behind the Big House, but had made improvements to the place, mainly in the form of being connected to mains water and electricity. They remained on friendly if distant terms with Marjorie and her husband, but generally invited Thaddeus over for Sunday dinner; an invitation he generally accepted.

Now, as he poured the tea, Thaddeus became conscious of his brother-in-law's discerning gaze. 'Heard anything from young Joe?' Bob asked.

'Not since he went back off leave. Still in the same place on the Rhine.'

193

'How long are we going on with this Army of Occupation lark?'

'God knows. At least they're not killing each other.'

'Reckon you could do with him here, couldn't you?'

Thaddeus grunted. 'Have a biscuit.'

'Trade looking up?'

'Can't say it is. Maybe it's still early days.'

'That one's a beauty.' Bob transferred his gaze to the new rose standing in the jam jar. 'What's it called?'

'Haven't got round to naming it yet.'

The sound of a vehicle drawing up outside made them pause. Thaddeus stood up and peered through the window. 'It's the military. Wonder if that's young Joe – '

Bob stood on tiptoe and peered over his shoulder. A uniformed officer got out, briefly appraised his surroundings then strode round to the front door, which was seldom used. Thaddeus opened it with an effort.

'Mr ah . . . Noggin? How do you do? I'm Colin Atherton, Adjutant of the Royal Suffolk Fusiliers.'

'What can I do for you?' Thaddeus eyed him distrustfully, then added, 'You'd best come in.'

They stood together in the front room that smelt of damp wallpaper and the officer removed his cap and said, 'Well now, Mr Noggin, I've called to see whether you can help us. I dare say you know that a lot of our chaps copped it pretty badly during the heavy fighting in Normandy. Place called Avranches. Yes. Right. Now the fact is this. Our Commanding Officer is arranging to co-operate with the French authorities in planting a garden of remembrance which will be partly dedicated to our chaps, and the C.O.'s particularly keen to have flowers and stuff from their own part of the world. You know the kind of thing, Suffolk shrubs, Suffolk flowers and so on. But it's proving easier said than done. Most of the nurseries we've approached have put up rather a poor show – haven't quite got geared up to peacetime – then someone told me that you grow roses as a kind of speciality so thought I'd pop along and give you a look-see.'

'Yes,' said Thaddeus heavily. 'How many would you be . . . ?'

'Oh, I should say a couple of hundred or so. Think you could manage that?'

Breathing hard, Thaddeus said that it might be arranged.

194

'Some nice reds and pinks that'll give a good show. You know the kind of thing.'

'Yes. I think I know. And when would you . . . ?'

'The answer to that is always as soon as possible, but you dig 'em up in the autumn, don't you?' The Adjutant slipped his hand inside his tunic and extracted a card. 'That's me. Perhaps you could give me a buzz on extension 205 as soon as you've had time to sort something out. You must be jolly busy these days, but I know the C.O.'s dead keen to get something sorted out pretty pronto – ' he strode towards the door, then looked back at Thaddeus – 's'matter of fact my mother's favourite rose was a neat little job called *The Fairy* – know it, do you?'

'Polyantha. Free flowering – '

'But I'm not too sure the chaps would appreciate having fairies in their memorial garden! Still – do what you can, won't you?' He bounded briskly through the front door, replacing his cap as he went. 'Keep in touch. Cheers.'

'What did he want?' Bob looked apprehensive. 'Joe, was it?'

'No. He just called to ask if he could make me a rich man. And I didn't say no.'

Thaddeus began to laugh, crashing his large fist down on the table so that the new rose leaped in its jam jar. 'A couple of hundred or so, he said!'

'What – quid?'

'No, rosebushes.' His laughter became a long bellow threaded with anguish. 'When that young fella danced in here I thought oh Christ, Joe, what've you bin up to . . . then roses, he said, roses for a place out in France . . . and when I asked how many, thinking he'd say six or seven – '

'All the way to France?' Bob reiterated incredulously. 'Don't they grow their own over there, then?'

'They want English ones,' Thaddeus sobered. 'Better than that, they want Suffolk ones and they're going to plant them in a memorial garden where the poor ole Suffolk Fusiliers copped it. He reckoned they'd like that.'

'Reckon they would, too.'

'It'll take pretty near all the stock I've got ready, but there's some nice little maidens coming on – '

'They'd like some nice little maidens, poor bleeders – '

They began to laugh again. Thaddeus swept aside the tea and substituted a bottle and two glasses.

'Snaps. Joe brought it home on leave last time. Fair takes the roof off your mouth.'

They drank, grimacing, and Thaddeus shook his head in wonderment. 'A coupla hundred straight off, just like that! Talk about miracles . . .'

'It's being wanted that counts,' Bob said. 'I know. I bin through it.'

Being wanted. That was the heart of it. Having skills, knowledge, experience, but perhaps above all the kind of loving respect for a subject that thrives upon being shared.

The thought of it drove him to work harder than ever. When November came Bob Turner lent him a couple of his men to help lift the plants and pack them. And when Dora informed the local press that a Maplestead grower had been given the honour of supplying roses for a memorial garden in France they published the story in detail together with a photograph of Thaddeus standing tall and inscrutable with secateurs in hand.

At last the long-awaited customers began to arrive. In ones and twos to begin with, bumping up the driveway and asking if this was the place where Mr Noggin grew roses. The ole gent, name of Pavlicek who lived at the Willows, brought a couple of his foreign friends and between them they ordered two dozen *Peace*, the great hybrid tea bred by Meilland that was not only a Gold Medal winner but, because of its name, regarded as a symbol of the future.

Thaddeus would leave his work and attend to their requirements, giving advice when it was asked for and inscribing each order in a big earth-stained ledger in the potting-shed that had now become an office. He found the same customers returning, and decided that it would be expedient to stock a few other plants as well, but only those compatible with roses. So he rigged up a stall and sold pots of delphiniums and marguerites, lobelias and pansies, then took Dora's advice and employed a professional signwriter to repaint the faded name at the gate: T. NOGGIN ROSE GROWER & NURSERYMAN. (He was tempted to make it T. NOGGIN & SON, but prudence prevailed. Joe didn't seem all that keen on the idea of growing roses, although once he got out of the Forces he might see things differently.)

196

It was on a day in early June when a midday shower had moistened the soil and raindrops lay glittering on the leaves that Thaddeus saw the blonde woman with the rucksack wandering along the paths between the roses. She walked musingly, with her head bent, and there was a curious kind of intentness about her. She appeared to be gazing at the roses without really seeing them, and when he finally stepped into her line of vision and asked if she was looking for anything in particular, she raised her head and looked at him unsmilingly.

'Yes,' she said. 'I am looking for the place where my husband worked when he was a prisoner of war. His name was Helmut Kubler.'

Apart from Dora, few women entered the bungalow and it was strange to see the blonde woman – Mrs Kubler, he supposed he must call her – sitting at the kitchen table smoking a cigarette.

'When I told him not to come back I was only kidding,' Thaddeus said rather awkwardly. 'No hard feelings, he knew that. So, where is he?'

'He died of cancer eleven months after he came home.' She spoke English with careful precision and only a slight accent. 'He only complained of feeling ill during the last few weeks.'

Thaddeus passed a hand over his face, then looked away from her. 'I'm very sorry to hear that,' he said finally. 'Very sorry indeed.'

'I loved him.' The woman sat staring at the smoke curling from her cigarette.

'Quite right too. He was a good little ole boy.'

'Little?' She appeared to examine the word. 'No, I think he was not very little.'

'Sorry, it's a way we have of talking round these parts. Fri –Helmut was a good friend of mine.'

'And a good little old boy.' She looked across at him with the ghost of a smile, and her eyes were a silvery grey blue. Then she suddenly added, 'Please, may I see where he slept?'

'Well. If you really want to.'

'It is important to me.'

She left her rucksack on the floor and followed him through the garden to the small outhouse that had once been her husband's

197

home. The bed was still there, the blankets folded as he had left them. She looked round in silence at the tea chest draped with the mouse-nibbled old curtain, at the tin bowl and enamel jug and small square of cobwebbed mirror. It was exactly as he had left it except for a pile of empty seed trays dumped in one corner.

'He lived in here, all that time.' She moved across to the bed, sat down on the edge and ran her hands over it.

'Not up to much, I know,' Thaddeus muttered. 'But we all lived pretty rough in the war.'

'Because of us,' she said. 'Because of German madness.'

He would have been happy to agree, but instinctive courtesy prevented it. 'It was a bad time for everybody.'

He stood looking down at her, then turned away as she took the top fold of blanket in both hands and held it against her face. She closed her eyes, breathing deeply like an animal trying to catch an elusive scent.

Helmut was dead. He couldn't believe it. Helmut, otherwise ole Fritzy, and this was his wife sitting here.

'I'm sorry,' her voice broke into his thoughts. 'I knew it would be hard for me to come here, but I had to.' Reluctantly she smoothed the blanket back in place and stood up. 'I will go now.'

'You can't go yet,' Thaddeus said, moved by her dignity. 'You'd better have something to eat first. And I've still got a bit of snaps left, if you'd like that.'

'Schnapps?' She looked surprised for a moment, then laughed. At least, it was almost a laugh. 'I don't drink spirits, but thank you, Mr Noggin.'

'You know my name all right, then.'

'Of course I do. Helmut spoke of you very often. And it was by your name that I found my way here.'

'How did you travel?' They walked back to the bungalow.

'The cheap way. Third-class train and boat, and walking. I like to walk, and at this time of the year the country is beautiful.'

'Where are you staying now?'

'Nowhere. I came straight here.'

'I dare say they might put you up at the King's Head. Nothing fancy, but – '

'I had not planned to stay.'

'Doesn't make sense to turn round and go straight back.' He

didn't quite know what made him say that, but he meant it. He made a pot of tea and got out the cups and saucers. 'What I mean is, you'll tire yourself out. No sense in doing that, so put up at the pub for a couple of days.'

'Pub?' She examined the word as if it were a strange insect.

'Public house.'

'That means it is free?'

'Well no, but they won't charge you more than a couple of bob –shillings, I mean.' He cut two slices of cherry cake from the tin.

'You are very kind.' She drank her tea and ate her piece of cake as if she were very hungry. Then leaned back in her chair and said, 'Please Mr Noggin, speak to me about Helmut. What he did here, what it was like for him.'

Thaddeus hesitated. She hadn't actually cried, sitting there on his bed – she didn't seem the crying sort – but he saw no point in upsetting her unnecessarily. At the same time he realised that to mutter conventional platitudes would somehow demean the relationship that he and Fritzy had built between them.

'It didn't come all that easy to start with – ' he pushed another slice of cake towards her – 'To be honest, I didn't want him any more than I reckon he wanted me. We just got shoved together because of the war. But we grew to be friends slow and gradual, the way you should do, I suppose – and I'll tell you one thing: he did more than work for his keep. Didn't need telling twice about anything, and once I'd shown him how to do a thing and managed to explain what I wanted – he'd go at it slow and steady and careful until it was finished. We had a bit of a job with the language of course, but we found a way round it and after a time he seemed to settle in quite comfortable. Kept himself to himself, rather the way I do, I dare say, but we got along pretty well and I was sorry when he went.'

He poured more tea while the woman sat with her head bent over her cake.

'I only saw him give way the once, and that was when peace was declared. I came in to hear the news and Fr – Helmut was already in here with the radio on and he just seemed to break down. Wasn't surprising of course, and truth to tell I felt a bit awkward about it – us winning and him losing, I mean – but never in my life did I see a man cry so dreadful.'

199

'He told me. He told me that just before the announcement they were playing Elgar, and it was the first real music he had heard for five years.' She looked up at him with her strange silvery grey-blue eyes. 'Helmut was a violinist in the Berlin Philharmonic before the war.'

'Oh. Oh – God Almighty.' Blinking rapidly, Thaddeus stood up. 'Whyever didn't he say something? Why didn't he tell me?' He stood looking down at the woman without really seeing her. 'I could have got him a gramophone or something . . . I mean . . .'

She shook her head without speaking.

'Christ, he must have hated it here – and me as well. I remember him coming in with damn great scratches on his hands, and then blisters, and I told him to rub them with paraffin to toughen 'em up. All that, and he never said a word!' Appalled and mortified, Thaddeus rested his head in his hands.

'Helmut always found it difficult to talk,' she said gently. 'Even to me.'

Very slowly the full realisation was beginning to dawn. Ole Fritzy, the poor ole Jerry POW uncomplainingly growing vegetables in Suffolk mud and rain when his proper job was playing on a violin. And now he was dead. A goner, after only a few months back with his wife. Tears pricked at Thaddeus's eyes.

'I will go now,' the woman said, and he heard the sound of her chair being pushed back.

'You can't,' he said harshly. 'It's too soon.'

'I have seen what I came for. The place where he lived.'

'I can't get over what you've just told me,' Thaddeus muttered. 'We grew to be mates, you see.'

He began to realise that he and the woman standing by his kitchen table had a kind of share in the man, and that pooling their memories of him was in the nature of a tribute and the payment of a mutual debt.

'Tell me about him before the war.'

'We met at a students' camp in the Black Forest. Helmut was studying the violin and I was starting my final year's study to become a teacher. I had already spent the previous summer in England. Helmut and I fell in love. Everyone was falling in love in that wonderful summer of 1936, and we married on the last day in November. We had a two-roomed flat and very little money but

200

we were happy. So happy.' She sat down again, then said, 'Please may I have another piece of cake?'

He offered it immediately, and poured more tea without being asked. His habitual reserve began to fade as he listened to her.

She had a nice face, cut on wide, generous lines and there was something uncompromising about the direct gaze of her light-coloured eyes. He had already assessed her age as somewhere in the late thirties, and her trousers and shirt, although much travelled and of a mediocre quality, were worn with an unobtrusive finesse that he had never been aware of in other women. He imagined that she was fussy about washing, and all that kind of thing.

'Go on,' he encouraged. 'Tell me about the rest of it – although not the private things, of course.'

'There was nothing very private about the war, Mr Noggin,' she said laconically. 'You may find it hard to believe but I assure you it's the truth when I say that we had no knowledge of what was happening until it was too late. Like everyone else we believed in the Führer. We all knew that our country needed rescuing from corruption and cynicism, and like everyone else we made the mistake of leaving him to get on with it. Once I saw some Jews beaten up in the street and when I was told that they were guilty of financial exploitation I didn't question it. I was busy teaching and I was in love with my husband, and when you are the child of a happy family background you do not suspect evil until it is inescapable.'

He was becoming accustomed to her precise, rather dry way of speaking, and found himself examining everything she said with deep interest.

'But Helmut was told that he must join the army – called up, you say? – and that was the end for us. I think we both knew it was so. I was so afraid he would be sent to Russia but instead he was in North Africa. He was taken prisoner there in the spring of 1943. So you see, he had more experience of being in captivity than of fighting. He was safe physically, but psychologically he was a badly wounded man. Or perhaps – ' she frowned – 'not so wounded as reduced to an emotional skeleton. All the things that made up his life had been taken away from him, and for him, those things were like the air he breathed.'

201

The woman was opening a world on to subjects previously alluded to with embarrassment, even scorn. Music meant at worst, hymns, and at best Bing Crosby or Frank Sinatra, and if the soul was stirred by the beauty of a sunset or a flower or a woman's face, it was thought wisest, in taciturn Suffolk, to keep the emotion to oneself. But there was no shame or embarrassment in the face of his companion. She might have been discussing the price of cheese, and the fact that she was doing so in a language foreign to her increased his silent wonder. He had never met anyone like her before, but was naturally incapable of saying so.

'My boy was at El Alamein,' he mumbled finally.

'You have a son?' Her eyes brightened with interest. 'And your wife?'

'She died when he was born.'

'That is sad to hear,' she said. 'But part of her is living in your child.'

'He's a good boy. And when he comes home he'll most likely come in as a partner in the rose business.' There was no harm in hoping.

'You love your roses, don't you?' Here it was again, that clear-eyed, straightforward ability to penetrate the heart of things. But he refused to be drawn.

'They're what I work at for my living.'

'They are more than that. Helmut told me about the roses in your little front garden. How you cared for them like children. Stern with them when you had to be – although I hope not too many parents pull their children from their beds and throw them on a bonfire if they don't grow properly! He also told me that you sometimes spent a long time looking into their eyes as if you were having a conversation.'

'Roses haven't got eyes,' Thaddeus said gruffly. Then relented slightly. 'I mean, Helmut was what they call artistic and all that. He'd got imagination, hadn't he?'

'It takes a lot of imagination,' the woman said, 'to hold a little brown twig in your hand and to know that one day it will bear a beautiful flower.'

In June the day melts unobtrusively into evening, and the hours seem to lengthen with the shadows. The last square of golden light slid from the wall opposite the window and left the kitchen washed

202

in a faded lavender. The cat roused herself from her cardboard box, stretched, and began to wash herself in readiness for the night's adventures.

'In Berlin we ate cats,' the woman said meditatively. 'They are like tough rabbit.'

She stayed for the night, vigorously refusing young Joe's bedroom and insisting upon sleeping in the outhouse that her husband had used. Thaddeus's protests that it was damp, dirty and mouse-ridden fell upon deaf ears. The woman jutted out her chin, clenched her hands and said, 'Please. That is where I wish to sleep. Otherwise I walk back to Harwich and wait for the next boat.'

He capitulated; her only requirement was to have the enamel jug filled with cold water. She had brought soap and a towel in her rucksack and seemed content to prepare for bed by the light of a solitary candle.

'Is this the one that Helmut used?' She stroked the tin candlestick with her finger.

'That's it,' Thaddeus said from the door. 'Nothing's changed.'

They bade one another goodnight and he closed the door and went back to the bungalow. But his sleep was uneasy, and broken by fragments of dreams. Neither Helmut nor his wife appeared in them, but there were roses, and then faces of women, some of whom he didn't know, and he woke more than once to lie in the gauzy summer darkness and think with almost a kind of horror of the strange woman sleeping in the outhouse among the spiders' webs and mouse-droppings. He didn't think an Englishwoman would do a thing like that, no matter how much she had loved her husband.

He wondered if she was lying awake too. Perhaps in spite of her brave determination she was frightened out there on her own. He hoped to God she wouldn't come shivering across to the bungalow and start pounding on the door. He wouldn't be able to deal with that kind of thing; he had lived alone for too long. Punching his pillow he turned on his side. When he woke up a golden pattern of leaves was falling across his bed; looking out of the window he saw the woman coming across the yard with her hands in her trouser pockets and her face upturned to the sun. He realised that he didn't know her name, except that she was Frau Kubler.

They had breakfast together, and Thaddeus suppressed a grin at the thought of Dora's reaction supposing she could see them. But Bob and Dora were taking a fortnight's holiday in Devonshire during the midsummer lull in farmwork.

As if she could read his thoughts the woman lit a cigarette to go with her second cup of tea and said, 'I must leave soon. Your friends will think that you are an immoral man.'

'I haven't got many friends,' he confessed. 'Don't seem to get the time.'

'We had many friends in Berlin before the war, but they are all gone now. Dead, or living somewhere else.'

'Do you still live in Berlin?'

'Yes. But not in the same flat because it was bombed. Everything was lost, including Helmut's violin.'

He tried to picture it. Tried to picture himself as poor old Fritzy, finally allowed to go back home only to find that he had no belongings any more; not even the tools of his trade so that he could earn a living.

'We didn't know the half of it over here,' he murmured.

'It was our punishment.'

There was no more to be said. Thaddeus prepared to clear away the breakfast things but the woman stopped him, saying that she was quite capable of washing a few dishes. So he left her to it, and went off to the rose fields to continue spraying fifteen hundred bushes with Bordeaux mixture as a guard against black spot, which had struck for the first time last year.

Common sense told him that he must start to think seriously about employing labour. He could afford it now; perhaps a couple of boys to train, or maybe one man who was an experienced worker . . . He was now a member of the Royal National Rose Society, his own hybrids were selling nicely, and the old, vague dreams of one day taking a stand at the Chelsea Flower Show were becoming more insistent. He wanted to move forward, and yet . . .

Switching off the spray he straightened his back beneath the heavy weight of the container strapped to his shoulders and looked round at the rose blooms shimmering in the dancing sunlight. A sea of red, white, pink and gold: *Hugh Dickson, Guinée, Frensham, Golden Melody,* and the new *Eden Rose* in the immediate vicinity, and over to the left, rows of his own children nodding and swaying as the breeze riffled through them.

And yet, he wanted to work in solitude. To keep the sense of personal responsibility and, yes, the privacy. It would be shattered anyway when young Joe came home; he was still only a kid and he would want friends round in the evenings. He would start courting, get married, have children, so in the meantime, Thaddeus told himself, he would stay here alone, however hard the work.

Then he remembered that he wasn't alone. Not at the moment. There was a widowed German woman over in the bungalow. He turned the spray on again, swishing it among the leaves, and the next time he looked up he saw her walking slowly and meditatively some distance away, her head bent and her hands in her trouser pockets. And she looked to him like the loneliest person on earth.

She stayed to eat bread and cheese with him, and listened carefully when he explained that in his father's day it had been known as bait-time. He found an increasing sense of ease in her company because of her obvious abstraction. She wasn't really attending to him, although she smiled politely, and he noticed with a trace of pity the way she would sometimes incline her head to one side as if she were listening for something. A voice on the breeze, a footfall in the old outhouse. She showed no sign of making herself a nuisance or of getting in his way so he felt no immediate urge to mention the subject of her departure.

The weather settled to a spell of warm sunlit days and misty, motionless nights. Late in the afternoon of her third day Thaddeus went back to the bungalow and found that she had baked what looked like a length of pastry curved round in a horseshoe shape.

'Apfelstrudel,' she explained, 'but it is not the correct flour. I found apples in your barn and helped myself to the other ingredients. But you had no cinnamon.'

'Smells all right.' He washed his hands and face at the sink, brushed his hair back between his palms and then unrolled his shirt-sleeves.

He persuaded her to share a bottle of beer with him while they ate the cold lamb, new potatoes and salad he had provided, and when they came to the apfelstrudel he was intrigued by German ignorance of traditional apple pie and custard, then compelled to admire the novelty of its flavour. He had two helpings, and afterwards they sat out in the garden he had made so hastily as a sanctuary all those years ago. The evening was filled with an incomparable blend of rose perfumes.

The woman pointed her cigarette at a bush bearing soft pink blossoms touched with gold. 'That one is beautiful. What is it called?'

'Haven't got round to naming it yet.'

'You mean, you invent roses?' Again that clear straight gaze from her silvery blue eyes.

'Sort of. Although the rose as a genus was discovered rather than invented about four thousand years ago, maybe earlier than that. I learned a lot from the little ole boy I worked for some time back.'

'Helmut must have loved them when they were all in bloom.'

'Reckon he'd have preferred his music.'

From the top of the barn roof a blackbird was filling the air with the richness of its song. Its voice was deep, rich and leisurely, and Thaddeus and the woman thought silently of the violinist who had been deprived of music. God knows what envy he had felt of the Suffolk songbirds pouring out their melody with a freedom denied to him.

The sun had set in a flare of gold and ultramarine, and the woman sat with her head cocked as if she were straining to hear another, fainter sound behind the blackbird's passionate voice. As the light faded, Venus, the evening planet, rose above the roof of the old outhouse.

'Not feeling cold?'

She shook her head vehemently, as if impatient of being interrupted, and Thaddeus sat watching her profile dissolving in the grey-blue dusk, her blonde bob of hair being drained of its life. She was a rum sort, but he was getting used to her and perhaps they had more in common than was immediately apparent.

His thoughts went back to the time when he lost Polly, and to the long cold months when it seemed as if he had died too. There is no comfort, no medicine, to ease that kind of pain; only the grim necessity of getting up each morning in order to work oneself into a stupor of tiredness, and if there is any mercy a new life may emerge from the ruins of the old one. A grey, listless, hopelessly inferior kind of life which will begin to improve with time and patience. He felt that he ought to explain some of this to her, but was unsure of being able to lay tongue to the right words, and was also afraid of intruding upon her privacy. Beneath the air of casual friendliness that he had catalogued as foreign – no woman from these parts would set off on her own for another country and doss down in the same place as a single man – he sensed something essentially private and untouchable. They had shared kitchen chores but had never touched hands, and they had even denied themselves the mild intimacy of using one another's name. They addressed one another as 'you', and left it at that.

The blackbird broke off its song in mid-phrase, and with a sudden startling scream sped down from the barn and made off to its roosting place. It was a time that Thaddeus had loved since a young boy, the change from day to night, with one set of creatures preparing to sleep and another waking to activity. Small rustlings, scufflings and creakings, with a small shadowy blob manifesting itself as a maurauding hedgehog coming up to sniff the motionless toes of his shoes. Finding them inedible, it trundled away.

The woman was no more than a faint glimmer when they said goodnight. As on previous evenings he accompanied her to the door of the outhouse, lighting the way with a powerful torch and then shining it into the interior while she lit the candle.

'OK, are you? Got everything you want?'

'Yes, thank you. Goodnight.'

He went back to the bungalow and gave the cat a saucer of milk, then remembered that he hadn't closed the greenhouse window. He didn't want her jumping on to his seedling lettuces.

The moon was up now, casting a splintering light over the countryside, and from over the fields came the yap of a fox. He walked slowly, the cat at his side, and on the way back from the greenhouse he paused by the door of the outhouse when he heard the sound of sobbing coming from within. He stood listening; the cat listened too, then abruptly darted away on a mission of her own. The sobbing continued, muffled and low. He stood motionless, irresolute, then turned the handle and went in.

It was very dark in there, and stuffy from the day's heat. The sound of her weeping was so terrible that he blundered over to the old makeshift bed and sat down on the end of it. 'Don't cry, my dear. Don't cry so.'

She was like a ghost glimmering in the darkness but she raised her arms to him with the instinctive gesture of an abandoned child. He held her close to him, and with the other hand smoothed back the hair from her hot, wet face. 'There, there then . . . Try not to take on so . . .'

She made no attempt to speak, but leaned against him as if she were relinquishing an intolerable burden. The hand that had been stroking her hair as if it could have been the cat's fur, hesitated, then passed down her neck and followed the contour of her bare shoulder. She jerked her head upwards, whether in surprise or protest he would never know, for their mouths met and her arms were no longer childlike but twining and grasping. They clasped him with feverish desperation and he responded, groaning with pain and a kind of madness after all the years of near celibacy.

They made love violently, each striving to satisfy a seemingly unquenchable thirst, and when at last it was over he lay on his side, staring at the shadowed contour of her body and thinking: this is Helmut's wife.

Well, Helmut's widow.

They spent the rest of the night together, sweatily entwined, and at the first hint of dawn Thaddeus stumbled off the bed and opened the door. A gush of fresh air hit his naked body and he stood breathing deeply for a moment before returning to the disordered bed. She was lying on her back with one knee raised and one arm flung above her head, and the joy of going back to her after just a few moment's absence was that of a young man.

He kissed her gently; her closed eyes, her small firm nose, her sleeping mouth. Once again he smoothed the disordered bob of blonde hair back from her forehead and she opened her eyes and smiled at him.

'Good-morning.'

'My name's Thaddeus.'

'Good-morning, Thaddeus. It's a name I never heard before.'

'After my Grandad. Good-morning . . . Frau . . .'

'Berta.'

'How d'you spell that?'

She told him, taking his large hand in hers and ticking off the letters on his fingers. 'Berta. After my Mother.'

They lay at peace, careful to keep the future at bay, but when the first beam of lemon sunshine touched the corner of the bed she left his side, saying, 'I am very hungry after so much energy, so I will cook breakfast.'

He watched her gather up her underwear, shoes, shirt and trousers and walk out into the new day with them under her arm. By the time he followed her to the bungalow she was trimly dressed, and bacon and eggs were sizzling in the pan.

She moved into the bungalow with him, ostensibly because the improvised bed was on the verge of collapse, but in reality out of deference to Helmut.

Helmut was dead, and love for him had impelled his widow to come to England on a pilgrimage during the course of which she had found consolation. She had found sympathy and a wordless understanding among the sunlit roses that now filled the fields where her husband had toiled to grow vegetables for the enemy, and as the warm days glided past there seemed less and less reason to reject what she had found.

And for Thaddeus too, the affair with Helmut's widow began to seem less of a betrayal than a subtle binding together of the three of them. He and Berta often spoke of him, and it was a source of wonderment and satisfaction that the image of a cowed, deprived Jerry POW should become replaced by that of sensitive musician. Under Berta's guidance he listened to a couple of classical concerts on the radio and found that he quite enjoyed them, and she tidied the outhouse and arranged a handful of roses in a jug which she stood on the old tea chest as if Helmut, wherever he might be, was still capable of enjoying them.

Because Bob and Dora were still on holiday and visitors to the nursery never came closer than the barn, which had now become a rough kind of office, Thaddeus and Berta remained in peaceful seclusion. And as Berta expressed no particular desire to leave the vicinity Thaddeus continued to drive down to Bures and into Sudbury on market day for whatever provisions were needed. The days passed as slowly and dreamily as the feathery clouds passed overhead; apart from spraying and feeding there was little work to do in the rose fields and Thaddeus concentrated upon preparing his autumn catalogue for the printers. He wanted to have it ready in good time, and Berta drew a charming little pen and ink sketch of an unfurling rose which she said should be his trademark.

The warm rose-scented nights were spent in Thaddeus's bed, loving, sleeping, and wordlessly appreciating the luxury of closeness and simple compatibility. Within three days Berta's skin had tanned to a honey gold which seemed to give a new translucence to her silvery blue eyes, and her bob of hair showed the first signs of sun-streaks. She moved and spoke with the same quiet and thoughtful deliberation, and although she seldom laughed, amusement would sometimes illuminate her face like the switching on of a light. She seemed to bear no resemblance to the harsh and humourless Hun of British stereotype; but then neither had her husband.

Continuing to avoid all reference to the future they lived each moment as it came with silent gratitude, knowing that it couldn't continue in the same way indefinitely. Bob and Dora were due home in a day or so, and already there might have been whisperings in the village about a strange woman staying up along Thaddeus Noggin. Country eyes were sharp.

In effect however, it ended on the late afternoon the local taxi bumped up the track to the bungalow and disgorged young Joe and two suitcases. Now Sergeant Noggin, he had broadened and hardened in appearance, and he slapped his father on the back with a hand powerful as a sledge-hammer.

'Hi, Dad! Pleased to see me, are you?'

'Very. But why didn't you let me know?'

'Thought I'd surprise you – '

'How long have you got?'

'Aha!' Another sledge-hammer blow. 'Got me discharge – *and* me gratuity *and* me demob suit – so I'm back for keeps, ole Daddy-boy!'

The plumpness of his face had the effect of making his eyes seem smaller, but his nicotine-stained grin was as wide and affable as ever and Thaddeus felt a great surge of affection for him.

'Glad to see you, boy.'

'How's the roses?'

'Doing fine. Orders coming in nice and steady and we've nearly finished the catalogue.'

'You're gunna need me to give you a hand and that's a fact,' Joe said. Then added, 'Who's we?'

Before Thaddeus had time to reply Berta came round the corner, hands in trouser pockets. She was whistling. The whistling ceased when she saw the British army uniform, and the two suitcases.

'This is Berta – Mrs Kubler – who's staying here,' Thaddeus said. 'And this is my son Joe I told you about.'

Slowly Berta extended her hand and Joe shook it politely. 'Pleased to meet you.' After a brief pause he bent to pick up his luggage. 'I'll just dump these in me bedroom – I mean, if it's free?' Obviously puzzled, he glanced back at them.

'Your room's same as it was,' Thaddeus said gruffly. 'Make yourself at home.'

Joe disappeared, and Berta turned away with a little shrug. 'It's over.'

''Course it's not!' Thaddeus told her in a vehement undertone. 'It's nothing to do with anyone else. Joe's come back without warning so he can just accept it or do the other thing. Up to him, isn't it?'

'It's over,' she repeated. 'Time for me to go.'

'You're not going!' He bunched his fists. 'You're staying here with me and it's nobody else's business!'

She turned to smile at him. A sad, wrecked little smile. 'All right. We'll see.' She walked away.

Thaddeus encountered Joe in the open doorway of his bedroom. The two suitcases were on the floor and his jacket was slung on the chair.

'Bed's always made up ready,' Thaddeus said.

'Great. Thanks.'

'Come and have a cuppa tea – '

'Hang on a minute, Dad. Who is she?'

Thaddeus shoved the door to with his foot, then sat down heavily on the end of the bed. Joe looked down at him, intrigued and kindly.

'She's the wife of the POW I had here, name of Helmut. Think you saw him once when you came on leave.'

Joe nodded.

'Well, she just walked in one day to see where poor ole Helmut had worked when he was a prisoner. He'd told her all about it after he got repatriated, but when I asked her where he was and why he

211

hadn't come too, she told me he was dead. Died of the cancer, poor ole boy.'

'Tough luck.' Joe took out a packet of Player's and offered one to his father. 'How long's she staying?'

'Not sure.' Thaddeus inhaled deeply. 'But Helmut had been a violinist, she told me. Used to play in a big orchestra before the war and then here was me getting him to dig and plant and weed and bugger up his hands good and proper. You never know, do you?'

'No,' Joe repeated. 'You never know.'

'What I mean is, you've got to keep your hands soft as a girl's to play the violin. But he never told me. Never said a word.'

'And now he's dead, poor bloke.'

Joe looked as if he wanted to say more, but instead began wrenching off his tie and tugging at the buttons of his shirt. 'Feel like getting into something cooler . . .' He flung the shirt down and Thaddeus saw that his son had flabby breasts above a moderate-sized beer belly. It shocked him.

'Looks as if you could do with some hard work, boy.'

'That's what I came home for. In the meantime, what's say we go down the pub and have a drink to celebrate?'

'I'll ask Berta if she'd like to come.'

'Sure.' Joe lingered, now clad in jeans and a T-shirt. 'The more the merrier.'

But Berta, who was cooking rhubarb for a pudding, smiled without hint of concealed reaction and said that she would prefer not to as she was rather busy. So Thaddeus and Joe went down to the King's Head, and it was beautiful the way they got on together again. Father and son, yet real mates who could afford to kid one another because of the depth of mutual respect they had, Joe having worked his way up to senior NCO in HM Forces and Thaddeus a rose-breeder and nurseryman who had done it all himself. Other locals who had dropped in for an early pint greeted Joe and offered him a drink when they heard he was demobbed.

'Best get back soon, Berta's cooking supper,' Thaddeus warned after a while.

'Supper?' Joe fed more coins into the old juke-box and added the voice of Doris Day to the general noise. 'Used to be called tea.'

'Got to keep up with the times,' Thaddeus said drily.

'Reckon I'd best go on a rehabilitation course.'

'Shouldn't worry. Still, I think I'll be getting back – no need for you to hurry.'

But Joe drained his glass, waved goodnight and walked back with him.

'Getting your leg over, are you, Dad?'

Thaddeus remained silent.

'Every man for himself these days, isn't it? Grab what you can while the going's good.'

'That's what they say.'

'Jesus, the tales I could tell you.'

'Yes. I dare say.'

'But I'm glad to be back, Dad.' And his use of the word Dad reminded Thaddeus of the old days, and the over-use of his name as if it had been some kind of talisman for Joe. They walked in silence.

'Coming into the business, are you?' Thaddeus asked eventually. 'Could do with another pair of hands and a better head for figuring than mine,' he added cautiously, hopefully.

'Thaddeus Noggin & Son Limited. Sounds all right to me.'

'What d'you have to do to be Limited? And what's the advantage?'

'Not too clear,' Joe confessed. 'But we'll find out. It must be something good or people wouldn't bother.'

They reached the bungalow. Berta had prepared an evening meal for three, a blend of English and German cuisine in the form of pork sausages served with some kind of chopped-up cabbage and onion steeped in vinegar. Joe accepted it with an equanimity which pleased Thaddeus; he wanted the three of them to settle down nicely together, and tried, in his taciturn way, to select suitable topics of conversation. The war was out obviously, and so was Joe's post-war sojourn in the Rhine army, which left rose-growing and the weather.

'Anyone hear the forecast?'

'Sleet and snow,' Joe said, shovelling.

'It does that here in *June*?' Berta looked amazed. 'It rained, but there was no snow when I last came to England.'

'You bin here before, then?' Joe asked.

'Before the war. To learn English.'

'Ready for the takeover, eh?' Joe spoke good-humouredly. 'Shame it was a waste of time.'

'No learning is a waste of time,' Berta responded politely.

'She's got me reading a book,' Thaddeus said. 'Knows a damn sight more about Shakespeare and Dickens than I do.'

'*Reveille* and *Titbits* does me nicely so far,' Joe helped himself to more sauerkraut. 'But when I get to Dad's age I might be seeing things different.'

He winked across at Berta, and the meal ended on a note of carefully maintained harmony, which was badly shaken when Joe became aware that Berta was installed in his father's bedroom.

'So you really *are* laying her? My God, I don't believe it – I thought she was kipping down in the outhouse when I looked in and saw the flowers on the dressing-table and the bed made up.'

He stumped out of the bungalow and into the garden. Thaddeus followed him.

'That's where she started off, but then . . . Dare say it's hard to understand, and all I can say is that it just happened naturally – ' Thaddeus stopped, despising the note of apology in his voice and attempting to replace it with a kind of waggishness. 'Ah well, proves there's life in the ole dog yet!'

But Joe's eyes were not admiring. His plump face, which army life had coarsened, bore a slightly sickened look. 'You could have chosen someone your own age and your own nationality,' he said, turning away. 'I spent over three years killing krauts.'

'So now's the time to start making up for it.'

'What'd you want me to do – start calling her Mum?'

Thaddeus clenched his hands, then relaxed them. 'Go and do your unpacking, then have a bath and go to bed.'

'Meaning I stink?'

'Yes, son. Of intolerance.'

'Intolerance – ' Joe mimicked him. 'Dad, you've bin learning some long words.'

'Just told you,' Thaddeus replied with determined good humour, 'I've taken to reading books.'

The spell was broken. Sometimes it seemed irreparably so, and at other times as if the situation might be stabilised with luck and careful handling.

They all tried their best. Berta spent a lot of time going for walks on her own so that Thaddeus could be alone with his son, while Joe refrained from further overt criticism of the relationship that had developed during his absence. They remained carefully polite, and it was scarcely their fault that so many topics of conversation were spiked with incipient danger.

It made Thaddeus recall Berta's fourth night of sharing his bed when, replete with love-making, they had lain side by side holding hands and staring into the darkness.

'Yes,' he had said finally, 'but Auschwitz, and those places. I mean, how did you . . . ?'

'I didn't. Any more than you beheaded your King Charles I.'

'That was hundreds of years ago. But Auschwitz – did you go along with it?'

'We all knew there were labour camps for foreign dissidents, but that was all. Our crime was in not discovering the details.'

'In which case, you'd have ended up with them.'

'No doubt. In the meanwhile, spare a thought for Adam von Trott and all the others connected with the von Stauffenberg plot who tried to rid the world of the Führer and were either shot or hung on meat hooks for their pains.' She turned her head and buried her face in his shoulder. 'Sometimes I feel that it is all too much to bear.'

'You don't have to bear it all on your own,' he said, stroking her hair. 'There must be thousands who feel like you do, and come to think of it, no country's perfect, is it?'

'I like it here,' she said in a muffled voice. 'People are kind.'

'Stay, then. I reckon we could fix things up.'

She had not replied, but he had sensed doubt and bewilderment in the way she moved away from him, bunched the pillow beneath her head and murmured goodnight. Since then they had said no more on the subject.

As for Joe, he told himself that he had got over the shock of coming home and finding his ole man tucked up with a kraut, but as the days passed, so did the exhilaration of being demobbed. There was nothing to do – a prospect that had once delighted him, but that now filled him with an increasing sense of futility. Suddenly released from the discipline of a rigid army timetable, the hours lost their meaning for him. As there was little work to do in the rose fields he too went for long walks, and grew irritable with himself for automatically falling back into the brisk marching steps of a military man with a mission in view. He tried to loiter, but found it difficult. So he called in at pubs and drank moodily and alone. The beer was rotten, and he thought with nostalgia of the Export variety available in the sergeants' mess.

He wanted a girl, but there didn't seem to be many about. Village barmaids appeared uniformly faded, fat and forty, and the lone girl he sometimes encountered riding a horse looked down on him with withering disdain. On the day he stepped off the verge and swept her a mock bow the horse shied and she called him a thoughtless bastard in a voice that crackled with ice. He replied that she was a toffee-nosed cunt and left it at that.

He began to watch Berta and his father together, covertly studying their attitudes towards one another during mealtimes. There was little outward demonstration of their feelings, but Joe became increasingly adept at interpreting the lingering glance, the private smile, the occasional discreet touch of hands. He felt irritated by them, and equally irritated with himself as voyeur, but found himself lying awake at night listening for tell-tale sounds coming from the other room. He never heard any; maybe he and Dad had built the dividing walls thicker than he remembered.

In an effort to pull himself out of this new and unpleasant mood of lethargy he borrowed the van and went to the Labour Exchange in Sudbury to look for a temporary job until the autumn work in the rose fields began.

The woman who interviewed him was also faded, fat and forty, and tended to treat him as if looking for a job was a new version of scrounging. When she learned that he had been an army sergeant she offered him part-time work in a fishmonger's; alternatively he could apply for the post of boilerman at Bellfields. When he asked what Bellfields was she sighed again and said that it was a private home for the insane.

So he thanked her and walked out (still trying not to march) into the big pub on the square and sat moodily drinking beer and watching women's nylon petticoats and knickers waving from the market stalls. Then he drove home and accused his father with rough jocularity of importing krauts for immoral purposes.

'You've had too much to drink.'

'One pint, that's all.'

'And the rest.'

Joe took a deep breath, then said, 'Listen. What I do with my own money is my own affair. There's nothing for me here, so even if I drank myself stupid and screwed every woman in sight it'd be nothing to do with anyone else because I'm a big boy now. See?'

Thaddeus nodded, and watched him with thoughtful eyes as he flung himself into his room and slammed the door.

'He is finding it difficult to become a civilian again,' Berta said when Thaddeus told her of the encounter. 'It was the same for Helmut.'

'He was ill. Joe's just sorry for himself.'

'No,' she said. 'He is sorry because I am here. Can't you see how difficult it is for him?'

'If he doesn't like it he can clear out.' He didn't mean it, but the words soothed him.

Berta shook her head. 'If anyone goes, I must be the one.'

'You're not going!' He grabbed her by the shirt-sleeve. 'You and I were getting on fine until Sergeant Noggin appeared on the scene and it's still going to be all right once he's got himself properly transplanted and settled in. God, me and my lot went through the same thing after the first war, and we were too damn grateful to be back to start behaving like a lot of spoilt kids.' He put his arm round her and hugged her close to him. 'Just give him time to get his roots down, that's all, and in the meantime don't let him upset you.'

She looked up at him with her clear eyes. 'You are the one he is upsetting.'

On the day that Bob and Dora returned from holiday Thaddeus drove over to see them. He barely recognised Dora beneath the summer tan and Bob was wearing a fancy T-shirt. They presented him with a pot of Devonshire cream and told him that they were going back to the same place again next year. 'And you're coming too,' Dora said. 'It's right on the seafront and the prices are very reasonable.'

He thanked them, then said 'Oh, by the way, Joe's home. Kept his demob a secret and just came stumping in a few days ago.'

He was planning to mention Berta too; to work her offhandedly into the conversation purely as his old POW's widow making a

217

sentimental pilgrimage, without going into explanations about subsequent developments – but somehow he didn't. Every time he prepared the opening words either Dora or Bob jumped in with something about Devonshire, and whenever a momentary pause did occur he found himself unable to get started. By the time he stood up to leave he still hadn't told them, and when they asked him and Joe over to Sunday dinner he panicked and said, 'No, no, not this time – but tell you what, both of you come over to ours for a change – '

They accepted, perhaps a trifle wonderingly, and he hurried away like a man with an urgent mission.

It would have been naive to imagine that Berta's presence was still unnoticed in the locality, and Thaddeus thought it more than likely that Joe had mentioned her in the King's Head, but introducing her to Bob and Dora was another matter. Romantic entanglement at the age of fifty-three was a bit of a laugh really (Joe obviously found it nauseating), but the real problem lay in the nationality of his choice. The war had been over for six years, but memories are not eradicated at will. He knew that, and it worried him.

Berta herself took the news of the invitation calmly, merely asking whether the guests would like meat or fish for dinner, and outside the bungalow Joe gave him a sour look and said, 'Hope you know what you're doing.'

'God Almighty, sounds as if I'm introducing a hag out of hell.'

'How d'you know you're not?' Joe slouched out, and that evening came back from the pub saying that on Sunday he was going off for the day.

'Where?'

'Fishing, with some mates.'

Exasperation tightened his father's mouth. 'You couldn't have planned it for some other day?'

'No. Why?'

'Because I want you here, that's why.'

'What for? To hold your hand?'

Both felt conscious of a steadily mounting tension. 'Look,' Thaddeus said after a pause, 'your Auntie hasn't seen you for best part of a year and she'll want to see you now. And I more or less said she would.'

Even as he spoke he wondered why it was so important to him to have Joe there as well. It could scarcely be in the hope that he would be on his side, supposing Bob and Dora cut up a bit rough. Joe had already made his own views abundantly clear, and Thaddeus could only suppose that the answer lay in a somewhat naive desire for peace and quiet. For everyone to settle down nice and easy together.

'So, will you be here?'

'Dunno. I'll see,' Joe muttered, without looking at him. He walked off, kicking at stones as he went.

The final explosion came two days later, and typically, was touched off by a trifling incident. Going into the big new greenhouse Thaddeus found Joe sellotaping a large coloured print of a busty nude over one of the workbenches.

'What's that supposed to be?'

'New form of rose tonic.'

'Take it down. It cuts the light out.'

Joe made no reply.

'Go on, take it down. Customers come in here.' He didn't mean to speak so churlishly; it just happened.

'No.' Joe turned to face him. 'You got your bit of home comfort, I'm going to have mine.'

'Well, if that's the best you can do . . .'

Another pause. Both of them aware that the last seconds of peace were ticking away.

'I'd rather have her,' Joe said slowly and distinctly, 'than a lousy second-hand kraut.'

'You're going to apologise for that.'

'Like hell I am,' Joe said, and grabbing at the nearest flower pot, hurled it through the opposite window. With a satisfying crash it landed on the path outside, and the sudden violence unleashed the storm. 'If there's any apologising to be done I reckon you're the one who should be doing it. Christ help us, is this the freedom I've bin fighting for – freedom for you to shack up with a German whore? They're all whores – I'm telling you and I know because I spent nearly two years out there – a kraut'll sell herself – she'll do anything you ask – any way, any how, any time – for a packet of fags or a bar of chocolate – and when I see *you* – '

'Shut up!' roared Thaddeus.

'When I see you and her together, shacked up cosy like man and wife – '

Thaddeus advanced, huge fists bunched.

' – and think of you fucking the wife of a bloody POW – the lowest scum on earth – '

Thaddeus lashed out. The blow went wide. Instantly Joe stopped speaking and assumed a defensive stance. Head lowered, fists raised, eyes murderous. 'Come on, then . . . come on, come on . . .'

'Stop it, Joe. For God's sake stop it – '

'Scared, are you? Not the man you were? Putting all your energy into getting that cow on her back, are you?'

Joe's rage came as a sweet and cleansing relief after the elation of demob that had so swiftly declined into ineffectuality, boredom and disgust. It roared through him with the old joyousness of punch-ups outside the NAAFI and the sortings-out of stroppy young National Servicemen who knew it all after three weeks' basic training. 'Come on then, if that's how you feel!'

He jabbed a blow at his father's chest, no more than a light tap which was supposed to serve as a warning, but it was sufficient to ignite in him the desire to continue. Rage and frustration poured out of him. He wished he was back in the army. Wished he was back with the lads where everybody knew what was what and exactly where they stood.

They fought grimly, murderously, for several seconds. Thaddeus had the weight but not the expertise, and stood awkwardly flailing while Joe spent his accumulated frustration in dancing jabs interspersed with vicious blows. Dazed with baffled fury Thaddeus reached for an iron-handled trowel and clumped his son on the side of the head with it.

Joe stopped dead, his ears ringing, then turned on his heel and lurched out. Another pane of glass crashed as he slammed the door behind him. Panting, Thaddeus stood looking at the trowel, then after a moment's consideration used it as a lever to detach the nude's photograph. It slid down on to the bench and he crumpled it savagely and flung it in the opposite corner.

They had eaten tea without saying much, but the mood was one of calm reflection rather than tension.

'Joe is not here?' Berta indicated the empty place between them.

'No. Be back later.'

They had made no further reference to him, and when the meal was finished Thaddeus had glanced round at the tidy kitchen – clean shirts and socks airing over the stove, the cat asleep in her bed –before going out to water the boxes of wallflower seedlings.

'Won't be long.'

'Fine. I have one or two things to do here.'

Evening had come with no more than a lengthening of shadows and a flaring of colour in the western sky when he walked down to the gate to see if there was any sign of Joe returning. The lane was deserted. He toyed with the idea of walking down to the pub – it was past opening time now – to buy him a drink and make up the quarrel if he was there, yet he remained standing irresolute. Trouble was, he could see both points of view, Joe's, as well as his own. He wondered, rather hopelessly, what Bob and Dora's reaction would be when they came over on Sunday. Well, it was up to them; all he wanted was for people to get along together.

But the fight with Joe had shaken him badly. He hadn't wanted it, and the thought of father and son fighting over a woman sickened him as much as the murderous light in Joe's eyes had appalled him.

He had walked back towards the barn and the old outhouse when he heard the sound of footsteps behind him. He turned, and watched her move slowly towards him.

'What's this, then?' He indicated the rucksack in place between her shoulders. Her shirt-sleeves were neatly rolled and her trousers were the ones she had arrived in, freshly washed and ironed. 'What's all this about?'

'I'm going home, Thaddeus.'

'Why? What for?' As if he didn't know. 'I mean, did you hear me and Joe in the greenhouse? That didn't mean anything . . .'

She smiled; that old smile of hers with downcast eyes and bowed head. 'No. It's just time for me to go. I've already been away for too long.'

'But it *is* because of Joe, isn't it?' he persisted. 'Well, don't take any notice of him. He's young and he doesn't understand these things, not like we do.' He tried to take her hand but she slipped it

221

into her trouser pocket. 'I mean, he's young and sees everything black and white – '

'Most people do,' she said sadly.

'But that's nothing to do with us! Why should it be? Not the way we feel, the way we are, and everything.'

She raised her head to look at him and her silver blue eyes were full of pain. 'It's just too soon, my dear. People who never knew of our existence have ordered our lives.'

He stood looking at her, still stunned by the fight with Joe and now silenced by the melancholy of her words.

She asked if he knew the times of the trains to Harwich, and he managed to rouse himself sufficiently to suggest that she went back indoors while he found out. Gently she refused, and his mind became filled with the question of where she would spend the night, had she sufficient money, how would she travel back to Berlin and what would await her there. But the questions died on his lips.

'I'll drive you to the station. We can find out about trains when we get there.'

'I like to walk.'

'OK, I'll walk with you.'

'No. It will be easier if you do not.' Already she seemed to be returning to the precise, pedantic speech with which she had arrived, and he fancied that her accent had become a little more pronounced; all as if in preparation for laying English aside and returning to her mother tongue.

'It's a fair ole step, mind . . .' He shook his head, then touched her bare arm and said, 'Stay with me, dear. Please stay.'

She removed her hand from her pocket and for an instant his hopes rallied. But she held it out to him in what he recognised as a farewell handshake between friends. 'Come as far as the gate.'

A small bed filled with the new rose ran alongside the barn. Silver pink flushed gold; fragrant; very full; upright growth; dark foliage; known merely as *Rosa X*. Thaddeus picked one and gave it to her. 'Matches your looks.'

She took it from him, unable to speak, and they walked to the gateway in silence.

'Goodbye then, Berta.' He touched her cheek and she closed her eyes. When she opened them again he saw her taking a last look over towards the outhouse where Helmut had lived.

222

'Goodbye, my dear.'

She turned away and he stood watching until she was out of sight, her head bent in the familiar musing attitude, her two hands clasping the rose he had given her.

Then the lane was empty, and he had lost both of them. He had lost both her and Joe.

1966

The publisher's office was a daunting block of cement and tinted glass off Bedford Square. Cautiously Thaddeus inserted himself in the revolving door and found himself inside a vast and artistically austere reception hall. A young woman looked up from behind a desk the length of a London Transport bus and asked if she could help him.

'I've called to see a lady called Eustacia Scarthe,' Thaddeus said. Then added, 'on business.'

'Your name?' Flicking the leaves of a large appointments book she looked up at him, pen in hand. Her eyes had some kind of black paint round the edges which gave her a vaguely Old Testament look.

'Thaddeus Noggin. It's about a book I wrote.'

But already she had picked up a telephone receiver and was speaking in dulcet tones. She replaced it, and asked if he would come this way. When she glided out from behind the desk it became apparent that she had no skirt on. Just long black stockings and high-heeled shoes and a kind of long black-and-white striped jumper tightly belted round the waist. The effect startled him considerably.

They went up in the lift together, then she led him down a long carpeted corridor where most of the doors they passed were open. He saw all the fascinating paraphernalia of the modern office: electric typewriters, plastic telephones, glass-topped desks and rubber plants towering ominously in the corners. More girls without skirts were passing to and fro, and his guide led him to an open space set with armchairs and low tables and ashtrays large enough to roast a duck in. Under her instructions he prepared to seat himself, and descended into almost limitless depths of yielding plastic foam. His knees met his chin. The Old Testament girl left him. He found himself studying an elderly woman with frizzed red hair and brass earrings who was holding a large mackintosh-covered portfolio. By her feet sat a small and shivering dog with protruding eyes.

'Nice weather,' Thaddeus said to the woman as their eyes met, 'for the time of year.'

The woman studied him in return. 'Is it?' Then her gaze drifted past him. The little dog nuzzled her beseechingly, and Thaddeus was interested to note that she was wearing a ring on her index finger. He transferred his gaze to yet another rubber plant of formidable proportions that was standing guard over a glass-topped table strewn with shiny magazines. More girls without skirts passed by.

'Mr Noggin?' A slim white hand was held out to him, attached to a naked arm. Her scarlet shift dress covered her from shoulder to crotch, and the dizzying length of nylon-clad legs ended in the kind of ingenuous strap-and-buckle sandals that Joe had worn as a child. 'I'm Eustachia Scarthe, Publicity.'

Thaddeus attempted to rise from the clinging confines of the chair and fell back. He tried again, and stood looming gauntly over Miss Scarthe. 'Pleased to meet you, Miss.'

'My friends call me Eustacia, Thaddeus.'

She led him back down the corridor and into one of the offices where she collected a doll-sized coat and a little red handbag. 'We all love your book, Thaddeus, and as you know we're zooming it at the Christmas trade. We want it to be a *big* seller.' She flicked her long hair back over her shoulders, smiled and said, 'Ready?'

The restaurant was crowded. The owner flashed a gold-toothed smile of welcome at Miss Scarthe – Eustacia – and conducted them personally to their table. Thaddeus saw that it had been reserved.

Seated opposite his hostess, he also saw that he was the only man wearing a tweed suit. All the others were wearing polo necked sweaters or open-necked shirts, and a man with heavy jowls peppered with bristle was wearing strings of beads over a long caftan. Thaddeus concluded that he was from foreign parts.

They ate lasagne and drank a flask of Chianti. Unfamiliar with wine, Thaddeus found himself growing accustomed to it with rapidity.

'. . . gardening and cookery books are always a sure bet for Christmas presents,' Eustacia was saying, 'and we're going all out to push your *Roses for Everyone* and Jemima Tump's *Cooking in Kathmandu.*'

'Is that a place?'

'Kathmandu? Oh yes, all the kids are going there.'

With a blurred vision of children with buckets and spades, Thaddeus nodded. He finished his meal with a large dollop of Italian ice cream followed by cheese and biscuits while Eustacia smoked a cigarette. After the plates had been removed and small cups of inky black coffee substituted, Eustacia pushed back her hair and said, 'Right. Now we'll get down to business.'

She had a lot of hair. A tumbling chestnut-brown mass of it that obscured her forehead and cheeks, and from between fronds of which her dark brown, highly intelligent eyes stared into his without a hint of constraint. She was rather beautiful, and used her beauty in a new-fashioned way that had not yet penetrated the regions of the Stour valley. Lots and lots of hair and no make-up except for a faint dusting of some kind of greeny-blue stuff round the eyes; an exaggeratedly large wristwatch, no skirt to speak of and a pair of kindergarten-style sandals. No, he had seen nothing like Eustacia Scarthe walking round Sudbury.

She took a notebook and ballpoint from her tiny red handbag and began to acquaint him with the details of his promotional tour. He leaned close across the table, striving to catch her words against the babble of voices. Four appearances on local radio, three press interviews, a women's mag thought they wanted to do a feature on him but weren't yet sure, and on publication day she had managed to get a book-signing session in a High Holborn bookshop. Hastily he strove to intercept the dates she threw at him and scribble them in his diary but she gave him a sudden heart-stopping smile and said, 'Don't worry, Thaddeus. My secretary will confirm all the arrangements by post.'

She flicked her fingers at the waiter and paid the bill by signing something on the piece of pink paper he gave her. They left the restaurant, and after glancing at her huge wristwatch Eustacia said that she must rush off to a meeting. She tripped away in her little-girl footwear, calling something that sounded like '*Chow*!' over her shoulder.

He stood on the edge of the pavement, an unusually tall old man wearing black boots and a suit made by a Sudbury tailor in 1938, and he had never met anyone like Eustacia in his life before. Drawing a deep breath he prepared to make his way back to Liverpool Street station.

His schedule arrived by post, and he was startled to realise that he would be travelling to Liverpool and back in a day, and calling in at radio stations in Birmingham and Manchester. An hotel room had been reserved for him for one night in London in order that he and the Publicity Manager might make an early start by train from Euston. The letter ended with good wishes for a pleasant and fruitful trip.

He had his hair cut, and bought a new shirt and tie under Dora's guidance. She also told him that he must wear shoes and not boots. The night before leaving he scrubbed his hard cracked hands and spent a long while extracting the last fragments of soil from beneath his fingernails. When he was ready to depart he looked at himself in the dressing-table mirror with an expression of dubiety.

A craggy face tinted by the weather to a warm near-cinnamon brown; the beetling brows of an old man sheltering eyes bright with apprehension; a powerful nose, reasonably good teeth and a firm chin rising from the new shirt collar and paisley tie that Dora had chosen. But he still looked what he was. A country clod. Ah well, he reckoned he'd done his best, and with that thought to comfort him he locked up the bungalow, issued final instructions to Pete, his foreman, and then slinging the small canvas bag containing his pyjamas and slippers into the car drove off to Bures station to catch the London train.

The London hotel was nice enough in its way, but unbelievably lonely. So many people dodging about and he didn't know one of them. So he retired to his room and spent a long while memorising the IN THE EVENT OF FIRE notice stuck on the back of the door. He read through leaflets advising him to visit the Zoo and Madame Tussaud's, but when he looked for reading matter of a less ephemeral nature there was only a Gideon's bible, for which he was not in the mood.

So he undressed and got into bed with a copy of *Roses for Everyone*, the book he had started to write over three years ago.

It had begun merely as a series of notes intended to jog his own memory regarding the vagaries of rose growth – *Madame Alfred Carrière* was not as happy on a north wall as some growers insisted – a strong decoction of elder leaves was still as powerful against mildew as many of the newfangled chemicals – and the notes had grown with remarkable swiftness. Sitting at the kitchen table during winter evenings he had covered page after page with the neat script taught all those years ago by old Miss Ball at Marling village school.

By early February he decided that he ought to put the notes in some kind of order purely for his own convenience, so he bought another exercise book and began to copy them out under various headings: Species, Varieties, Propagation, Feeding, General Maintenance, then Pests and Diseases. The final result, to his own amused surprise, filled six and a half thick exercise books.

For a laugh he showed them to Dora, and was mildly astonished when she appeared to take them seriously – 'You mean you've read the lot? Well, I'm buggered!' Good-humouredly he allowed her to have them typed (Dora now had three shops and employed a girl called Marlene to do the accounts and write business letters), and was humbly pleased when she corrected his spelling and amended his grammar. But he was not prepared to go further, and when Dora said one day over Sunday dinner than his notes ought to be published as a gardening book he told her not to talk so fancy.

'It's not fancy, and you'd see that if you had a grain of business sense, which you haven't. There's money in books, and besides it'll bring you more customers.'

'Don't reckon I want more. I've enough to keep busy.'

Dora told him not to be a fool and Thaddeus told her to mind her own business. Sometimes he marvelled that this firm-lipped, discreetly well-dressed woman should be the poor little ole Dora once so painfully in love with a married man, and he sometimes feared that Bob, for all his plump affluence, had a slightly browbeaten look.

So nothing more was said until the day Thaddeus received a letter from a firm of London publishers saying that they would be interested to consider publishing his book on roses.

'So who did this?' He waved the letter beneath Dora's nose. 'This is your work, isn't it? How did you come by my notes when they were on my table all the time?'

His indignation was so comic that Dora suppressed an involuntary giggle. Then straightened her features and said, 'I got Marlene to do a carbon, of course. And what's more, you ought to be glad.'

Correspondence then ensued with the publisher's editor, and various alterations and amendments were agreed (somewhat blankly) by Thaddeus. Suitable artwork was produced, and in due course Dora helped him to correct the proofs.

The pleasure came slowly, and took a long while to melt away the sense of outrage at what appeared to him an invasion of privacy. His notes were an integral part of himself; intimate, warmly attached, and liable to disintegrate under public scrutiny, and when he finally mumbled as much on the phone to his editor, the young man's voice said with disarming sincerity, 'That's precisely why we like the book so much. It's so obviously written by a man who loves his subject.'

And then the summons had come from Miss Eustacia Scarthe, Publicity Manager.

Lying in bed in the London hotel he marvelled anew at her official title. He had never realised that women could be managers any more than they could be vicars or coal miners. He wondered how old she was; looked about eighteen, but must be more than that, he reckoned.

He laid aside *Roses for Everyone* and turned out the bedside lamp. Subdued hotel sounds came to him: footsteps in the corridor, voices, and the rattle of doorkeys; the distant whine and clang of the lift and the stomach-like gurglings of hot-water pipes . . . he fell asleep trying to remember what he was supposed to do IN THE EVENT OF FIRE.

He took a taxi to Euston station early next morning and waited on a prominent seat as instructed. Fascinated and appalled he watched the ceaseless surging of commuters, then Eustacia Scarthe herself rose in slow splendour like the morning sun, stepped off the escalator and said, 'OK, Thaddeus, let's go.'

She had their train tickets and various other papers in what looked like a highly varnished Gladstone bag – strange how current fashion dictated a preference for either the minuscule or the monstrously large – and he followed her to the platform, then to their reserved seats.

'First class,' Thaddeus murmured.

'We only deal with first-class authors,' she replied with a grim little smile, and sinking into her seat opposite him put on a pair of dark glasses and laid her head back on the white antimacassar.

229

He couldn't tell whether or not her eyes were closed, but the sparkle that he remembered seemed to have died. The whole of her exuded a sense of intolerable weariness. As the train pulled out of the station he ventured to ask if she was feeling under the weather.

'Yes,' she said tersely. 'The party finished up at four-thirty.'

They remained silent until they had passed Watford Gap, then a steward came round with a trolley and Eustacia attempted to restore herself with a black coffee, two aspirin and a cigarette. Thaddeus drank a cup of tea and gazed at the surrounding countryside. Like his Publicity Manager, it looked wan and rather bleak.

By the time they reached Rugby she appeared somewhat restored. Without benefit of comb or pocket mirror she suddenly seized her long hair in a single hank, twisted it up on top of her head and secured it in place with the aid of some small unidentifiable object. She removed her dark glasses, recrossed her long legs, then removed the sheaf of papers from her Gladstone bag.

'So I've arranged for us to start in Liverpool,' she said, 'and sort of work backwards.'

'Yes. I see.'

He didn't. At least, he knew that he was due to perform on some sort of radio programme in Liverpool, Manchester and Birmingham, but nobody had yet told him what he was supposed to say. He had never been much good at talking just for the sake of it, and so far no one had even bothered to issue any kind of general guidelines. His sense of baffled insecurity increased as they drew closer to the West Midlands and Eustacia appeared to have sunk into yet another private torpor behind her dark glasses. He came to the conclusion that in spite of her citified ways she was not to be relied upon in an emergency.

But when at last the train drew in at Lime Street, Liverpool, she seized her bag and leaped on to the platform crying, 'OK Thaddeus, this is it!'

She bundled him into a taxi. Having naively expected architectural intimidation to match that of his publisher's offices, Thaddeus was surprised by the downtrodden downtown appearance of the first radio station on their list. Located in a back street among tattered hoardings and partially demolished terrace houses, it had a stale and seedy appearance that was enhanced by the large and sullen woman behind the reception desk. Under Eustacia's haughty London stare she ticked off Thaddeus's name in an engagement book and told them to siddown over thur.

They did so, on a shabby plastic settee drawn up to a chipped plastic coffee table littered with empty drinks cans and brimming ashtrays. Pop music scraped rather than soothed the nerves and Thaddeus glanced anxiously at Eustacia, hoping against craven hope that she would drop him a crumb of encouragement with which to face the unknown. He had given up any hope that she would tell him what he was actually supposed to *say*. But she had resumed her dark glasses, and sat tapping one sandalled foot – Oh the strange and wicked allure of those little-girl sandals – to the sound of adolescent male voices yelling '*Yeah-yeah-yeah!* until the record ended.

It was replaced by a man's almost insanely jolly voice imparting the latest news and weather forecast, then a young chap in jeans appeared through a door and beckoned to Thaddeus. Receiving no more than a limp hand-flick from Eustacia he rose to his feet and followed the chap down dusty passages and through pairs of double doors into a cluttered studio of asphyxiating stuffiness.

The man with the jolly voice was sitting before a microphone and a bank of controls, wearing headphones and an expression of unrelieved bad temper. Taking the seat indicated, Thaddeus listened to the swoop and lilt of his cadences as he imparted news of a traffic hold-up in the Mersey Tunnel, and watched the thunder in his profile as he flicked switches and growled 'Arleen you bitch, where's my fuckin' coffee?'

'Coming, Brent. Just coming,' said the girl's disembodied voice. Brent flicked a few more switches and resumed the tones of manic jollity. Fleetingly Thaddeus wondered whether it too could only be achieved by the manipulation of switches. Anything was possible these days.

'. . . and this is the spot in the programme where we're pleased to welcome today's guest – a, er, rosarian – which means someone who grows roses no less – with the name of – ' fleetingly he glanced at a copy of *Roses for Everyone* half-buried beneath a pile of papers – 'Thaddeus Noggin from Suffolk. Now, before we go any

231

further – ' he turned to the mesmerised Thaddeus for the first time, his features uplifted in grotesque bonhomie, 'the name Thaddeus is a bit unusual, isn't it – Thaddeus? Care to tell us how you came by it?' He nodded to the microphone placed before his guest.

Moistening his lips, Thaddeus said, 'It's on my birth certificate.' Then added desperately, 'I was christened it after my grandfather on my father's side, and his uncle – '

'Great!' said Brent. 'Really, great. And now Thaddeus, if we can call you that, tell us about your roses. I believe you've won some gold medals with them. Care to tell us about it?' A girl tiptoed in with a mug of coffee and tiptoed out again.

'I can't in just a few minutes.' Thaddeus eased his neck inside his collar. 'To breed a new rose takes years of work and it's mostly a question of trial and error. Of introdoocing the pollen of one plant into the waiting receptacle of the other. It's all a matter of male and female, and you can get some very funny results. There was one time when I – '

'That's amazing, Thaddeus! You're really telling us that all the beautiful roses we grow in our gardens originate from the same old malarkey as the rest of us?'

Mesmerised by the uplifted features and wildly assumed hilarity, Thaddeus saw Brent flick a few more switches before bellowing, 'Where's the fuckin' teaspoon? How can I stir the fuckin' sugar without a fuckin' teaspoon?'

The interview proceeded: a series of jerks interspersed by blasts of pop music and jets of local news, throughout which Thaddeus remained nervously pedantic. Outside in the waiting-room Eustacia flicked through last evening's *Liverpool Echo* then tossed it away and lit a cigarette. Blowing smoke rings in the direction of the receptionist she listened to Thaddeus's voice and was pleased. Exactly what she had hoped for. A rather shy, rumbling rustic voice with only slow country courtesy to show it the way. She had been quite right not to spoil it with hints about microphone technique or personality projection.

Thaddeus reappeared, loosening his tie a little and saying that he was sorry he hadn't made a go of it. He was unwilling to interrupt the debilitating melancholy of a Dusty Springfield record.

'You were marvellous,' Eustacia said. 'Anyone would think

232

you'd been doing it all your life!' She kissed his cheek, and he remained aware of the soft cool touch of her lips all the way back to the station.

He was deathly tired by the time they returned to London at eleven-fifteen. His legs ached, and his throbbing head was filled with jolting, kaleidoscope impressions of trains and taxis, cold railway platforms and hot studios. After the initiation in Liverpool, Manchester had been quite enjoyable; here, his host asked him to autograph his copy of *Roses for Everyone* – 'Don't get much time for reading myself, but the wife'll be pleased – ' and as his manner had seemed more genuinely cordial Thaddeus had relaxed a little.

But Birmingham had not been good. Another bully-boy concealed behind a pally exterior: without warning he had thrown at Thaddeus the jovial news that as they had nearly twelve minutes in hand they would end with a phone-in of listeners' rose problems.

He nodded to Thaddeus to put on the headphones lying among the empty coffee mugs and overflowing ashtrays, and Thaddeus had done so. They were too small. They pinched his ears with such brutality that his eyes filled with water. Three minutes later he heard an old and rather wavering voice asking him about white fly on brussel sprouts.

'Thad's really what they call a rosarian, darling,' chipped in his host, 'but I dare say he could give you an answer in three words, couldn't you, Thad?' Nodding and grimacing as though conducting an orchestra, he managed to extract the words 'Spray with malathion.'

'Mala – what, Thad?'

'Malathion – '

'Right. Spray with malathion, darling – '

'Or she could try dimethoate,' ventured Thaddeus, but Darling had already been replaced by someone called Mrs Goat, or possibly Coat, with a rose up her trellis that had gone back to wild.

'Grub it up,' Thaddeus said, conscious of his three-word limit.

'You mean, get rid of it, Thad?' prompted his host. 'Right, darling, Thad says dig it up and start again . . .'

It was astonishing how many callers could be jammed into such a short space of time. They all sounded like elderly ladies trying to reach him through a violent crackle and spit of frying bacon, and they all began by saying 'Oooh well . . .'

'Oooh well, I've got this pot plant me daughter got me an' it's gone all strange on me – '

'What sort is it?'

'Oooh well, I don't really know. It doesn't say, like . . .'

But at last it was over. Breathing heavily, Thaddeus wrenched off the earphones and wiped his tear-filled eyes. His host adjusted his bank of controls and the raucous voice of Tom Jones filled the studio. Thankfully Thaddeus took it as a sign to depart.

'Thanks, Thad. Mind autographing the book before you go? Don't get much time for reading myself but the wife'll be pleased . . .'

'Did they book you in at the hotel for one night or two?' Eustacia asked. The crowds at Euston had thinned. They passed a derelict youth leaning against a wall twanging a guitar and an old man in stockinged feet lying asleep on a bench. MAKE LOVE NOT WAR someone had scrawled above his head.

'Only the one.'

'It's a bit late to make Suffolk tonight. You'd better come back to my place.'

'Reckon I can find another hotel all right.' Dazed with tiredness he forgot to thank her for the offer.

'Please yourself. But I've got a studio couch that's doing nothing.'

He didn't know where to start looking for an hotel. Perhaps they would all be closed by now. Weariness ate his bones, confusion fogged his mind. 'Well . . .'

'Oooh well . . .' she said in a Brum accent, and taking his arm guided him into a waiting taxi.

Her flat was small, modern and filled with books. She went into the kitchenette and made a pot of coffee, which they drank in silence. Sitting opposite, he saw that her face was pale with fatigue and remembered that she had stayed up until after four on the previous night. He wondered what sort of parties she went to.

'Did I mention we're trying for a TV appearance for you?' she asked. 'I'll know for certain when I check in at the office tomorrow.'

234

'What's television like?' he asked, too tired to care very much.

'They serve a better brand of coffee.'

'This one's all right. Nothing wrong with it at all.'

'Thank you, Thaddeus.' She smiled at him with something of the sparkle he remembered from their first meeting. Tucking her sandalled feet beneath her small and skirtless bum she leaned back and lit a cigarette. The lamplight caught the stretched whiteness of her throat; maybe twenty-five, but not a day older.

'So the sensible thing is for you to stay in London tomorrow. I mean, you can look after yourself, can't you?'

'Reckon so.'

'Then if I can wangle the TV thing we can both go along together on Thursday.'

'What day is it now?'

'It was Tuesday up until half an hour ago,' she replied, glancing at her watch.

They finished their coffee, Eustacia showed him how the studio couch worked, showed him where the bathroom was and bade him good-night. He heard her whistling the Tom Jones song behind her closed bedroom door, then sleep hit him like the falling of a heavy blind.

He enjoyed the next day very much. A leisurely bath and shave after Eustacia had left for the office and a brief phone call home, then the freshness of London streets where plane trees were dripping pink and yellow leaves and iridescent pigeons, pompously full-breasted, marched among the human feet. Every now and then a cloud of them would take off and he would stop to observe them perching and preening on rooftops.

Ignoring Eustacia's suggestion that he should visit the Tate Gallery he wandered aimlessly and contentedly, looking at the old buildings rubbing shoulders with new glass and ferro-concrete blocks rising from cleared bombsites. Occasionally he passed one that remained untouched, and he would stand in grave contemplation of dying willow-herb and spindly buddleia that had somehow found sustenance among the tumbled brick and broken stone.

But the human beings were fine; they were flourishing like nettles in compost. He watched them too, and when any pair of eyes met his own he would automatically nod good-morning. The greeting was seldom returned, but he now had sufficient self-confidence to feel amusement at his own countrified habits.

London struck him as unexpectedly cheerful. Full of pneumatic drills and transistorised pop music, it seemed to be living the sixties in a mood of creative ebullience. The shops were busy and the coffee bars were full of beautiful girls like long-stemmed roses. He stopped for a bite of lunch in a King's Road pub and was astounded to see two young men kiss one another with casual grace. A man and a girl wandered by wearing long skirts and wreaths of flowers crowning their long hair. Their manner was dreamily unconcerned, but the flowers looked pretty well dead. He was partly familiar with this area of London because of the Chelsea Flower Show which he had attended for many years now, latterly as an exhibitor, and with three radio interviews under his belt he was perhaps no longer the typical Suffolk hayseed of old.

He meandered on his way, thinking about it. He was now the proprietor of a forty-acre rose garden and employer of seventeen workers, the bungalow now had an upstairs to it and they were on the electric, as well as mains water. And Noggin's roses were selling abroad, as well as over here. There was a border of his first hybrid planted in a bed in Queen Mary's Rose Garden up in Regent's Park, and bulk orders for the grounds of new hospitals, universities, blocks of flats and old folks' homes were now fairly regular. The money didn't mean all that much in itself; its greatest asset was in allowing him to continue the slow and absorbing process of hybridising while others performed the more routine jobs of pruning, feeding and spraying. They were also experimenting with the new system of container-growing, of setting the young plants straight into black polythene pots which could save the manic rush of November work, when hundreds of rose trees had to be dug and packed by hand.

And now there was the book. On the day of its publication he would have the right to call himself an author. He sighed, and wished he could send a copy to the Reverend Fiske, but he had died over ten years ago, drinking his early morning tea then resettling himself cosily among the pillows and murmuring 'Just another ten minutes . . .' According to the nurse he had departed this life with closed eyes and hands folded beneath his cheek like a contented child.

But Joe and his wife were pleased about *Roses for Everyone*. Janice was a nice girl from Marks Tey, and the firm of Thaddeus Noggin & Son Ltd had been in official existence for fourteen years. With two small grandsons coming along, the firm could continue indefinitely, with a bit of luck.

He had been pretty lucky so far, Thaddeus thought, sitting down on a bench. Sad parts too, of course. He didn't seem to have much luck with women, although he was a bit long in the tooth to worry about that now. He wondered how different things would have been if Polly hadn't died. Polly with the bouncing yellow curls and laughing blue eyes – would she have grown into a plump and garrulous matron with fancy bifocals and spreading feet? God forbid, he thought, as he watched a couple of miniskirted dolly birds swing past, then swore at himself for a dirty old bastard. He was too old. Too old. He was a grandad, and father of a chap already half bald . . . His mind drifted back to Hoppity May and to what might have been; to the sad, ultimately inconsolable Berta, the glimmering ghostlike figure of Lady Isobel . . .

Drawing his shoulders back he remembered that he had offered to take Eustacia out to supper that evening, and when later on he passed a branch of Marks & Spencer's he bought himself another new shirt in readiness for the occasion.

They arrived at her flat at about the same time, and he sat sipping the glass of white wine she had given him and listening to the swish of bathwater coming through the open door. He tried hard not to imagine her lying back half covered in bubbles and adjusting the taps with little pink toes. On the other hand, he had only to move ten paces or so and he would be able to see for himself. Marvelling at the trustfulness of such a sophisticated young creature he remained where he was, but when it occurred to him that she regarded him as a father figure only, he reached for the wine bottle and defiantly recharged his glass before switching his mind to the coming TV appearance she had fixed for the following day.

He was wearing his new shirt when he hailed the taxi to take them to the restaurant where she had booked a table. She wore a doll-sized dress of emerald green taffeta and a pair of unbelievably shiny black boots that reached above her knees. He couldn't keep his eyes off them, and failed to catch the gleam of delight in her eyes when he took out his purse to pay the taxi driver.

237

'I've never known anyone like you, Thaddeus,' she said as they seated themselves at the small, pink-clad table. 'You're like a character out of Trollope.'

'My mother was a real countrywoman,' he said. 'Able to feed a growing family on ten bob a week.'

'Trollope was an author,' she said gently. 'Now, shall we have an aperitif?'

He knew about apéritifs and he knew about authors because he was one himself, but he hadn't yet heard of Trollope. Give him time and he would.

They began the meal with whitebait and followed with roast duck. During the pause that followed Thaddeus took a coloured photograph from his pocket and handed it to her.

'My new rose.'

'*Gosh* . . .'

'Due to make her first appearance on our stand at Chelsea next year. She's already won the Best Seedling award.'

'It's striped – I didn't know there were such things as striped roses.'

'How about the *Gallica versicolour*? Then there's a pink and white striped rose named *Rosa Mundi* after Rosamund Clifford, who was the lady-friend of King Henry the Second, and he didn't live yesterday either.'

'I notice you call it a *she*.' Eustacia held the photograph closer to the pink candleshade in the centre of the table. 'What are you going to name her – *Rosa Mundi Mark 2*?'

'Oh no,' he said, 'this is a very modern lady. Firm and infrangible, as we say in the trade, brilliant colouring, continuous flowering, resistant to disease and indifferent to bad weather.'

Smilingly, she handed back the photograh. 'Sounds a bit like me.'

'Interested?'

'In what, precisely?'

'In having it named after you.'

'I'm interested in a lot of things relating to you,' Eustacia said slowly. 'And not just roses.'

They lingered over the meal, the waiter gliding shadowlike to refill their coffee cups. They had a brandy each, and Thaddeus leaned back in his chair and said, 'Well, I reckon I never met a girl quite like you before.'

238

'Then you can't have met very many.' She looked at him with her chin on her hand, pensive and rather sad. 'London's teeming with girls like me now we've received the official go-ahead to compete with men. Smart little brains and sexually explicit clothes – God, no wonder they call us dolly birds – and we compete with each other as ferociously as we do with men. We've joined the great human rat race, and I suppose there's no turning back now.'

'You hate it, then?'

'Can't pretend I do, altogether.' The candlelight enhanced the gleam in her eyes. 'I mean, it does have certain advantages over darning socks and pushing a pram.'

'Tell me some of them.' He wanted her to go on talking so that he could go on looking at her.

'Well. This, for instance. Going out to dinner with an attractive client in the guise of promoting his book.'

'I'm sixty-seven,' Thaddeus said gruffly.

She threw back her head and laughed, exposing the long slender throat he had wanted to touch last night. 'I know perfectly well you're sixty-seven, it's in your biog. notes.'

'Sixty-seven's too old.'

'Too old for what?' She stopped laughing, but the waiter had glided from the shadows with the bill and Thaddeus was already fumbling for his glasses and his cheque book. The price of the meal was astronomical and he wished fleetingly that he hadn't bought another new shirt. Then recklessness overtook him, and outside the restaurant he hailed another taxi although Eustacia said the walk would do them good.

Nightlit London flickered through the window and danced fleetingly on Eustacia's profile. They sat without speaking, and the knowledge that he was sixty-seven rang inside Thaddeus's skull like the strokes of Big Ben. He knew that it was going to happen; he wanted it to, and was only afraid that age and the years of abstinence would betray him.

Inside her flat she closed the front door with her foot, her arms already reaching out to him. Her long shiny boots squeaked against his trouser-legs and her lips parted under his in a quick, little-girl giggle. They undressed and fell into bed and he performed heroically, burying himself in her and rejoicing in the tumultuous rising and falling. Her skin was warm and damp and

239

smelt of apples, which was funny in London. Must have come out of a bottle. But the subtle, musky woman scent was there as well, and looking down on her flushed face and tumbled hair he felt like a man in his twenties. He kissed her with love and gratitude. 'Firm and infrangible . . . brilliant colouring . . .'

'Thaddeus, I adore you . . .'

They slept, then awoke in the early hours; this time he couldn't. It didn't matter. They lay close together, nuzzling and whispering, and it was the closeness that mattered, not what they did. She was out of bed before first light and he heard the bath running. Women in London bathed a lot. Or perhaps it was just dolly birds.

She brought him a cup of tea in the soft light of the bedside lamp, her diminutive dressing gown falling carelessly open; he had never known a woman who treated her private parts as if they were of no more account than a sheet of newspaper. Dora would have called her a tart, but she certainly wasn't that, for beneath the cool and casual exterior Thaddeus sensed a lonely little girl, top of her class at school but still ready to rush home to the sheltering arms of dear old Dad.

They breakfasted on orange juice and Ryvita, and on the way to the Television Centre at Wood Lane Eustacia once again donned her dark glasses and retired into herself.

The interview went off well. Bathed in the golden heat of studio lights he found less offhandedness, more willingness to support him. He was agreeably surprised to find that his interview was enriched by close-ups of his most successful roses. He chatted easily, sitting back in his chair and enjoying himself, and for the first time became conscious of a sense of loss when the interview was over.

'You're becoming hooked, aren't you?' Eustacia said when they met afterwards. 'Most people do.'

'What d'you mean?'

'I mean the self-esteem syndrome. You see yourself as another person, a new creation designed to fit the media and to be moulded into a bankable commodity.'

'I still don't understand you,' he said rather helplessly. 'All I know is you sound cross.'

'Not really, darling,' she brushed her lips against his cheek, 'and when I'm promoting someone who's – '

'Who's what?'

'Oh, never mind. We'll talk about it later.'

Back in central London they parted, Eustacia to call in at the office and Thaddeus to return home. She kissed him, and when he gently removed the dark glasses from her nose he saw their new relationship sparkling in her eyes.

'Don't forget I'm more than old enough to be your father.'

'OK, Daddeeee! . . .' she chirruped, and walked away from him swinging her little-girl's red handbag. 'Chow, Thaddeus.'

Half an hour after he reached Maplestead the phone rang. 'Thaddeus – that you?'

His heart jumped at the sound of her voice. 'Reckon that is.'

During the last couple of days he had discovered that a heavily accented Suffolk accent made her laugh, and as he loved the sound of her laughter he frequently employed it. She laughed now, but only in a brisk and businesslike kind of way, then said, 'Listen, we've just received a call from a firm of fertiliser manufacturers. They saw you on the box and wonder if you'd be interested in doing an advertising spot for them on TV.'

His immediate reaction was disappointment that her call was merely in an official capacity. 'Well, I don't know. I'd have to think . . .'

'Don't think for too long,' she said crisply. 'The money would be very good, and so would the publicity.'

'I thought you were warning me off that kind of thing. Media whatsit . . .'

'Worse people than you have become media fodder,' she said. 'Grab it while it's going.'

'So what do I have to do?'

'I'll give them your phone number and they'll contact you. Let's see, you haven't got an agent, have you?'

'No. Doan reckon to hev nuthun' like that, gal.'

She didn't laugh. 'OK, don't worry. I'll deal with them myself, or else get Samantha on to it. In the meantime, book-signing session on Thursday – I'll meet you in the manager's office at quarter to twelve. You can't miss the shop, it's near the tube station.'

'Look forward to seeing you – '

'Chow, Thaddeus.' The phone died in his hand, and he was left wondering why dolly birds said *chow* when they presumably meant cheerio.

The last gold of autumn had been stripped away by a gale, and now the sky hung low and weeping over the crawling London traffic. As if in recompense, the shops seemed suddenly to have dressed themselves for Christmas: red, silver and white shone from the polished windows and a one-legged man in Oxford Street was hawking plastic Santas to hang on plastic fir trees.

The bookshop was a large one, and Thaddeus was gratified to see *Roses for Everyone* arranged cheek by jowl with books about the Beatles and the Rolling Stones in one of the windows. He walked inside rather diffidently, newly conscious of being tweed clad in a lounge-suited world, but he was immaculately shaved and barbered and the nails of his large working hands were scrupulously clean.

Eustacia came forward with a warm and loving smile, both arms outstretched. She had no qualms about embracing him in public, which seemed a happy omen.

'Good boy,' she said, 'right on time, and every inch the country rose-grower – ' laughing, she held him close – 'I can even smell roses on your breath – '

'Not quite,' he said, and produced a narrow cardboard box from behind his back and gave it to her. She tore it open, and drew her breath at the sight of the striped rose inside. Long and tapering, the outer petals were still loosely folded round the heart of it, but already the sweet clove scent came drifting out to challenge the smell of new books all around them. Reverently Eustacia held the rose in her cupped hands. He though he saw tears in her eyes before a thick curtain of hair fell forward to hide her face.

'Oh my God,' she whispered, 'I'm holding perfection in my hands.'

'It's yours,' he said. 'All yours.' He helped her to pin it on the bodice of her dark green minidress, and noticed for the first time that she was wearing her child's sandals. Her legs looked longer than ever.

She led him to the manager's office where he seemed to shake hands with a good many people before being offered a glass of sherry. At three minutes to twelve he found himself back in the shop, seated at a large table containing a blown-up photograph of himself taken from the book jacket, and a stack of *Roses for Everyone* awaiting purchasers.

Everyone kept asking if he was OK – could he see, had he got a pen – as if he were some mossy old rustic dug out of a ditch, and the more vigorously he affirmed that everything was fine, the more his qualms multiplied. Supposing he had no customers? Supposing he didn't sell a single copy? Supposing he just sat there for the prescribed hour with fixed smile and uplifted pen and no one wanted to know. The few casual onlookers eyed him and his fancy set-up with no more than bored London interest, and he suddenly felt a rage of impatience and self-hatred at letting himself in for such a silly fandangle.

What in God's name was he doing here when he should be at home helping with the lifting and packing of non-container plants ready for dispatch – as if there wasn't enough work to keep them all hard at it until the frost got into the ground . . .

Then a lock of hair touched his neck and her lips touched his cheek as Eustacia leaned over him and whispered good luck, leaving behind a sweet breath of the striped rose's perfume. When he looked up there was a weatherbeaten woman in a brown hat standing in front of him and proffering a copy of the book for his autograph. Uncapping his pen he signed Thaddeus Noggin, and she scrutinised it carefully before moving away with a satisfied nod.

'Write *sincerely yours* in the next one,' whispered Eustacia. Obediently he did so, and a little old lady with a woolly scarf asked in a deferential whisper if he would put *To Vera* as well.

He paused, smiling. 'Who's Vera?'

'My friend whose husband's just passed away.'

The crowd increased, bulging in a queue and pressing against the table four abreast.

'Heard you broadcast . . .'

'Saw you on TV . . .'

'Can you tell me a proper cure for mildew?'

'Do you mind writing *Happy Christmas Mum* in it? She'd be everso pleased . . .'

He did everything they asked of him with a countryman's slow and somewhat obdurate courtesy, stiflingly hot in his thick tweed suit and laying down his pen every now and then to massage his cramped fingers. The heat in the shop seemed to him asphyxiating, and when a small child proffered her copy for signature he paused to ask her if she liked roses.

'No. But my father does.'

He signed *To Father – best wishes Thaddeus Noggin*, then told her that she ought to sign it too. 'What's your name?'

'Polly,' she said.

Polly. He closed his eyes for a moment against the heat and the noise and the press of customers, as if the name would bring back the cool of the river and the water meadows and the moonlit summer evenings, then carried on with the task in hand. *Sincerely yours Thaddeus Noggin . . . Thaddeus Noggin . . . Thaddeus Noggin . . .*

But he discovered that he enjoyed talking to his customers. He liked the unexpected sense of rapport, and they for their part felt that this slow-speaking old chap with the thick grey hair and faraway blue eyes offered a direct link with the world of their dreams – woods and water and wild flowers blowing in the wind; secret gardens spilling with roses and lilies and dreamy girls in long nighties musing among moonlit magnolias . . . Rattling tube trains to suburban housing estates seemed to fade in his presence.

The signing session was supposed to be for an hour but became extended to two and a half. His handwriting deteriorated to a cramped scribble but they didn't seem to mind, and when the cashier imparted the news that they had sold a hundred copies, flashlight photographs were taken of Thaddeus loomingly shaking hands with the latest purchaser while the manager and his staff smiled complacently. Every now and then he caught sight of Eustacia chatting animatedly to various spectators and once he even had time to notice that the striped rose pinned to her bodice had opened almost to fullblown. No wonder, in this heat. He felt a stab of pity for it, panting out its life when it might have been slowly burgeoning at home along with its mates in one of the glasshouses.

He went on signing until the last customer had drifted away and the manager shook his aching fingers and said, 'That was great Mr Noggin – absolutely great!' and led him away through the other brightly coloured Christmas books to a large storeroom where a long table had been set with a buffet luncheon. Champagne fizzed, and Eustacia with glass aloft kissed his cheek and whispered, 'You were absolutely *super* . . .' He began to feel like a film star or something.

He also felt extremely hungry. The sandwiches were very small and exceptionally delicious and he crammed three into his mouth at once, before taking another swig from his glass. He had no idea who the other people were, but they were all very nice and they all liked roses. At least they all said they did, and he listened good-humouredly to a lot of champagne-tinted rubbish about roses growing best on clay soil, roses responding to music, to being talked to, etcetera. Eustacia broke away from the group she was with and hissed in his ear, 'Keep going – soon be over, but the man over there is the editor of *Modern Gardener* and is going to ask you to do a weekly column . . .'

'Don't reckon I could . . .'

'Nonsense,' she said, 'you're an author.' Her lovely face looked sharp with fatigue as she raised her refilled glass to him. 'Come on darling, remember you're a pro now.'

Dazed by the noise he thought she said a *pronoun*, which was something about which poor ole Miss Ball had tried to teach them all those years ago. And now he had written a book and got it published, still not sure what a pronoun was. Made you laugh really . . . He reached for another smoked salmon sandwich, and a woman with a lot of teeth told him that she had planted one of his roses on her mother's grave.

'Thank you,' he said formally. 'Thank you very much indeed.'

'Mother would have been so – so pleased . . .' she said, and her eyes filled with champagne tears.

The party broke up at around half-past four, and they were ushered out of the trade entrance into streets shining with cold rain and the false beauty of neon-lit Christmas.

Suddenly depressed, Thaddeus reached for the comfort of Eustacia as she stood beside him. Her little-girl coat was slung over her shoulders and she groped in her mock Gladstone bag for an umbrella. 'I *loathe* rain.'

'Makes things grow.'

In the lurid lights he saw her shrug irritably. They paused at the edge of the kerb, and as she bunched her coat more tightly round her neck the striped rose fell unheeded from its pin and tumbled into the gutter. He watched with pain as a passing bus coated its dying petals with thin mud.

A taxi drew up beside them, the driver leaning towards them interrogatively.

'Where are we going?' Thaddeus took her elbow.

'I'm going back to the office.'

'What – now? It's only half an hour to closing time.'

'No such thing as closing time in my job, darling. Letters to sign, appointments to fix and on Monday I'm flying to Oslo.'

'Oslo?'

'Travel book by a Norwegian. It's coming out in a couple of weeks and we want to push it like mad . . .'

Some of her old friendliness had returned, but he was too disconsolate to pay it much heed. The taxi driver suddenly bawled, 'Well, do you or don't you?' then reset the meter with a fierce ping and drove off.

'Shall we meet after the office, then? Perhaps a drink and something to eat, or . . .' Can we just go straight back to your flat. I'm old and tired and muddled with all the people and the heat and the silliness. I just want peace in your arms.

She didn't reply. Still standing on the kerb, he strove to keep his tone as light as possible. 'Monday you're going, you say? That's in three days' time.'

'Yes, I know. And listen Thaddeus, I'll get Samantha to let you know the outcome on *Modern Gardener* – '

'What's his name?'

'The editor's?'

'No. Your Norwegian chap.'

'Lars Svertsen – why?'

'Just wondered.'

They began to walk through the jostling crowds, and all the way he felt her slipping irretrievably away from him. Her little-girl sandals squeaked lightly on the wet pavement and her umbrella bumped against his ear.

'Your feet are getting wet.'

'I've got some more shoes at the office.'

'Oh. That's all right, then.'

'I'd better get a taxi now.'

They paused again, and he read dismissal in her eyes. Behind them an open-fronted record shop blasted them with the *Yeah-yeah-yeah* of a pop song and he felt too old and tired to care about the young any more.

'Do you sleep with all your authors?' he asked finally.

She tilted her umbrella back and looked him straight in the eyes. 'Only the men.'

There was no more to say, yet for some reason they remained standing there uselessly and inconclusively.

'I don't suppose you want to call your new rose after me now, do you?'

'Oh, yes,' Thaddeus said. 'Yes, I do. Eustacia Scarthe's the perfect name for a rose that's firm and infrangible but impatient of bad weather.'

She grimaced; then smiled at him with a hint of sadness before jerking her umbrella at an approaching taxi. Just before climbing inside she turned to brush his cheek with her lips.

'Chow, Thaddeus.'

Oblivious to the false enticement of the Swinging Sixties blaring all around him, Thaddeus moved away to join the first home-going crowd of commuters on their way to Liverpool Street station. A copy of *Roses for Everyone* lay snug and reassuring in his pocket and he switched his mind firmly away from the poor little corpse he was leaving mud-soaked in a London gutter.

The roses in the glass bowl were now fully open and the afternoon sun was in decline.

'So let me guess,' Nanda O'Flynn said, touching one of them with her finger. 'This one's *My Ma*, isn't it?'

The bloom was circular, the outer petals disclosing a rich ruffle of inner ones, and in the centre a wicked little eye.

'That's her,' the old man said.

'And the aloof-looking white one's *Lady Isobel*?'

'Correct.'

'And how about this one . . . *Polly*?' The flower was turned towards her, its softly crumpled petals lightly pursed as if for a kiss.

He nodded.

'I bet the striped one's *Eustacia Scarthe* – so this pink and gold one must be . . . what was her name? Must be *Berta*.' The rose in question seemed to be staring past them, as if at some different time and place.

'And who's this one? You've got six roses in the bowl but you've only told me about five.' She looked at him accusingly.

'Ah, that's my new one. She'll be showing off her paces at Chelsea next year.'

'She? It's another woman then?'

'No call to sound disparaging,' the old man said mildly. 'Yes, this one's already been named. She's *Lady Noggin*.'

'Oh.' Nanda O'Flynn sat back in her chair and regarded him blankly. 'So you got married again?'

'Reckoned I might as well.'

'Well . . . congratulations, Sir Thaddeus.' The word *Sir* was hard to say because she didn't believe in privilege. Didn't believe in any sort of obeisance to the old class-orientated system of preferment.

'Thank you,' the old man said, and smiled at her. He looked across the garden with his faraway blue eyes. 'And if I'm not mistaken, I can see Lady Noggin coming now.'

Following his gaze, Nanda O'Flynn saw a smallish, dark-clad figure coming across the peppermint daisies with a tray in her hands.

Despite her age she was walking briskly, but with a little bobbing, hopping movement, and when she reached the arbour her face, delicately creased with age, broke into a radiant smile.

'I have brought us all a glass of sherry,' Hoppity May said. 'You poor souls have been working so hard . . .' Her gaze rested upon Thaddeus. 'And the phone has been ringing non-stop. All very exciting of course, but a little exhausting at our age.'

She seated herself, and Nanda O'Flynn thought, well, perhaps knighthoods are acceptable if they're awarded for hard work. For sheer bloody hard work with your own two hands. Otherwise they're just a load of capitalistic crap . . .

With a touch of youthful pomposity she raised her sherry glass and said, 'On behalf of the *Ipswich Bystander* and myself I offer congratulations to Sir Thaddeus and Lady Noggin. Looks like you've arrived at last.'

Hand in hand, they smiled at her.